W9-BEV-862

FAITH WALL

A NOVEL

TIMOTHY TAYLOR

THE
BLUE LIGHT
PROJECT

SOFT SKULL PRESS
AN IMPRINT OF
COUNTERPOINT BERKELEY

Copyright © 2011 Timothy Taylor

All rights reserved under International and Pan-American Copyright Conventions. No part of this book may be reproduced in any form or by any electronic or mechanical means, including information storage and retrieval systems, without permission in writing from the publisher, except by a reviewer, who may quote brief passages in a review.

This book is a work of fiction. Names, characters, places and incidents either are the product of the author's imagination or are used fictitiously. Any resemblance to actual persons, living or dead, events or locales is entirely coincidental.

Library of Congress Cataloging-in-Publication Data

Taylor, Timothy L., 1963–
The blue light project / Timothy Taylor.
p. cm.
1. Hostage negotiations—Fiction. 2. Psychological fiction. I. Title.
PR9199.4.T39B58 2011
813'.6—dc22
2010026378

ISBN 978-1-59376-402-9

Text design: CS Richardson
Printed in the United States of America

Soft Skull Press

An Imprint of COUNTERPOINT LLC

1919 Fifth Street

Berkeley, CA 94710

www.softskull.com

www.counterpointpress.com

Distributed by Publishers Group West

10 9 8 7 6 5 4 3 2 1

In memory of Ursula Lilly Taylor (née Kuppenheim)

For Brendan the Navigator
And for Jane, as always.

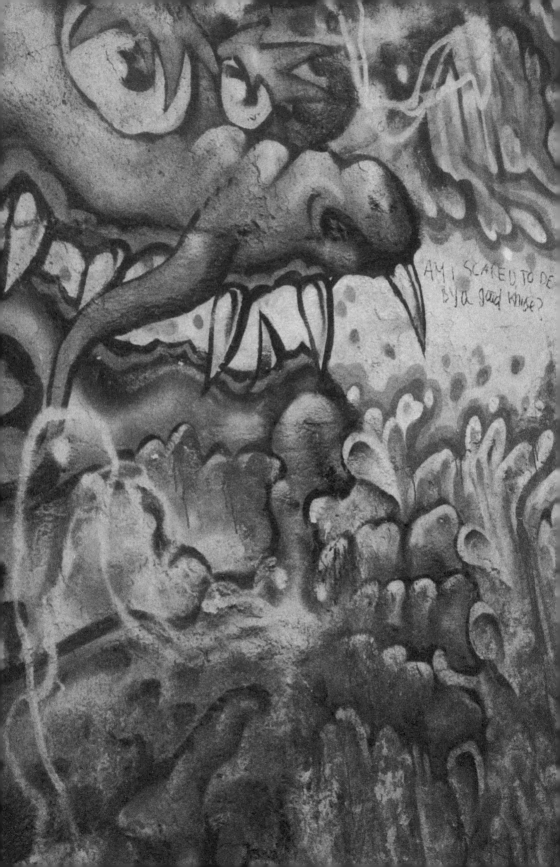

ROGER EBERT: *Send Us an Electrician.* That film was shot in Wisconsin.

WERNER HERZOG: Yes, and the dancing chicken was shot in Cherokee, North Carolina. When you are speaking about these images, there's something bigger about them, and I keep saying that we do have to develop an adequate language for our state of civilization, and we do have to create adequate pictures—images for our civilization. If we do not do that, we die out like dinosaurs.

From an onstage conversation between Werner Herzog and Roger Ebert, April 2004

E S S A Y

THE BLUE LIGHT PROJECT

PART I. The gold medalist

By Thom Pegg

She's beautiful. Let me just say that at the outset. A person could pretend they didn't notice, but that person would probably be lying. I've lied before. I've lied notably, some might even say *infamously*. But this is the truth: she's a classic willowy, green-eyed beauty. And she carries it in a way that might surprise if you've based your impression on the ads and the television spots. In person, there is nothing endorsement, nothing podium about her. No flashing of the winning smile. No casual glancing around for the nearest camera. In person, it's all about health and natural athleticism, straw-blond hair and a perfect dusting of freckles over tanned cheekbones. I've heard her described as having "Midwestern" looks, but that doesn't quite get to the essence of it either. The essence is that

This is the first of three excerpts from Thom Pegg's book, Black Out, Blue Light, *about his experience during the Meme Media Hostage Crisis, to be published this fall. Pegg worked for six years as a Senior Features Editor at L:MN, an entertainment periodical. He lives in Los Angeles.*

she seems beyond regions and sources. As if she came from everywhere and so belonged to everyone. As if, and this is related, she came from nowhere and belonged to no one.

I know how this sounds coming from a person like me, who has worked for years too long inside the machinery of fame, leaned in close against the grind and squelch of it. *The fan is always the mark. Celebrity is a con.* Who wrote that, years ago, as if it were a great insight? Me, of course. I wrote that years ago as if it were a great insight. Still, when I first saw her, I was hit by the whole suite of symptoms: the adrenal spike, the sense of brightening, of possibilities opening wide. And like the strike of a crystal bell in my inner ear, like a breath whispering through my body at the cellular level, I heard her name: Eve Latour.

Of course, everybody up in the Heights that morning seemed to be slightly lost. I'd been wandering the city myself since first light, a dread chill in the air, flinty breeze off the river, the skies above me all smoky and heaving. The pale October sun leaked only briefly through bruised and purple clouds before slouching away. I stood just a few blocks from the plaza, which had been the epicenter of the troubles, and evidence was still everywhere. Broken glass glittering in the street. Sirens scoring the air. Smoke rising. I saw the remains of a car that rioters had burned earlier, the interior gutted and blackened, soaked by fire hoses and steaming in the watery light. Police and troops wandering around. The recent events continuing to dominate every news broadcast. The Meme Media Hostage Crisis, as we were all calling it. On the hour and the half hour, they laid it out again and again, from inception to climax, and made no further sense of anything. You could see it in the anchors' faces. Incomprehension in the furrows between plucked eyebrows even as they tried to explain how events unfolded. The Meme studio theater stormed in ghostly silence. A strange pulse of energy felt on the skin by everyone in a six-block radius. And then the strange agitations of a stricken crowd: a vigil turned riot in the predawn blue.

We stumbled. We reeled. We looked into each other's faces for clues.

Eve Latour stood holding a newspaper in one hand. A fingernail of her other hand traced across her cheek as she read. Mill-town sky, the clouds sagging low behind her. She stood against this backdrop, tall and lean, with an easy grace and natural strength. While reflected in the broken front window of a dog grooming salon, I saw myself: addled, disarranged. My expression confused, smudged with lack of sleep. I looked as creased and untucked as my clothes. As lost as the one shirt collar point popping free of my jacket.

Police cars and fire trucks crisscrossed the hillside. Helicopters hovered watchfully, dipping down out of sight behind rooflines, or pivoting in place and angling off to other quadrants of the city. I could hear the city's landmark waterfall down at the river, the never-ending white keen of it. Eve stood calmly in the midst of this, reading, thinking.

I'd walked from the north side, from my hotel downtown across the river where the streets were almost untouched by what had happened here. I'd crossed one of the bridges and made my way through the inner-city area of Stofton, then on up into the gentrified Slopes. I knew these neighborhoods, having been born and raised here, long ago. Yet as I covered the ground, I'd slowly become aware of my own uncertainty about where I was exactly or where I was going as I pushed on, going block by block, turning down a street or cutting through a park. And everywhere I saw people who looked to be in a similar condition, heads turning, faces slack, drifting through the strange familiar.

There were no birds anywhere. No pigeons, crows, no geese or grebes. When I crossed the boulevard that marked the boundary of the Heights, a man stopped his car and rolled down the window to tell me that hundreds of people had been arrested and were being held in temporary detention centers down by the east side rail yards. I judged from his face—from his suit jacket, his car, his wristwatch with many dials—that he wasn't the sort of person who believed rumors easily, but that something had changed. Belief was now very close. Belief that some hidden badness had been flushed into the open and exposed. A hidden badness in us. A plague of ourselves upon ourselves.

I climbed up the streets and into the Heights. Traffic clotted and broke out of its patterns. The main routes up into the plaza were cordoned off, yellow tape shimmering in the light and wind. Armored cars were parked next to the fountains, between the park benches, in front of cafés. Troops wore gray-mottled city camo fatigues with black knee pads and throat mikes, helmet-mounted cameras. I took a random turn into a narrow avenue lined with high-end clothiers and boutique law firms, a cosmetic surgeon. Broken glass in the street. The air smelled of rubber, burnt sugar, nylon. Eve Latour didn't belong in the scene at all, I thought. She lived in my memory as a heroic figure on alpine landscapes with crisp air and wide sight lines. Yet as I stood staring, I felt that our arrival there had somehow been planned: place and persons, trembling moment.

She sensed me standing there. People who spend their lives in the public eye develop a kind of radar. They feel the eyes, the longing, the volatile desire. Some love it, thrive on it. Others are smartly wary. Eve Latour was wary, I think, but also kind. So she didn't ignore me or pretend to be distracted with something else. She looked up instead and inventoried me in a single glance. The clothes. That shirt collar point sticking up. Shoes, hands, face. History and disappointments. The fear and the fatigue.

Then she closed the distance. She stepped towards me and extended her hand.

Strange thing, that. They don't normally touch you, in my experience. I mean the really big stars. The name brands. The people of iconic wealth and wellness. The people who could surely envy only God. It's less a germ issue than it is a matter of observing the sacred separation between you and them. But Eve was going to surprise me in various ways, and the handshake was only the first instance. She took my hand, applied the faintest pressure. The nod, the rounded eyebrows to signal that we both understood at least one part of what the other was feeling. And then we had the same conversation that thousands of strangers were having that morning. We worked our way back in time together to where we'd been when the crisis began.

I told her that I'd been on the West Coast, where I lived. That I'd been on a date, at dinner. I told her about the unexpected phone call, the shock, the terrible dawning, the rush to the airport to fly here. But past that point, past liftoff—I remembered a cream leather cabin—my memory frayed and sputtered. My forehead twitching, my cheeks flushing with effort as the details jammed.

She said: Journalist. You're a journalist. We've met. Which sounded familiar, so I told her: Yes, I remember. Although I wasn't at all sure that I did.

And here she nodded and turned away, not coming back with her own story immediately, but waiting in silence for several seconds instead, the air textured all around us with radio squelch, rotor wash, the sound of the falls, all those uncountable sirens. I recognized in her pause the long habit of self-concealment around journalists. Forget about all those interviews and profiles after her gold-medal win in Geneva eight years before. The tide of curiosity as her athletic fame so quickly morphed into something bigger. The celebrity engagement to the French film director. The paparazzi outside her Paris hotel after he left her for the tennis player. Her high-profile term as a UNICEF Global Ambassador. She'd faced them all squarely, the photographers and the networks. She'd accommodated the local press on her return home from Europe, their loved daughter. Always gracious, never minding that they called her Evey like she wasn't thirty-two years old but still a kid. It was true that she had lived in the media, lived in our gaze. But none of it would have prepared her for this occasion, as we stood together in the post-normal. This lean, unwavering beauty. The slumped and damaged hack opposite.

Something blinked to life in my memory. Eve Latour had given an interview to a men's magazine several years before. One of those cleavage and six-pack catalogs. Eve Latour sitting in an old Ukrainian deli, a famous place in this city. In the Heights, I thought. Not too far from where we were standing. In the photograph, she was wearing an impressively ugly cable-knit sweater, her head cracked back laughing, mid-conversation with the old guy who ran the place. She told the interviewer that she planned never to leave the city again. She didn't want to. More importantly, she didn't need to. She'd seen the world and seen what it had to give. She knew now that everything required in life was right there close at hand, at home. And if it wasn't—whatever thing or experience—then she could certainly learn to live without it.

I loved that detail, then and now. That Eve Latour was the kind of person who didn't let herself be tormented by those desires that could not be satisfied.

Eve Latour continued to think of something else, a long loop of thought that took her away from me, her eyes drifting to the buildings opposite, to the sky, to a jet passing overhead. Military. Heading east. It made a sound like a God-scale fabric being torn down the length of its seam.

Then she surprised me again. She motioned we should walk. She took my arm. Again, the physical contact. Again the willing, familiar touch. This time with a new authority. So it was that I crossed the broken Heights, over to the shoulder of the hill, walking arm in arm with Eve Latour. And right at the crest—where the whole downtown delta was revealed, those high and magical spires, each one shimmering in its individual haze of sorrow and money, poised to carry on—right there, she started talking.

She'd been at home, she said. As for so many others, the first images of the Meme Media Hostage Crisis had flickered to consciousness in the upholstered safety of a living room. She remembered the fire, the first gunshots. All of which had been terrible, but not nearly as terrible as what followed. That spilling of events from the inside to the outside, that sense of contagion, violence spreading from one to so many and with such seeming ease. She wondered if it had happened that way, if people had lost themselves in these events, because so many of the hostages had been children.

I didn't say anything. I just kept walking as she steered us into the street, dead intersection lights overhead, swaying in the breeze off the river. Her foot crunched broken glass and pieces of brick. We crossed to the opposite sidewalk and she asked my name. And when I told her she repeated it quickly, as if it had been there, right on the tip of her tongue.

Thom Pegg, she said. And she turned to look at me, her eyebrows raised. She seemed, incredibly, to be finding some upside in the moment, to be tapping some secret source of hope.

But she didn't tell me what it was, just then. She only nodded again and tightened her grip on my arm, pulling me along. Towards something. That much seemed clear. But what was it? Where was it? I didn't ask, and she offered no answers. And while I might have pressed on another day, in another frame of mind, on that day, in that frame of mind—shifting gaps in my memory and a pervasive sense of being lost—I let myself be pulled down the street by this famous and mysterious person, this angel. I let her lead me, walking briskly now, dropping down the hill towards the river, the sound of the falls growing and growing. The wind unseasonably high.

PART ONE

"Keep up the good work! Keep up the good work,
you beautiful, beautiful young artists!"
Anonymous dancing woman, January 2008

WEDNESDAY
—
OCTOBER 23

EVE

—

EVE RAN THE STREETS in the earliest hours of Wednesday morning, a lean shape in black. Through the riverside neighborhoods, the Flats, River Park, Stofton, the lower Slopes. She slipped through on silent shoes, nothing to hear but her breath. She surveyed the walls. The posters and billboards, the cloud of advertisement hanging over every space in the city. But more recently, another phenomenon too: heaving seas of urban art.

Posters, photographs, paintings, sheets of words. Graffiti seemed to be the smallest part of it these days. Eve liked the long landscape banners in the alleys of the lower Slopes and Stofton, stencils of wildflowers and fields of long grass. Always one bunny, stamped in the corner. Or the poster series she'd seen in River Park that read: *You'll Find It Where You Last Saw It.* These words drawn in felt pen and ballpoint over a picture of keys, loose change, cigarette lighters, little love hearts and peace signs. Once, far east into the warehouse district, deep into a run, Eve was brought to a halt in front of an entire wall papered over with these. A hundred missing objects, ideals, notions. She stood looking up, breathing hard, hands to her hips, smiling at this crazy thing. If it didn't make any particular sense, Eve thought it made a kind of super-sense, responding to impulse logic just beyond the rational. And that made her think of herself at a younger age, ready to burst into action, to proceed in the face of disagreement. Sure of her heart.

Fast run, long run, rest day. Stairs, rest day, short run. Then, on the seventh day, the night run. Eve started as the light failed. She ran the bridges, the worn eastern suburbs. She ran the river and the inner city. She ran into the late night, into the early morning, and Nick would complain about her coming home so late.

Eve liked the photographs too. She saw shots of urban distress, textures, faces, construction sites, dumpsters. These were postered up near the places or objects they depicted, on a nearby wall, hoarding, bus shelter, train bridge, mailbox. Why here? Why anywhere? Most people had no idea these images existed at all. But Eve also knew you had to close your eyes not to see them.

Eve knew this art existed. She also knew that her estranged brother, Ali, had once been part of this world. And gripped hard by a recent inspiration, she was looking for him. So she ran the parts of the city he'd favored in those last years of contact between them. Seven, eight years ago, far too long. She remembered a wiry reed of a kid, urban explorer, wall climber, roof jumper. When they were teenagers, Eve had followed him everywhere. Up the East Shore radio tower once, highest point in the city at the peak of the ridgeline north of the river—350 feet. A four-sided tapering Eiffelized structure in steel. Up a dozen crisscross flights of stairs, up into the freezing night. She faltered at the final length of it, where the tower grew so narrow that you had to thread your way up thirty feet of ladder through a cylindrical lattice to the final platform, which Eve could see swaying against the blackness, nestled among the stars. Suddenly the whole business seemed crazy. And she froze, couldn't move a muscle. Tears squeezed out of her eyes and seemed to ice on her cheeks in the wind that whipped the deck on which she stood.

Then Ali came back and slipped a lean and muscular arm around her shoulders. She warmed immediately with his touch, with his words. "Don't worry, E. We'll stay here. I'll stay with you. Look at that. Look at the view. We're above it all."

And he'd been so right, saying so. Back then, they had truly been above it all.

EVE RAN AND RAN. Always alone, although never feeling alone. Where she last knew Ali had lived, in the oldest and poorest parts of the city, the streets kept you company. Eve would stop and show people the wrinkled photograph she carried. Her brother standing on a flat roof, hands on his hips, painted in orange streaks and blue shadows by the sunset off to the west. A man with the scent of boyhood still on him. So handsome. Eve loved the picture and showed it around with a trace of pride. "I'm looking for this good-looking guy who happens to be my brother. He'd be about ten years older now. Around thirty-six. Have you seen him?"

She ran with a water bladder strapped between her shoulder blades. Six months back at the running program, after letting it go for several years, Eve was closing in on something she remembered, a feeling like she could run forever.

"His name is Ali," Eve would say. Some old guy smoking on the concrete steps out front of a corner store still open at midnight. Sitting right where he'd been sitting for years.

"Ali as in Muhammad?"

"He was named after Muhammad Ali, in fact," Eve would say. "My father was a big fan."

"You Muslim?"

"Secular humanist. How about you?"

"I believe in God and Allah and all those. You sure you want to be running down here this hour?"

Dark streets, shining alleys. Eve alone and yet in the company of the city, its wall art, the shifting energy of its sidewalks where crowds gathered after midnight around the neon hum of the convenience stores. There was crime in the riverside neighborhoods, Eve knew. Stofton especially. But she never felt afraid, even miles away from the neighborhood where she lived in the western reaches of the city. Miles from its quiet sleep and private security SUVs, its shingled roofs and motion-activated lights that blinked on nervously over the wide lawns.

One night, just off Sixth Street in Stofton, not far from an intersection that served as an open-air market for drug dealers, Eve came across two young men putting up a poster on a plywood hoarding over an abandoned storefront. There was a crowd watching. Two dozen people standing in the low light, the wafting smells of the sewer and the riverfront. A bearded man sat on an overturned milk crate nearby. Somebody lay at his feet covered in a blanket, coughing and heaving in the chill. The poster was six feet wide and at least that high. It was made with dozens of single sheets of paper, each one a panel of the larger image, pasted up onto the plywood with a brush and a pot of glue. The final image only slowly made itself plain: a close-up photo of two plastic figurines blown to life size, gymnasts with their backs arched and hands extended in a flourish over their heads. There were large bold letters across the bottom of the poster. When the last panel went up, the young men stepped back and everyone could see that the words were *Freedom Is Slavery*. And the crowd began to cheer. The man with the beard yelled: "That is black and white!" Another man said: "Right on!" And a woman who had been standing nearby, tightly gripping two plastic bags full of clothes, put her things down and danced up the sidewalk, singing: "Keep up the good work! Keep up the good work, you beautiful, beautiful young artists!" Eve herself standing with a hand to her mouth now, a lump forming in her throat. The reaction rippled around her, so genuine and so passionate, that it infected Eve too. The woman twirling away up the street past a silent police car bathed in silver street light.

Onward. West out of Stofton. West through River Park, the Flats, along the boulevards that funneled into the West Stretch. She increased her pace, not to hurry but to hear her body in its solitary rhythms and pulses. She shone with sweat, with pleasure, thinking again of the two young men and their poster. The woman and her dance and how her feet had scuffed the pavement in circles, again and again.

Beautiful, beautiful. Down into the quieter winding streets, the looping concentration around West Slopes, then West Lake. Nick would be long snoring by now, lying on his back under his sleep-mask with his earplugs. Otis deep in the murmuring disquiet of his young man's dreams. Oats, they called him, his boyhood nickname although he was seventeen already. Young man enough to be aware of Eve and his father together and to poorly conceal his bemusement at that.

Down towards Angus Lake and towards the house, which had been Nick's parents' house, which is how Eve always read the lawns and the low expanse of building in those moments. She lived there. But it was *his* high square hedge. *His* family oaks and flower beds. Cored out by her run, dangerously emptied, with still no news of Ali, Eve felt now more alone for the effort of looking than she'd been when she started.

It was never her house at the end of a long night run.

THE REFRIGERATOR WOKE FIRST, the television on its aluminum face winking to life, a burble below. A long-familiar tune: war and financial turmoil. There were websites that could be consulted for maps and graphs, videos and the best advice of experts.

Eve hummed "Satellite of Love" while she dressed.

She knocked on the door of Nick's bathroom to let him know she was up, fed the old Alsatian, Hassoman, with his creaking hips and unfixed glaucomic stare. A golden capsule of glucosamine with the organic kibble. Then she went into the big kitchen at the back of the house to find Otis at the table already, hunched in front of his netbook, expression rapt, features luminous with screen light in the half-dark, playing MoleChess™.

Eve pulled up the blinds and flicked on the lights over the counter. "I hope at least you're winning."

He said: "Morning, Champ. Do I lose?"

"You want some breakfast?"

"Gotta finish this one."

"Oats, you own the site," Eve said. "You could adjust your score."

Molechess.com. The noble game bent to suit suspicious times. You owned a piece on your opponent's side, activated for a single move of your choosing. So were games upended by black bishops slaughtering their own, knights rampant behind the lines, queens killing their own kings at the crucial turn. Was it more exciting with traitors?

"Not traitors, Champ," Otis once explained, with the deliberate patience of a smart teenager accustomed to adults falling behind. "Here we are dealing with something more like a system imperfection. Like a program flaw or a defect. Which people really seem to like."

They certainly seemed to. Thousands of people were paying members of the site. Eve was forced to reflect on occasion what it meant that Nick's kid was well on his way to becoming independently wealthy, before university. He was, Eve supposed, enacting his family genes, moneywise at the level of their amino acids. In three generations of Nick's family: a mill owner, a land developer turned wine writer, and now an online-gaming entrepreneur whose skin complexion had not yet cleared. Eve didn't feel quite so competent being between careers herself, between phases somehow. Out of phase. She felt it in the morning especially, when the blinds first went up and the horizon presented itself. A person should be brimming with anticipation at that point in the day, possibility undiluted by fatigue or disappointment. Eve missed that feeling, having known it once. The morning pull of a purposeful heart.

Nick and Otis ate in the sunroom together, side by side at the long table as they'd been doing since Otis's mother left all those years before, when Otis was only five. Father and son behind their bowls, scraping and clattering and reading their separate screens or papers. Eve ate breakfast standing in the adjoining kitchen, not because Nick hadn't encouraged her to sit down, only feeling like she should leave them to their long patterns. So she leaned on the sink looking down the acre of lawn to the creek where the hedge stopped, where someone half-hidden was washing a shirt in the cold stream there. Frompton Creek. It had once held trout, when Nick was a boy.

It was a homeless man camping there, Eve knew. His back bent over his washing. Bare from the waist up. Eve thought of how in Stofton, at that moment, people were waking in parks and stairwells, in parkades and on benches. So many of them. She hoped Ali wasn't among them.

"They're putting up these posters downtown," Eve called over into the sunroom. "I saw them doing one last night. I'm trying to decide if they're political or art or what."

Nick sipped coffee. He looked into his bowl, then across at Eve. Then he started in again on his porridge.

Otis said: "Posters like of what?"

Eve came into the sunroom doorway. "Like these big black-and-white photos of toy soldiers and that kind of thing. With phrases underneath. Those famous newspeak phrases from the Orwell book. 1984. Remember 'War Is Peace'?"

"Like 'Ignorance Is Strength,'" Otis said.

"In the book, what was the guy's name?" Eve asked. "The girl was Julia."

Nick's face was pursed down around a mouthful of Irish steel-cut oats, cream, brown sugar, cut-up apples and pecans. Beside him, Otis ate dry bran flakes by the spoonful, each moistened carefully with a sip of milk.

Nick finished and swallowed, his features settling back into their handsome symmetries. "Was the guy's name Winchester?"

Otis said: "No, Winston."

"Winston," Eve said. "They were in love, Winston and Julia."

"I don't know about love," Otis said, his mouth full again.

"They made love," Eve said, "where no one could see them, although I guess the point was someone actually could see them."

"I think the point," Otis said, "was that given the circumstances, Winston and Julia were certain to betray one another. So their love, or whatever it was, certainly would not last."

"The poster I saw last night," Eve said to Otis, "was 'Freedom Is Slavery.' When it went up, people were cheering and dancing in the street. I'm not kidding."

Which struck them both as absurd, as things often did, making Otis and Eve start giggling, something they would have carried on had Nick not spoken up.

"Eve, you're going to meet those people today, right?"

Otis started eating again.

"Yes," Eve said. "I'm going." Moving back into the kitchen. Leaning again on the sink. Looking through her own reflection in the window, her face greened over by hedges and grass, laced across with branches of weeping willow.

Nick and Otis finished their breakfasts, their getting-ready routines, their goodbye routines. Otis gave her a point of the finger and the wink of one eye. He said: "Later, Champ." Nick gave her a peck on the cheek and squeezed her hand. He told her to call him afterwards. Then he did something he'd started doing lately. He looked into her eyes in what Eve assumed he meant to be a warm but knowing way, a glance to the soul of the moment's true meaning.

Nick said: "Feel good about this meeting. Don't dread it. People love you."

Eve tried to smile. Then, when they were gone, the sound of Nick's car having purred away down the driveway and into the morning, she cleared away breakfast things, made a fried egg sandwich and took it out into the backyard, where she found Katja, Nick's gardener, working the flower beds just off the main deck.

"For me?" Katja said, looking at the sandwich.

"I'll make you one," Eve said. "But this is for our visitor in the hedge."

"Aww," Katja said. "You're so nice."

Eve went down to the bottom of the yard, to the man camping there by the stream. He was fifty. Had been in the wars. Asia, the Middle East. He sat with his shirt off in the fall chill, his hands to the flame of a camp stove where his tea water was on the boil. His brown belly was an accordion of wrinkles. And when he thanked her for the sandwich, he spoke with the trace of an accent from far away.

Two days before, Nick had said to her: "He's got to go, of course. He can't live the rest of his life in our hedge. There are millions of people in need, homeless, unemployed. We can't have them all living in our yard." And Eve made Nick swear he wouldn't force the man to go until they'd had a chance to really talk it through. But she was silently furious with him, a reaction she struggled to justify even to herself.

SHOWERING. STANDING IN THE HOT WATER. Agonizing pointlessly over what to wear, then pulling on the usual jeans, faded cable-knit sweater, never fashionable, borrowed from her father years before and, now, never to be returned. Then out to the truck and eastward across the city. Up into the Heights, the ancient Heights. Time to face the music. Face the day. The meeting had been scheduled and canceled five times previously. Eve was out of excuses.

Double Vision: endorsements, promotions, campaigns, storytelling. "We've worked with many top former athletes," a young partner named Ganesh told her on the phone. "And I can tell you there is always an appetite for the right sort of former athlete. It's recession proof. It really is. It's like a hunger that doesn't go away. And your story . . . Eve, let me tell you, it's one in a million. It gives us tremendous material to work with."

Nick called when she was almost there. He had a way of pressing Eve while at the same time suggesting there was no urgency. This had once been part of what she considered his grounded certainty about what came next, a seeming immunity to doubt and the influence of others. More recently, Eve had sensed these comments to be colored with a different quality. A certain urgency Nick wouldn't have wanted to admit. So he'd tell her that it was good for her to work again. Good for her to be out and about, to move on now after what had it been, two years? The deceased Henri Latour, indefatigable to the moment of his death, would have agreed certainly that being busy was the key to being happy.

Those were Nick's words. *Indefatigable. The key to being happy.* He was in the car himself, heading to a warehouse south of the city to meet with a big area wine broker. A guy who had access to cult wines, secret wines. "Just checking in," Nick said, voice bright.

"I'm on my way," Eve said. "Nick, I'm in the truck. I'm almost there, honest."

Signs and messages all up the main drag through River Park and into the Heights. A show about cooks after-hours. A budget holiday destination. An ethical investment fund. A new cell phone, disposable, biodegradable. It was called the WaferFone: *Minutes to a Better World.* Up towards the crest of the hill, Eve noticed the renovation and improvement. New bike lanes and planters. A thicket of cranes on the ridgeline. It had been warehouses and tenements when she and Ali were kids. Work yards, an abattoir, a field where they'd once watched other kids burning tires. They used to take three different buses from where the family was living in East Shore, which was a new suburb then: modern houses, clean schools, fathers who worked just across the river at the university, or in architecture or journalism. For Eve and Ali, the Heights had been a secret playground. They ate Ukrainian sausages at Kozel's Deli. They trolled the alleys, looking at graffiti. They climbed the fire escapes of abandoned buildings, explored the hidden world of urban rooftops. Heard the pop of gunfire once in the street below.

Up to the top of the hill, utterly transformed. The dead buildings and weeded-out railway spurs of the Heights were now a nexus of impossible refinement, all glimmer and reflection. The tiny wedge-shaped galleries. The hanging coral glass sculpture in the restaurants. And at the heart of things, the resurrected plaza. No more wasting benches, dormant planters, dead fountains. No more daylight muggings or clusters of grim shapes, in-turned around needles and pipes.

Everything changed. Even sight lines in the main plaza seemed to have been radically upended. The old Unitarian Church was gone. And now the natural paths of the eye converged on the Meme Media complex at the western end of the plaza. Clad in silicon and titanium. Canted, billowing sheets. It coaxed the sun to life each morning and was a bier for its setting. The rest of the day, it was a city-scale fun-house mirror, reflecting the streets and buildings, the cafés and the people walking by, all in warped distortion. Meme Media was the home of *KiddieFame*: an idol show for the toddler to nine-year-old set. Naked yearning for status on the faces of parents and coaches. A show big enough to have its own protesters who dressed in black and gathered spontaneously, hoisting signs. Their objections to the show seemed to braid the rhetoric of the neo-anarchist anti-globalism movement with a moral denouncement of the show for being a kind of child abuse. They seemed opposed to fame itself, or fame's pursuit, a point on which Eve was sympathetic even if their critique was scattered. In recent months, the protesters had favored a banner and T-shirts that read *Celebranoia*, which Eve liked, thinking when she saw the word of how close she'd come once to marrying Reza, a French film director with three Palmes d'Or and at least twice as many girlfriends who'd once gone out onto the balcony of a hotel where they were staying in Avignon and aimed a rifle at photographers in the square. He'd been arrested and released, made all the papers and news channels, and later incorporated the scene into a movie. Any rational person who met Reza probably should be *celebranoid*, Eve thought. Although she thought better of buying the T-shirt when she saw it in the window of a rock shop.

Eve found parking on Jeffers Avenue, which ran due south from the square. Double Vision was in that first block south, on the east side of Jeffers in an old building that had been sleekly refurbished in the high-modern style. She rode the elevator to the eighth-floor lobby with its open expanse of glass looking north up Jeffers back into the plaza. As she looked, she remembered that when the protest groups became large enough, the media referred to them as "Black Blocs," but the group gathered today didn't look like it would earn the epithet.

The senior story manager came gliding out from behind a rice paper screen: choker, yoked shirt, wrists bedangled with awareness bracelets. A bearded twenty-five-year-old with an air of religiosity and the faint smell of hair product.

"Eve Latour," he announced. "I am totally, entirely thrilled. I've watched Geneva. What a story. A sort of come-from-behind underdog with suffering and justice. We're all enormous, enormous fans. Please feel no pressure, no pressure at all. My name is Ganesh. This is Marcus."

And here came the founder of Double Vision in his leather car coat and his rumpled shirt, white hair, uneven shave. He toddled in towards her, stood grandfatherly close. Eve smelled talc and cookie dough as he whispered: "I'm glad you're here, Evey. Are you well since your father? A terrible loss. Henri was so important as a journalist and a man, I feel I can really say that for the city, the whole country. For anyone who knew his drive and engagement. His essential what. His essential Latour truthfulness. Courage, yes. You look like him."

He took her hand in both of his without another word, only smiling softly. They weren't shaking hands. Or at least not in a way she'd shaken hands before. He seemed to be working it to and fro, testing the joints up her arm and back into her spine. As if he were gauging her weight before a chiropractic manipulation. And Eve felt an inappropriate laugh rising within her. A laugh she could imagine sharing with Otis later, who would see the absurdity of the moment. The packaging of her life story for sale by a company called Double Vision. Only she thought of the great Henri just then. The drive, the engagement. The essential Latour truthfulness. And as the Double Vision founder straightened and let go of her hand, the comedy of the moment died.

NICK WAS A FORMER GERBER BABY. His face on a million bottles of pureed peas, tomatoes and rice, chicken and pasta. To forestall any discussion of "destiny" or "luck," Nick would discuss this episode only in scientific terms: his infant head to body mass ratio, micronomically symmetrical ear and eye placement, and most important, the correct shape of mouth and lips. Nick, then and now, had a lovely smile. Eve would never have imagined herself with someone more than a decade older than she was, but the smile had certainly been part of it. From the first time she saw it—introduced by a friend whose husband played squash with Nick—Eve had read a graceful self-ease in that smile. Evidence of a man who didn't steal glances at his own reflection or worry overly about shirt choices. A couple years post-Reza, who'd lived almost entirely as if guided by the impression he made on others, these qualities in Nick, all captured in an easy, symmetrical smile, seemed to Eve most attractive.

Blind genetics, Nick would say, the program of cellular certainties. Nick was an atheist of the new school, which meant that he had moved past argument, finding anyone still harboring transcendental yearnings to be an acute embarrassment. So, while he courted Eve avidly, seeming always to anticipate her moods, to find the right idea for the moment—a quiet dinner or a day at the dog races—from their first discussion of it, he refused any suggestion of fate in his Gerber history. He'd been expertly selected, picked out of a stroller in a parking lot by an ad man whose signature was at the bottom of a contract Nick kept framed in his den. Berwick Chad, VP Talent Development. Nick went looking for him later in life and learned Chad had died of lung cancer some years before. Nick's own family, for their part, never discussed the Gerber business after the fact. Going back, they were landowners and operated a number of flour mills along the river. Nick's parents were astute with his small windfall, silently investing every penny, then passing away early. So they'd handed Nick his adult life in the form of a house and a tract of riverfront land where the mills had been, which became the first important area in the city for redevelopment. It all unfolded as if by plan. Build the condominiums. Sell them. Make the money. Retire to write the wine column. It read like self-creation, but Eve knew Nick occasionally experienced it as a mechanical given, something over which he'd had no control from the beginning. And that thought could make the days heavy, even for an atheist. Confining Nick to his den, deepening the frown lines and the silence.

Deep inside Double Vision, meanwhile—deep into a long montage of images and music that the story managers had put together about Eve's gold-medal race in Geneva—Eve herself was struggling to keep her thoughts on the matter at hand. She squinted in the lowered light of the boardroom and tried to focus on the film, a jump-cut affair laid over a soundtrack of pulsing urgency and cultural import. Didgeridoos and beatboxes, bassoons and a Franco-Celtic fiddle coloring aural depths beneath the grainy images of her famous race. She wasn't bored by the story or embarrassed to hear it again. She'd learned to live with its retelling because it happened a lot. But to have the visuals and audio ramped up to this degree made her distinctly anxious. The Double Vision folks didn't appreciate perhaps that Eve had the psychological interior of this event stamped on her memory. So, despite the soaring music, she knew what paralyzing nerves had threatened to overcome her there at the start of the pursuit portion of the race, her breathing obviously far too fast, her glances back towards the waiting pack of opponents far too frequent. Chief among these opponents, Giselle Von Kemper standing cool in her skis, rifle snug between her shoulder blades. A slab-muscled woman from Innsbruck, incumbent gold-medal holder, savage media darling. And still the strong favorite, despite Eve's having bested her in the sprint the day before. Eve at twenty-four was a wisp compared to her. She remembered thinking there in the tapering seconds before the starter's pistol how her own thighs were approximately half the diameter of Von Kemper's. And with that thought, the Austrian aimed a cool smile in her direction, said a word that Eve never caught, then turned her face back to the trail. Fatless, aerodynamic. A human bullet train.

Eve's eyes left the screen, again, seeking reprieve out the window that ran down the west side of the boardroom. There was a telescope standing at the window, a vintage touch in the modern boardroom. It stood on a tripod aimed out at the view, and Eve longed to get up and look through it at the roofs opposite, to look out over that same hidden world that she and Ali had once explored. And with that exact thought, something moved on the roof of the old Peavey Block directly across from Double Vision on the west side of Jeffers Avenue.

Eve was alert, all at once. Wide awake, curiosity alight. The Peavey Block roof was lower than the eighth-floor boardroom where she sat, so it was laid out for her to examine. And that was definitely a person over there, half obscured at the shadow line. And then, as it turned, or adjusted position, she saw that it was a young man: lean frame, down on his knees on the gravel and moss. He was muscled in over some business, hidden from street-level viewing. Eve guessed he was applying pressure to something, flexing his body, his shoulders hunched, his narrow waist twisting. While around him the rooftops seemed to join in a single surface, stretching across the ridgeline, then disappearing over the lip of the hill towards downtown. Roof ducts and ventilator shafts, air-conditioning units, satellite dishes. Eve imagined herself down there with the young man, looking over his shoulder as she might have done with Ali in their day: rooftop running, floating from parapet to cornice, from brick to gravel, shingle to sky.

In the boardroom, the on-screen music ramped and the Double Vision staffers hunched forward in their chairs. The visioning managers and plot leaders and product narrative specialists. All pulling for her, urging her on in the half-light. It was a miniature re-enactment of what had happened in the city those years before. Everyone had been paying attention to her training. She was the local girl. And the whole city had watched in amazement as she'd beaten Von Kemper in the qualifying sprints by five seconds, the rest of the pack another full twenty seconds behind them. A stunning, unexpected result. So now not only was the whole city watching, the whole world was watching as Eve was poised to start the pursuit. She would go first, followed five seconds later by Von Kemper, followed twenty seconds later by the rest of them in the order they'd finished the sprint. And in every watching mind—those rooting for and against Eve—it was a one-in-a-thousand shot she could hold them off. There were simply too many of them. And Von Kemper was too strong, too sure, too calm. So everyone leaned forward, tense and waiting, as the starter raised his arm. As the pistol cracked in the cold air.

Nick had once told her the circumstances surrounding his own viewing of this material on television. He was at the offices of the real estate development firm he was then working with, and someone came into his office to say the race was live on the television in the common room. Nick was game. He went down the hall. He remembered watching Eve's breath making ghosts in the alpine air. But he remembered a particular feeling too. Not love at first sight, Nick said, as if he needed to assure her on that point. But a certainty that they were going to meet. And the deep irrationality of that thought so unsettled him, as it was just a superstition in the end, an ignorant hunch, that he excused himself to the men's room before the race began, where he splashed cold water on his face and stared himself down in the mirror. *Snap out of it, man.* He returned just in time to see the race begin. In retrospect, he told Eve some months after they'd started dating, he also thought he might have had a touch of food poisoning.

Now the archival footage rolled, Eve surging across the start line and heading down the trail. Von Kemper quickly in pursuit, her skis raising Valkyrian plumes of powder as she tried immediately to close the gap. In Double Vision, Eve watched and relived those straining first moments. And then the shock, as Eve seemed to stagger, to jolt in her boots, then tumble with agonizing slowness sideways and off the path. There was a glittering aura of snow crystals and camera flashes. The air humming instantly with alarm and reappraisal as the French announcer famously pronounced, in just those opening seconds: *Eve Latour has fallen!*

Then the French announcer said it again. And as if to punctuate the epic seriousness of Eve's failure—including the failure of judgment implied by being born to a French family that had immigrated to North America three generations previously—he rephrased and focused the thought using the full version of her name, fully inflected with the mother tongue: *Genevieve Latour! Genevieve Latour will not win the biathlon gold!*

He said this because Von Kemper was hard on her now, storming past Eve in a mist of snow and heading down the trail towards the first targets. But even so, it was early for him to reach his conclusion. Like all those watching, live and on television, he didn't know what had really just happened. Eve hadn't stumbled because she was clumsy. She'd stumbled because something had hit her, just above the ankle of her left boot. Something small, hard and traveling at extremely high speed. Like a bullet, exactly. An instant curtain of pain fell over her. But as she lay on her side, gripping her ankle, she saw in the faces of the nearby officials that they hadn't heard a thing. Not a bullet from a gun, then. What? On the trail, right in the track left by one of her skis, lay a steel ball bearing. And all around the point of impact on her ankle raged a wildfire across frantic nerve endings.

Slingshot, it would later turn out. A rather serious-looking hunting slingshot made of aluminum and surgical tubing wielded by a crazy Belgian on a balcony with clear sight lines. Now here was a random piece of bad luck. A man obsessed with the beautiful Eve Latour, whose apartment was wallpapered with photographs of her. A crazy Belgian who decided a good way to get Eve's attention would be to take her opponent out of the race. He'd been aiming for Von Kemper, he told police.

But all that would take days to come out. Eve didn't have days, a thought that shafted through her as she lay writhing on the snow. And if it didn't quite ice the pain (bruised Achilles, hairline talus fracture), the thought did reorder the hierarchy of her senses. As Von Kemper blew by her, Eve's pain was forced to take its place behind other concerns.

And here it came. The heroics. Eve Latour skiing and shooting on what everybody would later understand was a broken ankle. Gutting it out into the history books. She followed Von Kemper around that course, closing, closing. Five times two and a half kilometers. She came magnificently from behind, her face a rictus of pain and concentration. And then the miraculous final sprint, passing Von Kemper on the down leg. The five-shot burst on the final targets, her breath ripping in and out of her. It was like shooting off the deck of a ship in a storm. But she knocked them down and sprinted for the finish line. Von Kemper dethroned yet somehow ecstatic, as if in relief. The Innsbruck Ibex scooped Eve up from where she lay crumpled in the snow on the far side of the finish line. Von Kemper hefted Eve as if she were a child. Kissed her neck, weeping, carried her around.

Eve escaped briefly to the window again as the film drew to its long-established close. Her eyes drifted out past the telescope to find the young man still bent over that same task, applying his strength to the same stubborn problem. Around him the littered evidence of human traffic. The empty drink containers and painted marks. The plastic lean-to abandoned in the elbow of a service shaft. The young man tremored, his back shifting and now, suddenly, unfurling as if something had given way. He might have been reefing on a stubborn lug nut, but whatever it was had surrendered, and the young man sprawled on his side in the gravel, then bolted to his feet, holding one hand, hunched over, grimacing. Then standing and staring straight up at the sky. Mouth open. Yelling out in exasperation, Eve thought, although she couldn't hear it. Now standing straight again, pacing and shaking his hand. Eve could see him more clearly now. Black hair, lean and wiry. Darker skin and taller, but otherwise so strongly reminiscent of Ali.

The film was done. The lights came up. There was a moment when a break for coffee was proposed, but Eve motioned for them to continue, her attention now hard split as the charts of personal data went up on the screen, the survey results, the storyboards of her life with turning points and moments of capsize. The way these meshed with the story requirements of existing Double Vision clients. A training shoe manufacturer, a climbing outfitter, a financial institution. The Chinese Winter Tourism Authority. Heathrow Airport. The list was preliminary. She could say no to anyone, they assured her. There would always be more.

Eve listened and kept her eyes in motion, nodding and communicating her full attention, while stealing glances at the rooftop opposite. The young man was in his late twenties, she guessed. And he had either finished or abandoned what had brought him up there because he was packing his things now, loading them into a black nylon knapsack, a certain irritable haste in his movements. And then, something unexpected.

He left the knapsack on the gravel and moved to the rear of the Peavey Block rooftop, to the very lip of the parapet, where he leaned over and planted his hands on the aluminum flashing. He gripped and regripped, as if testing the surface, then upended himself into a handstand, right at the edge of the rooftop, sixty-odd feet above a sheer drop to the pavement behind the building. His body rigid and quivering. His legs first straight, then spreading slowly into an open V. He held that position while all around Eve the air was filled with a discussion of her attribute catalog, known qualities and values. The number of hits generated when googling the phrase "I love Eve Latour," 837,578 as of that morning.

She was pulled back into the room, where Ganesh gave her two thumbs up. By the time she was able to check back out the window, the parapet was empty. And Eve's heart was instantly racing. She heaved up halfway out of her chair, about to bolt to the window, thinking that he must have fallen. Then she noticed that the young man's knapsack was also gone and she sank back into her chair.

MARCUS WALKED HER TO THE ELEVATOR, then rode down with her. He said: "Take time. Talk to Nick."

"I'm a little unsure."

"We won't push."

She finally let go the laugh. It cracked the air in the elevator. The Double Vision founding partner did not startle or wince. He laughed too. He was a natural.

She said: "I guess I'm having a mixed reaction. Licensing. Buying the rights to a part of my life story, to copy and reproduce. To sell. Is it just me or is that weird?"

She had words streaming through. *Movieland. Brands. Messages. Promises. Values.*

Finally she said: "I find it weird."

"Weird or threatening?" Marcus asked her.

Which was also insightful. At this point, Geneva was no longer a story she controlled, but the edited footage made it seem a thing over which she had never been in control. That, in turn, cast her future in a questionable light.

"Threatening," Eve said, relieved to say it.

"Think of magazines and newspapers. You give them interviews."

She nodded. Not so often anymore. But when they asked, she did.

"So you let them have your story. It's the same transaction that we're proposing. Just a different medium."

She was watching the numbers click. Six, five, four. This calm voice from the space just to her right. "The journalist asks you: Evey, where were you born?"

The elevator dinged arrival at the lobby. He held the door with a large white palm, then stepped out with her into the wide, shining room. Through high glass doors she saw the buses and traffic cones, the trenched-out sewer works of Jeffers Avenue which led up to the plaza.

"You say: I was a kid from the East Shore. Right? But I'd come across town and troll the Heights with my brother, Ali. We'd take pictures with an old camera we found at a junk shop. Buy copies of *True Crime* and read them over at Kozel's Delicatessen. Right? Maybe you say more. Maybe you tell them how you never told your parents where you were going. Or that Ali was your childhood hero."

Eve brought her attention back inside. "Did you talk to him?"

He shook his head. "We don't know where he is either. Both Nick and your mother were eager to talk, though. They're fans of yours."

"They're not *fans*," Eve said, voice sharpening.

"Supporters. People who love you."

Trucks were passing, sides painted huge. Courier services, commercial bakeries, moving companies. The one that stopped just now had a frog on the side, huge red eyes locked on Eve alone. A cable company. Eve released a long breath, stabilizing herself. She didn't show anger often, but Marcus had just pushed her very close.

"But it's still your story being sold," he continued. "To the magazines, the papers, then finally to the people who wanted it in the first place. The people who desire it. Key word *desire*, Evey. Desire is how your story achieves its highest natural value."

The frog was gone.

He produced a key card and buzzed her out. Then in the open doorway, he held the card out towards her.

"To come and go," he said. "If you can begin to feel comfortable here, I think this is a process you can learn to enjoy."

Eve took the card to finish their business. She submitted to the cheek kiss, a cool damp touch, wiped when she was safely away from Double Vision, well down the street.

OUT IN THE PLAZA there were flags fluttering and Eve had the sensation of having forgotten something, like where she'd parked. Or an errand she was supposed to run. But it wasn't either of those things.

Across the square, crowds had gathered outside the main doors to Meme Media, and she walked down through the sunken garden, past the empty band riser, the singing fountain and cubist waterfall until she was close enough to see the anxious queue, the show's black-clad protesters cordoned off to one side. This was the final procession of contestants in for the filming of another episode of *KiddieFame*. And even bundled against the fall chill, Eve thought she could decipher plainly enough every ambition. The aspiring soul singers and rappers, the six-year-old actors and models, the stand-up comics and celebrity chefs in waiting.

The kids moved and corralled, they hived off and re-gathered in front of tents and awnings, past the tables with the sign-up sheets and releases and waivers, onto the switchback ramp that led up the glimmering flanks of the building under the two-story banners that riffled overhead: *KiddieFame. You Should Have these Problems.* The words imposed over a picture of the cliché spoiled child star, pampered by staff, lounging poolside, tiles under the deck chair littered with twenties and fifties, spent candy wrappers and game controllers.

They filed inside with their voice and dance coaches, their prompters and image consultants and stuffed animals. Never with their parents, who were craftily banned from tapings. Whose presence, producers had long ago decided, made contestants too sympathetic, too human. Parents who surrendered their children to the *KiddieFame* machinery weren't even allowed to sit in the green room. They stayed shivering outside the building, smoking against a bank of outdoor toilets erected for their use.

Eve watched these parents and imagined their anxieties. The humming cameras inside. The 93 million homes into which their children would soon be streaming. These things would be on their minds. But none more so than the possibility that their children might succumb to what was simply known as a "Kill."

KiddieFame had its elimination mechanism, that necessary algorithm of the fame game. You had to kick people off the show in order to find a winner. *KiddieFame* was unusual, however, for having two methods. A competitor could simply lose in the voting that followed a set of performances. But then, in the show's signature moment, they could also be the target of a surprise Kill. These were rare because they followed not bad performances, of which there were many, but perfect ones: performances that received five stars from every voting remote in each of the six hundred seats in the theater.

Why eliminate a candidate who'd been judged perfect? There were PhDs written about the *KiddieFame* Kill, including one that received some internet notoriety for asserting that the show was inspired by "archaic sacrificial religions, which always laid the best, most beautiful victims on their altars." In any case, whether understanding it or not, the audience seemed to sense when a particular performer must go. And how harmonious the rounds immediately following a Kill then seemed to be, as if some sort of peace had been restored. While from the sacrificed, naturally, came snivels, and from their attendants muttered curses, knotted rage, the sense of the existential trapdoor having been sprung. The fall into invisibility begun.

Eve turned to leave, returning a wave from a traffic cop standing nearby—a touch of a finger to the brim of his hat, a shy grin of recognition—then she crossed back over the plaza and down Jeffers towards her truck.

She'd parked near the mouth of a narrow alley that ran down the side of the Peavey Block. She had her keys out, but she stepped into the alley, into the cold shadow, remembering the wet-paper smell, the floral ambiguity of the scent of garbage, the rust motes alive in the air, descending from the disintegrating fire escapes and window grates that spidered up the flanks of the building. Eve followed these with her eyes, up and up.

And there he was. A tight package of balance and nerve, poised high on the parapet, halfway down the alley. He was wearing purposeful clothes, she could see, like those of a specialized kind of climber. The shoes looked thin soled but grippy. The cargo pants trim to the legs. The hoodie functional and black. She noted that one of his hands was gloved but that the other was now bandaged, and she remembered him shaking it out on the roof earlier. She could make out his face from where she stood, although he hadn't seen her and was staring straight ahead as if the view down were of little interest. He had dark features and eyes that, though steady, seemed to fix in an expression of playfulness. Not much like Ali at all in that regard, who tended to be serious, except that the expression contained no fear. Even from that distance, Eve could see that the man was utterly certain about what came next. Certain and pleased at the same time. His feet parallel, the tips of his shoes lipped out a fraction over those six stories of brick below, six stories down to pavement where she stood. And she saw that he was bouncing slightly in place, completely at ease with his balance as if it were something that would never be questioned. He might have been contemplating a standing broad jump across the alley.

She wanted to yell: "Don't!" Or to shout up: "Stop!" But she didn't, thinking she might startle him and actually cause him to fall. But perhaps more because he was clearly going to jump no matter what she would say. And exactly as she had that thought, the young man stepped back off the parapet and disappeared from view on the hidden rooftop. Eve imagined him flexing his legs, a quick hand down to each ankle to stretch the quads. Limbering up. Eyes front, locked on the far side.

She made an involuntary noise, a choked and fearful squeak. But here he was again. He would have leaned forward a fraction before uncoiling. He would have taken about a six-step run-up. Bim bim. Bop bop. BAP. BAP. And bursting into view, into the open air. He made a long parabola against the gray and cooling sky directly above her. He filled the empty space, his arms spread for balance, his legs tucked. And then, impossibly, he rolled at the top of his arc. He flipped in midair, which brought about a microsecond of complete silence and stillness in her. The whole movement was completely dangerous and completely harmonious. And it pinned her to the spot.

Gone. Across the alley, through space, over the parapet of the far building. Without a sound. Without a reason. No motive, nobody chasing him. No audience that he could have known of, since he hadn't looked down to see that she was there.

It was breathtaking. The most beautiful thing she'd seen in years.

HOME LATE. Winding down the cedar-scented avenues. Nick came out from his den and made her an omelet and a salad, poured her a glass of wine, telling her about the grapes and the vintage as she took her first sip. Young vines, clay soil, surprising body. Fruit, acid, harvest times. A cold room lined with barrels of toasted oak. Nick journeyed the wine from its vineyard to her glass, then sat staring into the book-shelf over her shoulder, waiting for her to notice him. Waiting for her to speak.

Eve said: "Sorry."

"I can't make up your mind for you," Nick told her.

"I just have certain questions about the whole thing."

"Work is work."

"It's not the money. You want me back out there."

"I think it's healthy that you get back out there, yes."

"So I start peddling my former self."

"Former," Nick said. "What, is that person gone?"

"I mean all this business of my *story*."

"Not everybody gets asked to tell their story."

She chewed a mouthful of omelet. This little miracle of eggs and Gruyère on the plate in front of her. Golden yellow, flecked with green parsley, dotted with truffle oil. Nick was very good at this kind of thing. Every plate deliberately amazing. Every wine paired. Eve was good for making porridge. No Home Economics in her education. No box of recipes from her glacier-climbing, telemarking mama.

"Well, they asked," she said. "Marcus gave me a key card and said I should come and go."

"They respect and trust you. They want it to be mutual."

"But you don't do this kind of thing out of being flattered," Eve said.

"Maybe you do it out of why the hell not. Go down. Sit in the board-room. See how terrible it is. Or maybe you just do it because you're proud of who you are."

Eve chewed and watched him go into the kitchen for the bottle and a second glass. There were certain thoughts about Nick that she realized she cut off, afraid of where they might lead her. Why did he want this for her so much? She hated to think Nick needed her out there so that by her recharged public image, something in him might be renewed and recharged, validated by her recognition.

Nick returned with the bottle and topped her up, poured some for himself.

She said: "I'm not *not* proud of who I am."

Nick sipped and looked into the wine. "After your father died, you started to pull out of everything. You started to brood."

"UNICEF was always understood to be a term thing. Two years."

"Everything else, though."

"I needed new ideas."

"All right. So Double Vision. A new set of ideas."

"They call it 'personal story management,' did you know that? I bet Stalin could have made good use of a phrase like 'personal story management.'"

"In the end, it's just benign," Nick said.

"Your story is over, comrade. My condolences."

"They're just about what everything is all about anyway."

"Everything? What does that mean?"

"They're . . . charisma brokers," Nick said, pleased to have thought up the phrase. "So they find people who other people naturally like. Then they get those people linked up with companies and products that need access to some of the same goodwill."

Eve stared at her plate. It killed her appetite to hear Nick talk this way. It made her shrink inside. *Charisma.* Likeability. Did Nick think about these things more than she realized?

"They weave a tale of great courage into the selling of some basket-ball shoes. Who's hurt?"

"Great courage." Eve laughed.

"Sure, great courage."

"That's not what it was."

"You downgrade yourself constantly," Nick said. "More so since your father died. Like you're not happy with yourself in any setting. I really think you're having some kind of self-esteem crisis, which I just don't understand at all."

She put her fork down. She could challenge Nick on this point. If someone was having a self-esteem crisis, it wasn't her. But she hated arguing, so she said instead: "I just don't happen to see winning a gold medal as having anything to do with courage."

"No courage," Nick said. "None at all. She gets winged by some psycho with a slingshot. Falls down. People think it's over. Not just one person. Every single person watching. About a billion people think it's over."

Eve picked up her fork again.

"But not this young woman. So she gets up."

"I'll tell you one thing," Eve said. "I was pissed off."

"No doubt. You had a broken ankle!"

In the living room, down the passage, Eve could see the television flickering, sound off. Twenty-four-hour televised news because there was always news. And now, something, somewhere was burning. A car.

A building. There was a certain comforting structure to the images, bad news in recent progress. Someone ran across the camera's field of view, arms waving. It was possible to feel reassured. The world producing what the news needed, the news then delivering it back to the waiting world.

"This Ganesh," Eve said. "Have you met him?"

"Talked to him on the phone."

"He described Geneva as suffering and justice." She started laughing again.

"May I finish?"

She made her eyes wide. *Yes.*

"You continued the race despite the fact that by any reasonable estimate you were done, finito, kaput."

"Finishing is just what you do. I imagine it takes more courage to quit."

"Okay. I give up. Zero courage."

The news broadcast was back inside the studio. Man anchor. Woman anchor. Serious expressions. Eve was glad the sound was off. Maybe she could sit out this news item and never have to know the details of where in the world things were going poorly at the moment.

She looked over at Nick, voice and spirits suddenly brightening. "I saw the most incredible thing today."

He was closely reading the label of the wine bottle. Soil densities. Organic practices. She told him about seeing the young man jump. Late twenties. Lean frame, muscular. But how shocked she'd been at his power. How he exploded right off the edge of the roof, across the alley, and then flipped at the top. "Which is crazy. Right over my head."

Nick raised his eyebrows, twisting the bottle. "You're not saying that was courage, I hope. That's just daredeviling."

"It's called Parkour," Eve said, who'd been looking for the word the entire afternoon, then got it just as she was pulling in the drive. Parkour: from a show she'd seen on Discovery Channel.

Nick shook his head. No, he had no idea about Parkour.

"It's a sport. They jump off very high things. Run creatively."

"They run creatively."

"It's French," Eve said, but she knew there was no point. Nick had a particular expression, a holding expression. Like he knew he shouldn't interrupt, but that he was already wholly occupied with the next thing he was going to say.

He said it now: "Let me just say this."

Lights continued to flash on the television. Fire trucks. Police cars. Blue and red halos in the blackness. Orange flares and white head-lights, familiar as Christmas. The camera just now bucking at some nearby shock or noise, the light sources spinning. Pinwheels. Sparklers. Someone was shooting, Eve realized, recognizing it in the shape and shift of the images. Here we had something going badly, somewhere, and it involved guns. One of those stories they had all become tragic-ally used to seeing and hearing about. The man with a gun in his workplace. The kids in trench coats wandering into a school. Eve thought how utterly horrible it was that the news would be shaping up again around one of those stories.

"Let me just say that your father was never a daredevil," Nick con-tinued. "As a journalist he took more risks than most. But he was cal-culated. Still, of course . . ."

"Improvised roadside device," Eve said. "You can say it. He was one of three journalists killed in three separate incidents on the same day."

She ate the rest of the omelet in a flattened silence. She drank wine. Then tried again: "I don't look at everything in me now and see my father. And I didn't end my term with UNICEF because he died either."

"What about the weather announcer gig. Why'd you quit that?"

"I didn't mind doing the weather, actually. I liked going up in the helicopter."

"But you were always conscious of the cliché."

"The jock on TV," Eve said. "Talking low pressure systems from a beach somewhere. You're right. I mostly found it embarrassing."

More shots, Eve guessed. The camera operator was seeking cover, his picture all skewed. And now something else appeared to have gone up. The camera operator was running, lens on the pavement. Then back up and shooting. In front of a high building, glinting metallic in the grainy light, another car lay spectacularly on its side, engulfed in rolling black smoke and licks of flame.

"Where's Oats?" Eve asked.

Nick followed her eyes down the hall. "Watching online, no doubt. This looks vaguely CNN-able."

"Where's that look like?"

"Dunno."

"Is it happening now?"

"I guess."

Nick got up again. She expected him to go down the hall and find the remote control, toggle on the sound. Although at the same time she found herself hoping he wouldn't. That he wouldn't reveal whatever had suddenly gone bad in the world.

Nick moved the other way, back into the kitchen. He yelled back: "We could finally get married."

She squinted. The building behind the burning car had banners fluttering down its front.

"Okay," she said. "Wait."

Above their heads, in their bedroom, Hassoman levered himself from the bed and thudded to the carpet. He did this when events on the main floor corresponded aurally to certain canine expectations: dishes going into the dishwasher, the front hall closet door opening in advance of a walk. Nothing was signaling him now, but Eve could hear the dog move heavily on the floorboards into the hallway, over to the top of the stairs, where he stood and growled once.

"Good boy," Nick called from the kitchen.

"Nick, that's here," Eve said. "That's up in the Heights. I was there today."

"Come on, boy."

Eve was up and walking towards the living room now, arriving at the door just as Hassoman emerged at the bottom of the stairs, sniffing the air, then barking towards the front door. Once. Again.

Eve started looking for the remote.

More sound on the stairs. Otis coming down. Eve could see herself in a wide shot all at once, pulling up the cushions on Nick's parents' old couch while, for some unknown reason, a car burned in the plaza opposite Meme Media. While Otis stood in the doorway with an expression Eve had never seen on him before. All his teen-aged confidence gone. His eyes wide, mouth seeming to work at some immobilized word. And here came the anchors again, the situation-desk expressions, the pre-fatigue of some event they both knew they'd be talking about for many further hours, through the night. An event that already perplexed and astounded. Eve watched a graphic roll on the blue screen. Familiar queues of children. Then the incident banner. It scrolled across the corner of the screen like a sash. It read: *The Meme Media Crisis.*

Cut to the street, the reporter out of breath. Over his shoulder, three police trucks rolled out of Jeffers Avenue and into the square.

Otis was still working the words, lips opening and closing.

"Otis," Eve said. "Are you all right?"

"Hey, what's up?" Nick said, entering the hall. He was holding a small skillet and a towel. He put the pan down on a side table and picked up the remote from where it sat on one of the shelves of the bookcase. But he didn't key the volume just that moment, staring over at his son. "Okay. Come on."

Otis got the word, finally. "Hostages."

"Turn on the sound, Nick," she said.

But Nick just stood there, remote dangling. "Hostages what?"

Eve was nodding at the screen, just as Otis's mental logjam broke.

He said: "Hostages, Dad. In the TV building." Then: "They say a guy took some of those *KiddieFame* kids for hostage in the building."

And here Eve did something that she couldn't explain to herself then, and which she knew she would remember as a strange impulse later. She ran into the kitchen to look at the clock hanging there, to note the time. As if it were clear that the most pressing priority were to mark the beginning of this thing.

The clock, innocent of all knowing, had ticked its way past 9:00 in the evening and was heading towards 9:01.

WEDNESDAY EVENING

—

OCTOBER 23

GIRARD

—

LIKE THEY WERE ACTING SOMETHING OUT. Like they were part of the show.

They escaped by the rear doors of the television studio. Mad crowds, crazed. Adults and children. They slammed into each other and bounced, they grabbed each other and held, or pushed away. The only law governing their movement was the impulse to escape. To get out, get free. In that they were inspired by one another. Pushing and pulling, helping and not helping. The concrete stairs echoed on the way down, feet stamping and skipping and slipping. Some people were on their cell phones already, but there really wasn't anything to say. They didn't know anything, nobody did. So close were the performance and the feared reality, so close the entertainment and the violence.

So they yelled into their phones: *A man with a gun!* But they also added other things, voices scrambling out the words: *As if he had been choreographed! Just like it were part of the show!* And they forwarded pictures and video clips too, out there in the rear alley and the side street, but these images didn't reveal anything. Grainy figures in black, curtains of smoke. Terrible audio. They were dream sequences.

At first people thought it was a Kill that launched the terrible events, a Kill so early in the taping that it had been a complete surprise. Viewers generally had to invest a few hours before the factions began to form, the feudal hatreds, the necessary sacrifices. But not in this case. She was that good. A ten-year-old version of any number of top-level soul singers, but different too. Hyacinth was her name. Tall for her age, with skin toned the color of creamed coffee, gorgeous cheekbones and a high-beam smile. And as the studio audience learned in her preamble comments, she lived in the eastern foothills of the Rockies, a few hours on horseback from the Continental Divide. Her ancestors were the indigenous people of that area, having been there for over ten thousand years, and she had herself learned to sing by listening to thunderstorms and hail, the power of the wind in the towering forests near her home. That and Celine Dion, she said. But mostly nature. And with her mouth open full aperture, lungs in full release ("The Power of Love," 1984), it became clear she was beyond the standard herself. By the time she'd climbed to the summit of that first chorus, people weren't just swaying in their seats compelled by the rhythm. They were being pushed and pulled by the sheer pneumatic force of the kid's pipes. She moved the air in the theater, in great tidal fluxes. And when she hit that apogean note—so many registers above them all, lordly in its duration and clarity—the crowd was at once buzzing, aware that a talent of religious proportions had been unveiled, a talent that would certainly destroy them all if it weren't first destroyed.

The assembled competitors and coaches, invited guests of the studio and all those who'd won their tickets on radio call-in shows or had convenience store scratch-and-win tickets, simultaneously had the knowledge. She was too good. Her story was too good. Hyacinth had to go. So they floated to their remotes, before the voice had fully drained from the room. They keyed in their scores and they knew.

She killed. And they killed. Five stars came in from every voting seat. And there it went. Flash pots exploded, the surround-sound speakers rumbled to life, a loop of helicopter rotor noise shook the building as if it were under attack. And on the massive flat-screen monitor at the front of the theater, where the contestants normally appeared in close-up, there were images of soldiers storming through the backstage area, heading towards the studio theater. Figures in black combat fatigues charging through corridors, shouting and brandishing their weapons. And seconds later, those same figures were storming into the theater itself. There were only six of them but they seemed to flood from everywhere at once, and as they scattered, waving their weapons, they swelled in the senses to become many more.

A THIRTEEN-YEAR-OLD BOY, GERRY—full name Girard, rarely used—was sitting in 14G, watching this with a wry smile. He turned to his six-year-old sister and her best friend. "I've seen this before," he told them. "They had it on CNN." It would be many hours later before he would wonder what he'd meant by saying that, because he'd never seen a *KiddieFame* Kill on CNN. Only real soldiers.

But here they came, seeming to charge directly off the big flat screen at the front and out into the theater through its three sets of doors, one at the rear and two on either side of the stage. These men and the chaos of their soundtrack. So it was that happy delirium and pyrotechnic bedlam coexisted for a while, the audience cheering as the soldiers ran up and down the aisles and yelled back and forth and waved their assault rifles in the air. They looked quite real, these men and their weapons, as real as in the movies. Which was exactly how everybody knew that they were actors hired by the studio to carry out the Kill. People understood it, instinctively, Gerry included. These six men were part of the show.

It was only when the seventh man took the stage, not from any of the three sets of doors, but from the right stage wing, ambling rather calmly across the boards and seeming to observe the action from a critical distance, that the first trace of unfamiliar scent began to taint the air.

Gerry might have been the first to sense it. He watched that seventh man and immediately felt his smile fall away, his brow wrinkle with suspicion. Now here was a person who seemed to carry something in with him from the outside, a whiff of the real. Gerry arrived at this thought in a glancing way. He first thought of how he hadn't wanted to be here in the first place, and how his father had insisted that he accompany his younger sister and her friend. Only then did he register a smell. A sweaty canvas smell, the fragrance of unusual oils. And having sensed that, all the other details began to cascade. The man onstage wore different clothes than the actors. He had on a rumpled suit with a balaclava pulled over his face. He didn't just have a rifle snouted out casually over the audience; he also had an aluminum briefcase held tightly in his other hand.

These were the wrong details, Gerry knew. Just as it was wrong that the singer Hyacinth and her entourage weren't immediately rounded up to a corner of the stage and escorted out of the building, cameras swiveling and scuttling to catch every detail. In fact, the whole performance seemed now to veer in the wrong direction, the whole cycle of fake threat and artificial violence not wrapping up as it should, but seeming to deepen instead, yawning open suddenly to new and troubling possibilities as the man with the case and the gun pushed the girl Hyacinth back into the audience, into a random seat. And rather roughly too.

That was a turning point, which Gerry felt even if nobody else did. There was still a lot of cheering going on at this point, delighted expressions, horror-show screaming. But Gerry felt it like a draft, new information blowing through the room. *The seventh man is not an actor.* And he reached for his sister's hand, something he may have done only

once previously in his entire life, in the back seat of the car on that day
a year before when it had been decided that she would go live with
their father. He took her hand then, just as he did now, and pulled it
to his lap. Holding it between both of his hands very tightly.

There was a suspension in the air. The volume fell off sharply.
Murmurs and questions swept the seats around Gerry. Regret, it
sounded like. Guilt about triggering the Kill and now finding the
victim still among them, smile extinguished, sobbing uncontrollably
in her first-row seat, her face cupped in slender hands. But real uncertainty too. And that was made worse by the odd pattern that now played
among the soldiers. When Hyacinth was pushed clear of the stage,
pushed back into the audience and not removed, those six men registered the seventh man onstage for the first time, and all of them immediately stopped shouting and running about and *acting* like they
had violence on their minds, just as an actor would if he were interrupted by a heckler or a technical mistake that raised the houselights
in the middle of a performance. Now they were looking at each other,
gesturing back towards the production booth. And all of that would
have gone on for many minutes had the gunfire not started. Cold
cracks in the agitated air, and not from the speakers either but from the
man onstage, who was calmly triggering his weapon into the ceiling.

Was this still the Kill? Clearly nobody thought so any longer as all
visible action moved hard towards what people remembered, from
movies and television, was supposed to happen when actual violence
was under way. There was glass coming down. Bits of soundproofing.
A lighting unit dropped from the ceiling and shattered in the aisle to
Gerry's right. And sometime in the previous minute or so, the camera
operators around the theater had abandoned their viewfinders and
stretched out on the floor. The producers in the production booth
must have done the same because the flat screen at the front of the
theater now showed only the ceiling where one of the cameras had

been left to point: blank acoustic tiles punctured here and there by bullet holes, hanging cables, broken lights.

Gerry thought that the blank screen was what did it for the rest of the audience. A switch was thrown. Suspension of disbelief collapsed. And there was a sudden release, a sudden unveiling. People burst into whatever action had been queued up in their systems waiting for the adrenal trigger. They ran to whatever set of doors was the closest, or they ducked for cover. Children were grabbed or they were not grabbed. There were bumps and shoves and entreaties and curses. All behaviors evident in the same moment as if from the same organism.

It was a good thing (Gerry thought later) that he was holding his sister's hand already or his legs might have carried him out the door without her. As it was, she was dragged behind him up the center aisle, bits of ceiling falling here and there, all the way back to the rear doors and into the crush of bodies there. Gerry pushed his sister into the mass of people, yelling at her to go down the stairs, to keep running. She was screaming, but with no words. Although everyone was screaming and no single voice could be heard. He pushed her again, physically driving her into the vortex of bodies and watching to make sure she was swept to the top of the stairs and pulled downwards with the flow. Then he ran back to their seats and began to look for his sister's best friend. But she was gone.

Shots again from the stage, lacing lower over the crowd. And now a tidal shift of motion swept the room. Most of the hundred and fifty people in the theater dropped to the floor, clutching their heads or pressing themselves down over smaller children. A few stood bolt upright, frozen in the thought of flight, or yelling, or trying to speak calmly to those around them. Others didn't move at all, sitting placidly as if nothing had yet registered.

Gerry was on his stomach, flat to the concrete floor at the end of his row with a good view up and down the aisle. Here he saw several of the original six actors crawl by on hands and knees, heading towards the rear door, one of them sobbing. He saw the producers and technicians come creeping out of the production booth at the back of the theater. And here an incident ignited that hurried things from chaos to their brutal order. The senior producer, creator of the show, and a man of significant fame for doing so, lumbered to the top of the center aisle, not far from the end of Gerry's row, purple with rage and shouting. He demanded an explanation. And when no response came from the stage, no anger, no immediate move even to make him stop, he tipped catastrophically into his own fury, spit flying, wattles shaking, threats blazing. If this jackass up there, with no authorization to do what he'd done, if he didn't, this second, this fucking *instant* . . .

So the shots began again, with an almost lazy, painterly quality. A flourishing spray over their heads, chips flying, electrical complaints from the production booth. Gerry saw it all. A final spray of bullets that struck the senior producer in a cluster at the center of his chest and dropped him where he stood. A few more bullets pocked the floor around him, skipping and whining towards the rear where there was a final shattering of glass.

And here the sound fell to near nothing. A terrible falling, a loss of hope. These were what some would later remember as the first moments of the affair. When the man fell and the sound failed. The first moment at which everybody understood new events to be in motion, launched in their uncertain, irreversible sequence.

The producer continued to breathe while Gerry watched, tears and whimpers spreading through audience members around him. The producer breathed through holes in his chest, in shallower and shallower breaths until these stopped and Gerry understood that he was dead. He saw combat boots running rearward, the final actor exiting. And then the noise reduced to a shifting, seething mixture of repeated words. Some people repeated the word *no*. Others repeated the words *oh God.* Others the word *please.* Just breaths really, throat singing in the crumpled air. *No. Oh God. Please.*

The seventh man came down from the stage and circled the theater, weapon loosely trained over the crowd as he worked his way to the rear. Gerry watched what he could see of him from the floor. At the rear doors, he set down his weapon but not the briefcase. And using his free hand, he locked the handles of the doors together with a black bike lock he removed from a pocket. Then, retrieving his weapon, he returned to the front of the theater and did the same to the door at the right of the stage, the one that led to the storage and technical areas. Leaving the final door unlocked, the one that led out into the side lobby and from there into the plaza, he remounted the stage and disappeared for a moment into the wings.

Nobody moved. And when, seconds later, the houselights began to fade, every remaining child and adult wondered with the slow pixelation of light what new type of show had begun.

The man re-emerged and set his weapon down again. Then he pulled his balaclava free and showed his face. It was by now in shadow, and the light was withdrawing fast from the room. But here he was briefly revealed, neither happy nor sad, not frightened or madly emboldened by what he'd done. He seemed merely placed in the moment, more or less content as he pulled on a pair of night-vision goggles. No evil genius in it. No accented arch-villain. No edge of insanity that could be seen.

And that detail was the one remembered by the final person to escape the theater in those opening moments of the crisis. A woman in the very front row, in the seat all the way over and against the left wall nearest the exit that had remained unlocked. She was unconnected to any of the children, unconnected to the show in any way except that she was the maid of one of the line producers, and after she had cleaned up the mess following a party he'd thrown the week before, he'd given her tickets to the taping.

"Bring your children," he told her.

"My children are in the Philippines, sir." And with the rest of her life to think about it, she'd never be able to explain what made her get to her feet at that moment, as the light in the theater failed.

Gilda was her name, and she believed in enormous mysteries. Strength that rose from the deep, lurking energies of the soul. To be feared certainly, because while they rose from within, they did not belong to the person in whose depths they lived.

Up to her feet, across the maroon carpet. She saw the man's chin move an inch to square with her, saw him shift on his feet. But he didn't make a move to stop her. Didn't say a word. So when she reached the door, all that remained to be done was to grip the handle, push outwards, and pass on through to freedom.

Out into the lobby. Through the glass doors and out onto the marble front steps of the Meme complex. Gilda was free. Although the first place she entered in her freedom, that wide public space in front of the television studio, didn't seem to be the same one that she'd left. The plaza was full of lights now, reds and blues. The orange of a flare line. Two enormous bonfires in the street were belching black smoke. Not bonfires, cars. She squinted at them, unable to understand how this had happened. The broken windshield. The flames enveloping the interior. The details were slipping past her somehow, streaming away with the long blue shadows she was casting at the convergence of many hot white lights. There were bullhorn words winging in. And with a swoop, sudden and shuddering, a rush of shapes enclosed her, holding her arms as she collapsed sideways, carrying her. She was on a stretcher. She was in an ambulance, voices and faces all around her. A young man came closest, short hair, trimmed sideburns, nose like a blade on his face. Handsome in all the wrong ways. She found time to distrust him just as the questions began, as her own houselights began to fade.

Why had they let her go? What did they say they wanted?

She was tumbling down the staircase of symptoms, freezing and shaking, her ears full of white noise, her vision messed up as some density rose inside her, clamping closed the avenues of sense.

"In Manila I was an ER nurse," she told the young man. "I'm going into shock."

"Tell me what they wanted."

But that was the point right there, she wanted to say, as the man's face came close enough for her to feel his breath, her own words failing in a storm of sensory overlap and overload. She wanted to say: The point was that it wasn't *they*, it was *he*. And it seemed clear to her that *he* didn't want *anything*.

RABBIT

—

AFTER HE BROKE THE UNIT he'd been trying to install on top of the Peavey Block and banged up his hand in the process, Rabbit paced and swore and stared at the sky briefly as if it might offer an explanation for his own stupidity. And it was this irritation more than anything else that inspired him to jump across the alley and onto the roof of the adjacent building. With a front flip, no less, which was insane on every level. Insane to risk being seen in the middle of the day. Insane . . . well, insane to risk dying.

But he hadn't been seen, he didn't think. And he hadn't died, clearly. So he ran home, loping along and cooling down. Rabbit was twenty-six. Lean and muscular without bulk. Gray eyes, solid chin, black hair and skin that tanned easily to bricky brown. He was handsome, but this derived less from his form than it did from his balance somehow. The way he ran: controlled strides with much reserved energy, like a jungle cat. He was stealthy, Rabbit. And when he reached his apartment building on Third Street down in Stofton, he climbed the fire escape without releasing a creak or a rattle, keyed the padlock and let himself in the window. There he slipped out of his clothes and into his sleeping bag, which lay on top of an old futon in the corner. He slept immediately and deeply for several hours. And when he woke up in the cool darkness with mercury lights bleeding in from the rail yards, a decision was already shaped in his mind before full consciousness: tonight, Rabbit would run the Easter Valley Railway Tunnel.

Why just that moment? It was past eleven on a Wednesday night. Rabbit knew he should devote some time to replanning instead, given that the unit he'd broken that afternoon had been the last part of an installation he'd been working on for almost a year. The whole thing would have been ready to turn on, to release into the world, if he hadn't stripped a damn mounting bolt and smashed a critical compon- ent made of glass and steel and electrical contacts. But all that would have to wait, because the tunnel was there in his mind on waking, and Rabbit responded to these instincts.

Superstition, his friends would have said. Rabbit was thinking of Jabez and Beyer in particular, two very different people, who had no taste for one another yet somehow maintained a great interest in him. Jabez the born protester, and Beyer the born entrepreneur. But both men had separately observed Rabbit's life to be thick with private rou- tines and secret penances. These two warring would-be teachers who hovered and cajoled, who beckoned him towards their perfectly oppos- ing views of the world.

But superstition wasn't quite right, anyway. Rabbit had arrived in the city eighteen months before, a bearded, long-haired stranger having last lived in Oregon. (Shaven, trimmed and smoothed, Rabbit was now, strangely, much harder to see at night.) But he'd never been the coastal bush mystic that they originally imagined him to be. What looked occult to them about Rabbit—general appearance, mumbled words, small repeated hand motions, running the tunnel—was in fact the product of a coder's mental tic. *If that, then this.* Rabbit had left his old life behind, rigorously: all technology and its discontents. But even in his new, no-tech life—no e-mail, credit cards, driver's license, nor any surviving official record of his university degree (MSc, Big 12 school)—he had yet been unable to shake that one: *if-then*. Rabbit did things according to mental patterns and apparently nothing was going to change that.

So: *if* he had messed up the whole project right at the moment he thought it was finished, well, *then* clearly he had to do the one thing that had yielded calm insight to him in the past. That meant running the Easter Valley Railway Tunnel, two miles of near blackness, 100 feet below the eastern suburbs and deep in the city's bedrock. Twenty minutes from end to end, the maximum time allowable inside given rail schedules, a time that had to include however long he stopped in the very center of the tunnel to pay his respects. And a chorus of sirens up the hillside seemed to herald Rabbit's firmed-up commitment to do just that.

Rabbit went to the window, wondering if he saw an unusual glow up the hillside or just the normal reflection of city light onto low cloud. Then he returned to the narrow kitchen of the studio apartment, where he stood at the counter and turned his attention to fueling up for his evening.

Rabbit had changed the way he ate since arriving in the city. In school and then in Oregon, where he'd worked his one job until that imploded, fat, sodium, sugar and caffeine were the only food groups. So he'd lived on wasabi peas and pizza pockets, Toppo Japanese chocolate sticks and slender cans of NitroGlo, which combined the effect of six cups of coffee and about nine regular colas into a single aluminum sleeve. Now, living with a good deal less money, Rabbit ate what he thought of as bulk urban survival, which meant whatever he could get from the back of a supermarket warehouse where he'd gotten to know one of the forklift operators. Cash or weed, the latter of which Rabbit got in small bags for free or next to nothing from Beyer, who had a complex network of suppliers branching out in all directions around him: marijuana, but also booze, sushi-grade bluefin tuna and a myriad of other products and services his lifestyle demanded. So Beyer helped Rabbit out with a little weed from time to time. And Rabbit traded that for flats of multivitamins and fish oil capsules, plus the fixings for a dish he called ramen-oni, which you made by combining a box of Korean spicy ramen noodle soup and a box of macaroni and cheese dinner. Call it 1800 calories with a couple of eggs. Rabbit ate one of those a day and carried a plastic bag of trail mix for snacking. He drank tap water. He'd lost a bit of weight, but it wasn't a diet he intended to maintain for years. Rabbit had a plan, and that plan didn't involve living this way forever. That plan involved a garden with real vegetables, just like when he was a kid. It involved self-sufficiency and being many miles away from here. But he hadn't reached that point in his plan quite yet.

Now Rabbit checked his front-door locks, bolts and bars. Then he slipped out the fire-escape window and padlocked it behind him. When he climbed down to the alley, he did this in a way that would have startled anyone watching. Rabbit vaulted the top railing, six stories above the pavement, and grappled himself to the outside of the metal framework. Then he dropped, floor by floor, one fire-escape landing at a time, his feet and hands touching the rail and decking in unison, but with such lightning brevity that he looked, as he plummeted, like some kind of bouncing spider. Then the dismount, a spring and twist of the body, Rabbit sailing over a parked car and landing on the lid of a dumpster, where he rolled on his shoulder and flipped down to the pavement. Animal fluidity. One touch, balls of the feet, and off he went.

Fifteen minutes to the Easter Valley Railway Tunnel. Rabbit had this run well clocked. East out of Stofton into the warehouse district, then across the boulevard to where the tunnel entered the hillside on

the opposite side of the valley providing a connection to the coal shut-
tles that serviced the river terminals. Schedules long memorized,
Rabbit knew he wouldn't meet a train tonight if he kept up the twenty-
minute pace once inside.

In he went on those short cat-like steps, designed not for speed or
distance, but for control and quick changes of course and speed, something Rabbit did frequently, monkey-vaulting a park bench up onto a
wall and over into a hidden alley. Or carving off sharply down a side
street by making unexpected use of the walls. These were Parkour
moves, although Rabbit didn't use that term. Freesteal was what people
around Rabbit called what they did: a combination of running, climbing, exploring places off-limits to the public, and leaving public art on
the walls wherever they went. Freestealers were pacifists, craftier and
less territorial than graffiti writers. Freestealers didn't tag. And they
didn't steal either, unless you counted the wall space itself. The art was
a gift to the cityscape so that the free eye might freely find it. And
Rabbit, who wasn't disposed to clubs or gangs or affiliations, still
thought Freesteal came closer than anything else to defining how he
wanted to fit into the world. Making his quiet way without confrontation, leaving his marks for those who would see.

In the tunnel, Rabbit was keeping up a decent miler's pace along
the rails. He was in deep. Long past the graffiti that scored the entrance to the tunnel, then grew sparse as the air cooled and thinned,
then vanished where the walls began to seep black, coated with the
residue of diesel fumes from big turbine engines that came through at
the head of the coal trains. Rabbit was now far past the point that any
tagger was willing to go, into a place where the air supply seemed to
tighten, where the lungs came alive with invisible motes and particles,
diesel and clay, steel and creosote. Where the slick black mucus of the
earth and the fungal heaviness of the soil became the actual substance
of the air.

There was no light here, natural or artificial. And Rabbit didn't carry a flashlight either. But at forty yards in, the eye found resources it didn't normally use and a surface glow could be detected on the rails. Rabbit followed these to the half-mile point, where a new glimmer appeared in the steel. A blue ghost cast out by a single blue light at the center of the tunnel. Here Rabbit picked up his pace and reached the middle of the tunnel in a few minutes.

He stopped there, as he always did, staring up at the wall: not at the blue bulb itself, which was a railway safety installation, but at the magnificent thing that the light revealed. In iridescent greens and yellows, with licks of red, silver and gold, massive interlocking letters shaped a name. Graffiti pieces were not so interesting to Rabbit normally, but this one had him. It was as impressive as the greatest works of art Rabbit had ever seen, not for its strokes and lines, but for its location. That is: precisely where nobody would ever see it. This piece had obviously been painted with no intent on the part of the writer that they be known or admired for their effort. And that was a new kind of image, Rabbit thought. A lodestone of pure creative will, a suggestion of motives and meanings beyond the world itself.

If-then. The writer of this hidden graffiti hadn't been saying: *if* you are seeing this *then* I am truly alive. The statement here was radically different. Rabbit thought it was: *if* I am to be truly alive, *then* this is what I must do, whether you see it or not. And that idea enthralled Rabbit. It sped his heartbeat and fired his imagination.

The name on the wall was Alto. And as he'd done before, Rabbit stood in front of the piece, a sense of bright certainty enveloping him. And he read that name to the blackness, his only witness, the tunnel echoing *Alto* back to him in long parabolic waves.

AFTER RABBIT RAN OUT OF THE TUNNEL, he jogged across town to Joey's Panda Grove, where he found a corner booth in the basement bar and turned his attention, at last, to the critical matter at hand. The big project, his installation. Rabbit unfolded a city map, which he smoothed onto the table in front of him. And there he sat for some time, hardly moving, tracing the map's many lines and markings with one finger. He sat in the low light under the gaze of a dragon his friend Jabez had painted on the wall years before and which nobody dared paint over. That dragon, Rabbit had often thought, was an expression of Jabez's righteous anger at the world's injustice. And nobody had the nerve to create an image to rival it.

Jabez, as he always did, sniffed from upstairs that Rabbit was there and came down to find him. Rabbit had occasions to wonder if his friend had the place tricked out with hidden cameras. Jabez seemed always to know so completely what was going on in the Grove. But then, the Grove was his. Impossible that he could own it, Rabbit had decided, since his friend never seemed to have any money. But he had somehow secured its use. He ran the illegal bar and the hall upstairs. Most important, Jabez ran the walls, which were postered and painted, over and over, with the work of a hundred street artists. And all of it administered by Jabez in accordance with some code of rivalry and usurpation—an algorithm based on the length of time a piece had been up and the original prestige of the artist who'd made it. Nobody messed with this Jabezian order, because to do so meant you'd never set foot in the Grove again. Which is why every graffiti writer and wheatpaster, every muralist and photofreak, lightboxer and landscape painter, all the sloganeers and wall journalizers, even the tagger kids who came in from the burbs to leave their plague of marks like dogs pissing on hydrants and unable to stop, all of them accepted the hovering authority of this local prince, whose office was up in one of the crudded-over spaces of the hotel overhead, who came and went by a private freight elevator, who stumped around, his signature stilt and list, gimp leg fluttering behind him like a broken wheel on a shopping cart. Signing constantly with his hands.

Oh yes, Jabez was deaf, a source of yet deeper authority. To be pegged by a freight car in the yards while painting a grain hopper, to lose your left leg from the knee down in service of the craft, that conferred a certain status. But to be able to read lips at forty feet was a different kind of power altogether. Rabbit had many times seen people talking at the Panda Grove with their hands over their mouths. And the dumb-luck coincidence that Rabbit's childhood best friend had also been deaf, and so Rabbit had picked up some rudimentary sign, this cemented his place in Jabez's rigid affections.

"The ID sniper is a rifle designed to shoot a traceable microchip into the human body so a person can be tracked," someone was saying at the bar, where debates about conspiracy and subterfuge held never-dying allure. This rifle, the man went on to say, had recently appeared at a weapons trade show in Germany and it was understood that American and Canadian law enforcement agencies were very much interested.

Rabbit kept his head down, poring over his map, its streets and avenues, squares and boulevards. The map was scored with marks and connections. Numbers and arrows, a hieroglyphic tangle to any eye but Rabbit's. Almost twelve months of his life up on cedar shakes and asphalt shingles, gravel on tar, sheet metal. All over the city. In Angus Lake, the East Shore, the warehouse district. Downtown, River Park. And right there in Stofton too, the Slopes, up into the Heights. Rabbit knew the city from its roofs. And when his index finger had traced all those lines and still found itself bouncing on top of the Peavey Block, right there immediately south of the plaza, the solution to his troubles was plain. He simply couldn't call the thing finished without that unit in place. So he'd just have to return to the site and reinstall the thing. Which meant building another one. Which meant, against all good sense, that he'd have to borrow more money. And it wouldn't be from Jabez either, who had many things in abundance, none of them being money. It would be instead from the ever-liquid Beyer.

"There is a system of tunnels and storage areas under the city," somebody over at the bar was saying just that moment. Yelling really — there seemed to be a disagreement on this point. "It was built by federal authorities —"

And then they stopped. Which Rabbit could easily interpret: that would be Jabez crashing into the room and causing every speaker to consider lines of sight and what exactly was being said. Across the floor he came now, directly towards Rabbit, hands already in frenzied motion, twisting and whirling. A cyclone of sign. And the message was clear. The world, as long predicted, was coming apart at the seams.

Don't joke about it, Jabez was saying, noting the suppressed amusement in Rabbit's expression. This time, the terrible news was terribly true.

RABBIT WALKED TO THE RIM OF THE PLAZA. He stood at the south end, in the mouth of an alley, and looked down across the sunken space with its spreading trees and calling fountains. Scattered crowds already, a sense of early gathering. Rabbit could only shake his head. Soldiers, people gesturing, agitation. Rabbit wondered what reflected the times more: the fact that someone would be desperate enough about *anything* to take children hostage, or the fact that Jabez and his crew had so quickly found a passionate reason to turn this incident into an angry protest.

Back in the Grove, that was just what Rabbit had seen: real anger. Sure, people hated whatever lay at the root of these events. Whatever it was that made people shoot up a hotel, or call out the helicopter gunships, or take hostages. But people more recently, especially people like Jabez, splintered so quickly on where to finger the blame. That was the contemporary difference. Sitting in the basement of the Grove, Jabez had hardly finished telling Rabbit what he knew — theater, kids taken hostage, guy with a gun — and he was past those details, on to what might lie behind. Shadowy forces. Hidden causes and secret triggers. Powers and authorities. Nobody used the word *conspiracy* anymore because it had become a self-defeating cliché. But suspicions turned quickly inward. Things were never believed to be as they seemed.

Rabbit thought about the kids. Five, six, seven years old. He'd watched *KiddieFame* maybe twice in his life, never liking the show even back when he'd been interested in television. But he knew that even those seeking the tackiest variety of renown did not deserve this. Standing where he was, Rabbit could see the full face of the Meme complex, and the shape of the Peavey Block just half a block down Jeffers to the south. He again considered skipping that last installation, sensing a high-strung, volatile tension in the air. It was a terrible time to be climbing roofs in the neighborhood. Snipers had probably been deployed. But Rabbit also knew he would not have finished what he'd started if he didn't climb that roof. And that was true no matter what Jabez thought of the project.

"You just sitting down here in the dark," Jabez said. "Doing what? All this stuff going on. The army's in town now and you're down here in darkness all sipping tea and looking at a map."

Jabez tried to get a peek at his map, but Rabbit folded it quickly away and into his bag, causing his friend's face to pull back into its default state. His brow open, unfurled, his eyes brimming with the possibility of offense. He signed: "God, please don't tell me this is more work for Beyer. You working for Beyer again?"

Rabbit rolled his eyes and sat back himself. They'd been through this one before. Yes, he'd once done some work for Beyer. But no, the map wasn't it.

Jabez was dubious: "So why'd Beyer send one of his goons down looking for you?"

Rabbit sat forward. "Beyer was looking?"

"You scared?" Jabez asked. "Hiding out?"

Rabbit forced himself to sit back. "I'm not hiding," he said. "And I'm not scared."

"Why's Beyer looking for you if you aren't hiding?" Jabez pressed.

And here came the speech about crew and family, which Jabez unrolled reproachfully from time to time. He, Jabez, was the founder of a crew. They called themselves the Poets. They worked together and lived together. They supported and protected one another. They were like family. Rabbit, on his arrival in the city, had been invited to join this crew, this family, and thus embed himself in the safety and love that they had to offer. Yes, love. Jabez used the word often, without irony or shaded meanings. He was a protester. He had ideals.

So: love. And Rabbit had turned them down in favor of this thing. This what. This adequate image he was trying to make.

"Adequate images," Jabez said, repeating the phrase Rabbit had used so many times. "This idea comes to you after seeing some film."

Rabbit didn't mind acknowledging the debt. It was a Werner Herzog film and he liked remembering it.

"It's called inspiration. The guy said, if we don't find adequate images, we'll go the way of the dinosaurs."

Jabez looked at the ceiling. Rabbit had explained it before, but he didn't think his friend wanted to understand. Still, he gave it another try. It meant breaking the cycle of images that they all ingested every day, on television and billboards, in every magazine and newspaper they read. The hypnotic cycle. Rabbit said to Jabez, "We have to take back control. Make those adequate images and save ourselves."

"As if the Poets' images aren't good enough."

Rabbit didn't say anything. Jabez was a friend. He wouldn't have continued reminding Rabbit about the Poets if his affection wasn't real. And Jabez too, perhaps, sensed there was no point arguing. He went atypically still in the booth opposite Rabbit. Working towards some thought. And when he was finished, he produced it in the form of a question. Right to the heart of the matter.

"So this new thing, your new type of image. What's it called?"

Rabbit now stood at the rim of the plaza remembering the question. Jabez had leaned forward across the table, his face a foot away. Rabbit's balding, irritable friend. Warehouse sleeper, bin diver, street artist, devout believer in a revolutionary god. This Prince of the Grove. Rabbit kept his voice low, but shaped the syllables for lip-reading clarity.

"The Blue Light Project."

Jabez breathed through open lips, his eyes going past Rabbit, through him, imagining, picturing what the name could mean. And with a rare smile too. Jabez, it seemed, was made a degree happier just thinking about the Blue Light Project, without even knowing what it was.

And here in the plaza were all these other lights. The white halogens against the Meme complex, the flashing reds and yellows in the plaza. The whole machinery assembling itself, blinking into existence, some terror rousing itself in response to terror. Rabbit watched it for many minutes, during which time dozens more people, more vehicles, more cameras and lights arrived in the plaza. These were the old images, unfolding as always with such eager industry. Sadly and terribly familiar.

Then Rabbit went to find Beyer.

PEGG

—

THOM PEGG'S PHONE, having rung twice already and been ignored, seemed committed to spoiling his evening. He was on the West Coast, where he lived. But this was Spratley calling from the East Coast, and right in the middle of Pegg's dinner too. In the middle of a date, if that was the right word for whatever this was.

"I say, you," Pegg said to the woman opposite him, whose name splendidly enough was Chastity.

"You say me what?"

"I say . . . you sparkling rainbow of wit and beauty."

She leaned in against the small table. "Mmm?"

Pegg made an apologetic face and cricked his neck downwards to indicate the ring tone coming from within the rolling folds of his suit. A Barry White groove. He said: "Would you mind terribly if I deal with this?"

She lolled her head to one side, eyes wide. And here Pegg fished into his inner pockets to find the fibrillating deck of his phone. Hauled it out. Then stared at it irritably. Yes indeed, Spratley. Like you need to hear from your editor once, let alone three times in an evening.

Maybe if you worked for the *New York Times*. Maybe if you still had that kind of career. Certainly not working for *L:MN* magazine.

Finger to the Ignore key. Depress. Goodbye, Sprat-man.

"Now, as I was saying . . ." he said to Chastity, who had just now speared up a quarter-pound prawn and was easing it between her lips.

She said: "Uh-huh?" And as her teeth closed, a little cocktail sauce sprang to the corner of her mouth.

Pegg began coughing. He said: "Oh my, blossom. I just went entirely screen saver there."

She chewed. And chewed. Then swallowed. Then licked her index finger and middle finger in considerately slow motion. She said: "Well, you know what to do when your screen saver comes on, don't you?"

He was killing here. He couldn't believe how well it was going. Or no, check that. He could believe how well it was going. Because he was such an evil genius at this kind of thing. He'd asked her for her views on health care, the environment, the situation in the Middle East. She was simply paying back accounts now. That was the wonderfully brilliantly terrible accounting involved.

He said to her: "No, darling, I don't know. Tell me what to do when my screen saver comes on."

She leaned forward, her breasts settling on the tabletop, nosing the edge of her plate. She said: "Well, honey, you just jiggle your mouse."

Yes. Yes. Oh my goodness me. How nice was this? Very nice. She had virtually the best of everything Pegg had ever seen in the physical flesh. Yes indeed, this epitomatrix opposite was a model. A model. And more (more!), she'd been linked to one of those twat stars. It was a tabloid story, but still. The guy was what mattered. Some beardo with an ass about six inches across. Some guy with a lot of street, a lot of *right now*, a lot of meetings for all the agents he suddenly needed. Pegg knew how it worked. He wasn't passingly familiar with the celebrity machinery. He *was* the machinery. And the machinery towered over these people.

Towered, well. Just to be clear, Pegg wasn't a big man. His game in these situations wasn't stature-dependent. He himself was no epitome. Pegg in the steaming, inhospitable jungle of his recently divorced career-tanked mid-forties was 45 percentile for height and 75 for weight. Shaved head. Pale skin. Christ, this girl here was about six inches taller than him. Coming in earlier, he'd seen the man at the front do that eye-flick business. Up and down, up and down. Didn't matter. *L:MN*, Senior Editor. Pegg had a certain warily acknowledged clout in this town. So he duked the guy a fifty and they got the booth. There were A-listers all around the place. And some of them looked. Oh sure they did. Have a look, fellas. Have a long look. Chas-titty.

But no. Pegg didn't flex muscles to get what he wanted. His was a guile play. All brain work and expertise. Much harder, Pegg knew, than it would have been if he were handsome or actually had any money. An actual movie star closed the deal in ten minutes, five if he met Chastity in a hotel lobby and one of them was already a registered guest. Pegg? Well let's be honest, Pegg didn't engage the enemy on the open desert. It was black ops all the way. It was the deployment of every psychological tactic in his interviewing repertoire to get them there over the second course—truffle risotto being massaged to completion somewhere by a chef with his own cooking show who drove around in a titanium SUV—and he was *still* playing about a sixty, maybe seventy percent chance of getting the flop he needed.

"You know what I was thinking?" he said.

"About what?" She was on prawn number two.

"Well, I was going to tell you."

"I have to pee."

"No, actually. That wasn't it."

"I do, though," she said, her words just a bit smudged around the edges.

He intercepted the pained expression that was about to unscroll itself across his face. Like a judo move, you sort of had to move with whatever was coming at you. Irritability, then, became—with a deft adjustment of the eyebrows—a different expression. Like a thoughtful person with epigastric distress. A monk with colitis, he thought, seeing himself in the mirrored wall opposite. This business of having to shave his head certainly contributed to the effect.

"Well off you go then, my juicy pomegranate, and I shall think of you every moment when you are gone."

And off she went, more than one or two sets of eyeballs swiveling in their sockets to watch her pass. Pegg imagined air molecules bowing their heads and parting to accommodate the swaying, feline length of her, and he found he disliked the air molecules for doing so.

Around the corner. Out of sight. She disappeared and Pegg went into the side pocket of his jacket and palmed two airline vodka bottles out and over to his water glass where he poured them carefully into the ice. He wasn't *drinking* tonight, he'd agreed with himself earlier that evening while stowing only six such bottles on his person (two more in each inside breast pocket) and one emergency flask of cognac down his pants (only for afterwards, if there were an afterwards). But having just picked up that his date might be encountering the world through her own preferred veil of intoxication, he wished briefly that he had more.

Nova Scotia. Would you believe it? His pour complete, half of its slurry beneficence burning pleasantly down his hatch, the empties discreetly stowed down the crack in the seat cushions. He thought: Would you believe the father of this beauty actually fished lobsters out of the ocean? Not as a joke or for a television show, either. For a living. The week before, when Pegg had phoned a photographer friend to get Chastity's number, he couldn't believe that part when he heard it.

"Say though, Pegg," the photographer friend had said. "You're not asking about her because you're interested in buying lobster."

Well, no. He was interested in meeting this girl because next to the phrase *dirty bomb* in the dictionary, there was a picture of her. But also because it fell under the heading of *things Pegg did on occasion* just because his situation sometimes afforded the opportunity. There was a kind of payback in it. So you're in an editorial meeting. Copies of the new July issue are all over the place. You notice the Herculean beauty on the cover. Nothing monumental here, yet. *L:MN* often ran full-paged leggy reasons for teenage boys to throw themselves off a bridge. It was sort of how the magazine worked, how it bridged from straight gossip and industry chat to that coveted ignorant-spending-male demographic. Every now and again, there would be a cover with a woman licking a golf ball or lying naked in a bathtub full of chili con carne.

He made some calls. *Who is this girl?* Chastity Something-or-other. Then he forgot all about it. Then he was in another editorial meeting and the cover of the last issue was on the wall, in a frame, larger than before. As if she had taken a step or two towards him, closing the distance. As if she were—yes, Pegg thought, that was it—as if she were laying down some sort of a challenge.

Pegg was drinking quite a lot at the time. But that wasn't the reason he took her up on it. That's just the way it was with celebrity and Pegg, by that point in his life. He would be the first to admit it, if anybody asked. Although Pegg wasn't asked much anymore. He knew his nickname in the *L:MN* art department, the one they used behind his back. They'd say: Pebialta. Like the name of a Mediterranean resort or an Italian scooter. He wondered about it for quite a while before learning it was an acronym. P-B-I-A-L-T-A. Pegg Briefly Important A Long Time Ago.

All right, fine. It had been brief. There had been the syndicated column. There had even been TV appearances. There had been a time when questions had been asked of him about corruption and deception in our time, about the erosion of public ethics and private decency. They called Pegg "the Lie Detector." But the generic term was *muckraker*, someone whose output was provocative even if their follow-the-victim ethic was suspect. And Pegg certainly made a business of victims in those days. He found them. He found their tormentors. And there was invariably a story at that intersection.

People liked these stories. Pegg had an entertaining, flowing style. He had a way with stinging words. But the stories also satisfied the single common certainty of the day: that the social rot was advanced. People didn't just enjoy Pegg's writing. They were reassured by it, people who believed nothing more strongly than that they were being routinely lied to by authorities and institutions of every kind. And on the talk shows, Pegg had examples, cases, stories to tell that were much listened to and pondered and rehashed as evidence that a great darkness was stealing across the face of the deep, and that light was a thing sorely needed.

The light of Thom Pegg.

It was a career's worth of recognition, even before the Pulitzer. How close Pegg had come to that senior accolade. He learned he was a finalist. He took the phone call telling him he'd won. He danced around the room, told his wife, drank champagne, then booked his flight to attend the awards luncheon at the Low Library on the Columbia campus. And then his whole life careened off the rails, almost immediately, upended by a prizewinning story about shameless lying that had a shameless lie at its very own heart.

Maybe it was a tiny untruth compared to the whole, as Pegg at first believed. It was fatal, nonetheless. Were there widely publicized cases of innocent citizens whisked free of airport security and ending up in one of those special hells that had winked into existence all over the world? Black sites, they called them. The land of exception, supra-judicial, supra-jurisdictional. People tortured without charge, stooped in concrete rooms not high enough to stand. Ninety-six-hour interrogations, fake electrocution and drowning, dogs and excrement, bloody floors and three years gone, slipping away like consciousness. Were lives lost?

Oh yes. There were names and stories that had made the papers, printed and online. And many more that didn't. Young men, typically brown and bearded, faithful to the other God. But not always. The black sites could subsume anybody. And people knew them to exist. The toxicity of this awareness had leached into the public soil and people were sick with it, sick with knowing.

But did Pegg technically have access to a civilian interrogation contractor who had participated, who had hurt people, who had ordered up the canine units and cold cells, slammed shut the steel doors? Did he have that man who had accumulated the secrets about foul doings and rank humiliations, even deaths, and then broke under their weight?

Such men existed. Pegg knew it. Everybody knew it. They had to exist because humans were the creatures that they were: they changed their minds, they had regrets. *Homo paenitentia.*

But no, technically, Pegg hadn't actually found such a man, hadn't found that story. So he listened to the winds of truth and wrote down what he heard sighing there. He made the man up.

Who cared? Well, nobody and then, later, everybody. People loved the story. One victim caught in the machinery of an entire hemisphere gone wrong. It was the world illuminated as the world was understood to be. And that was the story's undoing right there, its dangerous proximity to the cliff of truth. Pegg was known. He was respected, admired even at this point in his career. He'd just won a Pulitzer.

But here came that very different thing: Pegg briefly famous for reasons having to do with the opposite of truth. So he learned what that was really all about. What it means for others not to want what you know, or what you have, but to want your actual existence. There is hatred in the construction of celebrity fame: a love that is resented by all those it infects. Some really famous people handle it. Pegg was never a man for subtle ways, delicate handlings.

So Pegg learned a harsh lesson. It was a violation of trust to make bogus election promises or harass whistleblowers, to pollute the environment or imprison people without reason or rhyme. But it was a crime of a higher order to be a journalist reporting such a sad story and citing a made-up source. As his story itself became the story, as his phone began to ring and ring, Pegg made a cascading series of bad choices, covering track after track with new sources, new victims. Composites, full-on fabrications. The lot.

It blew open. It hurricaned onto shore. Pegg's house crashed down and no one rushed to his aid. He had defiled the suffering of those he'd tried to help. He'd compromised the credibility of their story by telling it his way. He'd sacrificed them again, in effect, to the greater cause of getting his version out there and restoring order and sense to the world. And having polluted that sacrament, so too was Pegg laid on the altar in the name of order and good sense.

At his peak Pegg's column had run in 157 newspapers, from Bangkok to Baffin Island. It took a few weeks for that number to shrink all the way to zero, even less time for his Pulitzer to be withdrawn. Truly scandalous. The furor raged briefly online. Articles about his misdoings written by colleagues and even former friends. But then it died, all at once, as these things do. His phone quivering to a deathly silence.

Yes, it was his own fault. That wasn't the difficult part to accept. What hurt was his unconditional exile by even those who had thought his original project a humanitarian, even a noble thing. Noble Pegg.

"These affairs cause great damage to journalism itself," another journalist wrote on the editorial page of the *Times*, one of the final pronouncements on the affair that Pegg had the stomach to read. The man's name was Loftin, and he was, as painful coincidence would have it, originally from Pegg's hometown. "But we journalists must realize," the man went on piously, "how even that pales in comparison to the damage Thom Pegg has done to the very victims his own column had ostensibly been written to aid and reinstate."

Ostensibly. So now even his original motives were impugned.

Pegg went home. He shut the door behind them. He wondered what would happen next. He soon found out.

"Careers are tidal, Peggy, they ebb and flow," his then-wife Jennifer said, not weeks before she went slack tide on him and disappeared over the lip of the shining mudflats that had suddenly formed all around his person.

How do these dramas unfold? Professional ruination, divorce, bankruptcy. The big house they shared, she could have it. But then, on account of his drinking, which had punched through epic to apocalyptic around this time, she took his boy too. She took his love and hid him away. And Pegg could still crack and spill like a soft-boiled egg thinking about that one. Micah Swenson Pegg. Micah, Micah. The first six years had been so good. He read to the boy aloud from the canon: Mencken, Perelman, Carlin, Hitchens. They went to cafés and winked at girls. All gone, it seemed to Pegg, in minutes. In seconds.

Spratley was from school, and a timely sliver of fortune that was too. Knowing Pegg from so long before, when they had co-witnessed so many behaviors they wouldn't really have wanted known outside their dorm clique, Spratley never mentioned the public shaming, the criminal suit (dropped), the civil suit (outstanding). But then Spratley had also carved a career in journalism out of less high-minded material—his first job was with *Penthouse*—so he was disinclined to judge. What Pegg himself never understood until he was on the job at *L:MN* magazine was that Spratley had offered him more than a financial lifeline. Pegg had been given a job that came with levers and buttons, a mechanism that could be worked to extract occasional compensation from fame itself, from the fact of its perplexing, poisonous appeal. Payback, yes indeed. Sometimes it involved publishing grotesque pictures of a famous person's failed plastic surgery or writing a story about their meth addiction. Other times it just meant scamming a dinner with someone like Chastity and hoping for the best. Either way, it was payback. And Pegg had become an expert.

There were only three rules for interviewing celebrities, Pegg quickly determined, having reverse engineered the techniques he'd used for previous subjects. Only three things you had to do to inspire the on-message famous person to open up, to search for truths that might impress you. One, start with an early question about something outside their area of expertise. Two, express interest in something irrelevant to beat them towards something better. And three, turn off the tape recorder before the interview was actually finished, while still taking mental notes. Flattery, manipulation and deceit. These worked.

"All the best celebrity hacks hate stardom to their bones," said Spratley, whose creviced features lent themselves to creviced pronouncements on the culture at large. He made this particular one holding a stingingly potent drink with an umbrella in it. Pegg was on his second.

So, Chastity. A few e-mails and phone calls later, he had the damsel in his sights. The agency wrote: *You'd like to shoot her again?* To which Pegg responded that no, he didn't want the girl for a photo shoot. He was looking for an interview.

Rule Number One in action, right there: ask an early question outside their area of expertise. With actors that question was invariably about politics. How they loved to sound off on the workings of the world from which they wanted to scurry away, lurking in character or in trailers, angling with their agents and dealers, checking available reflections, and groping the makeup technicians.

Models, to this cultural haute bourgeoisie, were like aristocracy. And just like peers, having inherited everything, they were vulnerable too. They didn't create or absorb the culture in which they thrived. They were its purest reflection, defined entirely in the eyes of those who set the model in her coveted place. And at the moment this all occurred to Pegg—hungover at an editorial meeting, feeling a bit nasty—he saw the application of Rule Number One in the case of models as being a simple matter of asking them *anything*.

"ALL RIGHT THEN?"

And here she came, this vision, this perfection. Approaching his table just now, having peed. She had a nasty little smile of her own on too, as if she had made for the contents of her own pockets while out of sight, and now felt it all might be working out just the way she intended.

She said: "I feel great." Little slanting smile.

"Do you . . . ?" Pegg started, but then the damn phone was going again. And this time, it was hard not to interpret the vibration against his ribs as a very special kind of bid. Spratley might as well have been telling him: your former fame against my possibly sexual relationship with our billionaire publisher. Bets to you.

"Blast," Pegg said.

"To answer your question, though," she said, making no move for that last prawn.

"Which one was that?"

"You asked: Do you . . . ?"

"Right, well . . ."

"Yes. I do."

Pegg started coughing, which invoked a certain pain under his right ribs that he'd been successfully ignoring so far that evening. Ouch. Wince. Out with the hanky. Out with the phone. He held one finger up for Chastity, then pressed a key.

"Sprat-man," he croaked. "I'm halfway through my appy here."

Spratley let the line run silent with rebuke and emphasis.

"Oh all right," Pegg said. "You're up late. What is it, then? Something good, I hope."

And here it came. Something not so good, as it turned out. Something *KiddieFame* related. For a moment, hearing none of the details, Pegg was forced to consider what he had done in life that it might come down to him writing about that loathsome show, for what crimes did his punishment continue.

He cut in, right on top of something Spratley was saying with an unusual, quiet insistency. Pegg caught Chastity's glance and winked at her, pointed at the phone with a slight shake of his head. Then he said to Spratley: "God man, really. It's just, you know." And he was thinking: It's just that I'd rather poke my eyes out with pencils than have to interview one of those brats trying to angle their way into the fame business at the age of five.

But then Spratley, who was normally inclined to let Pegg have his tantrums whenever a story didn't suit his mood, did not stop talking at all, only raised his voice. Spratley, the icy, sarcastic queen, was *yelling*.

Orders. He was yelling orders. Pegg would zipper-in his plans for the evening. Pegg would extract his credit card and pay the damn bill. Peg would get himself out onto the sidewalk and into a taxi and over to the airport that goddamn instant.

"Airport?"

Private aircraft departure terminal. There was a plane waiting. Warmed up, ready to roll. Interesting detail, this one. The plane belonged to the feds. Seemed they had some kind of standoff. Bunch of people being held all cooped up in a television studio in a city in the middle of the country where people were generally a lot nicer than that. *KiddieFame*. Yes indeed. That show. Yes. Hostages.

Pegg pressed his little finger deep into his free ear and closed his eyes. He said: "Hostages. Like when they want money?"

Like when they want *something*, Spratley told him.

"But why," Pegg started. Then tried again: "Why would we be interested in a hostage story?"

Spratley was one hundred percent preparation this evening, despite his fouled mood. "Well it's really the hostage taker that we're interested in here, Peggy."

And why was that? Pegg wondered.

"Well because . . ." Spratley drew it out, deadpan incredulity. "Because the hostage taker seems to be quite interested in *you*."

Pegg squinted and winced and tried to focus again. He wouldn't have been much to look at just at that moment, he was sure, in the middle of that room full of robotronic showbiz perfection. There he was, a short and frankly overweight gentleman about to field a massive stroke.

Wanted to talk to him, yes, Spratley was saying. Won't talk to anyone else.

Coughing again. Ribs. Ouch. This was bad. It was like something was lodged in there. A wad of last night's takeout burger mixed with shredded tinfoil.

Interested in him? Thom Pegg? He flashed on an image with this unhappy news. A strange one, from the beginning of what had become decidedly the strangest part of his life. Not long after the Pulitzer was yanked from his fingers and the ensuing scandal had flared and fizzled, a few weeks after he'd been given the *L:MN* job. He'd been on a subway platform in a city out East, there on a story. He had finished the painful interview: some Canadian singer, new show, a little shrew, ninety pounds and pathologically self-involved. And as he stood there waiting for his train, thinking only of the spot he would shortly fill at the hotel bar, his situation seemed suddenly

most exposed, his own sense of himself gone radically third-party perspective, out of body.

As these things work, the reason for the fast-dawning sense of himself in place—an awareness of how he might appear to other people,
holding certain anticipations and regrets inside, bad memories hovering still—came to him just at the moment he realized he was being
photographed.

He turned to find the lens. Not one but two. Odd detail, that, he
would consider later, as he tried to force his mind to other things. Odd
that two people would recognize his only very briefly, very moderately
famous self, on the same platform at the same time, and think to lever
up their long telephotos at once. Two oily black eyes peering at him
around different pillars at the far end of the platform. The snick, snick,
snick of the autowinders finding him through the sifting crowd, which
then crosscurrented with the arriving train, bodies tumbling from the
sliding doors, pushing him aside and away, around a corner. Burying
the whole episode entirely.

Spratley was still talking. They were on to details. But Pegg stayed in
that other thought-stream instead, all the way out of the restaurant and
to the curb, into the taxi and out onto the freeway. Some long-standing
trickle of dread now accumulating into a more substantial flow.

Interested in him. Pegg wasn't sure there was a worse thing that
could be said about a person.

RABBIT

—

FINDING BEYER WAS EASY ENOUGH IF HE WAS IN TOWN. He was generally at his apartment or over at the Lagoon Sushi Bar, blocks apart on Caledonia Street, a hip thoroughfare bisecting the most gentrified part of the Slopes. Designer boutiques, wine shops, doggy day cares, spas. Rabbit had put up artwork in the Slopes, but avoided the area otherwise. Everything was too expensive, of course. But it was also the kind of neighborhood that liked to pretend it was part of a bigger city, one that was photographed more frequently and featured in more movies and magazine shoots. The Slopes embarrassed Rabbit, the same way people did when they revealed their impossible yearnings.

Beyer didn't answer the buzzer at his apartment, so Rabbit headed over to the Lagoon, where Beyer also wasn't, but one of his mooks was.

The mooks were funny, with their low jeans and sleeveless undershirts and their hip-hop girlfriends. Rabbit didn't know where they all came from, only that Beyer had apparently gotten so big that people were coming from all over to work for him. Beyer the business guru. And the mooks all treated Rabbit like he were fragile, one amusing aspect of the present situation, which was otherwise a little tense.

They all thought Rabbit was on special assignment for Beyer, and for some reason Beyer wasn't setting them straight. He wasn't telling them that while he'd hired Rabbit on a project a year previously, and advanced him significant money doing so, Rabbit had never produced a damn thing.

So this mook in the Lagoon spied Rabbit and immediately made for the door, doing that gawky rapper thing with his hands, saying: "Yo bra, I'll go get Beyer."

And he was out the door. So Jabez probably hadn't been exaggerating about Beyer sending someone down to the Grove looking for him. Beyer really did want to talk.

Rabbit settled onto a stool at the end of the long glass bar with fish arranged on ice under it. Tuna, octopus. The sushi chef, who'd seen Rabbit around enough to know he didn't drink, slid a mug of green tea in front of him, waving off payment, nodding to the overhead television where coverage of the Meme Crisis continued. The chef said: "You believe this is happening here?"

"Terrible," Rabbit agreed.

"My uncle used to be a cop," the sushi chef said. "He told me people might have set this up."

Rabbit's eyebrows went up. "What people set what up?"

"You ever see that documentary about that hostage-taking in Moscow?" the sushi chef said. "Done by these Chechen dudes. They took this theater full of people. Kids and adults. What was that, ten years ago?"

"Eleven," Rabbit said, doing the math. "That was terrible too."

"Yeah, but who all got killed in the end? Some of the leader dudes. Whole bunch of kids and people and such. But not the worst of the guys. The worst of the guys, some like super-Chechen badasses, their bodies were never shown out for the cameras. You understand what I'm saying?"

Rabbit did understand what the sushi chef was saying. He was saying that the super-badass dudes weren't shown on camera because they weren't dead. And the reason they weren't dead was that, according to this conspiracy theory, the Russians had hired them. Authorities in Moscow had arranged the hostage-taking so they could later look like heroes setting the hostages free, while at the same time demonizing the nation with whom they were just then fighting a costly war.

"You really believe all that?" Rabbit asked.

"Believe it? Man, I know it," the sushi chef said. "It's all like that now. Lies and deception and large amounts of money. Do you want me to make you something? I got beautiful toro today. Sweet stuff, man, you should eat."

"I'm okay. Not really hungry."

The sushi chef crossed his arms and looked at Rabbit. "So what've you been up to? What're you working on?"

"Difficult to say," Rabbit told him.

"Ah, right," the guy said. And he smiled, but nervously, revealing a certain wariness, since he too believed Rabbit to be some kind of Oregonian backwoods mystic. John the Baptist of the western forests who came tripping into town with nothing but a Thermos for his tea. A man who'd apparently wigged out of his last job and ended up living rough in the Tillamook State Forest, or maybe it was the Oregon dunes with the mighty Pacific thundering in his dreams.

"But I will tell you something," Rabbit offered.

The man grew serious, just a degree unsettled by the notion of having to hold in his brain anything that came out of Rabbit's.

"No big thing," Rabbit said. "It's just that after I'm finished this thing I'm working on, I'm going to leave the city."

"To go where?"

"To the bush," Rabbit said. "My parents died five years ago. They didn't have much, but they left me a little property with a house out in the bush."

"Back out West in Oregon?"

"Up north," Rabbit said. "My family was originally from north of here. I was only out West for work. And near where I was raised, there is a little house on some land. And that's where I'm heading."

The sushi chef had been concentrating hard during all this, almost to the breaking point. Now he glanced over Rabbit's shoulder and back, a quick flicker of the eyes.

"Anyway," Rabbit said. "Nice place. Up this country road with blackberry canes. Just a cabin with an outhouse, basically. We used to go there when I was a kid. And now I'm going to go again, full time."

And here he thought of forests and arriving in darkness. He thought of the spot where the train slowed to navigate the switch. The grass-grown country lane, the place to turn in where no gate was visible. The hidden keys and no plan for after that.

Was he saying all this for Beyer's benefit? Beyer crossing the room now. Rabbit could see him in the mirror. But when Beyer's hands went onto his shoulders, he pretended to startle. Hey, Beyer! And here it came, the basso profundo. Beyer in a steadily worsening mood. His first question, hands firming up, gripping Rabbit just a little too tightly.

"So, drinking tea means you're broke, right?"

BEYER. BEYER.

Beyer was what? The opposite of Jabez, who was all heart and feelings. Beyer was a machine, the whole illustrated flex of him. The artillery shell of his head. The lensed eyes, scanning the world. The sheath of ink-work that was his skin. Beyer had tribal half-sleeves, Celtic braids around his wrists and ankles, a full nelson of reptiles at his neck. His torso was stitched with crosses and names, phrases in Hebrew and Arabic. Iron pumper, ink absorber, financial news scanner. A guy who'd come out of the hardcore punk scene oddly primed for the business world, for the mosh-pit pursuit of relative wealth. Beyer was an anarcho-entrepreneur, Rabbit had decided. Although he was hardly in a position to feel morally superior given Beyer was also the single contact through which all Rabbit's income had derived for almost a year at that point.

Rabbit had to reflect from time to time on the income situation. He and Beyer had moved in exactly opposite directions this way over the eighteen months before and since they met. Rabbit on the West Coast was very much not broke. He remembered his pay stubs. Beyer at that same time, Rabbit had since learned, was a penniless street artist, part of an art crew putting up these huge Nazca line drawings on the gravel roofs of the big-box stores out near the airport. Inspired by the ancient ground drawings found high on the Nazca plateau in Andean Peru, this was art to be seen from the air, although not by the gods in this case but by people in commercial aircraft on final approach. That was their big idea and nobody paid them for it. A huge eye, a hand, a lizard. A hundred, a hundred and fifty feet long. Some of these were apparently still out there, having survived the elements, although Rabbit had never actually gone to look. But that art certainly wasn't what made Beyer who he was now. All the while Rabbit was having his crisis, leaving it all behind, becoming a wild Oregon dune man, then going frankly nuts for a while before drifting back East, Beyer had been accumulating. And by the time Rabbit stumbled out of the prairies and into the city, Beyer was a man with treasure, land, vassals, women and spreading reputation.

And he got it all by handing out stickers.

"Not stickers," he'd say. "It was a phenomenological project."

Perhaps so. Four-inch-square cards on heavy waterproof stock with peel-off backs that allowed them to be adhered to virtually any surface. Beyer's stickers went up and they were maniacally resistant to removal. So they gummed the side of lampposts and mailboxes. They fused to buildings, telephone boxes, train stations, buses, rail yards, churches.

The image on these stickers was of Beyer himself, although artfully fiddled with in Photoshop so that what remained was a pixelated rendering not of any single lantern-headed punk in the middle of an open-mouthed scream, but of all people frustrated everywhere. A lot of people saw their own face in the face that was Beyer's face. Then they read the line below and they wondered about that.

The line read: *Faith Wall.*

What did that mean? Well, nothing actually. Or: nothing and everything. Nothing except for its everythingness, which had to do with the fact that Beyer had managed to distribute 6.4 million of these stickers over a three-year period across the Western world, entirely by word of mouth. Yes, he was keeping track: 6.4 million and counting. And at 6.4 million units and counting, anything meant something. For a while, early in the game, a lot of people wanted to know who Beyer was, hiding behind his anonymous e-mails and websites. After three million stickers Beyer was closer to a national emergency than most hurricanes. After five he was an out-of-control virus, he was contagious. Surf and skate sites, music tie-ins, online games. At six million, he was beyond phenomenal. Whatever the stickers meant to people was what the stickers were about. Beyer's Faith Wall stickers spread to the backs of stop signs and the sides of convenience stores from Vancouver to Tampa, from Stockholm to Johannesburg. On the backs of cell phones, lunch boxes, school binders. On the sides of hopper cars crisscrossing North America. Blown up and plastered over billboards. Faith Wall. And then the fortuitous day when Beyer was in a SoHo gallery and overheard two art types talking about how powerful the whole Faith Wall campaign had become.

Campaign. That was the turning point. If you'd pressed him when he first started with the stickers, Beyer would have told you he kept doing it for the pure pleasure of seeing his mark proliferate and spread. But at that moment—eavesdropping in a SoHo gallery—Beyer understood that he'd done something much bigger. He'd made something with no particular meaning that people would automatically fill with meaning of their own.

And that's right about the point Beyer transformed into a person with clients, people who wanted the wall and the faith that some were prepared to place in it. It was a coveted demographic, that one. Scooter manufacturers wanted it. Music labels. All manner of electronic consumables. Those sharpies who came up with that disposable biodegradable phone with prepaid minutes. The WaferFone. There was a mega-billion-dollar global company behind that one, but when they started thinking about street-level promotions, they didn't hesitate. The Shock Beauty campaign, they called it. And to design that program and get the message out there, they wanted the Faith. They wanted the Wall. In short, they wanted Beyer. It had been about a year before, that one. Beyer's biggest gig by far to that date. But also the assignment that resulted in his thinking about creative associates for the first time, a process that eventually led him to Rabbit, that strange young man who'd heaved himself up out of the oceans of the West and onto the shores of the city those months before. Beached with, the story went, no personal belongings whatsoever except a Thermos and some crazy-ass idea for alley-long posters of wildflowers and mountain fields.

Rabbit's landscape phase: innocent, bucolic, pure. When this first street art idea took its full shape, Rabbit was living in the Poets' warehouse, having been befriended by Jabez only a few days after arriving in the city.

Rescued more like, Jabez would have said, who liked to give Rabbit a hard time about it. "Guy was sleeping under a bridge. Only he's so dumb about life on the street, he's sleeping under a railway bridge, which is not so great when it rains."

Rabbit remembered sitting up sharply in his sleeping bag to find Jabez standing quite close, staring at him. "Who are you?" Jabez signed, index finger fluttering in front of his mouth, then pointing.

Rabbit didn't know Jabez read lips at that point. And he hadn't used sign since the last time he'd seen his deaf friend back in junior high. So he self-consciously signed his name: one fist to each temple, hands opening flat twice to indicate the floppy ears.

Jabez laughed until his eyes were running. Only later did Rabbit sort out that having made the sign with his palms facing forward, he'd actually been telling Jabez that his name was Donkey.

Jabez liked or disliked people instantaneously, Rabbit would quickly learn. And the fact that Rabbit signed, even badly, put him in a special category of like. So Jabez invited him to move into the Poets' warehouse, where Jabez himself lived, into a corner of one of the abandoned mezzanine offices, where Rabbit found a huge box of old-fashioned flat-bed printer paper. Everybody in the place was working on some kind of art or other, stencils or text banners. Rabbit looked at this paper, which interested nobody else, and he decided he'd begin to paint.

"Paint what?" Jabez asked, for whom any painting that wasn't graffiti was a rare street art form.

"The before picture," Rabbit answered. "Before the buildings and cars. Before the freeways and cell phone towers. Before you and me."

Since Rabbit couldn't move the box of paper, he returned again and again to scroll off lengths. He boosted paints from an art supply store. Model paints, kids' finger paints. Anything but spray paints, which were stolen so often by graffiti kids they were guarded by eye-in-the-sky surveillance bulbs. Anything else with pigment, Rabbit used. And for brushes, he worked with whatever came to hand. Rags and toothbrushes, a dish sponge, a box of tampons, his fingers.

Did he know how to paint? Not technically. But this wasn't a technical project. It was a gut inspiration. So he started putting colors down on paper, thinking of the wide fields and plateaus, the ridges and valleys that lay under the city: moss-green expanses against the powder blue of the sky, thousands of blades of grass painstakingly applied and spackled with bits of color that shaped themselves, in their hundred-fold repetition, into flowers. Indian paintbrush, tiger lily, bluebell, daisy. Rabbit would post twenty- or thirty-foot lengths of these, gluing them to alley walls with a slurry mix of cellulose powder and water. They added a note of striking color when they were new, and dissolved attractively when it rained. Somebody wrote up the "flowering alleys of Stofton" in a local paper, tracked him down and quoted Rabbit saying: "If we don't find adequate images, we're all going the way of the dinosaurs."

Beyer hadn't met Rabbit at this point. But the story interested him when he read it the morning it was published. Not the quotation particularly, but the fact of the press. Very unlike those Poet freaks, Beyer thought, with whom he understood this new young artist Rabbit to be bunking. Very unlike Jabez in particular, a name Beyer could not bring to mind now without a wince and a shudder.

Still, Beyer wouldn't have done anything about it if Rabbit hadn't decided to move his postering up out of Stofton and into the Slopes right around that time, and ended up postering a twenty-foot length of brickwork in the alley behind the building where Beyer lived. Kids' stuff, Beyer thought. Look at those lines, those amateurish clouds. He tore the thing down. Sure enough, Rabbit re-posted a bigger one just a few days later, fifty feet long. Beyer waited a week before buffing the whole thing off the wall again. Then, sometime that same night, while Beyer was sleeping a few floors above, Rabbit returned and did the whole alley, carefully posting over doors and utility boxes, across loading bays and trash cans. It was a massive thing. A vista view of what might have been seen if the city were not standing.

Beyer took it in, down in the alley with his morning cup of coffee. Still kids' stuff, but the idea had a stimulating effect on him. This imagining of what might be visible if the whole city were razed to the ground. Beyer thought: The kid has ideas, but he also has a sense of *scale*. And to Beyer, scale was the thing.

Over at the Poets' warehouse, meanwhile, with the exception of Jabez, who had adopted Rabbit as his younger brother, to be schooled and guided, the rest of them kept their distance. They were a suspicious crew, all ex-something. Ex–juvenile detention. Ex–gas huffers. Ex–wards of the state. They tolerated Rabbit because Jabez had brought him in, but they didn't think much of his landscapes. As a group, they were heading in a different direction from vistas, backwards glances, faint regrets. They disdained any approach to street art that made it suitable for positive media coverage, anything vaguely commercial. Beyer, good example. They had a dartboard with a picture of Beyer stapled to the middle. Fame and ambition for the Poets? Never.

The Poets, instead, were into something like an updated Pichação graffiti attack, based on the work of São Paulo inner-city graffiti gangs. And as it was for their distant South American heroes, for the Poets there was no brotherhood without revolution. So they didn't paint, they bombed. And not just walls and alleys, bridge stanchions and railcars. Their unit was the entire building, whole structures. And these bombings were completed with paint, but more importantly with words. Teams of a dozen in their climbing gear, toting ladders and ropes, armed with banners and stickers, braille dots and pictures of hand signs. Never their names, ever. And never poetry either. Always some text chosen by Jabez from the small library of philosophy books he hoarded and which were stacked all around the warehouse. Rabbit watched them hit a bank branch in the east suburbs. He watched them ladder up onto ledges and climb on each other's shoulders. When they were finished you couldn't make out the windows from the walls. The place looked like it had flown into a spider's web of words and been wrapped up tight in loops and coils of text, enclosed and stored inside the writing: . . . *since the struggle is substantially a race for reputability on the basis of an invidious comparison, no approach to a definitive attainment is possible.*

Thousands and thousands of dollars in damage. Rabbit was incredulous. They knew what they were doing. They knew something destructive was let loose in the world by their own actions. But such was their texty agitation, the Poets. Their holy revolutionary fire.

Afterwards, back at the warehouse, there was silence between Rabbit and Jabez, until Jabez finally put his right index finger to his forehead, then both index fingers touching and springing away. Think + opposite = disagree. *You disagree.*

Rabbit made a sign in return. He could have spoken, but the hand motion was on occasion much stronger. Flat palm, fingers to his cheekbone and flicked away towards Jabez. The shrug. The mouth downturned, ambivalent. *I don't know.*

He went back to his landscapes. Working his alleys. And one Wednesday night, middling temperature, no stars, this mug in black warm-ups with a gold chain busts Rabbit mid-post. Coming in over Rabbit's shoulder, voice deep with authority: "So I finally meet my neighborhood alpine wanderer."

Rabbit heard glass breaking in the middle distance, a dumpster slamming closed, the voice of an MC smacking on the night air. Beyer was drinking a beer. He leaned in very close to the wall as if checking the brushstrokes. He said: "If we don't get adequate images we go the way of the dinosaurs. You believe that? Like, art doesn't innovate, then art dies out?"

"More like if art doesn't innovate then we all die out," Rabbit answered.

Beyer invited him up. Converted loft building. Fancy. He was married. He had leather furniture and some kind of rare continental mastiff that ate three pounds of raw meat a day. Beyer had two fridges, he showed Rabbit. One for human food, the other just for dog food, beer and bags of pot. It took Rabbit a few minutes to process exactly into whose apartment he had been invited. Then he saw the room-sized rendering of the Faith Wall sticker. He stood and stared.

"That would be me," Beyer said, handing him a beer, which Rabbit still drank at that time.

No, Rabbit wouldn't have seen him down at the Grove. Beyer hated the Grove, made no bones about it. The Poets with their text-and-paint religion. Beyer was moving way past that. And he was doing this without superstition and tributes paid to dead gods. Jabez. He spit when he said the name. Were Poets looking for innovative images? Of course not. But Beyer was. That was the powerful thing that he and Rabbit had in common. And that's why they were standing there on Beyer's deck looking down over the city sipping an expensive north European lager.

"You're the guy who's always tearing me down," Rabbit said. "You hate my work. I hate your neighborhood. Actually, I don't hate it. I just don't like it."

"You hate this apartment?"

"I must admit I like the fact you have hot water."

"I tore your shit down because it's sentimental crap," Beyer said. "Naive is not the innovation you're looking for."

"And Faith Wall is?" Rabbit said. "I hate to break this to you but I'm not putting up stickers for you. Thanks for the beer . . ."

No, no, no, Beyer had said, smiling. Not that. Just listen. Just hold still.

BEYER TOOK RABBIT DOWN to the far end of the Lagoon, out of the sushi chef's eavesdropping range. Then he went up to get himself a drink, vodka rocks. When he returned Rabbit was sitting with the strap of his bag over his shoulder, looking like he was ready to bolt, and Beyer said: "Don't run, Rabbit. Not safe to be out there. Soldiers and angry crowds. Makes for trouble. They say the Meme studio is all wired up with bombs by now. Special Forces in town. But they arrived awfully quickly, didn't they? Very strange."

"Jabez and the Poets are heading over to the plaza. Some kind of street art protest," Rabbit said. "You might want to join them."

Beyer sipped and scowled, a crease of concentration falling between his eyes. Then he said: "You know what really grips my shit? A kid walks into a school and starts shooting. A guy opens up from a tower on a quad full of preppies. People are always crying, wondering why these things happen."

"Not you, though. You know why these things happen."

"I do know," Beyer said. "They happen because people are angry. Most people are angry most of the time. You're shaking your head."

"You should try leaving the mosh pit from time to time."

"Life is a mosh pit, Rabbit. You'll learn. What the hell happened to your hand?"

Rabbit told him the short version: socket wrench slipped, racked his hand.

"Doing what is the question but don't tell me. Don't jeopardize yourself."

Rabbit reached across the table and took Beyer's glass. He took a smell of it, then put it back down. "I used to drink this stuff. Copious amounts."

"Out there in Oregon, all messed up. Poor little Rabbit. What were you doing before you went nuts? Must have been good but I forget this part of the story."

Rabbit smiled. "I've never told you that part of the story."

"So here's my guess," Beyer said. "You're not here today because I wanted to talk to you. You're broke. You need money. And of course you can't ask Comrade Jabez so you're here to ask me, who you treat as if I weren't a friend at all."

"I'm not broke," Rabbit lied. "I have a job."

"I know you have a job because I got it for you by introducing you to my wife. So you have a job *and* you're broke." Beyer leaned into the table, hand working in the pocket of his thigh-length baggies. He produced a money clip, a big brass dollar sign, and rolled out four twenties onto the table. "A gift. Okay, my friend?"

Rabbit stared at the money, then palmed the bills into his pocket. "Thank you," he said. "I admit it. I'm short."

"Like I'm stupid," Beyer said. "But the seven grand I advanced you a year ago on the WaferFone gig? Not a gift. Plus you took that whole box of phones. I still can't believe you did that. Those are actually worth something."

"Beyer, listen."

"No, you listen, Rabbit. Seven grand isn't chump change. After a year, it's reputation money. I don't get it back, my reputation suffers. I can't have that. So here's what I needed to tell you. You are going to pay me back. And I'm going to help you do that. As of next week, you're not working for Angela, you're working for me, full time."

"What?" Rabbit said. "Angela hasn't said anything about this."

"Angela will do as I tell her," Beyer said. "You stop by the Slopes location and there'll be some severance money waiting for you. I'm being generous here, Rabbit. I'm making this easy for you. And I don't have to."

"But Beyer, Jesus," Rabbit said. "I'm working on something. It's Shock Beauty."

"You think the client cares a year later?" Beyer said. Then he laughed loudly. "They've long gone and hired someone else. I paid them back their advance out of my own pocket, you dopehead. How do you remember where you live? How do you remember your middle name?"

"I quit smoke almost a year ago, you know that. My memory came back zing."

"Oh right, all super straight now. Parkour straight-edge superman. That's our Rabbit."

"Not Parkour. Freesteal."

Beyer made a face of ultimate weariness. "Whatever," he said. "You're my crew until we're square. Make it seventy-five hundred with interest. You work that off."

And even though Rabbit had not agreed, Beyer then chose not to press any further for a commitment. It was his way of persuasion, Rabbit knew, having watched Beyer play people like fish. Reel a bit, then let them run. Rabbit knew he was running now, while Beyer leaned back in his seat and drank down his drink, and then a second. Talking shit. Talking shop. Because they had a chance to really move this thing forward together, didn't they? They were going to wrap street art back around on top of itself like a goddamn Möbius strip. And when it came time that Rabbit knew he had to be out of that room, Beyer begged him to stay a little longer.

Have a drink. Come on. Get you in the zone. Tell me a bit about what it is you're doing. Come on. Paint. Wheatpaste. What. Nothing at all?

All right, later man. Give me a hug. Come on stand up and hug your brother Beyer because you are my brother and I mean that. No. I mean it sincerely. Jabez will never love you as I love you.

Truth. Word.

And then they were apart, Rabbit in familiar streets, down the far east side. Eighty dollars in his pocket. An hour walking, sirens all around, lights flashing past him going the other way. Police cars and vans. A truck painted green with soldiers inside. He felt the city contorting, a mood spiraling out of control.

Alto, Alto. He thought of that name, painted in that hidden tunnel, his hand folded over Beyer's bills. He made a general request for peace to the saint of this holy darkness, these Alto's own streets, his own secret night. And it didn't seem eccentric at all that he should make this request. Let Beyer and Jabez war. Let them commerce and revolution each other to death. Rabbit would quietly pay his respects to Alto. A new way.

No traffic where he was just then. Upturned shopping carts, mattresses, dead tires, major appliances rusting through. Railway transformer twelve feet high that someone had freshly postered over entirely to look like an enormous clock. Dialed in to 9 p.m. The beginning of the night. This night. The final night. The inauguration of designated time.

He was running now. All the way out to the hardware store at a steady sidewalk canter. All the way out to that big place the size of a bus station on a huge parking lot next to a huge furniture store next to a huge place that sold nothing but gas fireplaces. They called it 24/7 City, because it was always open. And there you could find the hardware store to end all hardware stores. Rabbit walked from the darkness into the brilliance of its parking lot lights, in through doors that sighed and parted, into air that was fridge cool. Rabbit walked between shelves the height of cathedral walls. That wood and fertilizer smell, the paint agitated into the atmosphere by a machine that wobbled at blinding speed.

A whole section devoted to lights. Here, look at this. There was a banner hanging from the ceiling so high overhead it looked like sky writing and it stopped Rabbit every time.

It read: *Illuminate Your World.*

THURSDAY TO FIRST LIGHT

—

OCTOBER 24

EVE

—

IN THE PLAZA EAST OF MEME MEDIA, the police laid down a cordon of concrete median dividers, about half a ton each. They arranged these in a long line, end to end, locked to one another with hook-and-eye loops made of rebar. Then they strung long spools of barbed wire over the top. They blocked the alley mouths too and began herding the gathering crowds down to the southeast corner of the plaza, down past the band riser and towards the fountains and waterfalls. The protesters in black resisted, chanting. Others who'd arrived since the story broke stayed in their quiet groups, perplexed and watching, as if they'd come there at someone else's bidding and were now waiting for instructions.

Someone yelled: "Information! What we want is honest information!"

The police arrested a man who'd been seen tipping over a mailbox. A woman blowing soap bubbles nearby was also held but then released.

A bulldozer roared and chattered and scraped. Men in combats stood on street corners. One of the bars on the side of the plaza had a lawn-bowling green on the rooftop patio, league games normally in progress at that hour under the lights. The police had shut it down and commandeered the greens as an assembly area. Men and women with pint glasses stood on the sidewalk outside a side door facing away from the plaza. They didn't seem to have any idea what was happening.

"Why have regular police SWAT units been replaced with military units?" asked a reporter from a local channel at the first news conference. But there was no answer, or no possible answer. There was an appeal for understanding instead.

"Guys," the police spokesperson said. She waved her hands. Her name was Pam Pavich. "Guys, there isn't much to report here. The situation is very fluid. I'm being told that there's been no contact with the hostage taker. So we're all totally in the dark."

Pavich was local, raised out in the east end. Nice-looking lady in her fifties. Redhead. Maybe five foot three but not to mess with. By midnight she'd been replaced. The colonel who stepped in had to deal with everyone's dismay that he wasn't Pam Pavich, which is to say cute, gutsy, local and candid. He was dour and stammered and had hardly anything to say. Journalists took his presence as an indication that things were going poorly in some way hidden from them.

"Sir, I wonder if you can tell us what rules of engagement have been given to the troops arriving, and what units these soldiers have been taken from."

No answer. Can't answer. You have to understand the position here.

All of this at the same moment a fistfight started between two men at the end of the square, although nobody could agree on anything except that the fight started without warning. The men were watching the front of the studio one moment, then swinging punches at each other the next. It was maybe a political disagreement, or one of them had been blocking the other's view. Nobody jumped in to stop it, in any case, because right then there were shots from the top of the square and the world froze.

A policeman brought on this incident. One of the remaining local cops at the barricades, thirty years in the force. Several cameras caught him as he did what he did. As he lumbered to his feet and put his gun down on the hood of a squad car. As he squared his shoulders with resolve and began to walk towards the front steps of the Meme complex with his hands held high and wide, palms open to show he was unarmed. At the top of the steps, he cupped a hand over his eyes and peered inside. Then he yelled: "Come on out and talk. Let's just talk this whole thing through."

Thirty seconds passed. Maybe a minute. Then there was a quick movement behind the glass, far enough back into the darkness of the lobby that it barely registered on the broadcast footage later. A shifting shadow, then the crack of gunfire. A ragged flare of orange. And the whole sheet of glass in front of the officer exploded and he went onto his back and rolled down the steps. Two more shots came out over his head while he scrambled behind a barricade. Unhurt but shaken, although that was not the story told and retold afterwards. It was instead how in the silent seconds that followed, while the entire plaza, the entire watching city dropped a degree in temperature, broken glass in the front window, a ragged aperture, everything poised, a voice cut through clearly: "Don't fire. Do not fire. Cease fire."

Many people heard the words. But nobody could sort out who had spoken, who had called off the storm of violence formed and ready there, sharp and immediate in those quivering seconds. Everything locked up with the words and in a double bind. To act or not to act. Knowing either way innocent people would die.

Don't fire. Do not fire. Cease fire.

Everything locked up tight for seconds, for a minute, while the cameras moved to better positions and glossy-haired anchors spun in their chairs to face the lights, lips already moving around the lines they were about to say.

Five, four, three (two, one). Action.

Shots have been fired . . .

A burst of gunfire has . . .

Reports of rifle fire . . .

More disturbing news from the Meme Media complex this hour as . . .

The world listening, listening. Straining to understand.

EVE STAYED UP, exactly what Nick told her not to do. She stayed up and stayed in front of the television. She phoned her mother and got herself exercised. Nick was asleep, motionless on his back. He slept like a computer battery recharging, very sensible, very like his family, who were all brains and chess and classical music and eight hours a night. Nick had winter tires, he had photocopies of all his credit cards and his passport in the top drawer of his desk. He had a natural disaster kit stored for each of them under the stairs, individualized duffel bags with sleeping gear, extra clothes, water and emergency rations. (For that unexpected trip across town during complicated weather, he once said, which was an oddly poetic construction for Nick.) He ate slow carbs, no piece of meat larger than a deck of cards. These were the deliberate patterns he'd learned from his parents.

No such lessons possible from her own family. In Eve's childhood, somebody was always up pacing in the living room in the middle of the night, worked up over something. An argument certainly, although never about staying out late or borrowing the car. The Latours addressed themselves to higher matters. Truth and liberalism, the fading of religion, the building of a better world. Eve had friends visit the house who showed no enthusiasm to return. She knew why. Because her father might demand an opinion on euthanasia or the death penalty.

One world government, an evolved idea or oxymoronic? The guy locked in Henri Latour's steel-blue gaze for that one was a nineteen-year-old jock at the local college, accomplished at being a running back and very good looking, Eve thought. After that evening the relationship sputtered. When they spoke, his eyes flickered around for safe places to alight.

Such was the House of Latour, the house of ideas and queries, knowledge and endless dissatisfaction. Statues of the Buddha, framed Sanskrit verse. Enlightenment thinkers on the shelves of her father's den. No refuge anywhere inside from the great quest for understanding, that sifting of causes and effects.

For Ali, unlike Eve, there finally came a breakpoint. The blowing of a fuse. Her brother was in the fourth year of his undergraduate degree, English/philosophy with plans for a law degree out on the coast. He talked about doing work that challenged the status quo. Socially relevant work. All of which made their father proud, while it lasted. Then Ali quit, grandly, sweepingly. Not just school, but the whole family program of events. Dinners, disputes, the assorted agitations. He went proudly to live in derelict Stofton, where a completely unforeseen artistic career was to be born.

Nobody in the family saw him much anymore, although Eve managed to keep contact alive for several years. Then, the year before Geneva, Ali began to fall away from her, no longer returning phone calls. Eve was training at a facility out West in the Rockies. Loping down the groomed tracks. Popping off the targets. She had a resting heart rate of forty-nine. She loved the feel of the rifle in her hands.

The last time she saw Ali in person he was gaunt, skin gone ashy. He said he was working on artwork that could only be seen from the air. His hands fluttered unnaturally as he spoke, churning the space between them. Eve knew nothing about heroin addiction, only that Ali had lost a quality. Some shade having bled out of his skin and his voice.

She remembered Ali on his rooftops, executing his pointless, perilous climbs. These were the things she loved most to remember about him, but she couldn't see this person doing any of them.

Eve went to Geneva, stayed away for less than a year. By the time she returned to the city, by the time Geneva and Reza and UNICEF were all over, Ali had vanished. And by that time, Eve thought now, she was the one who'd started to lose a quality. And it was the exact one she'd once seen in Ali and copied from him. What was it exactly? A willingness to act. To celebrate the momentum of her passions.

On television now, Eve watched the camera pan to the top of the square, to the front doors of the Meme complex. The face of the building was flattened and frozen by spotlights set to either side. Dark spaces beyond the doors were visible through the broken front glass.

Eve caught her own reflection in the gold-framed mirror near the fireplace, clutching herself and rocking in place. So Ali fled the house of dissatisfaction. But what could that have meant to their father, in the end? What did the memory of a Buddha in the backyard mean to a person whose body had just been blown free of a jeep? Fifty feet. Dying in the air. Dead in the air. Dead in the sand beyond. A man of so many thousands of words and no final ones himself.

These were useless thoughts, and she knew it. She paced into the dining room, into the kitchen, back into the den. The images of the Meme complex were still there, and Eve felt faintly guilty for letting her mind wander from these events to family matters. But no sooner had she registered this guilt than her mind wandered again. Ali, Ali. He had stormed back into her life, hadn't he? She remembered the moment. Sorting through old boxes that had belonged to her father. Files, correspondence, tax returns. Buried in there was a clippings file with all Eve's press. Interviews, profiles, newspaper accounts of Geneva. Eve pulled out a set of stapled pages, recognized the photo from Kozel's Deli. She remembered the journalist, a more likeable man than he wanted her to believe, disheveled, whiff of hangover, faintly posh accent possibly acquired later in life. But it was the pull quote that caught her, standing there in the half-light.

The question: *So where do you travel next?*

And her answer: *Nowhere, I hope. I'm at the point I just want to stay home. I figure if I can't find it here, I can learn to live without it.*

So glib, so over-confident. Ali came crashing back into the room of her conscience. She saw his face clearly. Remembered his voice from close. Whispered words of reassurance, high up a tower in the freezing wind. *Don't worry, E. Look at that. We're above it all.* Only Ali wasn't to be found here. And what a terrible thing that she had learned to live without him.

On television, the images already assuming a grainy, archival quality, even as Eve watched. They seemed to suggest in advance the number of times they would be pored over later. There were live shots of the gathering crowd now from various cameras around the plaza. Shapes moved against the mercury streetlights and voices echoed. A chant came from somewhere nearby and Eve thought how incredible it was that protesters would be there, growing in numbers, their agitation pooling and gathering in the granular light. There were soldiers in the plaza, barbed wire and concrete slabs. It was just like the movies, Eve thought involuntarily. Then wondering who wrote that people always compare traumatic moments to the movies because they cannot help comparing the *real unreal to the unreal real.* Some favorite of her father's.

Here it was not quite clear which they were watching. Real or unreal. She sat in the shabby gentility of a West Stretch living room, flat-screen television glowing from on top of the old cabinet hi-fi that had belonged to Nick's parents. There was a cordon around a building. Riflemen in the shadows. Soldiers no doubt creeping through the sewers. Commanders and officers leaning over a table somewhere with a situation map. Those were the familiar images.

Not a word from inside the theater, or none that was being acknowledged by authorities. And from the outside, a strange pattern prevailed. A large number of people had been released early on, so many that there was confusion over how many remained inside. People coming out of the theater couldn't help much. They came out blinking and blinded and confused about what they had just experienced. Were there bombs inside? Somebody said that the floor was laced with wiring. Others disagreed. An expert said this was how memory worked under these circumstances. Robbed of details, it would cut and paste, mix and match. It would paint into place the specific threat that otherwise could only be felt.

"The whole point of taking a hostage is to give yourself a shield to protect your life," another expert said, "which generally suggests that hostage takers aren't suicidal, as in the cases of gunmen opening fire in a public place."

"So we should feel safer knowing this?" asked the host, brow deeply furrowed, baritone full of doubt.

"The situation is still dangerous. But it's rare for the primary objective to be the death of the hostages, since it would necessarily mean the death of the hostage taker as well, who would no longer be protected by their shield."

Why no demands, then?

"Well," the expert said. "I'm speculating. But he could be waiting for attention to be brought to bear, for the media to gather."

They went to commercial and Eve muted the television, listening now to the interior of the house, the usual hums and creaks. The gentle breath of night, now failing to reassure. The expert saw a storm being called up, a dense pressure system, patiently awaited. This stillness then, Eve thought, was the eye of the storm.

"Champ?"

She jumped and turned and there he was.

"Oats, hey. You still up?"

Otis moved past Eve to sit in Nick's reading chair near the bookshelf against the far wall. He settled into the leather.

"Watching upstairs?"

"Yeah," he said. "Deeply sickening."

"They're going to end it soon, I bet."

"I don't know," Otis said. "Very risky."

"But what else?"

"Negotiate?" Otis said. "What's a million bucks, or fifty million?"

"Unfortunately the guy hasn't asked for anything."

"Everyone wants something. So this guy wants something. They just gotta figure out what it is."

"I suppose," she said. And although the announcers were back on-screen, Eve didn't key on the sound. So they continued to watch and discuss the silent images, comparing perplexed thoughts and hopes for resolution. And after several minutes, a silence came that Eve thought would end when Otis told her what was really on his mind.

He sat nodding in the semidarkness of the room, as if agreeing with her decision to leave the television muted. Then he said: "About this man living in our hedge. You and my dad were arguing about it."

She turned to look at him. "What about him?"

"My dad thinks he's gotta go."

"It's not decided. We're discussing it," Eve said. Otis didn't take his eyes from the television, so Eve let her gaze drift back there too. The west end of the plaza, the face of Meme Media and the wide steps leading up to its smashed front doors all laid out in brilliant white and harsh shadow. Dark shapes moving in the foreground. The blackest possible sky overhead. The same starless sky that was over them. The same night hanging over this house.

"And what do you think?" Eve asked.

Otis shifted in the chair. "I think I see my dad's point. One person comes. You let them stay. You end up with a campsite. There are a lot of these people out there."

Eve nodded, still watching the television. The anchors were back, making conversation out of the scant information available.

"I mean," Otis continued, "that there really is a limit to what we can do to help others, even in difficult times."

"All right," Eve said. "And what are you suggesting?"

Otis raised his hands, palm out. "I'm not. I'm trying to make a different point."

Eve thought the anchors betrayed uncertainty. There was an ad hoc quality to their movement. The cuts and cues not quite right. It was getting very late, people were obviously tired.

"Go ahead," she said.

"My point being that I admire you for disagreeing with him. For resisting the obvious logic."

Eve turned back to the young man who sat opposite in his father's favorite leather lounger, his knees squared and open in front of him, one hand hanging over the end of each chair arm, like a miniature Lincoln Memorial. It made her want to laugh. Not at Otis's expense at all. But in just the way they would have laughed together if they'd seen someone else sitting that way and sounding so grave.

"Well I don't necessarily think the logic is that obvious," Eve said finally. "But please, Oats. Why don't you just tell me what's on your mind."

He sighed and rubbed his chin. If it weren't so dark in the room, Eve was sure she would have seen the red rising in his cheeks. Otis blushing. "I guess I just think that acting on your gut, because you think something's right . . ."

"Yes?" Eve said.

"I guess that's what I think you're really like. What you had to be like to win a gold medal. Kind of stubborn. Kind of irrational but, in the end . . . right."

He was standing already. He was walking past her, touching her shoulder briefly on his way to the door, to head upstairs, to return to his chat room, his MoleChess™, his CNN watching. Whatever it was that made up his nighttime routine.

Just passing her, Otis said: "Which is something you don't want to lose."

Twenty-five more people released in the hour following midnight. They came out in twos and threes into the chill of the square. A person with a heart condition. A woman who'd fallen in the original moments of the incident and broken her wrist. All the show's remaining technicians and producers. Not much pattern to it: men and women, black and brown and white. Locals and visitors. Some children too. Blinking out into the light, blinded. About fifty people were left in the theater, it was said. And even this took on an ominous cast. Fewer people than before, was that good? Or did that mean they were closer to some final number? Some hard-set bottom line.

Eve took the phone outside to the back deck. Low concrete lines disappeared into the roll of the lawn that stretched down to the stream, to the lake beyond. No sign of movement, no wink of flashlight inside the tent. She thought of walking down, making a noise. He might wake up. She phoned her mother instead, out on the West Coast.

"Your father?" her mother said. "Well, he'd probably be inside the theater by now, interviewing people, looking very serious and unafraid."

"Did you admire that he was like that?"

"Oh, sure I did, Evey."

"Why did he take the last trip to Afghanistan?"

"Same reason he took all the others," she said. "Curiosity and indignation." No, she hadn't worried. It wasn't her job to worry then. He'd gone to live with his girlfriend.

"You still talked, though."

"We talked incessantly, that's why we couldn't stay together. I hope you and Nick don't talk nearly so much, although I suppose you probably don't because of the age difference."

"Did Dad feel like he was changing things, going over?"

"Oh, Evey, it's late there. Something horrible has happened. People worry it's all coming to an end at times like this. It never is."

"I really want to know," Eve said. "Like Dad felt he had to be involved, that it would be wrong to sit by quietly."

"Your father went places where there were wars, and reported what he saw. Change? I don't know. But he always said, 'I'm not a doctor. I'm not one of these heroes from Médecins Sans Frontières.' Those were the people he admired."

Eve was nodding, listening. She caught herself biting her fingernail and slipped her hand into her pocket.

"Of course he also admired you, Eve. He loved your athleticism. You ran like the wind. You skied and swam. And the fact you could shoot. We were pacifists, politically. We would never have sent you to that summer camp at all if we'd known they had guns. Then you come home with some kind of medal. And all these targets. He was horrified and he was delighted. That's how it was with him and you, all the time."

"And Ali? He was athletic too."

"He admired Ali's independence. But Ali wanted out. That makes fathers very defensive. They tend to forget their own desperation at the same age."

"Ali never measured up."

Eve's mother sighed. "You should go to bed. What time is it there?"

"Just one," Eve said.

"They're releasing people. You see, this is good. But I'm watching here and it's only eleven, which is reasonable. I hope you're going to bed now."

Eve walked back inside and looked around the corner at the television. "A woman said they were sitting in utter darkness. Some guy with a gun up there, saying nothing."

"Well I hope the guy gets jailed for life."

"I hope they shoot him dead."

"Don't say that, Eve! Nobody dies justly in these situations. Everybody is a victim."

Eve didn't think she agreed, but didn't argue the point. Time for her to say what was really on her mind. "I've been looking for Ali. Two months now."

Six more people were released from the front of the theater, and they came scrambling down the steps in a knot. Her mother said: "You see. Here come some more. They'll let them all go. It'll all be over."

But then silence, as Eve might have predicted. And it was possible for Eve to feel a distance close between them as their eyes rested on those same images, pulled quite tightly by them into a shared and troubled world.

Her mother sighed. Then, finally: "Maybe you should forget Ali and concentrate on yourself."

Eve pulled the phone away from her ear sharply and held it in her lap, the wind taken out of her. Exactly the kind of comment her mother was capable of making, the kind that had reduced Eve to tears numerous times as a teenager. The unexpected revelation of her mother's misgivings.

Then Eve picked up the phone again and put it to her ear, gently, firmly. Sometimes you just had to be stubborn. "Ali is still here," she said.

"You've seen him?"

"Not exactly, but I sense it. And I'm going to find him. That's what I've been trying to do and it's what I'm going to keep on doing."

Her mother didn't respond. Maybe she'd known for a long time that Eve needed her brother, to hear his voice, to be inspired by him as she had once been. The person she had so idolized through her youth.

Or maybe her mother just didn't know what to say. Eve heard her breathing in and out there at the end of the phone line. And when they resumed talking, it was as if they'd said all that needed saying on the matter. The vanished son and brother who condemned from a distance. The center of the silence that finally followed, even after their father's death, after all those stories in the paper Ali could not possibly have missed. He was out there still, Eve knew. And he might not deserve her looking, but things tumbled to a point—here and everywhere, the world alight with countless brushfires, nothing extinguished without something starting new—when Eve no longer knew what to do, what to feel, without him. And when she'd said goodbye to her mother and promised that, yes, going to bed was probably a good idea, Eve went outside again to contemplate the blackness and her brother, and to remember times they had shared.

Ali?

Yeah, girl.

Ali, I'm scared. Like I'm really scared here.

It's safe. It's a ladder. Ladders are easy. Look.

He stood smiling with his hand on one of those final rungs up to the top of the East Shore radio tower. She was freezing up, she could feel it. The wind didn't help. It was bitterly cold at that height, at that hour. It contributed to the sense of being blown free of the city, wafted over it like a leaf. Everything lying far below, the city lights, the black shape of the river. And the tower seeming to sway too. She could feel the staircase moving under her. Not inches. Eve guessed it was feet either way. They were bending back and forth. Ali was smiling, looking up through this spindly tube in which the ladder was mounted. Twenty-five or thirty more steps to the very top, a final push that Ali was assuring her was worth the effort. They were above the city now. But up there, that one level further, they would be among the stars.

She said: "I can't."

And he didn't go up without her. He had been many times before, but this trip had been for her and he didn't leave her to gain the summit alone. He came over to where she stood at the rail. He slid his arm around her and said: Let's just look from here, then. Don't worry. We'll stay here. I'll stay with you.

The platform was rocking under her. She didn't take another step, just held the railing with both hands where she stood. As she stood now, for the final minutes of her evening, before going inside and pulling the door shut behind her. Before raising the remote control to have done with it. One push of the button. With a zap, a wrinkle of static, burning the scene right off the surface of consciousness, dissolving it into the air.

RABBIT

—

RABBIT ASSEMBLED A NEW UNIT to replace the one he'd broken. He worked in silence in his apartment, hunched over a table made from an empty cable spool. His hands moved quickly and precisely in worn patterns. The bead of solder, the frame bolts. He had a solar panel ripped out of one of those lawn lights you see lining people's front walks out in the suburbs. He had a top-mounted halogen light wired into the works, snips and dabs, the solder silvering the joins, elements fusing into a whole. Effects to causes to causes and other causes.

A WaferFone sat next to him on the table. Rabbit consulted a list, then marked down the numbers on the side of the map. He bleeped in coordinates, juicing the phone with its future tasks. He cracked open the back with a jeweler's chisel and connected the trigger wire of cable with two more drops of solder. Then he rolled the phone in bubble wrap and creased it shut into a resealable sandwich bag, the cable trailing free. He slipped this package into the bottom of the housing, which he had cut with scissors out of a silicon baking sheet. Waterproof and heat resistant, it would sit and wait where it was installed, faithful to the end. One last check of the wires, the closures. Then into the knapsack with his gloves, clipboard, overalls, knee pads, bolt cutters, extra wire and batteries, aluminum sleeping foil in case he ended up camping out.

He left through the window and dropped down the fire escape to the alley, with grips and swings, the balls of his feet to the railings. One twist and jump from the lowest landing, one bounce off the lid of a dumpster, and he was in the alley running. The engine of the city humming around him as he entered the street, trying not to think about technical mess-ups, wet batteries, dead light panels, bad solder. It would work. It had to work. And he thought of the mystery artist Alto again, as if to call on him for strength, for an example of commitment.

The streets were amber with an alternating blue and red glow across the brickwork in the distance, helicopter rotors overhead. Rabbit worked around the hillside, staying below the plaza, zigzagging south and east. Finally gliding to a stop in a loose crowd that stood on the corner just outside the café where he worked part time. Angela's. Beyer's Angela.

Ten or fifteen people, all staring up towards the brow of the hill where the light intensified. All distracted, talking. Voices on top of other voices. Many ideas loose among them. Militia arriving. Snipers on the rooftops. The Meme Media owners were Jordanian, apparently. Major sponsors of an area politician who'd lost by a hair. What did these things mean? People were running the numbers.

Rabbit squeezed past a guy wearing a cell phone earbud, relaying the local news to someone far away. A lone perpetrator. Fifty-plus hostages, still. For sure they were storming the building that night, he was saying. They weren't going to leave the nutcase in there to stew things over. And this business of releasing hostages. That wasn't good news. Felt more like a cull before the killing. The man said into his phone: "Guy's got a death wish, I'm telling you. They should just go go go. Of course I'm right."

Inside the café, voices were low. Rabbit heard: "Wait until tomor-row. They're going to be showing us satellite pictures from Saudi Arabia or somewhere. They'll find a cube van at the airport with a passport. We've heard this story before."

The man was talking to a woman who was staring down at the counter as though the tiled surface had failed her, gone blank and silent just when she needed it.

He was listing facts: "They lie. They say anything. There'll be an arrest somewhere nice and safe and foreign. Some poor sucker in Kuwait or wherever. They whisk him off to some black site where he'll confess to everything."

Angela wasn't in and she hadn't left anything for him either. Rabbit wondered if she knew about Beyer's plan yet. Either way, if he knew Beyer, which he thought he did, Angela would indeed fire him. Which meant Rabbit himself had a problem going forward. He tried to re-member if he'd ever had a good plan for how to complete his project and pay Beyer back all in a year. He wasn't sure he had, beyond blind faith in creativity and good intentions. He hoped that faith wasn't a fatal flaw that would bring him down.

Rabbit returned to the sidewalk and felt the increasing tension there. The upended, turned-out streets. People standing where traffic usually flowed. Clustered in intersections, under blinking yellow lights. Or standing out in front of restaurants and bars, looking up to-wards the plaza. There were street food carts out past their normal hour, and the smell of brats and onions hung in the air, the black edge of a carnival feeling. Scared people often laugh. And now people laughed in groups here and there, televisions hanging over their heads in the background, showing the skip and hurry of things unfolding. Rabbit didn't want to know if some new thing had happened. A de-velopment, as the newscasters would say. He broke into a run again and made his way by alley to Jeffers Avenue, then cut north towards the plaza, stopping half a block short on the west side of Jeffers in front of the Peavey Block.

He tied his shoe at the mouth of the alley that traced the southern wall of the building, glancing up and down, checking for security. But he couldn't see anybody obvious. Nobody scanning the sidewalks, watching for specifics. Nobody looking his direction, then away quickly while flipping open a phone.

Rabbit stood slowly, then slid into the protective shadow of the alley, his shoulder to the bricks as he considered his next move. During the day, Rabbit knew, the roof could be accessed through the Peavey Block itself using a set of service stairs. He'd done exactly that the day before. And since a language college was housed there, Rabbit had attracted no particular attention as he made his way through the crowded hallways with his knapsack.

Different story at night, when the building was locked. Rabbit considered climbing options as he walked farther into the alley, tracing the south side of the building, slipping past dumpsters, ignoring the rusting fire escape, which was too exposed. At the rear of the building there was a chain-link fence that closed off the yard. Rabbit peered through it and saw that just inside was a drainpipe running six floors down from the roof in an open brick shaft about two and a half feet across.

Rabbit reversed his pack, so that it was strapped to his front. Then he counted off thirty seconds, watching the yard and the alley for any movement he might not have noticed before. When he was sure he was alone, he vaulted to the top of the fence in a sudden unfurling of limbs: a flex of the legs, hands to the top of the fence, a rattle of chain link, a twist of the torso. And he was up, standing on the top of the fence with one hand to the brick wall. A brief pause. Then he fell forward, grabbing the drainpipe and swinging himself into the shaft. Feet to one wall, back to the other. And immediately in motion, spidering skyward. The grind of dust in his collar, the trickle of blood on a knuckle where the brick had rasped his skin, sweat and the delicious sense of space opening below. Then the parapet, and quick now. No hesitation. Two hands up here, a final surge and grip. Rabbit swinging free over the alley. Once, twice, and up to the flashing. Foot hold, slow flex of the shoulders and hips, and he was over. Sliding down to the gravel of the Peavey Block roof, where he rolled into a ready crouch.

The roof was empty. Nobody there to see him as he crossed over to the elevator housing and climbed to the top, as he set down his pack and removed his tools, then the unit. Quick movements, steady and sure. Re-drilling the pilot holes for the metal screws, re-fitting U-clamps over the base of the bracket and cinching these down. When the unit was mounted he slid the silicon sheet into place and sat back, only just that instant feeling the surge of completion. Pride, sure. Excitement, yes. Relief, definitely. And his feelings were importantly augmented by the view, that guttering symphony of city light. Downtown sparkling across the south branch of the river. Towers rising, bridges plugging in below. Traffic pulsing up the black boulevards, out of the western reaches of the delta, across the flats, then seeming to vault upwards to join the illuminated density of the urban core.

On any clear night, Rabbit could see this surface as a patterned copy of the stars above, its galactic center swirling, tendril arms tapering into the absolute zero of suburban space and farmland beyond. The mechanical below a copy of the super-mechanical above, each light dancing in the matrix of law that brought it into being. His own work, now finished, was suspended between them, stretched taut as a drum skin. Waiting for the stroke that would give it voice. That would reveal it.

BEYER HADN'T TRICKED RABBIT into accepting that original seven thousand dollars, that one long year prior. Rabbit thought about this, taking a moment's breather on the top of the Peavey Block before descending. He knew he'd chosen the path a year before, and now he had to walk it. But he also thought how ironic it was that if he hadn't accepted Beyer's offer, Jabez would not have been provoked to take him through the Easter Valley Railway Tunnel. And if that hadn't happened, Rabbit would never have discovered Alto. Since Alto was the inspiration for the Blue Light Project, Rabbit was forced to accept that no Beyer meant no discovery of Alto, which meant no Blue Light Project, which meant he wouldn't even be up there in the deep blue of night, breathing the chill air over the city, his project finally complete except for activation. It was paradox certainly, but nonetheless true. Such, Rabbit supposed, was the black magic of the big idea involved as it was born a year ago.

Rabbit had moved by then out of the Poets' warehouse and was living even further down the socioeconomic ladder in Stofton, almost at the river. He remembered a sloping floor and intermittent plumbing. He slept curled up on a futon Angela donated. She gave him three shifts, all the barista time he could handle. He took home enough to pay his rent and eat. But when the power went out in his building in November and stayed out for forty-eight hours, he went up the hill and threw stones against the glass until Beyer came to the window, high over the alley, and called down: "You realize some people have buzzers?"

Rabbit remembered vaulting up the fire escape while Beyer watched and shook his head.

Beyer was in his kitchen making pasta by hand. There were eggs and flour and milk involved. He was white to the bottom of his Tahitian war paint and had an apron on, music pounding, hardcore. Angela was out. This was linguine, Beyer explained. It was going to become linguine vongole, which he would have ready for Angela when she got home. "A bottle of wine, a little pasta," he said, slinging the dough into a sheet of cling wrap to cool in the fridge. "Life is good."

Beyer knew why Rabbit was there. Rabbit knew he knew. Something was poised in the moment, in the warp of things. Circumstances and meanings about to change. So Beyer cleaned up and, since Rabbit was still smoking then, they smoked together and Beyer exploded into a short arc of cosmic intensity, crackling, hissing, popping. He turned the music off so it would be just him. And he echoed in the loft, Beyer now working on the cork of a wine bottle clamped between his knees, hopping to keep his balance.

He said: "You roll into town. You start hanging out with Jabez and the Poets, doing your pretty flowers. But you realize you're sick of being broke all the time. Sick of doing work that gets torn down in a day."

Rabbit remembered feeling warmth, if not safety, as he listened, as Beyer circled the room, heat-seeking, homing in. Master of disaster.

Beyer had continued: "We have archaic creative threads in our DNA, you and I. We're the guys who would have been cave-painting, laying out rocks in lines, making circles in wheat fields. We're creators, not destroyers, we reveal and don't hide. We're the people bringing the world those images it needs for survival."

Rabbit had been high, but he'd still been able to appreciate the craft there. Beyer folding Rabbit's own words onto themselves. Beyer about to kill.

"We're surrounded by advertisements," Beyer went on. "They assault and insult us with bad products. But then I'm contacted by someone who's got this incredible thing to sell, this phone, man. It's like that small. And biodegradable. Use and lose. Sixty minutes' calling time anywhere in the world and you throw it into your compost. *Minutes to a Better World*. And I'm supposed to reject this opportunity because I'm an artist? No! I reject that thinking. I reject Jabez telling us we should continue being poor, misunderstood and looked down on. That we should continue suffering for some kind of *cause*. We're not flipping to the dark side converting part of that daily storm of advertisement into something beautiful. Adequate images. Fucking right. We're adding beauty where there is none, Rabbit. We're turning the motherfucking dark side into light. Work with me, man. I got a feeling about you and me. A strong feeling."

Rabbit said: "WaferFone." He was smiling. So Beyer said, "That's the one. Shock Beauty. You know it's a good idea."

And it was a good idea. It was a very fine idea, that little WaferFone. So Rabbit took the money, way up there in the gentrified Slopes, high on good weed and sipping wine. And all the way down the hill in the rotting streets of Stofton, in the basement of the Grove, Jabez apparently sensed the transaction instantly. As Rabbit remembered how these things unfolded, he could only explain it that way, that the second he folded his hand around Beyer's check, the second he hit the street with that box of phones, credit card thin, a thousand units a box, Jabez knew. And he tracked Rabbit down.

Rabbit remembered Jabez coming over to his apartment. They had to talk, he said. So down to the rail yards they went.

"Here comes the speech about Beyer," Rabbit had said.

"Here's what you need to understand about Beyer," Jabez had said, "that he's taking the walls away from us. Sell your art in a gallery. I'm down with that. People have to eat. But turn street art into advertising and every square foot of wall in this town is going to have market value. Street art is a criminal offense now, fine. Nobody cares. I get arrested. I get released. Turn street art into the theft of somebody's profitable walls and trust me, lots of people with a lot more money and power than you and me will care very much."

"It's one lousy campaign," Rabbit had said. "One stupid phone."

"Maybe if you failed it wouldn't matter. But you won't," Jabez had replied. "And there will be others. You do this thing with Beyer and succeed, sell a lot of phones, it'll be over for everybody."

Jabez was less angry than Rabbit might have expected. Rabbit remembered him seeming only sad as he said those important words that came next: "I need to show you something. I don't do this very often. Easter Valley. The railway tunnel."

Rabbit had never heard of it at that point, but he remembered thinking that it was exactly the kind of thing that Jabez would quietly know. He loved trains. He loved their arcane and secret ways and maybe nothing more than this tunnel which plunged down into the cool and hidden. So off he'd stumped, Rabbit in tow. Into that tightening air, his lungs laboring. Jabez floating in the blackness ahead as the tunnel bent away endlessly into the earth. And when they reached the middle, the blue light, the glorious thing by the mysterious Alto, where Rabbit had stood with his mouth open not even understanding then how enormous his discovery would become, Jabez had just kept on walking.

Rabbit had run after him and grabbed him by the shoulder. Throwing his flashlight onto his own face, so his lips were clearly visible. Did you see that piece? Who is that?

Jabez did the same, turning his own light up and onto his own face. They stood there like two jack-o'-lanterns. Rabbit mouthing words in his light. Jabez making compact one-handed signs in his. He said: "No idea. Some kid. Not the point. Will you follow me, please? We're on a schedule here unless you'd like to get pegged by a coal hopper doing twenty miles an hour."

Rabbit remembered how they'd walked for another five or ten minutes through the damp and black, and how he couldn't tear his thoughts away from what he'd seen. *Alto.* Why was it there? Why would anyone make the effort? Eyes down in the small pool of yellow light afforded by his flashlight. The only bit of the future that he could see.

Jabez had arrived at a door in the wall ahead. Next to it, a keypad. He tapped in a security code and pushed open the door. They entered a passage that angled down towards a control room, dust covering everything. No graffiti. Jabez put his light on a shelf so he could sign with two hands.

"Just the beginning," he said. "There are tunnels dropping out through there and over there." He cracked the door into one room and Rabbit saw a round hatch in the middle of the concrete floor. It had a circular screw lock, like you might find on a ship.

Rabbit shone the light on his face and asked: "Why are you showing me this?"

Jabez nodded. "Because it's important. We're not going down the tunnels, don't worry. You're not ready for that."

"I'll never be ready for that," Rabbit said.

"But you have to know it's here. You have to know that we're standing at the beginning of a network of hidden passages and rooms that really do exist even though people don't know about them. Long spaces in the rock below. Abandoned bunkers and storage vaults."

"Okay, so I know," Rabbit said. "So what?"

"Think," Jabez had said. "Beyer is up there on the surface. He's about what the eye can see and what his brain can understand. Money, cynicism. I'm about down here, Rabbit. I'm about mysteries and secrets, sacred objects in a hidden world."

And to cement this point—as Jabez had surely planned it—on their way out Rabbit remembered how they'd run into a train. How could he ever forget that? The tunnel bending away endlessly. In the darkness Rabbit's thoughts had drifted. And then, quite suddenly, he'd sensed that another light was present. Not a flashlight, far too bright. The entire wall ahead starting to glisten, shining with its thousand rivulets of water, rising up to a glare out of the blackness, the tracks alive with light now too, shooting forward in parallel arcs towards him.

Rabbit groped his way towards the wall as a thunderous sound rose. He was, for a moment, unsure where to go. Then Jabez had leaned out of an alcove and hauled him in. He had Rabbit in one arm, gripping him tightly, holding him in against his chest. Then he slid his other hand over Rabbit's mouth, pressing there. Do this, the motion said.

Rabbit did it. Leaning into the wall, rough-textured rock here, gripping his own mouth now against the rising fumes. His head immediately swirling with them, going dizzy with them. Jabez was braced against the two sides of the alcove and Rabbit did the same just in time to appreciate the reasoning. You began to fail in those minutes. The fumes began to kill you. He felt himself slip, the downward rush of asphyxiation. And then he could feel that the weight of the thing had passed. He'd hardly registered the passing of the sound itself: the battleship-sized rattling, the shifting of plates of steel, the screaming of bearings and joints, the slow slop of cables, the grind of the wheels. He felt only the blackness clear at the opening of the alcove. It cleared to a blacker blackness and Rabbit was gasping. But he'd been laughing too. What Jabez had told him would stay with Rabbit. But what Jabez had shown him, without even knowing it, that was the more important gift.

Rabbit remembered breathing the word right there for the first time, feeling its possession. That name at the invisible heart of things. Citizen of the hidden world. It was all coming together.

Rabbit had whispered: *Alto.*

TIME TO CLIMB. Time to shimmy, time to rock. Rabbit blinked back to the present. He stole a last look at the stars, at the city. He then strapped his pack tightly to his chest again and leaned over for a final inspection of what he'd reinstalled there on the Peavey Block roof. His unit. Secure and patient. It would wait for the call.

Then he jumped down from the elevator housing. A gentle thud to the gravel roof and a forward roll, then he was up and on his feet and heading for the top of the drainpipe. He planted his hands here and vaulted over soundlessly into the brick shaft and was already sliding down when he realized that the fenced-in yard behind the building was no longer empty. It was, in fact, milling with people.

Rabbit froze instantly, feet and shoulders braced against the brick. What was this? But no heads swiveled upwards. None of the movement below stopped or changed in its patterns. Maybe twenty, twenty-five people. But then Rabbit, straining now, quivering in place, took in more details about these people that he wished he didn't have to see. Black fatigues, knee pads, balaclavas, tight-fitting helmets with goggles and mounted cameras. They were performing a ritual pat-down, each checking a partner: harnesses, straps, snaps, firearms, ammunition. Pat to the shoulder, turn. Check, check. Pat. Roll. Thumbs-up.

He couldn't go down, and he couldn't stay where he was, so Rabbit began to inch upwards again. Hand, foot, push. Gentle now. Hand, foot, push. He'd have to move quickly mounting the roof. He'd have to act without thinking or he knew he would fall. He counted off ten arbitrary seconds and then swung free, weight on his hands where he gripped the flashing. He was a black silhouette dangling over those other black silhouettes below. Back and forth, once, twice, building momentum. Then the kick up and the foot to the aluminum flashing and he was over. Down flat on the gravel, but hearing nothing. No sudden silence below. No hurried feet on the stairs.

Rabbit sat with his back against the parapet and thought about options. Soldiers, obviously. But soldiers you weren't supposed to see. These tight and lethal communities. Delta Force, Alpha Group, JTF2, SBS. The Black Hats.

He crouched low, palm flat to the roof gravel, working it through. If they were in the yard, then they were clearly using this building. Which meant the building itself would be secure. Which meant that each floor would have been searched. Which meant . . .

Rabbit's heart loped up to a sprinting pace. Which meant they were going to search the roof. Not later, but immediately. Any second now.

He swallowed and worked to govern his breathing. A sensation like this had taken him only once before, a brief but complete feeling of being out of control. He'd been at the top of an abandoned grain silo that time, out at one of the old river terminals. He'd crossed a narrow concrete beam over a hundred feet of blackness to reach a door that he understood would open to a catwalk on the far side. But he never found out if it did or not because, at the end of the beam, stones pinging downwards in the murk below, he found the door was locked. Turning and retracing his steps had not been in the plan. But after the heart-rate spike, the dawning awareness of what you had to do, you just did it. Your options whittled down to one, you took the last option with what remained of your confidence and all the care you could manage. Do it. Do it now. Don't rush.

So now Rabbit stood and moved quickly to the roof edge nearest the alley, where he'd been less than twelve hours before. Fifteen feet away and six feet down, the roof of the next building began. It was angled gently towards him and covered in gritty tarpaper, which had given him landing grip on his jump the previous afternoon. Although that had been in daylight, when he could actually see the surface approaching. He couldn't see it at all now. He wondered if he might see it halfway across, three-quarters. Maybe not until the instant before impact. Or even then.

Rabbit winced and looked around. He was aware of himself suddenly as if from an outside perspective. Doing his own pat-down. Checking straps and shoelaces, smoothing his hands over his face and clothes as if to streamline himself further.

He took one last long look at the hard roofline opposite, the pool of black beyond. Then he turned and paced off six long steps back from the parapet, where he stood with his hands dangling, shaking them, trying to loosen up, trying to breathe deeply. He reached down and took each ankle in turn, stretching his quads. He listened to the door opening behind him at the top of the elevator shaft, looking slowly back over his shoulder to see this for himself. No yellow light blooming. Only the darker shadow of the door intercepting street light. Charcoal on slate gray. Shapes coming clear too, moving in casual silence. One, two, three. Fanning towards the far roofline, nearest the square. Rabbit had time for a single thought: the reason why these soldiers were so effective had less to do with their being unafraid, and more to do with their having no anger. In their smooth movements and stable pace, Rabbit thought, they revealed themselves to be utterly calm about their relationship with death.

Rabbit turned back, square to the alley. He knew he could do this with barely a sound until whatever muffled bang he might make at impact. No time to calculate the risk there.

Six steps. Bip bip, bap bap, bam bam. Air.

And no memory of it, particularly. Rabbit, afterwards, could recall only snips from the beginning and the end of his flight. The cold moment of contact between the ball of his foot and the concrete parapet. Then the approaching pool of black shadow, and in it a glint of metal. A shred of tin foil, a beer can, the tip of a hypodermic needle. Rabbit never determined what, exactly. But it winked at him, like a runway light through the fog. This bit of refuse that had found its way onto an anonymous rooftop. And Rabbit tucked his feet up, and hit the surface hard. Then rolled, sprawled, bled from the nose. Dragged himself into the black shadow of a wide brick chimney. And for several moments after that, not daring even to roll his head and look back the way he'd come, he lay completely still.

EVE

—

FIRST LIGHT, AND THE STREETS around the plaza were taking
on a certain slow seething energy. The press had been arriving since
late the previous night and another rush was expected when the first
flights started coming in from both coasts and overseas that morning.
Already the white vans were queued along the side streets, their satellite dishes telescoped high into the billowing gray sky. Already there
were miles of cable underfoot and chairs set up under tents, cameras
draped in plastic against the threatening drizzle. And everywhere,
spots of white as updates and hourly briefings were completed, some
bright-eyed person haloed in light, beaming back the troubling news
to a waiting world.

Eve picked her way through the crowd, noticing how people were
showing up with different, often conflicting expectations. There were
chanters and singers, vigil keepers. There were placards angry and distraught, but all tuned to some separate motivating wavelength that the
Meme Media Crisis emitted. Scattered hundreds beginning to cluster
and mix at the cordoned-off eastern fringe of the plaza, furthest from
the theater, and at the barricades that blocked other streets. The air was

pregnant with suspicion and fear. And in the cafés and on the street corners Eve could hear arguments and position taking.

A man outside a convenience store was gesturing, face animated: "They simply have to go in. You cannot negotiate with these kinds of people."

"Well then the blood will be on your hands," came the reply.

At which point the first man brushed past the second one, jostling him as he did so. Careless or out of aggression, it hardly mattered. Now they were pushing and shoving. People were yelling. Friends pulling them apart. Eve was frozen, staring at this spectacle. Horrified. Disgusted to see civility stripped so quickly away. Both men were right, to a point. You couldn't deal with people who took children as hostages. And if one mistake was made, then blood would indeed be on all their hands. But the implied stalemate had the effect of making Eve quietly angry.

Nick would be asleep again by then. He did that well too. Resumed rest. No matter that the disagreement had been sharp and unresolved between them on her leaving. He counted up his investment in every dispute and knew when to stop his losses.

The other thing Nick told her not to do: don't sleep on the couch. You'll wake up after four hours with that television still going. Same broadcast, same news, which Nick somehow felt was unhealthy.

Eve did wake up on the couch, although the television was off. But then she turned it on immediately. And there were the same tired, concerned anchors. The same exterior shots of Meme. And this had an effect on her that suggested maybe Nick had a point. Maybe it was unhealthy to greet the day with images of a world still shaped around the tragedies and impasses of the day before.

She woke Nick before leaving and he did something she'd never seen him do in the years she'd known him. With her first touch, he came instantly to consciousness and seeming lucidity. He pulled off the sleep mask. He sat up, night-tabled his earplugs, popped free his mouth guard and fixed her with a comprehensive stare. She had to wonder if he'd been awake the whole time, waiting for her to come upstairs. But then the sudden rush of words. And these didn't come from the meas-ured Nick, the careful and self-aware Nick. They came from the one still easing free of his dreams.

He said: "Don't go, Eve. Please don't. I know you're showing around pictures of your brother to people. I trust you of course. But Stofton. Eve. There are drugs and guns down there. And nothing we do changes that. What time is it?"

She sat on the edge of the bed and stared at him. Dimple in his chin. Every hair in place. "I fell asleep downstairs," she told him. "I'm heading out early."

"What? Eve."

"I want to be there in the morning, first light. I want to see who else arrives. Who else wakes up needing to know what happens."

He was awake now. "You mean your brother. But why wouldn't he watch it on TV like everybody else? Why do you need to see him so urgently?"

She put her right hand on his where it lay on the sheets. Then she pulled her hand away: "I have a feeling."

"I have one too. It's called anxiety. About you lately."

"When I last spoke to him, things weren't going well for him. And I didn't help him much."

"It's history. What is it, five years ago?"

"Seven. Almost eight. Far too long."

"But you can't keep worrying about him. Or whatever it is you're doing about him."

"He was so convinced it was all going wrong. Railing on about, I don't know what. Agribusiness. Show business. All the businesses."

Nick rubbed his eyes. "I don't understand what this has to do with anything."

"If he's still here he'll be drawn to this thing. To the crowd. The vigil or protest, or whatever it is. I'll see him down there. I'll run into him in the crowd."

"What's the news anyway?"

"Not much more," Eve said. "But I feel charged by something."

"By what? By whom?" His voice was raised now. In the next room Otis stirred and muttered something. Not yet awake, but close enough to the surface to hear and reflect his father. Anxious, confused, agitated.

"By an energy. I realize this sounds manic."

"You've never been depressive, I'll give you that."

She got up off the bed, sharply. "How did you know I was showing his photograph around, Nick? I don't recall mentioning it."

He blinked at her. Apparently this detail hadn't risen with him from the gray zone of near sleep. He reached for the water. He held it in both hands on the sheets in front of him. "Katja's husband. I asked him and he did me a favor. I was worried."

"You had our gardener's husband follow me. Why not just ask me?"

"For me, since your father . . ."

She waited while he finally took the sip.

"Since your father, for me, that period of time hasn't been so good," Nick finished.

"You mean us not getting married."

"Of course I mean us not getting married. It was what we had planned. And while a six-month delay because of a death in the family is understandable, a two-and-a-half-year delay is harder to explain."

"Explain to whom? I don't think I owe anybody an explanation."

"And that makes you feel better about things? Your hallmark of successful living: zero obligation to explain yourself to others."

She was at the stairs already. He was calling after her: "Eve, I'm sorry."

Still in bed, though. Still sitting in bed while he called the words.

—

EVE DROVE EAST, the city alive in all the wrong ways. Traffic surges on the boulevards where there should have been nothing but the earliest of morning traffic. People trying to get close. People going the other way too. Eve worked these currents, cutting north to try a different artery, to no effect. The city was out of its ordinary rhythm. Traffic rips and whirls, freak waves. And up ahead along the road, she could see stop and go. She could hear honking and see the flashing lights already, police checks high on the hill.

Eve had prepared for the possibility that she couldn't get the truck close. So now she pulled down off the main road and into the maze of one-way streets in the West Flats, down towards the condo-town of River Park. Here you crossed the last major east–west street and headed down towards the river, and there was suddenly no traffic at all. Streets silent and gray, lined with parked cars. Glass towers sleeping, restaurants dark. The only sound came from the exhaust fans ventilating deep-buried parking garages, rumbling to life and fading away, low moans from beneath the surface of the earth.

She found a parking spot in front of a condo called the Paradise and pulled in. Then she climbed between the seats and back under the truck's low box canopy. She sat there in the close darkness and pulled on her running things: tracksuit and trainers, fleece gloves, wool cap. She popped the back hatch and climbed down onto the cool pavement, jogging in place for a moment, eyes across the river to the downtown spires. Then she locked the truck and padded off up the street, parallel to the river.

It took her about thirty minutes. Across the old dockyards area, on into Stofton, then up the hill directly towards the plaza in the Heights. The morning air cycled through her, cooling and replenishing. She could smell the river, which since the death of the old industry along the southern waterfront—there had been mills and foundries, brick and cattle yards—had developed an urban water smell of its own.

Stony, minerally, grassy. Traces of petroleum too, like memories released to air by the old timbers of the wharves that remained undevel-
oped there.

She watched the walls, instinctively. The art swelled in waves as you
exited the western stretches of the city, the walls growing busy. She ran
by one of the long flowered fields, an old one, parts of it peeling away.

Eve was climbing now, enjoying the uptick in her body's own industry. System temperature rising, a light sweat sheening her neck and
face, a pleasant low burn in her calves as the grade steepened up
through the loft apartments of the Slopes and the streets changed
around her. The drug trade falling behind. The endless hand-to-hand
exchanges, the near-silent mutterings of that inextinguishable market.
Now there were furniture upholsterers and auto body shops, then bars
and dollar stores. Cafés, restaurants. And on up towards the plaza,
where Eve pulled up finally, hands to her hips, a new scent with each
breath. Cologne, coffee, baked goods. Her breathing even and almost
at resting pace by the time she reached the barricades, the police
checkpoint where people were showing ID.

"Where're you heading? You live around the plaza?"

"Work," she said. "I'm starting early." She told the cop she worked
at Double Vision.

Early twenties. Probably his first year on the force. He turned her
ID in his smooth hands, neat nails, no calluses. He looked at the picture again. "Take off your hat, please."

Eve's father had a family-famous sore spot with anybody in uniform,
ever ready to make life difficult over a traffic ticket or a border crossing.
This had to do with early-life war protest and what was left of his revolutionary tendencies. But as these things go, by midlife he no longer
wore his prejudice as much as it wore him. So cops tended to quickly
sniff on him the scent of resistance. They quietly firmed up, needed
no further provocation. Once, after minor vandalism at the house,

which Eve's mother had phoned in (a kid cut off a dozen of her mother's peonies, probably to give to a girl), the squad car arrived and they climbed out with that insinuating slowness of the cop mid-routine. Her father hackled. He ended up in cuffs inside fifteen minutes.

"If you'll just calm down, sir, I can take these off."

Eve never shared her father's angle on these matters. And he reversed his position entirely by the end of his life, particularly with respect to soldiers, writing many long and sympathetic dispatches from hot zones and bunking with twenty-year-old riflemen who took to his interest with fond regard. But she still couldn't have anticipated how differently her own relationship would develop with the serve-and-protect classes. One gold medal, one parade through the center of town, and she was never forgotten. She smiled and agreed to have arms thrown around her shoulders, to have herself pulled a little close. They adored her for it.

Eve took off her hat. The young cop looked up at her, finally, making the eye contact that is reserved for just the moment required. Then he grinned. "I thought it was you, Evey. I just never knew your full name was Genevieve. Now put your hat back on. You're going to want to take a left at the block there and skirt the square to the east, all right? To the west is trouble and the square itself is all blocked."

She asked him about the crisis, assuming it to be his foremost concern. Out stopping citizens in the predawn blue. But he was still grinning and she realized she wasn't being heard. He said: "Hey, Steve."

And his partner came over, bobbing his head, boyish. She didn't mind any of this particularly. It had become a habit to answer the questions the same way. She still ran and trained, sure. Yes to still skiing. No to shooting. And like a lot of people, in keeping with a pattern that still amazed her, this all slid reliably towards a single conversational moment when they would both remember for her exactly where they had been when she won. "When you crossed that line," the partner said, his cheeks flushed. "Ah, let me tell you. We were all cheering. My gosh, that was something."

After which the conversation rolled to its second waypoint, people revealing with body language that they'd exhausted their polite curiosity and could think only of questions they didn't necessarily want to ask. They shifted on their feet, sometimes turned away a fraction, unsure how to withdraw from the little pool of light cast by her celebrity.

Such that it was. Eve moved away from the checkpoint carrying a typical bemusement. She had never had a single hero other than Ali. Ali the smart, the brave, the fast. Ali of no fear. When he reached the platform near the top of that skeletal tower, he stood up and turned and beckoned to her. She was eclipsed with fear, gripping that railing. Everything in her wanted to follow. The wind surrounding them and making a sound like the inside of a seashell. Eve could remember his face so clearly now as she walked away from the barricades, the shades of first light rouging the eastern cloud. Ali in silhouette against a warning sky. And she was pulled by the image, lengthening her stride, but not breaking into a run. Pulled by it and towards the floodlights, the idling armored personnel carriers, the charged stillness, the tension of the waiting plaza.

PEGG

—

PEGG JOGGED AWAKE IN THE WIDEST airline seat in which he'd
ever had the pleasure to pass out. Not a government plane at all, in
the end. While those had definitely been federals of one stripe or
another sent along to escort him, and whose opaque scheming
seemed to be driving the whole adventure, it was his own publisher
who provided transportation. The owner of the magazine. Pegg was
stunned. He'd only met the man once and then briefly, and didn't
recall much of the conversation, having had it towards the blurry tail
end of whatever evening it had been. But he couldn't previously
have appreciated just how much of a plaything, an ornament, a trin-
ket the magazine was to this man who had clearly made his money
at altogether more serious gaming tables. Pegg's last tether to sol-
vency—this job, Spratley's goodwill to retain him in it—was an oli-
garch's toe-bauble.

He looked around, wiping crust from the corners of his eyes and
mouth. He saw cream leather upholstery. He saw a long passageway
connecting different cabins. A bar up front. Sleeping rooms to the rear.
He thought: Bulk arms sales or private security services. But he didn't

have any further opportunity to speculate along these lines, as a face came hovering in.

Or, a non-face. Pegg remembered that just before he had fallen asleep he'd started to think that none of them really sported faces in the conventional sense, these men and women sent along to shepherd him. They moved and shaped their features into various expressions, but not as faces did, which in Pegg's experience was a process that you could observe to operate just beyond the owner's control. You said something funny, normal people smiled. You spun a sad yarn, they shed a tear. Not these faces, which moved only in response to what was carefully authored within.

He was looking at the face now, the non-face. He was thinking: Passed out. Yes, that was it. These were brutal hangover symptoms after two hours' sleep, the rapid calculation of how and who. After a good one out on the tank, he was usually numb throughout his core. Which he sadly wasn't now. He was sore from his nipples to the roll of his waist. Stormy pressure systems roving up and down his right side, then sweeping around to his shoulder blades. Sprinklings of sensory rain. The pitter-patter of drops before who knew what deluge.

"Ah," Pegg said, then coughed. Then coughed again.

The non-face said: "You're awake then."

"Up, yes," Pegg answered. "Or rather. Yes, up."

"We'll be on the tarmac in forty minutes here. We have things to cover."

"Right," Pegg said. "All right, cover."

The non-face withdrew, leaving Pegg to his computations. If he'd passed out, surely he had given them all the information they needed to have changed their minds about him by now. They would have phoned ahead and switched the teams to Plan B, or C or D or whatever they were down to by then. Released the gas or whatever non-lethal method had been dreamt up most recently for snatching

hostages from bad guys. *Forget the gossip jockey*, Pegg imagined someone important saying to somebody else important, tight lipped. *He's
no use to us. He was unconscious minutes after takeoff when we were in
the middle of his briefing.*

Pegg winced in shame and self-reproach, a finding of guilt by an
inward-pointing judiciary he no longer trusted. He impulsively pressed
with his fingers along his rib line, tracking the snake of pressure within.
His internal organs chatting amongst themselves on that favorite topic
of the worried and ailing everywhere: their worries and ailments.

He distracted himself from the disquieted murmur, as always, by
listening to other voices. And there were plenty now babbling from
within his cringing memory. He'd fled the restaurant and Chastity
with dignity and composure more or less intact. But then at the airport,
in the long white foyer outside the ramp, he'd seen them, those federal
non-faces. And his heartbeat had sped and thinned, gone fluttery. Five
white shirts at the end of the hall touching their ears and talking into
their lapels. He felt clandestine airways jump, crosshairs on his scalp.
He felt branched out and connected to problems around the world,
through them, through these agency types with pistols tucked into
their armpits. He didn't like the feeling at all and had to fight the urge
to turn and run. He had a real moment of calculation there. Insane
arithmetic. He could be outside the terminal in fifteen, ten minutes to
find a taxi. Safely into his second vodka-seven at Giggles around the
corner from his apartment in forty-five minutes tops.

He made his way to the men's instead. Into a stall to figure out a way
through all this. "Gravol," he said. And he took a handful of those, but
also downed his remaining pocket bottles and binned the empties.
Then the little safety flask of cognac too. Then the rest of his Gravol to
keep him from ralphing it all up again.

Aboard the aircraft, minutes later, he was just processing the environment for the first time, escorted to a seat, given some papers to

look over. The plane surged but nobody stopped talking, nobody stopped this rolling business of tearing him out of his life.

She spoke. This one who had regarded him the most coolly of the bunch, whose nose seemed to twitch at the first scent of him, first whiff of Chastity's lingering and incriminating odor. "Not entirely new to you, though, is it? This working in the hot zone. You've worked a few hard stories in your day."

That's right. That's right, Pegg answered. A few really big ones. But then he realized he wasn't talking. He was only thinking and staring. He was hearing takeoff noises, his head bending over onto somebody's shoulder.

AFTER HIS FALL, AND STILL LATER, after his strange encounter with those photographers on the New York subway platform, Pegg had been forced to work on himself a bit. He was ruined. He was recovering. He wasn't going to let a string of statistical anomalies ruin him again, even if life seemed to be throwing them up in a provocative way during those months. White vans parked across from his house seven mornings in a row at the same hour, flashing their lights as he stepped to the street. Wrong-number calls for a man named Rufus, through February, then again in April. And then an even stranger one. Unsettling, sure it was. There was a day in June, a very hot day, sticky, when seven people came up to him in the space of a single afternoon and asked if they could borrow his cell phone.

What were the chances of that happening randomly? Or, the more important question: of what cause could that conceivably be the effect? Because things came into the world via causes and nothing irritated Pegg more than people who believed otherwise, except perhaps people who stated causes without proof. Such a position was a belief, an article of faith. Pegg didn't have any. He militated against them. You didn't trace the causal chain to sources outside of your own system, beyond proof and accountability. This way madness lay. He'd written much to that effect, weaving it into the narratives of his various victims. God wasn't responsible. That company over there was. That government. That police department.

Still, the matter was not sealed in his mind until the bit of street theater he seemed to have stumbled into in New York City. On Avenue of the Americas, as it happens. A kid—typical: hoodie, slouch, droopy drawers, tongue gavel, nose screw—stepped up to him at the curb and showed him a hundred-dollar bill. Just like that. Snapped it between his thumb and middle finger. Then tugged it taut between two hands.

Pegg ignored him, as anyone would. Turned back to the flying street, buses, cars, taxis. The usual. Very busy. Very loud. Very comforting.

And then the second one appeared. Minor variations on the theme: mixed martial arts T-shirt, sunglasses, white ball cap, one arm in a cast from the wrist to the top of the knuckles. And he said: "You want to know why my friend showed you the C-note?"

Pegg looked for the pedestrians' walk signal, but it did not hurry to help him. "No thanks."

The kid said: "But I think you should know."

"Well I don't want to know, so could you please leave me alone?"

To which the kid sucked his teeth and responded: "I think I'd better tell you now."

Pegg was struggling not to curse, not to lose his composure. "Well I guess I can't stop you, can I?"

And here he looked again for the walk signal, sure that he had been waiting long enough. But he did not get it. So he was able to hear clearly, just as a brilliantly chromed bus howled past, feet from his face, throwing up grit into his eyes, his teeth. He spun free with his eyes pinched shut, hand to his mouth. And he heard the words, unmistakably.

"That was the hundred bones some dude in Washington Square gave us to push you in front of a bus."

Pegg staggered away from the curb. All the usual symptoms. Coughing, belly flaring. When he labored his eyes open both kids were long gone.

Here was the Google search later: "threats" + "white vans" + "cell phone prank." Three-quarters of the way down a bottle in his hotel room in his shorts, his situation briefly wobbling at the precipice of becoming much worse.

The result on thirty-odd thousand hits: Gang Stalking. With capital letters. Pegg was apparently being Gang Stalked. Followed by some amorphous group that might include some of his friends, neighbors and colleagues, but (according to this literature) certainly did include elements of the government, the police and the fire department. Pegg was instructed to watch for vans with a single hubcap missing, which he then saw. Clicks on his phone, which he was in fact hearing. Cameras trained on him in public places, people approaching him with crazy questions, theatrical disruptions in the everyday. Check, check, check. They made themselves known, that was their point. They called their technique FACT, First Amendment Chaos and Tactics, a template for harassment apparently modified by the militia movement from an original set of techniques developed by the Ku Klux Klan. The phenomenon had history and experts. And they had a name for him, these thousands of people out there who were assiduously documenting their own harassment. Pegg was a Targeted Individual. Or just a TI for short because this conversation had been going on for so long now that it had adopted abbreviations, time-saving measures so that the truckloads of documents and pictures and videos and chat-room transcripts could be disseminated and processed.

That cell phone trick, people coming out of the weeds to ask him for one? That was called anchoring. The mind-control technique where a word or action or object was milled through repetition into a psychological trigger. Repeat the gag twenty times and they'd be able to induce in Pegg anxiety and heart palpitations just by showing him a phone. Ditto the vans, ditto the day four different people called him Larry. Boilerplate Gang Stalking. It was all in the literature.

Thom Pegg, TI.

Did he believe any of it? That someone was working him over? Giving him the treatment? That forces shadowy and large had turned their attention on him? He might have. Pegg lost a good many months thinking that something, someone, was indeed closing in. Belief veered close, perhaps as close as it ever had for Pegg. But in the end, wasted again in his apartment with the blinds drawn, he walked into the bathroom and looked in the mirror and chose not to believe. It was pretty much as simple as that. From that moment forward, he did not believe. The phenomenon was nine parts psychiatric to one part real, he told himself. Which it had to be. Didn't it? Of course it did. So bring on the phone-line clicks. The e-mails sent to himself that took seventy-two hours to loop through the local fiber and back. The world might be toxic in just this way—full of shadowy forces and hidden agendas—but it was beyond Pegg's ability to prove. It would require faith. And victims, Pegg now knew better than perhaps any journalist alive, were always the ones who at first believed.

Pegg, looking in the mirror, knew all at once the saving truth about himself. He did not believe. And a week later, two weeks later, either a hidden spook machinery or Pegg's own tortured imagination granted him reprieve. Perhaps both. In any case, his tormentors disappeared.

"WELL ALL RIGHT THEN. You good? Can we get going here?"

When they came back into Pegg's cabin and started taking their seats again, Pegg registered that the speaker was one who hadn't been in the room before. Slightly different in frame and focus than the others. He was a little more boxy around the middle. Nicer suit. Better shoes. Quite nice shoes, in fact.

Agency man, Pegg thought, waking hard. Vision shaky, organs a-chatter.

"Brother, you look awful," the guy said.

"Yeah. Gravol kicked in hard."

The man laughed, pleasantly enough. "My goodness, did it. I'd say you were allergic."

Which made them all laugh. A short, tapering convulsion, like a group of actors doing a first read-through and encountering the word "laugh" in the script.

"Bruce," the man said, hand extended. "Bruce Haden."

Pegg was decent with accents, but Haden's went right by him. Distantly Caribbean, American Southern, trace of Asia and a good school. Maybe a slice of English on his mother's side. A global hybrid in fancy clothes, Haden also wore an unusual pin in his left lapel: a sterling silver frog with gemstone eyes. Pegg wondered if this whimsical detail was designed to put people at ease, in which case Haden was suffering under a grave misapprehension as, for Pegg, nothing would at the moment.

"Are you my handler?" Pegg asked him.

"You could say that," Haden said, still smiling.

"Where are you from?"

"Oklahoma originally," Haden said. "You?"

"Boring story. Is coffee possible?"

Somebody produced coffee, which Pegg fussed with, then partly spilled, then sipped and burnt himself and dribbled on his shirt. Nobody spoke, so he did first. He said: "Well I'm sure you can all imagine that I'm wondering very much what the hell I'm doing here."

Haden nodded and stopped smiling. He considered the matter briefly while tapping a folder on the low table between them with his index finger. Then he took a slow breath and said: "I voted against getting you involved."

Pegg nodded, eyebrows raised. There had been no vote, he was sure. But he didn't mind Haden saying it so casually, because that meant Pegg had at least one piece of vital information about the man opposite: he lied with ease and practice. He lied like a professional.

"But it seems an interview with you has become the only thing we can give the hostage taker," Haden went on, "because it's the only thing he will tell us he wants."

"He being who exactly?" Pegg asked.

A bit unclear, although this didn't seem to concern Haden overly. They had a dark theater, people coming out reporting all kinds of different things.

"So they're letting people go?" Pegg said. "That's good, isn't it?"

"Not always," Haden said. Lunatics came loaded with lunatic logic, he said. And since this one probably wouldn't have bothered getting kitted out for killing if he wasn't planning on doing any, the pattern of releases only suggested he was whittling things down to some favorite pattern.

"His favorite number," Pegg said.

"His favorite hour," Haden said. "His favorite astrological pattern or numerological sequence."

Who knew what data stream he might be drawing on? They had people working on the pattern, how many released and when. It might suggest something, but Haden wasn't holding his breath. The key detail was that they had someone in there. Someone who had discharged his weapon and killed at least one person. Someone who now still held forty-odd people hostage and who wanted to speak to Thom Pegg.

"So, some logistical things you'll need to know." Another voice, this one behind him. Pegg didn't look.

"Hang on," Pegg said. He was heating. Haden was good. Move on through the flattery. Don't linger. But the coffee was working and Pegg had biological malfunction on his side, making him brave. He was deliciously hungover on almost no sleep. His organs alight with unknown acids. And the plane had just nosed down now to begin its descent. That long ramp down to the ground, to whatever was waiting there. As his ears popped he let himself go.

"You realize what I do, right?" he said finally. "My regular day?"

Haden was nodding, eyes closed. Yes, yes. We know.

"Two hours' access with a couple of publicists hovering. I sip a cup of tea near a pool then I bugger off and write something that flatters without fawning."

Haden's eyes popped open. "Is that what you do, flatter? I thought you more liked to fuck with them a little. On occasion, even go for the jugular. Take someone down."

"However I do it, the fact is my job is generally senior-ranked among those things that the nutcase class hates most about us. I mean of course what they crave wholly and then blame us for making them crave."

"Showbiz, you mean. Hollywood," said Haden.

"The whole structure: red carpets, swimming pools, soundstages, publicity, fake tits."

"He may not be like other guys who've done it before."

"He has to be like them in at least one way," Pegg said. "He thought of it. Which is why they call it terrorism, folks. Religious or political or psychotic. It's just some color of hate. And I don't care if it's Aryan Nation or Army of Christ or the Brotherhood against the Infidels. Because approximately everybody in the world has a reason to hate us, and by us I mean you and me, and I assume by now you've checked online to see who's boasting about this one. Somebody posting out of Idaho or Gaza, Afghanistan or the Kootenays."

The unintended effect of this run through the numbers was that they all laughed again. Only this time, it was a short nervous laugh. There and gone.

Haden looked to his left and nodded. Someone spoke again from some intermediate distance over Pegg's shoulder. He didn't turn.

There was no point. "Not terrorism, Mr. Pegg. It's just not a word we're using. It's a hostage-taking."

Pegg felt a slight pressure in his head. All that knowledge swirling and adding mass in a container of decidedly fixed dimensions.

Haden leaned in, elbows to his knees. Chin to folded hands, bridged index fingers to his nose. Frog lapel pin widening its gemstone eyes in the light.

Haden said: "You hate your work."

"I don't exactly."

"I know, it's complicated. You hate your subjects."

"Whether I do or not—"

"We're eight, nine hours into a bad situation here, Mr. Pegg. Are we now wasting jet fuel? Nobody wants to force you. Nobody *could* force you."

Pegg let his eyes refocus on the unflappable Oakie Reggae Thai. There was more. He knew he was about to get the last part of the pitch. And he wanted to hear it too, since he knew already what it was. And he hoped very much that it was true.

"You end up being part of the solution," Haden said. "I didn't see this at first, but there it is. You're part of bringing people out. Kids without food or toilets, sitting in the dark. There's a lot of crying going on in there, we hear. A lot of fear. Holding up very strong, but nine hours. Try to imagine hour forty-eight, hour seventy-two."

"But there won't be any hour seventy-two," Pegg said. "Will there?"

"You don't help people because you have perfect information, do you? Sometimes you step in to help people because you think it's the right thing to do. We all remember this in theory, don't we? Doing things because they're the right thing. Sometimes doing more than we should do. All because of a conviction or a need."

Pegg and Haden made a short bridge of their stares. A Checkpoint Charlie at which they met and made the trade.

So the briefing properly began, as the pressure rose against their eardrums, as they hit a spot of turbulence and shuddered through. And the only surprise to Pegg then was the kind of information Haden chose to share from his various folders, handed to him by the others, laid flat open on the table in front of him.

First, the clothes. Yes, it seemed they'd gathered a lot of information about the perpetrator from the civilian clothes retrieved from one of the cars that had been set alight in the minutes before the whole thing began. A diversionary tactic was their best guess. But what was inside offered clues. Running shoes, jeans, khakis, college T-shirts, button-downs, hoodies, anoraks, a wool hat with a Green Bay Packers logo. No foreign brands. No foreign labels. And a short silence dropped as the air howled past outside. They were tunneling the freezing clouds towards a nightmare that could now be considered in this fresh light: a nightmare of us, dreaming of we, desperate to wake of ourselves.

Next, theater layout. Seat sections and aisles, exits and service doors. Where people were sitting, or were thought to be sitting. And then the bomb, while Pegg struggled again to curb a flight response. Nowhere to go while the people around him discussed explosives, possible trip wires, trigger systems. They thought the man was carrying a single large charge. Big enough to take down the building, said the man next to Haden, leaning forward to plant his finger at the center of the seat map spread out in front of them. The God Charge.

Pegg swallowed coffee. He coughed. His organs, he noted, were silent. He said: "I have this terrible feeling . . . that you might possibly think I'm going to enter the studio, actually go into that theater."

Pegg had imagined himself in a tent somewhere. In a parking lot around the corner from the theater. On a phone. With someone like Haden right there at his elbow, handing him his lines. He'd imagined all this taking place on a set.

Now Pegg slid his coffee mug away, as if he had just tasted a dangerous flavor underlying the breakfast blend. He surveyed the non-faces around him. He spoke again, although now even he could hear that his voice lacked conviction, that it revealed him to be aware of a trap. "And if that's the case, well then, you'd all be mad, wouldn't you?"

But they were all leaving the cabin now, gathering up their papers and filing out. Taking their seats up front. Pegg could hear the buckles snapping and the tray tables being stowed. He registered the placeless ding of the overheard light: fasten your seatbelts, we're about to land. Although nobody came back to remind him or to check. And he didn't do it either. He just leaned over to the window, let his face slide in close. Bare dawn over the rising city, the shape of it gradually making itself clear in the rosy murk. A shape in lights elbowed in around the black river, the downtown core, the bridges. He watched as they angled down into these lights, flickering in over the warehouses and the dusty residential neighborhoods that clustered near the airport. And noting something just in that last minute. A last thought before the wretched thump. Before the spill of something inside him, organic disputes renewed.

Images scattered, off-grid patterned. Appearing, disappearing.

No. Yes. He looked away, looked back. And there they were again. Ghosted outlines in white, floating, flashing to the retina and disappearing. A hand. An eye. A lizard. Nazca lines on the big-box stores. A retinal malfunction to accompany his many others, surely. Please, not this. Pegg squeezed his eyes shut again, then popped them open to shake off the clinging illusion, as the plane lowered itself towards the blurred ground. A robotic face. A spider. Sparking to life, streaks on the invisible landscape below.

A man with his arms up-stretched as if in surrender. Both hands open, one missing finger.

There and then gone.

LOFTIN

—

A SPASM WAITED IN THE AIR. All the news agencies seemed to agree.

Already by Thursday morning, any report or talk-show feature that didn't concern the Meme Media Crisis aired with a discernible trace of apology. The story about head lice in local schools. The guest appearance by the author of a book about organizing the clutter in your closets. These conversations continued, but were worried and frayed at the edges. People seemed to doubt the normal life to which these conversations pointed hopefully. And on the hours, news anchors made the mood official, cutting back to the wider tragic moment, clouds leaning low over the plaza.

A throat was cleared. An earpiece adjusted. Here came the update. Thursday first light, the opinion of all newsreaders and analysts sharply converge:

Strangely unsettling lack of activity.

A mysterious lack of official response.

The weather coiled and waited. Bruised cloud in the east, sloping gray strands beneath. In and around the plaza, the streets were frozen in uncertainty. People stood in groups on corners and outside cafés, talking in low voices or saying not a word. Shifting on their feet, shaking their heads.

"Most of us will remember an incident like this from some other time," said a security studies expert on one of the international channels. "Moscow, Breslin. Even Entebbe or Munich. This is different because there are no demands or negotiations. Officials still haven't been able to contact this individual, and that's a source of concern on this side of the barricade."

The *KiddieFame* banners fluttered now in a steady wind. The titanium flanks of the building were dull and smeared. The smashed front glass of the lobby doors kept the eye nervously focused there, one's gaze never flickering far before wandering back to watch and to hope.

Those released continued to emerge, but at a trickle now, in ones and twos. It was all happening against some calculus nobody could figure out. Released hostages were whisked from the front steps and into the backs of waiting minivans. Driven over to the command center where they saw doctors and were questioned, twice, sometimes three times. Made to produce ID. Nobody had the whole picture. They reported what they knew to everyone who asked, sipped tea or juice, wiped their eyes.

Inside the theater, it was reported, people cried or slept or fidgeted. Nobody was planning to fight back. Raised voices lasted fifteen minutes at the beginning. Objections and hostility. Twelve hours in, everyone was stupefied with fatigue. People dozed in their seats, waking only to imagine that they could see the faint outline of a figure onstage, briefcase across his knees. But they couldn't see this at all, in reality. It was only a retinal memory of those final seconds as the light fell. Some still believed they'd be released. Others didn't. Others worried only that the story might be long unfolding. Children cried. On and off, everybody cried. Released hostages spoke of having to use plastic garbage bags at the back of the theater for relieving themselves. The place smelled awful. They said that cookies had been distributed. But bland, like sawdust. One of the adults released early Thursday, whose family made a practice of laying away food in preparation for crisis, recognized the texture and the taste. So the story was out. The perpetrator of the Meme Media Crisis had thought to bring survival rations.

The news seized on the detail and re-ran the numbers.

Prepared for the long haul?

The stranger and stranger story of the silent hostage-taking.

Not a shot had been fired since the one that came through the front glass just before midnight the day before. Not a word said by the hostage taker for public consumption. Crowds grew dense in the south end of the square. Hundreds of people saw the armored cars of the militia units pull in from the north and south, saw them park on the lawns there near the public gardens, saw troops fan out. Federal politicians were known to be in town, huddled in the government buildings downtown. Black SUVs were seen crossing the bridge at high speed, flashers on. A story was suddenly circulating that SWAT and anti-terrorism units were training at a theater in the eastern suburbs. They'd set up a black tarp to block any view from the street. They were practicing the storm in there. Sweeping in from doors and the stage wings. A number of journalists made their way over to the theater that morning, but there was no tarp or anything else unusual to be found.

Among the journalists who didn't follow that lead was a man named Loftin who wrote for various newspapers and magazines of reputation. Loftin was well known in the press corps for his award-winning political and human interest pieces, and for the fact that he seemed always to find the more illuminating story that lived just off the shoulder of the one everybody else was writing. A journalist's journalist—enough so to be asked by the *Times* those years ago to weigh in on the Thom Pegg scandal—Loftin was comfortable in front of heads of state but found his most natural cadence with the second-in-commands, the supporting characters at the fringe of the action. He was an angle jockey, virtuoso of the surprise point of view. His book of collected essays was called *Oblique Angles*, a big seller. Now other journalists listened when Loftin asked questions at press conferences, sussing his take on the material at hand.

That day, the reason Loftin didn't bother heading over to the theater in the eastern suburbs was that he knew already the SWAT team wasn't there. And he knew that already because Loftin always had the right source.

Pam Pavich. That local police force spokesperson since replaced by the colonel. Pavich, who also happened to be someone Loftin had known since college. Yes, Loftin was a local too, although now based in London, married to an American woman with three kids from a previous marriage he'd met through EpiscopalianSingles.com. Loftin was pretty much over the thwarted first-year college crush he'd had on Pam back in the day. But he still talked to her once every few months, catching up on doings in the center of the country because Pam heard every rumor and seemed to know personal stories about every senior law enforcement official in the region.

When this particular crisis broke, Loftin was especially attuned. This was hometown news. When he called Pam, he found that she'd been up all night, following developments with mounting concern. She asked Loftin if he was coming in, her voice distinctly on edge. Loftin told her he was already at his hotel, having been on the last flight in the night before.

The information Loftin then received couldn't have been more timely. Don't bother with the SWAT team story, Pam told him. They've moved to another practice site already and I can assure you they'll never let local SWAT guys take that theater anyway. Listen up now. There's a lot more going on.

Which is how Loftin came to be striding into his first press conference less than an hour later, loaded up with a dark and vibrating energy. There was indeed something going on. And it was something not quite right.

The colonel sat at the front of the pressroom, the largest room in the hotel's convention area. He was flanked by two other military men, who were in charge of overhead maps and diagrams. Yes, they were examining all options. No, they wouldn't say what all those options were at this point. And now, the colonel said, he'd like to pass the floor to Army Reserve Captain Massri, who'd be giving a summary of Command and Control functions and would sketch for people the perimeter that had been established.

What about non-lethal techniques? Would they consider those?

Loftin waited until about the ten-minute mark, when the tide of frustration had washed through the room. When he stood, the colonel saw him and shifted in his chair, cleared his throat. Mr. Loftin? The room grew still.

"Colonel," Loftin said, speaking with the old-fashioned courtesy that was his trademark. "Sources indicate that the hostage taker contacted national law enforcement officials in the very earliest hours of the crisis last night. I wonder if you could throw some light on what was discussed or demanded. Also, would you comment on why that conversation has been kept secret?"

The collective intake of breath was sharp. The room swiveled to look at Loftin. Then everyone swiveled back to the dais. The colonel's mouth opened, then closed. Then the silence evaporated in a cloud of questions and toppled chairs. The sense of something withheld caught and burned in every imagination, suspicion spreading through the room. Why had that conversation not been mentioned previously? Who was the hostage taker? Where was he from? What did he say?

It wasn't satisfaction Loftin felt as he sat back down and the room unraveled. He hadn't received any answers himself, after all. But the colonel had confirmed that he wasn't authorized to answer Loftin's particular question, and that was actually worth a great deal. In Loftin's mind, it endorsed some of the other frightening bits of information Pam Pavich had passed along.

Were they sending people in? It seemed certain, Pam thought. Nobody from the local police supported the idea, but there was a lot of gung-ho talk from the out-of-towners. Pam slowed right down when she got to this part. "I think they know who the guy is," she said. "As in, they know he's dangerous."

Up front, Captain Massri was now announcing that the press conference was not canceled, just postponed, and that details of a follow-up would be circulated shortly. Questions kept coming, but these were now left to dangle in the confused air.

Loftin made his way towards the door, feeling some crucial phase change, the crisis having morphed dangerously. And he was right too, even if he didn't realize it. Because just that moment, across the plaza, an off-duty paramedic rose from her coffee and sandwich, left a twenty-dollar bill on the table, exited the diner where she'd been eating, crossed the plaza, breezed through the troops, climbed the barricade and walked calmly up the steps of the Meme complex.

Nobody later remembered anything agitated about her manner. And no official could explain how she did it with all that security except to note that the woman was just off-shift and still wearing her uniform, so she might have slipped through unnoticed, unchallenged. In any case, she was at those glass doors before anybody noticed, and then everybody noticed her at once, earphones suddenly hissing and crackling around the plaza. But she didn't pause there, didn't call out to announce herself to those inside. She just put her hand on the tall glass door and pulled hard to open it, shaking free pebbles of safety glass that skipped and glittered across the pavement and around her heavy-soled boots. And in she went, vanishing instantly.

Silence stretched out tight over greater silence. And then a phenomenon that didn't make the news because, while the cameras were all recording, it happened so quickly it was hard to interpret, even in the memories of those who produced and witnessed it. The crowd across the square, seeing the woman top the steps and stand for a moment outside, lost itself in a mournful murmur. The sound of pain swirled. And when she moved forward, swinging the door and entering the building, the crowd noise vaulted upwards in anger and agitation at the sight, at the sudden speculation about what this must surely mean. Every placard on display now went up again at once, jagging towards the lowered sky. Every sign reading *War=More War* and *God Hates Islam*. Every one with *Give Peace a Chance* or *Children Are Our Sacred Duty*. The anguished voices rose until they seemed to blend all peak emotions: fury, vengeance, excitement, even trace elements of something like joy. It was a sound so loud, so penetrating and strange as it crested, that people spilled to their windows in the buildings around the plaza, people came to the doorways of stores and restaurants. With light in their faces. A wide hope briefly flickering that a breakthrough of some kind, of some profoundly unlikely kind, must surely be at hand.

Everybody saw the flash first. Or did not see, exactly. It was so instantaneously there and gone that it was experienced as a thing in the past, never in progress. A ragged ripple of white that cast no shadows but filled the dark front foyer of the theater. Three flashes, as if one tripped the others. They blew out briefly in electric shades, yellow-white. Followed a split second later by the sound of an almost dainty explosion, which cracked in the sudden vacuum of crowd silence. Snapping the air, pricking the eardrum. Small caliber. The sound needled home.

THE BLUE LIGHT PROJECT

PART II. The map

By Thom Pegg

"There is one thing I've been wanting to ask you," Eve Latour said to me.

We were in Kozel's Deli. After I had first seen her by the newspaper box and been briefly but so intensely overwhelmed, this was where she'd led me, holding firmly to my arm.

Kozel's. Brilliant idea. We walked in the door to the smell of schnitzels and goulash, smoked meats and strong fresh coffee. The presiding Kozel (grandson of the founder) came out and kissed Eve on both cheeks, holding her shoulders gently. Then he took me by the shoulder as well, less gently, and pointed us into a booth.

I was now trying to eat a bratwurst with sauerkraut, although I seemed to have lost the technique somehow. The cupping of the bun towards the face, the angling of it so you didn't end up

This is the second of three excerpts from Thom Pegg's book, Black Out, Blue Light, *about his experience during the Meme Media Hostage Crisis, to be published this fall. Pegg lives in Los Angeles.*

with mustard on your shirt. I levered it up and lost some kraut, then the sausage began to come loose. And as I grappled with it, mustard finally did work its way free of the other end, stippling my shirtfront.

"Damn. What did you want to ask me?"

But by then the room had already stolen her away, and she was wrapped up answering a question from the people at the next table.

We had walked to Kozel's together, down over the shoulder of the hill from where we met in the Heights. I'd already learned a number of things about her. She attracted people, which is less obvious than it sounds. People didn't like her just because they'd seen her face on billboards and in commercials. They liked that well enough. But when they met her, they liked her spontaneously, without encouragement, without mediation. Here, I think, is an important finding. Eve Latour emits something—without strategy, maybe beyond her power to control—and we are all subconsciously but forcefully grateful to receive it.

How this plays on the ground is that you can't have an uninterrupted conversation with Eve Latour in public, ever. Try it. Walk down the street chatting with her, and people will appear with pressing things to say. On the street, yes. But here in her private haunt too, where the regulars call her out. Here at Kozel's: the retired couple in the corner, the young woman at the counter, the man pushing the broom up and down the aisle between the booths. And to each of these people, Eve Latour will speak without self-consciousness. Never cracking once, never asking for a break with her eyes, with the shape of her shoulders. Never splitting to her own thoughts mid-sentence, eyes drifting for freedom in the clouded front glass.

All that, plus talking to me, plus carrying on another conversation with Kozel himself, which ran superscripted over all other communications despite the proprietor's standing at the very far end of the counter where he was punching totals into the push-button cash register, skewering the receipts down onto a silver spike.

"You've been keeping?" he called.

"I'm all right," Eve said.

"Terrible business."

She nodded.

"Anything?" He tossed back an imaginary swig of beer. They had a row of Russian bottles behind the counter.

Eve asked me if I wanted anything.

"What time is it?" I asked. It was darkening outside. Perfect time for a whiskey and soda. But my body had its other ideas.

"Pepsi," I said.

"Pepsi," she called over.

"Pepsi!" he yelled at the ceiling, as if the person responsible for drinks was in the apartment upstairs.

Eve circled in her thoughts. She took a dexterous bite of her smoked European wiener, extra-hot mustard, no kraut, no onions. We settled into an unlikely mutual comfort. I didn't want our time together to end. But I was also ashamed to catch myself thinking such a thing, which only made me think further of life's luck, of failure and of how miserable I had always been with beauty. I was hopeless.

"What was the one thing you wanted to ask me?" I asked her.

She nodded. Another bite of sausage, a sip of ginger ale. A finger to the cheek again, a nail to that depression beneath the cheekbone, to stroke back, to find her temple and rest.

"You used to live in this town," she said. "You know it pretty well."

"I did live here," I said. "And I suppose I do know the place. Or I did once. At the moment . . ."

Eve looked at me slowly, gently. Waiting. And here's what I thought in those moments, hunkered in again above my sausage. The kraut still letting loose its vinegary steam.

I thought how changed we were from before, but how differently we had been changed. Eve had cleared away recent doubts. She had been liberated, charged with certainty. I was more lost than ever.

Of course, my situation was the more common one. Everywhere, doubt was the new reality. On the television news it was all rumor and suspicion, versions and tales. Reports and counter-reports. Disagreements over everything from who had died to where and how and by whose hand. Had bodies been found deep in the earth, beneath the theater? In the tunnels? Bodies or a single body, or none at all? Rumors swirled. One body, somebody claimed. No, it was a homeless man locked in a closed-off storage cave, hidden between toxic bins. And here the story spun out in the other direction. And there could be no coherent outrage at any of this because doubt swirled immediately to snuff it out. No official calls for calm, because these would have been pointless. What did it mean that crowds were still sporadically looting at midday? What did it mean that a dozen people had been killed by small-arms fire in the day since all of this was supposed to have been over? Twelve people. That was a war zone number. Who was shooting whom? Even with all the names lined up, perpetrators and victims, I knew it wouldn't be clear.

We had walked together across the littered plaza and partway down the long hill. It had been late morning then, and we were deep into the cool afternoon now, shadows stretching. The sky was clear, but the wind was very high. Outside Kozel's I saw pages of newspaper flying high, strung out along the power lines. And the smells of the city spun around us, smells of strain and distress. Sweat and gasoline, fumes as if the old mills and factories along the river had sprung up from the dead. As if the city were remembering itself with occluded weather, smog reinvoked and lying close, held in tight.

—

Eve had returned to her sausage. She took a look up at me once in a while during my long loop away from her, into the morning and back.

Finally, she said: "Are you all right?"

"Yes, I think so. I burnt my mouth on this."

"Had you forgotten it was hot?"

"Completely."

"How is it?"

"It's good, it's very good. This is called weisswurst. I kept saying bratwurst to myself, knowing it was wrong. Couldn't get the other word."

"I meant how is that," she nodded, eyes up on my forehead. "Your head."

"Is it obvious?" I asked her.

"You seem a little spaced out, yeah."

"My memory has gone patchy, but it's returning. When I woke up first, I lost my name. They asked me about a dozen times in the ambulance and I couldn't answer. But it came back."

"You didn't tell me any of this. The ambulance."

"It's really only just coming clear."

"You don't remember that we've met, either. Not today. Before," she said.

"Here in Kozel's," I said. "Sitting over there at the counter."

"In a booth. But yes."

"You were laughing," I said. "I remember you laughing."

"You were telling stories. Pretty good stories."

"About what? I haven't a clue."

"About your work," Eve said. "About the celebrities you meet. About the celebrities you meet and you never like."

"I'm an entertainment journalist," I said.

"Yes, you are," Eve said. "You interview famous people and make fun of them."

"Do I really do that?"

She said *Mmm*. Eating sausage again. Neatly, like a big cat.

It was coming back. "Okay," I said. "Right. They assigned me to write a profile of you."

She smiled, chewing.

I looked at her. "I didn't say anything horrible or spiteful, I hope. I'm afraid I've done that on occasion. Sometimes, in the mood, I've been known to take people apart. Take people down."

"To me, you were remarkably kind," she said. "Although you quoted me saying something that surprised me later."

"So where do you travel next?" I said, remembering this all at once and with complete clarity.

"That's the one," Eve said.

"And you answered: Nowhere, I hope. You said: I'm just at the point where I want to be home. I figure if I can't find it here, I can learn to live without it."

Eve was looking at me with a trace of sadness.

"I loved that line. I'm sure you said it," I told her.

"Oh I probably did say it," she said. "I just didn't know yet that it wasn't true."

I nodded. But I could take her point. I was sure that I wanted it to be true of her. But I was also sure that her view, from inside as it were, would always be more complicated.

It was a city map. That was the one thing she'd been trying to ask me about. She had in her possession, it seemed, a rather unusual city map. And as a journalist and a former resident of the city, Eve wondered if I would look at that map to help her determine exactly what it meant.

"What it means how?" I asked her.

"Just look," she said. And out it came. Unfolded from a side pocket of her coat and smoothed onto the tabletop. Unusual indeed. Scored with lines. Red marks and blue circles, with words and numbers in green down the margin. As I looked at it, my fingers lightly brushing the paper, I had a dream-like idea, a plausible imagining. The map was the plan for the city's demolishment, for new zones, for new boulevards and public buildings. Sites circled and connected with lines. Scribbles and thoughts, and sequences of numbers. It was a vision of a future. A prediction. A premonition.

"Where'd it come from?" I asked her.

"A friend."

I looked across the table at her, an eyebrow raised. "A friend who won't explain?"

"This friend is a bit mysterious. Also . . ." she said, taking a small breath and seeming to test her next words for how they made her feel. "Also this friend has gone away."

She touched her hair and looked out into the street.

I nodded and leaned in again over the hieroglyphic markings. "Had you ever seen it before?"

"Not to look at closely."

"So he'd never shown it to you."

"I never said it was a he."

She'd done interviews before. She had certain skills. But that didn't change the fact that we both knew it was a he.

Eve closed her eyes for a second or two. Opened them. "He left it behind. He left it for me. I'm asking . . ."

I smiled at her. "I'm yanking your chain."

"All right," she said. "So what's your best guess?"

Eve shifted the map in front of me so she'd have a better angle to view it herself too. We stared down at the thing together for a few moments in silence. I traced lines that connected buildings. I traced lines that connected other lines to lists of numbers in the margin. The person who'd prepared this had worked on a blueprint or two in their day, I decided. They'd looked at the plans for elaborate objects yet to be built.

"I think," I told her, "that your man was planning to build something. Or perhaps it's already built, which I must tell you, as this thing would appear to lie directly over this very city, I find a faintly unsettling idea."

I glanced up at her. Hoping to provoke. To drive some

remembered detail out of her in keeping with the words I'd said. Unsettling. Something built.

But before she could respond, Kozel was calling over again from the counter.

"You lost?" he joked.

"Course she's not lost," said the man at the next table. "Eve knows this city better than anyone."

"Everyone gets lost sometimes."

"She knows where she is."

"All right. Stop it now, you two," she said, still staring at the table. But with new focus now. The index finger she'd been using to trace one long red line now tapping in place on a single central point, where a great many lines and swiggles intersected. She'd found something. I felt certain of it. She'd found the key. And I deeply wanted her to have it too.

Let her have the key, I thought. Watching her. Waiting for her to speak. Please, God—or whatever quantum particulate factor we are to accept must cover these sorts of moments—please, someone or something or whatever you are, please let her have the key.

PART TWO

"You can't win, Darth. If you strike me down, I shall become more powerful than you can possibly imagine."

Obi-Wan Kenobi, *Star Wars: Episode IV*

THURSDAY

—

OCTOBER 24

RABBIT

—

SOMETHING FLUTTERED ACROSS HIS EYELIDS, a moth, a bat, and Rabbit blinked awake among the roof ducts and ventilator shafts, gray silhouettes rising to a stained sky. He'd had a good fast sleep, which, considering he'd been forced to stay on a roof overnight, meant that he hadn't been discovered or lost any of his gear. He checked inventory and everything was where it should be. Pack tucked tight under his head, foil wrapped around his shoulders. No face hovering, grooved with disdain, waiting for an explanation or worse.

Only birdsong, high clouds. The weather had been threatening each morning, but had not yet broken.

Rabbit rolled to his knees on the gravel and began to pack his things. He was under the overhang of a storage compartment built into the side of the service shaft, where he'd crawled after making his jump late the night before. Nothing broken, but he'd landed hard and the bridge of his nose had made solid contact with the corner of a duct housing. He'd stayed there in the shadows, bleeding and motionless, watching the roofline of the Peavey Block back across the alley in darkness behind him. He'd waited many minutes like that, holding a cramped position on his knees and palms until he was sure he hadn't been heard.

Nothing. No radio squelch, no silhouettes above the brickwork. So he was safe but trapped. Forget the alley-side fire escape. Forget going down through the interior of the building in the middle of the night. There was a software company in the top three floors, a temp agency below that. Both would be burglar-alarmed with monitored security. So he'd known immediately he had to sleep there and gone about finding a hidden spot, deeper darkness under a lip of cover. And there he'd made his nest. Foil, extra layers.

Now, in the thin and still-grainy light of the morning after: fresh problems. How to get down? Going down through the building the day before had been a straightforward matter of what Freestealers sometimes referred to as "credibility engineering." Software meant cubicles, disc towers, cables underfoot, people faced in to screens. It meant young staff and no dress code, so he wouldn't look particularly out of place. He'd simply gone down the roof access and walked out into the main room. He crossed that space in view of dozens of people, moving quietly, as if he'd done this a hundred times, talking in a low voice into his phone and gesturing once with his free hand. Confidence, self-possession. Rabbit knew these qualities were among the most reflective, and that people who belonged in these spaces would reliably turn them around, matching and endorsing them, awarding him the legitimacy he had originally copied from them.

So, the day before, he'd made it easily across the entire sixth floor to the elevators before he heard a word from anyone. He was still talking into the phone. Held up one finger, scanning available information, imagining the trade, the what for the what. The *if-then* statement. She was maybe twenty-three. Hardworking, going places. First year with the company. On her way from a meeting. Hurrying back to her workstation. Her question left a neat furrow in her brow, the place where patience temporarily alighted.

"This is a restricted floor. Can I help you?"

"Babes, can you wait a minute?" Rabbit had said into the phone, which was in fact turned off. Then holding it covered with one hand, he'd allowed an expression of deep embarrassment to cross his features, mouth sloping, a glance to the side and away. He looked back at the young woman and said: "Not unless you want to talk to my wife here and tell her that I didn't get the job."

And off he went to the lobby and the welcoming street.

Of course, Rabbit thought—shouldering his pack and looking around himself in the light of this new day—talking your way out of it was a game you could play to win, but not two days in a row in the same place.

He checked his phone. It was just coming up to seven. Not many people would have started below. The elevators would still be quiet. He climbed out from under the overhang and made his way to the roof door. Inside and down one flight, there was a landing and another door into the elevator room. It was locked. But just as predictably there had to be a safety key nearby. Rabbit found it in less than a minute, fingertips surfing the top of the doorframe, the underside of the lintel. Then he noticed the electrical panel mounted low on the wall, popped the door and there it was.

Rabbit let himself in, closing the door behind him, then toggled on his flashlight to assess. It was a two-car elevator system built in the mid-seventies. Both elevator pulleys were spooled in cable but weren't moving, which was a good sign he'd beat the morning rush. Better still, at the top of each shaft, next to the pulleys, there was a small access door.

Rabbit got onto his knees and inspected one of these. Padlocked. And this time there was unlikely to be a key nearby as the doors would rarely have been used. Elevator inspectors and repair people would normally access the shafts from inside the cars, through doors that opened in the top of each. Breaking one of the key rules of Freesteal then, Rabbit extracted bolt cutters from the leg of his pants and snipped one of the padlocks free.

The door swung out towards Rabbit, releasing several decades' worth of dust, which glinted in the air around him. Suppressing a cough, he rolled away from the opening, covering his mouth with one hand while fumbling in his side pocket for a dust mask with the other. He pulled it into place, snapping the elastics back and over his head, his breath suddenly alive in his ears, the heat of it against his face. He went back to the opening and stuck his head and shoulders through, shining the light down into the murk to find the cars below.

The one in the shaft he'd chosen was just twenty or thirty feet below, waiting at the fifth-floor doors. This position high in the shaft was good news and bad news. Bad if someone decided to take the car up while Rabbit was in the shaft. He'd have no time to react and would be crushed when the car reached the top. But it was good news in the sense that he'd be exposed to that risk only for as long as it took him to get down to the car using the service ladder that ran down the wall of the elevator shaft. Once he was there, Rabbit knew, he could use the maintenance override panel on the top of the car to take control of it, freezing all the buttons inside the car.

Rabbit pulled himself out of the doorway and checked his things a final time. He knelt, listening to the building, to ambient groans and creaks. Nothing regular like a footfall, like the murmur of conversation or a radio. No steady tones from the plumbing, flushes or running taps. Then he rolled into action. He swung his legs through the small door and shimmied back on his stomach, holding to the doorframes with both elbows and stretching his feet down into the blackness to find the rungs of the ladder.

Once he had a toehold, he eased himself back, reaching down with one hand to find a rung. And when he was fully in the shaft he dropped down quickly rung by rung, flashlight bobbing, painting the walls and cables in streaks and loops as he descended to the car. The instant his foot hit the cold surface, he knelt and steadied the light. Control panel, here. Toggle main control from Operate to Inspect. Roll the red Inspector switch from off to on. And the car was his.

Rabbit knelt in the dim light on top of the car, allowing his breathing to steady. With every shift of his weight, the car swayed on its cable, guide wheels knocking the vertical tracks and releasing a metallic *wow* that looped up the dusty shaft and back to him, then down to the bottom and back again. Rabbit's light caught the rising particulate matter. Hardware encased in grease. Ducting. Sheathed cables. The busy, invisible workings, the inside of the machine. Much more beautiful than people imagined, Rabbit thought, these true interiors. The gut reaches of a building shared something with the deep interior stretches of a natural landscape that way. In Oregon, Rabbit lived for months in places that were miles from the nearest footprint, deep among the trees, inside walls of vegetation. In the dunes, where at night the sand shelves leaned over with coarse grass, and a person could hide his body from his own eyes and look only outwards. Outwards across an immense plane. It wasn't a sense of isolation that made him seek those moments and still enjoy them now. Rabbit thought that all places beyond the common path—beyond roads and trails, outside of the stairwells and between the floors, shared a similar potential: connection and trespass combined.

Rabbit breathed in and out through his mask, felt the moisture of his own breath, from his own mysterious inner regions. He was aware of himself swinging gently, suspended at the center of a mechanism, condensation and dust all around. Clouded in fundamental particles.

Time to move. He brought his attention back to the controls. Flashlight tucked under one arm, he pressed the Down and Run keys simultaneously, and the elevator whined to life, the car now dropping smoothly, the counterweight shooting past the other way, scything into the darkness that bloomed overhead.

He counted floors. Five, four. He stopped on three. He could have tried riding to the lobby at that hour. Probably nobody waiting there. But a middle floor was safer, more likely to be quiet. So he released the switches, the car jerking to a stop, sounds reverberating through the shaft. He toggled the panel back to default settings, then popped the roof hatch and lowered himself into the car. Here, his light and mask stowed, a quick look at himself in the distorting brass plate around the floor buttons, he pressed and held both the Lobby and the Close Door buttons for five seconds to switch the elevator to express mode and off he went. Down to the empty lobby. To the front door. And out into the new light, pack swiveled around and onto his back. He was free.

Walking clear. And in doing so, he thought of Alto again, as if that mysterious figure could give him wisdom. Walk calmly. Swing the arms just so, not too high, not too low. Strides about the length of a shoulder width. This was the geometry of innocence, or so it seemed to Rabbit. No edges or lips, no crevices or rough patches on which the glance might snag, over which a thread of curiosity or imagination might catch and pull. Alto would have walked this way instinctively, swinging the arms, loose and low. Stepping with the whole foot, not rising onto the toes or hitting the heels with any determination. Neither hurrying nor stalling. It was a gait for slipping through the world.

Rabbit walked a half block south of the plaza, then stopped for the light on Jeffers. He was almost ready to let himself feel satisfaction, the project finally complete. It was last night's feeling intensified further, a view of the stars, rooftop moss underfoot, his last unit in place and beginning to charge, ready to activate as early as that evening. Rabbit was smiling.

The traffic lights changed and he stepped out briskly into the intersection. And his mind was just cycling back to the day at hand, lowered skies and threatening weather. Black smoke and the smell of gasoline, the sense of atmospheric pressure and alert nerves, poised fear. But these thoughts were interrupted almost the moment they started—thoughts of children, gunmen, cordons, consequences— because as Rabbit reached the far curb, a car door sprawled open in his path and someone climbed out and stood in his way.

Blue uniform, wide stance, a routine grained into every movement. The hand to the gun hip, the other one raised to catch his attention. Now the voice, no rush or alarm in it. A steady insistence: "Just a moment, please."

Rabbit raised his eyes and brought them level. He smiled again to indicate calm and an easygoing nature. And he kept that smile in place while the questions started. Where he was going, where he worked, where he lived.

"Just down in Stofton," he said. "I'm going there now."

"You work nights?"

"Just getting some air."

"You have some identification?"

Rabbit went under official observation there. He felt the patterns adjust. The partner climbed out of the far side of the car and circled around until he stood directly behind Rabbit. They cordoned him off and contained him with their eyes, their physical frames. The questions veered.

"No ID. None at all. You forgot your wallet at home?"

"I don't carry a wallet. I don't drive. I don't use credit cards."

They closed off routes back to the ordinary.

"You illegal? Where're you from? Please keep your hands where I can see them."

Real tension here, Rabbit realized. He heard the police officer behind him shift on his feet, open palm to the top of his nylon holster.

They wanted to know why there was grease on his hands. Why was there blood on his face?

"Put your hands on the car," the cop said, and when Rabbit did so, the other one began to pat him down. "Any weapons? Any drugs? You high?"

Rabbit kept the responses coming. Calm and cooperative. The cop behind him had removed Rabbit's pack and handed it to his partner. He'd begun his frisk, down Rabbit's arms and back, closing within inches of the map in Rabbit's waistband. The emergency of the moment was suddenly very clear to Rabbit. The pack held items that would be difficult to explain. The map with lines and numbers and sites would be a different kind of trouble altogether.

The air crackled. Static. Voices. Rabbit's pack was open now and here came the contents. Foam and foil. Bolt cutters, wires, batteries.

The cop behind Rabbit stopped his frisk and stepped clear. Rabbit sensed the moment that a handbook precaution was suddenly deemed necessary. One officer should stand aside and cover. One officer to continue the search.

The cop with the pack said: "And this?"

In his hand now: a WaferFone with the outside casing removed. Wires soldered into the works now tremoring in the rigid air.

The cop's head went over to the mouthpiece on his shoulder. Words and numbers. Codes and directives. Rabbit felt the city alive with hidden action, forces opposed in complicated arrangement. He flashed on Jabez the protester and Beyer the entrepreneur. The endless disagreement, isolating him in the space between them. He thought of words painted at the heart of a tunnel. Words that inspired and drove him. And as the officer cocked his ear to his lapel and held up a hand for quiet, Rabbit whispered the name: "Alto."

To which there was, then, a surprise response. Not from the person in question. And not in words. The answer came with her appearing. It was the only sense he could make of it. Rabbit spoke the hidden word and she emerged into his field of view, coming up over the shoulder of the cop in front of him just as Rabbit raised his eyes.

Here she came. With such an intense look of interest that he lost other details. Was she near or far? He couldn't be sure, only that he was observed in a way he couldn't remember having been observed before. She wasn't seeing through him but around him somehow, back to his beginnings. And when she spoke finally, the fact that she called him by an unfamiliar name wasn't strange. Rabbit accepted that it was the right name for the moment.

The cops turned, seeing her there. If Rabbit had been watching them closely, he would have noticed them both loosen in their stance, open in their expressions, as if her arrival had already relieved some tension in the moment.

She wasn't looking at either cop, though. Only at Rabbit. And no mistake on her part when she spoke, either. She hadn't taken him for someone else. She was telling Rabbit instead about a person he brought forcefully to mind. A person who, in response to the complicated joint needs of the moment, his and hers, Rabbit would now briefly become.

She said: "Ali."

PEGG

—

THEY CHECKED PEGG INTO A HOTEL. A nice place. Crisp white lobby, staff liveried in chalk stripe.

His handler checked him in, that placeless man with his frog lapel pin. He walked him to the elevators. Then Haden said to Pegg: "Make yourself comfortable. Things have gotten a bit hairy and I'm not sure when we can get you in. Will call, yes?"

Pegg went to his room and lay on his back, hands folded behind his head. Tremendous bed, he thought. Then immediately he sat up, phoned Haden and asked to be picked up. He didn't like the sense of being a payload in a silo, nice and cool and tuned up, ready to launch. Up there in the pressroom he'd feel more autonomously engaged with this thing, like he really was a journalist with a story to cover. Like he really was choosing to help.

One of Haden's people picked him up and drove him over. They left him with the others in the press pool area, a conference room in another hotel just off the plaza, long since booked to the rafters with media. All the typical event squalor, Pegg noted. Stubbed-out smokes in coffee cups. Trampled paper underfoot. Cable and phones and open computers. The bank of newsreaders working their lines, twenty of them all looking exactly the same with their big blond hair and coral nail polish. Orthodontic perfection. Pegg had hit on one of them once, drunk in D.C. He thought she was the one sitting second from the left but couldn't be sure because her mike with the network insignia was hidden from view. He rated the energy alive in the air as he passed people in the pit. Something registered, then reregistered. But nobody spoke to him. Nobody said: My God but they really burned you down to the ground, didn't they? How'd that feel, the flames licking up around your ass?

Pegg walked and they moved their chairs. Faces he recognized, by name and by type. The writer from a news magazine he'd played cards with once in Saskatchewan. He wondered why they'd both been there, couldn't pull it back. Then these two jokers: a couple of guys who must still have been in school when the personal shit hit for Pegg. They were checking him out.

Yes it's me, Pegg thought. Yeah you heard correctly. I fabricated a source. But in service of the truth. Black sites, did I make that shit up? No I did not. Like none of them had ever published white lies before. That was why it was never a good idea to get any of them drunk. Or at least, never let them get drunker than you were at any given moment. Pure misery, listening to the disappointments and disillusions of the copywriting classes. God, give me an actor any day, Pegg thought. It was naked truth from actors, including the aspiration to celebrity, whatever he thought of that. They never denied wanting fame, prestige, status. It was all in the collective gaze for actors and they knew it.

Pegg was heading towards the far wall, towards a door where he was going to stand and wait for Haden to show up. Stand under the frame like there had been an earth tremor, with aftershocks to come. But Haden was nowhere.

Pegg made his way through the mess of chairs and tables. Body odor. Boredom. Give me a perfumed PR flack, he thought. Give me a junket interview and an *L:MN* name card, for Christ's sake. Maybe he'd tell all this to Haden in the way of a confession. He'd tell Haden something like that and crack him open a bit, get him to talk. Get Haden to explain for real how the world had wobbled in its frigid arc such that Pegg was now involved in this business. Kids in a theater, crying. Was he supposed to feel grateful for this opportunity? He did not.

Because the hostage taker seems to be quite interested in you. He wondered if Spratley were somehow involved. There would be obscure reasons for these kinds of things. Haden trafficked in obscure understandings. All the myriad connections between things, commodity prices and rotten mortgage securities, central bank scheming and a storm brewing among the gang lords in the slums of Rio. A micro-burst over the Persian Gulf and soldiers were exploding out the backs of a hundred Bradley fighting vehicles in Bakhtaran. The rational brain demanded that these events all be related.

"Doing all right, Peggy? Just look at you here."

Thin purse of a face, high shoulders bent against invisible wind. Pegg had to think who this was, which meant he was from some very serious zone of print. One of the intellectual magazines with articles thousands of words long. Writers with war zone routines and jackets to match, all the patches and pockets. Gore-Tex boots. The name was coming to Pegg. The man was local originally, now a big name in London. Oh yes. Here it was. The man who'd put the last knife in when Pegg was going down. Right there on the *Times* editorial page. Pegg had every word etched in his memory, something no amount of drinking could erase . . . *how even that pales in comparison to the damage Thom Pegg has done to the very victims his own column had ostensibly been written to aid and reinstate.*

"Well hello, Loftin," Pegg said. "Still going after the truth, I see."

"Read about you. Your what is it, notoriety?"

"Yes, well, I gathered you did," Pegg said. "I read your ruminations in the *Times*."

Loftin smiled falsely. "Of course that all had to be said, Peggy. Even though it wasn't a bad story except for the . . . you know."

"The central character not actually existing," Pegg said.

"Yes, that pretty much killed it," Loftin said. "Shame, though, since it had within it . . . how to say this . . . DNA trace evidence of truth."

Pegg looked away and smiled at someone he didn't recognize. He knew Loftin wouldn't haven't crossed the room for the sole purpose of heaping scorn, so there would be more to come.

Loftin, finally: "But all that's history now, hey? On your feet again, I see. *L:MN* magazine, is that the one?"

"Yes, indeed it is," Pegg said, trying for a tone of bright satisfaction. "Spratley and I were at Oxford."

"Right, right. Spratley still . . . ?"

Loftin meant: is Spratley still rumored to be sleeping with Filipino boys? But Pegg only laughed through his nose and put a hand into his side pocket. There were no miniature vodka bottles there, he knew. He said: "So what's the business here? All kinds of nonsense in the air. No money demands. No get the troops out of Iran. No organ-harvesting screeds. No Islamophobia. No Jew baiting, flights to Jordan, unmarked bills. It isn't a side of architecture grads from Saudi Arabia or there'd have been a bloody big bang by now. And I thought of white supremacy wingnuts but only for about a second because they're much too self-apocalyptic to take *hostages*. Wouldn't you say?"

Loftin's expression had been hardening over during each of the seconds that Pegg spoke. "Well, you make various good points. General confusion and speculation. Although I suppose you could say this is where we've been heading for some time. School shootings. People storming their own workplaces, labs, trading floors."

Pegg nodded. "It's in the breeze, so to speak."

"If you're mad enough to do it off the cuff, no reason not to wait for a few hours before starting."

"Sure, sure. Wait for you and me to pull in."

"Exactly. The international coverage."

"Makes you wonder though, doesn't it," Pegg said. "Motives. The construction of the thing."

"It does, Peggy," Loftin said, muscles in his jaw working free each word. "Especially those of us milling around out here. Those of us dealing with the colonel. Those of us without the gilt-edged invitation."

Pegg heard "guilt-edged" and thought for a moment that Loftin was being impossibly clever. Then he refit the word to the circumstances and something important came to him the same instant. The fact of his access was a story that had just broken. The inexplicable reality that it was he, Thom Pegg, who was going in. That explained the way people had been looking at him, moving their chairs to let him pass, averting their glances. They couldn't believe what they'd heard: that it was Thom Pegg who'd gotten access. This dawning sense was like a private spring, only for Pegg. They were incredulous. And they were envious.

Envious. Sweet Jesus. The same people, like this jackass Loftin here, who'd so happily put the boots to him those few short years before. Here was something Pegg could savor about the moment. Not redemption. Payback. Quite different.

"What'd they say about the person inside, then? Who is he? What does he want?" Loftin was pressing quite urgently. He had canted in towards Pegg while Pegg had been skipping through the alpine field of his own delight. Loftin now looked distinctly, agitatedly curious to know if Pegg was going to share anything he'd learned about perpetrators, motives, modus operandi. And Loftin was anxious too, asking his questions. Because for all his skill with sources, for all his vaunted reputation, for all his *money,* it was pretty clear that Thom Pegg wasn't going to tell him anything.

Pegg pretended to cast his mind back as if making sure no detail had escaped him. Then he shook his head firmly and smiled. "I just assumed it was a fan in there, you know. Someone who reads *L:MN.*"

"Right, right," Loftin said, flushed, hands into his pockets, wanting the conversation over. But unable to resist a comment. He tried. He paused for a second. Then he let it go, a poison dart in every word. "Always wanted to ask you one thing, though. What it stood for, *L:MN.* Like, Little Men, you know. Teenagers whacking off in their mother's john over one of your famous spreads."

It was a delicious turning point for Pegg. Something he'd never experienced previously. He said: "Have you always wondered that? I mean about the name?"

Loftin's expression had gone hard and blank as a sidewalk.

"Because it's quite fascinating really," Pegg said.

"Really."

"Yes, well there are those who say the one thing, right? And then those who say something completely different."

The man's eyes were dead slits. "Right," he said.

Pegg plunged onward, gorging himself on a moment. "But really," he said. "I've always tended to think, you know, that *L:MN* stood for *Lick: My Nuts.*"

"Thom, Thom. Come on now."

This was Haden, finally at his elbow. Haden, whom Pegg had watched coming across the room while he spoke and not recognized until the very last moment. Stepping between chairs and through conversations without raising a single glance. He looked different than he had on the plane. Younger now in a sweater, wool cap and jeans. No frog pin either. He might have been the correspondent for the local campus paper. But more importantly, he was invisible. Seen by only those who had a need to see. Haden, it seemed obvious, was good at his job. Pegg wondered what that was exactly.

He took Pegg's elbow and steered him out into the hall. Haden said: "Yes, yes. It's out there. Some tabloid grunt has been given access. There are ways to handle the publicity that will make it easy and ways to handle it that will make it hard."

"Tabloid grunt," Pegg said. "You don't offend me, if that's what you're trying."

The conference room across the hall was still emptying. But already Pegg found his pleasure in the moment fading. Trumping the Loftins of this world, whatever. Loftin was a prig. Fucking puffed-up Loftin and his famous book. Six national magazine awards and a bunch of money. Wife and kids. Whoopie fact-bearing, bestselling, Episcopalian shit.

Haden guided him down the hall to a door, then through that and into the alley. Here, against the rank brick, he leaned a shoulder. Ten yards away, under the overhang of an entrance to an underground parking garage, a soldier trained his weapon on the pavement, looking back and forth. His eyes drifted over them professionally, lingered for the seconds required, then continued their steady patrol.

Haden shook his head before starting. "Try to keep it together. Things are only going to get more confusing here for a while."

"You seem rather calm though," Pegg said.

Haden's expression went opaque and distant. He glanced down at his own shoes. This next bit, Pegg thought, is full-on bullshit.

Haden said, quite clearly: "Brass is worried that he's started to kill the kids."

Pegg hadn't seen that coming at all. He swiveled sharply away from Haden and put his hands to his face, leaned into the railing. He could barely manage the words. "God," he said. "I can't do this."

Haden didn't answer right away. Pegg could hear the wind pick up, knocking a downspout against a wall somewhere nearby. He let his hands fall away from his face. He croaked: "Kill them, like what do you mean?"

Haden shook his head. "Like executions. Like he's getting impatient."

"Have released hostages been reporting this?"

"Nobody has been released in four hours and the idea is that this might have started within the past hour."

"An idea based on what evidence?" Pegg said.

"Well, not much really. I never said I believed the story."

"Fucking hell," Pegg said, staring at Haden. "What're you telling me for?"

"Just giving you the picture, Thom. It's what people are saying. Best guess at numbers is under a dozen remaining now. And the thinking is that these situations work down to some significant configuration. Then they resolve for lack of material."

Pegg breathed deeply, several times. "You are fucking with me."

"I'm not. You're here because the man asked for you," Haden said.

"You know what I think?" Pegg said. "I think I was your bright idea."

Haden nodded like he'd expected Pegg to say this eventually. "I'd like to say yes. I really would. As an idea, you would have been a good one."

"He asked for the *New York Times*, didn't he? He asked for the *Washington Post*. For the BBC World Service. And they all said no."

Haden found a vial in a hip pocket and unscrewed the lid, extracted a tightly hand-rolled cigarette. Darkish paper. He lit up and offered it to Pegg, who shook his head but knew the sweet scent. Beedis. Pegg thought: Please may I one day know what kind of federal operative, what the fuck kind of gray-zone emissary smokes beedis on the job.

Pegg said: "I'm having a hard time placing you, to be frank. In the scheme of things."

Haden inhaled the clovey smoke and held it, nodding. He released the lung-load while talking, his words sculpted in gray eddies and whorls. "My line is more creative than it used to be."

"And what line is that?"

"Think like human resources."

"You mean I could hand in my letter of resignation?"

"You could but you won't," Haden said. "You've been in that press-room. You've seen the envious looks. The *Washington Post* said no? What are you, out of your mind? There isn't a paper on the planet that wouldn't kill for what you have right now. Right in front of you."

Pegg glanced away again. The soldier near the entrance to the park-ing garage was gone.

"You've got the whole thing read," Pegg said. "Simple, simple."

"I didn't say simple. I see a situation here that is many sided."

"Do you really? I sort of see it having only two sides myself. Some lunatic threatening some other people who are probably not lunatics even if they are *KiddieFame* contestants."

Haden pressed out the cigarette on the sole of his shoe. "I'd be the last person to try and dissuade you in a moment of moral clarity. But you're really a spectacularly arrogant prick, aren't you?"

Morality between the garbage bins. Talking to a guy who got trained up at some private farm in rural Virginia or in the lake country outside of Regina. Knows fifteen ways to kill a man with a safety pin or a gelato spoon. Running down this line of reasoning, Pegg had a thought. The guys in the pressroom, the ripple of awareness when he'd entered. The galvanizing flash of his own resolve on sensing that he was the center of an envy field, his situation profoundly desired by all those arrayed around, arms hung over the backs of chairs, phones flipped open, screens flickering a thousand news feeds from other parts of the world, an endless loop on Meme Media. Whose eyes in that moment had just swiveled onto him, onto Pegg. Who never questioned why they all wanted it so much, the rare chance to go verbal with the real thing, the man with death on his mind, yours and his. They all wanted that. It was the thing coveted above all.

He asked: "Why tell anyone that I'd been given access?"

Haden looked at his watch and then the lowered sky. He said: "We set the information free. I mean, either that's the answer or: does it matter anyway?"

The drops of rain began to strike the alley garbage and the sheet lids of the dumpsters and Pegg himself. He does his job well indeed, Pegg thought. Haden calls the rain down. Haden darkens the mood. Haden pulls something small from his inside pocket that he wants carried inside.

"You must be joking," Pegg said.

"It's not a weapon," Haden said. "It's a voice recorder."

"I know what it is. I have my own, thanks."

"Of course you do. This is your own."

Pegg took the tape recorder and rolled it in his hands. Japanese mini-disc, ten years dated although it still worked well. Omnidirectional mike and a dozen hours' recording time on long play. Pointless to ask how Haden had gotten it. The fact was he had gotten it. Although nothing looked jigged or souped or tricked-up about it. Pegg paged through the storage folders, all empty as he had left them, except for Folder D. And there it was. The single recording that had survived all purging. A snip of audio that had traveled with him and lived on this machine while it recorded other voices in Bel Air haciendas and Park Avenue triplex palaces, in warehouse lofts on Queen West. And before that, in places where the real victims had been. In poisoned lives and toxic landscapes. This thirty-second clip had comforted him before sleep in an uncountable number of hotel rooms before his fall and since.

"Record your conversation with the man," Haden was saying. "He'll expect that."

Pegg's thumb brushed the buttons.

"Then at some point, when the moment seems right," Haden said, "play your little clip there."

Pegg looked up at him. "Like a signal."

"The man is wearing night-vision, we believe," Haden said. "We'd like you to confirm that, perhaps at a moment when you and the man are separated from the others by some distance. Night-vision, Pegg. If yes, hit Play."

"And you'll hear me."

"As long as you're carrying that device, we'll hear you loud and clear."

"And what will happen?"

"Something sudden, Thom. But you mustn't be frightened. Wait for that critical moment. Then hit Play."

Pegg's eyes returned to the silver surface of the voice recorder, the places worn gray where his thumb had so many times carried out its fractional movement. He pressed Play, right there, like a practice run, releasing the warbled voice into wet air. Three years old when the recording was made and an impressive grasp of fundamental things for a kid that age. He knew how to sell a punch line, that kid.

"What did the skeleton say when he walked into a bar?" asked the boy. One beat. "Give me a beer. And a mop."

And there it was. The sound of his boy laughing. Micah Swenson Pegg. A delight, a joy. There was nothing else. And you could hear it in Pegg's laughter too. Booming in the background. Pegg a hundred years younger than he was now. A hundred shades lighter. Pegg laughing with his boy. Jennifer looking in through the door from her office, a half smile on her face.

Had they been happy? They had been ecstatic.

PEGG HAD AN ERRAND. Twenty minutes, Haden told him. No longer.

The Pig and Python. Typical turnkey bar that belonged to the international Celtosphere. Pegg knew it was there. He had no idea how he knew. He was sure he'd never been there before. But as he forded the rivers of rainwater and floating garbage, found the alley mouth and surveyed the street, he sensed it just to the corner and left. Fake gold leaf. Fake red velvet booths. Fake fiddle music. Fake cheer. The place was perfect. They outdid the Irish in every respect and that's what the Celtosphere demanded.

Irish whiskey, he thought, as a matter of gratitude and respect. One slender half-pint pocket bottle for each side of his long overcoat, which was too hot for his situation but which he found himself unwilling to remove. Sweating in place at the bar, leaned in over a triple for the road. Neat. No ice. He was perspiring and palpitating, struggling to keep his breathing non-critical. He was gulping at the whiskey, waiting for its cauterizing magic in his middle regions, a certain slow calming of the troubles there, the shifting allegiances and betrayals of his inner works and yards. All the while his eyes were locked on the three white swallows that adorned the label of the bottle that had been poured. Their shapes lithe and perfect, flitting around one another in a rosette of purity, making sense of the universe with play, with a circular arrangement of their spotlessly iconic selves.

Pegg struggled with emotion, sipping. Then sipping again. Unfamiliar feelings and his movements to deal with them were not grooved by practice either. Swarmed by . . . what was this? Some kind of sorrow or grief, as if he had already done something for which an avalanche of guilt had been released. He swallowed and coughed, choked, then fumbled out a handkerchief to cover his face. After a few seconds, face buried in this scrap of once-white cotton that hadn't seen the laundry in many months, he made to blow, but had an epiglottal misfiring doing so, a loud and messy effect. He produced a throaty blatt and left a rivulet of snot across his lip and chin. Agh. Damn. Wiped away. Glances now from the college-aged bartender, who had questioned the triple with an eyebrow spasm and an

involuntary look at the clock over Pegg's head. Whose glance now had
no resting place, bouncing around the room and checking his brunch
crowd for reaction. English tourists. Little jars of jam with toast and
porcelain pots of tea.

Pegg gulped down the last of his drink, then exited to the street and
found his corner, his fetid alley mouth. He entered and passed a
dumpster he had somehow not noticed when heading out. A typical
metal bin, reeking and sordid, but which someone had artfully postered over to make it look like a piece of Louis Vuitton luggage. Must
have taken hours getting all those sheets of paper lined up, getting the
seams just right. Hours certainly to get that perfect-hued effect.
Magnificently in place while being out of place, luxurious pebble-
grained leather against the muck.

Onward. No time to linger on the seething streets in this most seething town. He was past and moving on towards the back door of the
hotel. Steeling himself, by the step. Unused to the procedure, but wondering if his display of emotion back at the bar might have been useful,
in its way. He was done with the self-pity now, Pegg thought, his mind
flickering forward to what nobler spirit must now be stockpiled in preparation for the events ahead. Which was a line of self-talk that might
well have continued—Pegg was nothing if not susceptible to his own
reasoning—if half a dozen steps farther down he hadn't been stopped
by what the alley wall next threw up for his consideration. A large
poster had been mounted on the brick. Eight feet high by five feet
wide. Styled as if after a thirties-era election poster, all face and slogan,
black and white. The double jab of a political rhetoric aimed at those
with guards held low.

Under a picture of what looked like two small figurines of circus
strongmen, barbells aloft, the slogan: *Ignorance Is Strength*. And plastered across the center, a new picture, recently appended to the whole:
a not particularly flattering photo of Thom Pegg.

He was now awake in a different way than he could remember being for a long time. Ripped off a website, scanned out of an issue of the magazine, candid maybe, although it had to be said, however the photo had been obtained, Pegg himself was looking just a shade less well than he would have hoped to appear in print. A bit bruised under the eyes. A bit florid and blossomy across the cheekbones.

Pegg was trying to deal now with new currents and fluxes within, adrenaline, random synaptic firings. Someone in the press pool, the jealous bastards. But an old dread was coming again to life. Pegg knew exactly what the feeling was: the dread sense of being watched, followed. Pegg felt targeted. And he longed for home just then, staring at this thing. This gag. This taunt. He ached not just for the city where he lived, with its hot breezes, palm trees, tanning lotion, exhaust, Mexican food, reefer, public-beach porn. He was longing even for his own cramped apartment with the crushed furniture and the empty refrigerator. Three hundred and fifty square feet of gobbed Kleenexes and spent pizza boxes. Kitty litter. Empties. A ceramic model of a Chinese lady holding a lantern. She had a cork in her head, had once held liqueur. And thinking all this, Chastity came back to him, but only for the briefest moment before Pegg chased her from the room of his recollection. Not now. Not even that.

No time to linger. Pegg was now being spoken to from close, with urgency. Haden was there. Two other men. Then a fourth man in uniform, who would take Pegg the final distance. Helmet, face gear, black fatigues. He had a weapon that suggested a great deal by its completely unfamiliar shape. What trickery was there in this tiny rifle that seemed to mount itself to the man's arm, a slender, serpentine thing that glinted blue in the failing light? What evil had we here, Pegg wondered, what elegant and hidden industry of malfeasance in that smooth shape?

"Ready," someone said. Not a question. A radio squelching quietly in behind the sound of water trickling in the sewers. They crossed the street and into another alley running parallel to the plaza. Around a corner to a dead end. There were loading bays and various men in blue arrayed about. They didn't take their eyes off the rear door of the theater as Pegg approached. None of them but one man standing facing the other way, circling and scanning the rooflines, rifle raised.

The soldier guiding Pegg had his hand on Pegg's arm, holding him back. He motioned and Pegg leaned close to listen. Through these doors he would find a warehouse with another single door at the far end. Through that second door was a hallway. Through that hallway was the foyer of the studio theater. The only door into the theater that wasn't locked would be right there at the top of the foyer. Announce yourself, loud and clear. Then go inside. Pegg would be on his own at that point and in blackness.

Pegg felt the pressure of the soldier's hand change as this information was transferred. The hand went from holding Pegg in place to pushing him forward, first gently and then with frank authority. *Go now.* So Pegg was walking. Moving forward. He was entering the shadows of the loading bay. And since nobody said good luck, he said it himself. *Good luck.* His voice at a trembling whisper. To the door and through it. Down the hallway and into the empty foyer. His blood moving in coarse surges he could feel in his neck and his temples. *Good luck, Thom.* Through the silent foyer and lobby, past the empty leather benches there. Hand to the surface of the heavy wooden door, fingers shaking violently. Quivering, dancing, shimmying just over the polished surface before they steadied on contact with the wood.

Good luck.

And into the blackness, blind and gagging. Pegg entered the theater and the latrine stench of a closed space rolling towards its second twelve hours. His throat convulsed and he groped to cover his mouth and nose.

"Hello?" he tried, muffled through his fingers. He felt his heart rate spike, his hands shaking again, his whole organism polluted with adrenaline and anxiety. Around him there was no light at all.

"Hello?" he said again. And hearing the sound around him shifting now too. Some snuffled breathing from far away. Then a voice. But close. It might have been inches. It might have been inside his own ear.

"I'm here."

And a hand on his arm again, but this time closing over his bicep in a firm grip.

Pegg screamed. That's what his body threw back at the moment. A torque of the shoulders, a strangled call. His belly inflamed and his back in spasm with the sudden touch and sound.

He went to his knees. And from there he fell, toppled sideways and lay. He felt tight carpet grain at his cheek, smelled industrial glues and cleansers and the spreading mystery of building materials. Concrete, rubber.

And it was only there—laid out, blind, exposed—that Pegg heard himself in place, for the first time among them. Through the black space around him, a sprinkling of human sound, scattered scrapes and tiny voices. And the truth of it crushed Pegg flatter still. KiddieFamers, children. In their tiny individual fidgets, a constellation of sound: shoe shuffling, nose blowing, low moans. And crying. All around him, issuing forth from hidden souls, the steady trickle of invisible tears.

EVE

—

EVE TOLD THEM RABBIT WAS HER COUSIN. It seemed like the best story for the moment. They hadn't cuffed him, but Eve thought that was seconds from happening. The two young cops were tense. They had his pack turned out on the hood of the cruiser. Eve saw tools and wire. These things signaled bad ideas premeditated.

But they hadn't committed to any action by the moment Eve arrived. And without planning it, without knowing specifically what she hoped to accomplish, Eve interceded on instinct, on impulse.

"Ali," she said again, which flushed through her an intense variety of excitement. The young man looked like he had some of Ali's personal material. Declining to look worried, although the situation was obviously serious. Acting as if things were under control, when they clearly weren't. That attitude was all Ali, all the time. Eve enjoyed seeing it for the way she seemed to immediately tap the energy and feel more certain herself.

So Eve said the name of her brother and made this young man into a cousin. To her own surprise, the whole story was ready to roll there, waiting. Father's brother's son. Known for exploring places he wasn't supposed to explore. Known for not carrying identification. Then, to emphasize, Eve stepped between the two cops and took Rabbit up in a sisterly embrace. She could hear him breathing in her ear. But he held her firmly, this stranger. He played along. And when she let him go to arm's length and asked about her fictitious uncle, he replied with just the right sheepish tone. Doing fine. Don't tell him about this, please.

He was much less like the Ali she remembered at this close range, in fact. Same unruly loose black curls, but more relaxed than Ali. Smiling evenly, easy in his stance. Open, tan face, full lips. Gray-green eyes. Bigger than Ali through the upper body. She could feel the cops shifting on their feet behind her, loosening their grip on the situation as Eve promised to return the moment to normal.

"Don't forget this," one of them said, handing Rabbit his pack. He thanked them. He apologized. He offered to show up at the station in the morning with identification.

They waved it off. They weren't smiling. A heavy residual of cop doubt remained. But he was with her and that counted. So they clipped off their suspicions and let Eve make everybody's life easier. They said to him: "Get going."

She took his arm and they walked away, north towards the plaza, bumping shoulders the way you might with a family member you hadn't seen in a while, a family member with whom you'd once been close. And when they were half a block north, just passing the doors of Double Vision, Eve suddenly felt that she had to be out of the sight lines. She popped the key card and they stepped into the cool and neutral lobby. Here she paced away from the young man, looking at her reflection in the doors leading into a bank branch.

When she turned back to him, the young man had gone to one knee on the marble floor. He had his pack open and was rearranging things inside. There was urgency in his motions, as if he needed to confirm that everything was still there. Then she watched as he withdrew a

scored city map from his waistband, opening it and refolding it carefully before sliding it into the pack. It was marked with many numbers
and lines, but she had only the briefest glimpse.

He said: "Thank you."

She shook her head.

"Do I know you?" he asked. "Because why . . . ?"

She said: "Because I saw you jump yesterday."

He looked up at her sharply. Then he got to his feet. He said:
"Where?"

"From the Peavey Block and across the alley. To the next building."

He made a face, a minor wince of self-reproach. "Where were you?"

"I was in the alley," she told him. "You scared me."

He was looking at her with a new curiosity. He recognized her face
but couldn't place it. He said: "I should probably get out of here."

"No," Eve said. "You walk with me a bit. I need to talk to you."

They skirted the plaza. They crossed an invisible perimeter that
marked the press zone. White vans with satellite dishes cupped towards the lowered skies. Then another outer perimeter that seemed to
mark the very eastern edge of the conflict area itself. Beyond that, in
steadily more dirty streets, the city grew quieter, the Meme Crisis a
disturbance still, but at one critical remove. They reached a small
park, down into the east end. A stamp of muddy green. Eve had never
been in the area before and noticed the sadly sloping houses and storefronts, nothing painted recently, every second building for sale. She
asked: "Where are we going?"

He stopped and gestured to a bench. "Here," he said. "Let's sit here
for a bit."

They sat, just as a cop car pulled out of a side street and turned its
flashers on, then sped off west towards the plaza.

Rabbit ran fingers through his hair, watching. "It's as if the city has
been taken over."

"That's because the city has been taken over."

"There are people waiting to do this kind of thing, always," Rabbit said. "Roll out the threat. Roll out the response."

The bench where they sat was opposite a three-story parking garage with an open concrete stairwell that ran down the outside. Half a dozen young men were taking turns running the stairs from top to bottom. They were doing so with different flourishes and vaults. One running down the concrete rail. The next swinging over the side of a landing and dropping to the one below. At the bottom they challenged for the highest dismount, one guy sailing from ten feet, fifteen feet up the structure and onto the grass there. Tucking and rolling and walking free. Rabbit watched. Eve noted how there was no applause or high-fives when somebody nailed a move. This kid in the tuque here, swinging free of the top landing, hanging from the rail, then bouncing with his feet, creating a kick of momentum and flying across the entire flight of stairs below to the far landing where he hardly touched down, only catching the railing again and swinging back. Landing by landing. Spider-Man was never this agile. Then down to the grass and up on his feet. Nobody even smiled. And Eve understood that it was enough just to do it and keep on doing it. To jog up the concrete apron of sidewalk. To mount the stairs and take position at the back of the queue.

She said: "Parkour. What you were doing."

Now half a dozen people dressed in black jogged down the street towards the plaza. Black handkerchiefs across their faces. Black Bloc, Eve thought, wondering at the magnetic pull this crisis was proving to have. A thought that came to her just as a police van pulled to the curb across the park and two men began unloading gear.

Rabbit was squinting into the low light, watching these same crosscurrents. He answered her finally, saying: "Not Parkour. Or not just that. We call it Freesteal. Freedom of movement. Stealing time and views. It's about getting in places. Getting out. Leaving a poster behind or some writing or whatever it is."

Eve looked over at Rabbit. "What about doing a handstand on the parapet of a building six stories above the alley? What's that: free-suicidal?"

Rabbit nodded and frowned. Then he slowly turned his head to meet her gaze. "All right, I'm curious. How'd you know I did that?"

"Before I saw you jump across the alley, I was in the eighth-floor boardroom of the building across the street. How'd you hurt your hand?"

Rabbit nodded and pursed his lips. Then he looked back towards the kids climbing the parking garage. "I just got it. UNICEF posters. You're the skier. Goodwill ambassador to the world."

"Don't make fun of me," she said. "What were you doing on the roof? Do you have any clue why I might care to ask, having just bailed you out of being arrested?"

Rabbit nodded and rubbed his eyes, but didn't answer. Eve watched him in profile, estimating character from features and expression. No longer the cocky indifference he'd shown the cops, more observant now, reflective and removed. He was often alone, this young man, Eve guessed. He was often in a place just outside the general field of view, on tar and gravel, on parapets, looking out over the teeming plane of the world. She thought of her night runs. Her own peering in. Her own solo searching.

She said: "I competed in biathlon."

He looked at her with a hint of a smile. "I remember now."

"And you? What do you do? What was that map all about?"

"The thing on the roof is an installation." Then he turned to her again, his expression migrating again. "Gold medal, Geneva. Your name is Von Kemper."

Eve had to laugh. "Von Kemper was the other one. Close."

He put up his hands. Sorry. But he was remembering details now. Psychopath with a slingshot. "You finished that race on a broken ankle." It was all coming back.

"Very good," Eve told him. "What were you, like twelve at the time?"

He raised his eyebrows and looked over at her. Then his eyes roved for an instant, a quick flicker of the gaze. Checking her out. Eve was surprised to find she didn't mind.

Rabbit said: "What were you, like sixteen?"

"I was twenty-four."

"I was eighteen," Rabbit said. "Tell me your name."

"Latour," she said. "Eve Latour."

He smiled and said the name, still looking at her. His eyes weren't gray-green, Eve decided, they were sea green, a mineral color. He said: "I'm Rabbit."

"So what about the hand, Rabbit?" she asked him.

He held it up. "Flesh wound," he said. "The important thing is that it's finished. I've been working on this for almost a year now. Now it's time to throw the switch."

Eve's eyebrows went up. "It has a switch?"

"It gets turned on. It gets activated."

"And I'm supposed to be very calm about that idea," Eve said. "An installation that activates."

Down the street a van pulled up and parked, brown with windows tinted to black. A man climbed out through the side door. He had a camera with a long telephoto lens hanging from his neck. He looked into the park, then up one of the side streets. He saw the police van parked on the corner there, the group standing. Then he walked off in the direction of the plaza.

Rabbit looked at her and held her gaze. Neither of them was smiling. "I could lie. I could tell you I just work at a coffee shop," he said. "But after what you did back there, I suppose I owe you the truth."

In a side street a bus pulled up and a dozen or more police climbed out wearing blue overalls. They began to rank up on the sidewalk, partly obscured by the jungle gym and the leaning trees. Some of the Freestealers stopped to watch as the men kitted up: shields, batons, heavy gloves, helmets.

"I used to paint these landscapes," Rabbit told her. "Alpine fields, high detail. All the flowers, bugs, whatever."

"Did you study painting?"

He made a noise through his nose. "Not quite," he said. "Engineering and physics. Then I had a different idea."

That different idea was to make art. He shook his head saying it, like it still surprised him. But there it was, a burning idea. He wanted to paint a picture of the city before the city was there. So he began with the landscapes, which he'd post in alleys, twenty or thirty feet at a time.

"They actually wrote about those ones in the paper, the flowering alleys of Stofton. You see that?" he asked.

Eve was staring at him. She said: "I'm still stuck on the engineering and physics part."

Rabbit shrugged and scratched his chin, then looked away. "Changed my mind."

"I run at night," she told him. "I've seen your landscapes near the river in Stofton. Always one little bunny in the corner."

"My signature," Rabbit said. "Your parents give you a hippie name, you roll with it."

"Not an Updike tribute, then."

Rabbit laughed. "Unlikely. But no big deal, I like bunnies."

"So why not call you Bunny?"

He smiled. "Now you're making fun of me."

"I'm not really," she said. "I loved those landscapes. I wondered who made them."

The ranked policemen were moving in a choreographed pattern. One step forward and a tap of the baton to the plastic shield, the pace of a heartbeat. Rabbit's expression was sloping towards concern.

"So who is Ali?"

"My brother," Eve said. And she gave him the wrinkled snapshot, which he took in careful fingers. Ali had been a street artist too, she told him. And Rabbit bent to the photo with a fingernail on its surface, frowning and focusing. Ali in the land of rooftops, sunset off to the west. Rabbit's finger traced a lip of tar and gravel just over Ali's shoulder, the smudge of a white line visible near the edge of the roof.

Eve told Rabbit that the photo had come seven years before, attached to an e-mail. It was just before Ali vanished.

"Meaning he could be anywhere by now," Rabbit said.

"But he's not," Eve said. "He's back here."

Rabbit thought about that for several seconds. Then he seemed to drift away, leaning back, shoulder blades hitting the back of the bench. She felt the length of his body lever the boards, which moved against her own back and under her thighs.

The cops practiced their advance and retreat, thumping their shields. Then a man spoke on a bullhorn and the men all squatted down on their haunches or sat on the curb. The young guys on the parking garage continued to jump and swing throughout the police drills, but something had agitated their performance. They were hitting the landings harder now, trying for radical moments of air. Bare elbows and knees. Scrapes and blood and laughter. The whole energy of the ritual had changed. A guy spilled badly, turning over on his ankle and limping to a bench. Another fell dismounting the railing. He hit the stairs and sprawled down, chest to the concrete. Then he rolled on his shoulder and up onto his feet, holding something over his head in one hand. It was dripping with blood. A tooth.

Rabbit moved suddenly. A breath in, a quick unfurling, as if readying himself to run. But he held his position for several seconds, hands on the boards to each side of his tensed legs. He said: "Eighteen months ago I was in Oregon working for a company that designed telecommunications equipment."

She looked at him steadily. "Okay."

"Now I'm here." Rabbit's eyes were focused on a very distant point, past the cops, past the kids climbing the parking garage. "It's been a weird ride."

Eve smiled. "I know the feeling."

He turned and looked at her. Eve saw gray skies racing in from the east. They were poised there for a second or two. Then Rabbit was on his feet. Eve was up too, something coursing through them both, an energy similar to that of the first moments they'd met. The cops standing around. Everything undecided, but action spooled up surely between them, ready to roll.

"Beyer," Rabbit told her. "You want to find your brother, then the man you have to see is called Beyer."

THEY HAD TO STOP TO PICK UP HIS PAY at the café. Eve watched from a front table as Rabbit greeted the woman who owned the place. She was pretty. Lean and athletic. When they embraced, Eve thought the woman held on to Rabbit for a second or two longer than necessary, one hand on his waist and the other in the middle of his back, pressing. Now they stood together at a side counter talking. The woman had just given Rabbit an envelope. Eve couldn't see his expression, but she wondered from the furrow in the woman's brow if this was bad news of some kind. Although Eve then also noticed the intensity of her own watching and turned away.

She pushed her eyes to the front window and watched the strange scene shaping on the streets outside. In addition to all the other groups, there were now hundreds of people standing silently on the sidewalks with their hands and eyes raised to heaven. Their lips moved but they made no sound. Eve assumed this was some kind of mass prayer, but she'd never seen anything like it in the city before.

She turned back to look for Rabbit and he startled her by being right at her elbow. He'd come up so quietly. Eve saw the woman still standing at the counter. Their eyes met for an instant but they both looked away.

BEYER WAS WAITING FOR THEM, sitting at a corner table in the Lagoon under a long fish tank with assorted tropical specimens and brilliantly colored anemones. The air smelled like air fresheners and cologne, upholstery and a distant hint of miso. He stood when Eve approached the table, took her hands by the fingertips, bent slightly at the waist. Then sat again.

Movieland, Eve thought. Double Vision. Brands and messages. Promises and threats. She wasn't entirely sure why she was having this reaction, but it suddenly seemed to her that Beyer was acting, showing chivalry like wise guys he'd seen in the movies.

"Got your check?" he said to Rabbit, with a smirk.

Rabbit nodded and patted his front pocket from which the envelope protruded. "Thanks," he said.

"I'm generous, I told you that."

"You're an amazing person," Rabbit said.

He doesn't trust this man, Eve thought. An opinion she was inclined to take seriously, despite having known Rabbit at that point for only a few hours.

"And what can I do for you?" Beyer said, fixing Eve with a stare.

Eve pulled out the photograph and put it on the table in front of Beyer. "This is my brother," she said. "I haven't seen him in quite a few years, but I'd like to find him. Rabbit said you might be able to help."

Beyer looked at the photo. "So you're starting Monday?" he said to Rabbit, without looking up.

"The picture was taken out by the airport," Rabbit said. "Plus you can see the markings on the roof behind him. That looks like one of your Nazca line jobs, so I figured you would have known the guy."

"You figured that did you?" Beyer said. Then he glanced up at both of them. "Want something to eat? Sit down at least."

Eve pulled out a chair and sat. Rabbit went into the booth on the far side of the table, back to the wall. Beyer looked at the photo again.

Rabbit said: "You can see a white line, right there. You can see the river. It's definitely near the airport."

Beyer took his time. Then he nodded again. "Okay," he said. "I do remember him."

Eve sat forward. "When did you see him last?"

"Oh God," Beyer said. "I don't know. Ages ago. But Rabbit's right, the photo was taken by the airport and this would be one of the Nazca line installations. Maybe the lizard on the Staples store."

Beyer smiled and slid the photograph back across the table to Eve, but she didn't pick it up.

"Can you tell me anything else?" she said. "Did you work together?"

"He was on the scene, yeah," Beyer said, shrugging. "But we weren't friends. What was his name?"

Eve told him. Beyer squinted. "Ali. Rings a bell."

"Any idea where he might be now?"

Beyer gave all appearances of racking his memory. "China? Korea? I vaguely recall hearing he went to Asia at some point." He scratched his chin. He pulled the photo back over and stared down a second time. Then his head popped up to meet Eve's gaze. "Named after Muhammad Ali. This is coming back. Your old man named your brother after some boxer who took so many punches to the head he can't say his own name now. Sad story. You like boxing?"

Eve sat back in her chair and didn't respond.

"Beyer," Rabbit said. "Can you help her out? She has questions."

"Like do I know if he's still alive?" Beyer suggested.

Eve felt the question hit her chest, a short, sharp impact. She waited a few seconds before replying, watching the fish tank above and behind Beyer where a yellow fish was sailing silently from left to right. It didn't move any fin at all. It seemed merely to will itself through the water.

"All right," Eve said. "Do you know if my brother is still alive?"

"Honestly, no idea. But with junkies it's tricky. Even alive, they're not very alive."

"Could you excuse me for a moment?" Eve asked. And she got up and walked the length of the restaurant, all the way to the front door. But she didn't leave. She stopped there, thinking. So there it was. Junkie. Had she suspected all along? Probably, but never dared use the word. Still, did that explain why this guy was being such a jerk about it? His resistance made no sense to Eve until she thought again of Rabbit. And with that, her heart slowed and her breathing steadied. A calm descended, just as she'd always felt when a bull's-eye settled into place behind the crosshairs.

She walked back to the table. She sat down. "I don't know you. And you don't know me," she said to Beyer. "But I've been looking for my brother on and off now for many years. This is important to me."

Beyer was looking at his fingernails. "How long have you known Rabbit?"

Eve nodded slowly. "I understand."

"I doubt you do," Beyer said, his voice deepening as he A-framed behind his hands and fixed them both with a glare. Eve smelled a bluff and prepared herself to play it.

He was talking about business now. Some speech that could not be avoided in its full form. Here were some things she had to know about the business. Debts and obligations.

"Beyer," Rabbit interrupted, "I won't work for you. If you want to take this money back, go ahead."

Rabbit pulled out the envelope and slid it onto the table.

Beyer didn't pick it up. His eyes closed briefly, as if he were calling on reservoirs of patience. Then they opened and he continued where he had left off, only with more intensity. And so Eve heard about WaferFones and contracts, lost clients and work to which Rabbit had agreed but never done. And while Beyer was talking, Eve watched the yellow fish trace his long way back from right to left and thought she was starting to like Rabbit more for each minute Beyer spoke, more for whatever mysterious thing he had gone and done with Beyer's money. Rabbit had snubbed Beyer. He'd hurt his feelings. That was the gist of it even if whatever Rabbit had done was no doubt more than Beyer deserved, a better ending to the story than Beyer himself could have ever devised.

Beyer was finally finished and sat breathing deeply, some punk sense of injustice greatly stirred. Eyes on Eve. Hurt blue eyes.

Eve sat motionless, knowing that they were close to that moment of transfer when Beyer would release whatever final information he held. It was only up to Eve to make this happen, to say the right thing.

"All right," she said. "So you hired my friend Rabbit here to do something, and he went and did some art instead."

"I have no idea what he did," Beyer said. "I just know it's not what I paid him to do."

"And now you want him to work off the debt, but he's not interested."

Beyer stared at her.

"I could buy it from you," she said.

"What?" Rabbit said. "No, listen . . ."

Beyer sat forward. "Come again."

"You don't want whatever it is, so sell it."

Beyer's eyebrows went up. He pulled on one earlobe.

"I'll pay. That puts you square with Rabbit. Then you tell me, plain language, where I go to find my brother."

Beyer's face slowly relaxed, his hands spreading open on the table. "I like this woman."

"Cut the crap," Eve said. "Price, please."

"Ten grand," he said.

Rabbit stood up. "Forget it," he told Eve. "That's ridiculous, way high. Besides—"

"Including interest," Beyer continued, voice raised, "my time and the value of a lost client relationship."

Ten grand was crazy. But then Eve knew she'd never been this close to Ali before. She suggested six thousand. Beyer countered at seven thousand five hundred. And Eve, who had no experience with negotiations and didn't know she had the skills instinctively, heard something ring quite clearly in the air: Beyer finding middle ground closer to her original offer than to his asking price.

She wrote a check. Seven thousand even. Fully aware how wasteful a thing she might be doing as she signed her name and handed it to Beyer, who took it without a word, folding it into a billfold and slipping it into his pocket. But then something did shift in the room, the balance between them was rearranged. Because Beyer pushed the envelope on the table back towards Rabbit. And he gave Eve the information. The name she needed.

At which point, no reason remained for them to be there. So Eve put a hand on Rabbit's arm and they both stood up. And as Beyer looked in the other direction, they both moved together through the Lagoon and out into the street.

EVE AND RABBIT, sitting in her truck down in Stofton. Rabbit still absorbing the shock, still shaking his head. "I can't believe you did that," he said, finally.

Eve couldn't believe it either, really. It was still humming through her. The buzz of foolishness and daring. Seven thousand dollars. "It better be good, whatever it is," she said.

He looked at her. "It's good."

"So Jabez." She said the name that Beyer had given them.

"And that part is also very strange," Rabbit said. "Beyer sending us to Jabez. Those guys *hate* each other."

Eve was waiting for more on this point, but then her phone rang. And it was Nick, just as the afternoon shadows started to lengthen. If he hadn't been paying much attention to anything other than getting her back to work recently, night approaching now signaled to him that things were more seriously out of whack. She'd been gone all day. She'd been gone over dinner time. There was a nervous warble in his voice.

"We had pizza," he told her. "Katja stayed because she was working late cleaning up the hedge. Now she's gone home."

Archaic fears, these. Woman on the cusp of doing something terrible. Another couple hours, as the light fell and Nick's circadian clock cycled around in its relentless grooves, she would no longer just be away from home. She'd be into some darker category of absence entirely.

A man stood across the street looking in their direction. He had a camera with a telephoto lens around his neck. Eve wondered if he'd just been taking pictures.

"I'm sorry about all this," Eve said. Then: "Cleaning up the hedge where, Nick? Katja, I mean."

Nick didn't answer, so Eve pressed, the matter taking on importance. He finally told her: cleaning up the mess left by that man who'd been camping there.

"Where did he go?" Eve asked.

"I have no idea, only that he's gone and I'm glad because he was a health hazard."

"You asked him to leave," Eve said.

"He was trespassing!"

"Nick, why did you do that? We agreed to talk about it further before doing anything."

"Well, you're not here to talk to, are you?" Nick said, his voice raised. Anger right there, closer to the surface than Eve had imagined.

Rabbit touched her shoulder and gestured towards the truck door, indicating that he could wait outside, but Eve shook her head.

"I know. And I'm sorry, Nick," she said. "It's just . . ."

"Here's a good sign that things aren't going the way they should be," Nick said, still sharp. "You find yourself apologizing all the time."

Eve felt intensely fatigued, all at once. She closed her eyes, pinching the bridge of her nose. She steadied herself and opened her eyes. She tried to tell him what was going on. "Nick, I think I've found Ali. I'm really close."

Nick made a noise. Exasperation. Frustration. The desire to punch a wall. It was the sound of very alien emotions flushing through Nick.

Eve kept going. "I showed that photo to someone . . ."

But Nick really didn't want to talk about that photo. He had a list of other things to say, and he let these go as if they'd been queued up and waiting to roll. Nothing he said was obviously wrong, either. It was indeed thoughtless of Eve not to be home. Not to have called. Perhaps she was also acting out the stress of the moment. Eve could even accept that she was still in one of the stages of grief over her father and that her timing couldn't possibly have been worse. Only she couldn't stand the tone developing in Nick's voice as each minute went by. A rising desperation.

"Where's Otis?" she asked, to divert the conversation.

"He's in his room," Nick said. "You're worried about Otis?"

"I'm not worried," Eve said.

"You should be worried about yourself," Nick said.

Eve inhaled sharply and didn't speak. She thought: *I am worried about myself. That's why I'm here.*

Sensing in her silence that he'd touched a nerve, Nick chose to plunge onward. "Do you have any idea what's happening in the world? The city is under siege. The police are asking people to stay home. Don't you think you have some obligation to act responsibly? You of all people. You've got a special place in this city. You're a public person. You owe something to your public even if you don't think you owe anything to me." And his voice was again raised sharply by the end of this speech, more evidence of that new anger in him. Although much worse to Eve, evidence that Nick had become what she most feared: the very opposite of what his calm, symmetrical smile had once suggested to her. Not removed and assured. Agitated and fearful instead. Driven by desires and insecurities he couldn't express, but which he looked to her to satisfy and resolve.

Nick was still talking. He was on to the Call now. Thousands of fundamentalist crazies, Nick was saying, all praying at once, chanting and holding their hands to an imaginary heaven. He was trying to make fun of them. He was trying to get her to laugh with him at their foolishness. But Eve didn't, knowing that the discussion between them was over. She didn't need his support to do what came next any more than she was able to be the person that he wanted her to be. She would find Ali. She would end what had soured between them.

"I'm sorry, Nick," Eve said. "I'm really sorry."

With the phone clicked shut, she covered her face with her hands. And Rabbit watched her for a moment, watched her shoulders silently heave. Then he took one of her wrists and gently moved her hand away from her face.

"Tell me something," Rabbit said. "Why go looking for your brother now?"

She let her gaze drift out the window again, thinking. She wouldn't normally have answered that or any other personal question from a near stranger. But this one here, sitting in her truck, brought something out of her. It was impossible to really justify, but she wanted him to know. She said: "After Geneva I almost got married. He was a famous film director in France. Very good looking, very fun, very unfaithful. It didn't work out at all. I stayed in Europe for a while, then came back here. Which I did for all the things that I expected to be familiar about this place. I wanted things nice and familiar. Safe, I suppose."

She was looking past Rabbit out the window. Scored walls. Drifting sidewalk traffic.

"But it wasn't that familiar at all, I discovered," Eve said. "A lot had changed. My parents had split. My mother was on the coast. My father, a journalist, was back in Afghanistan. My brother vanished. No phone, nothing. His e-mail canceled. I talked to the police and they came back three weeks later and told me they were at least sure he didn't die here."

"But you kept looking for him."

"Eventually I had to give it up," Eve said. "I had to try living my own life again. So I got a job in television. I met someone. Nick. And he seemed to have this quality."

She laughed silently and shook her head. "Stop me. This is too much information."

"It's not," he said. "Go on."

"So I thought I was in love and I moved into his house. He asked me to marry him and I said yes. I mean . . . I wanted to when I said yes so I suppose I was in love. Anyway, I think back now and definitely see that I was trying to replant myself here."

The man on the sidewalk with the camera was now walking away from them. At the corner, Eve recognized the brown van with tinted windows from earlier in the day. The man stopped at the passenger side window of the van, seeming to talk to someone inside.

"Then something happened," Rabbit said.

Eve nodded. Then she told Rabbit that about a year after getting together with Nick, and only a few months after she moved into his house, her father died in a roadside explosion near a small Afghan border town recently retaken by Canadian troops. She told Rabbit about the shock of it, the impossible reckoning. The strange stoicism of her mother. She told Rabbit about planning the funeral, about her brother not being there. She told him what it felt like to pick up the search for her brother again only to give it up a second time. To try that resumption of the normal against a growing background noise. A floating sensation. An unbearable sense of drift.

"Like you'd lost track of what you cared about," Rabbit said.

Eve turned to look at him.

He said, "Like the last time you could remember trusting your gut was when Ali was around."

Eve nodded. "Yes, that's exactly it."

Over Rabbit's shoulder, the man by the brown van was standing with his hand on the side door. He appeared ready to climb inside. But just at the moment his weight shifted, the moment the action seemed certain, he turned and presented the camera squarely. No mistake. No ambiguity. Eve saw the sequence unfold: the sunglasses, the dark sweater, the black jeans, the camera going up to conceal the face. She couldn't hear the shutter but she felt it snatch at her. A sensation flushing to the surface of her skin.

She wanted to be gone again. She knew exactly the feeling of wanting to be away. And Rabbit's eyes followed her gaze, but the van had pulled away and around a corner, out of sight.

"READY?" HE SAID. And she was. Eve was ready.

Don't be alarmed, he told her. And in they went. Into the Grove, but not the bar. Into the hidden spaces upstairs. In the hallway Eve stepped around stalagmites of pigeon guano and dodged drips of water from the stained ceiling overhead.

Jabez occupied the most chaotic living space Eve had ever seen.

Evidence of a creative process exploding inside its own container, again and again. Aging computer carcasses were stacked to the ceiling in the center of the room with only narrow corridors between them for movement. The walls were densely cross-hatched with drawings and writing, schematics and plans. There were several hundred photographs of women's lips collaged onto the inside of the door. A low worktable was covered with beer bottles, a mounded ashtray, rolling papers, tobacco, Sharpie pens, X-Acto knives, protractors, condom packages. A blown-up picture of a human eye was papered over the front glass, as if a giant wearing lacquered mascara were peering in the window.

Jabez shook her hand, then motioned to Rabbit that they needed to speak in private. He turned away from Eve but she could still see the signing as it began, the agitation plain. Jerks and stabs, scrapes and chops.

"Just look at the photograph," Rabbit finally said, breaking the oddly pixelated silence. But the signing continued and didn't appear to change much in tone.

Eve excused herself into the rest of the studio, squeezing between the gutted CPUs and the dozens of keyboards that had been stripped of their letter and number keys. "Wow," she said aloud, leaning in close to examine a dense map and legend of what appeared to be a fictional subway system, ready to be pranked into a bus shelter somewhere. Then a wall of books, beat-up paperbacks, dime-store volumes about half of which appeared to be copies of 1984. She stopped to run her finger along their spines, struck with a sudden and pleasant sense of recognition. A single large poster filled the entire wall, floor to ceiling, just peeking from behind the bookshelf. It was mounted to stiff cardboard, so Eve was able to slide it out a few more inches, then a few more feet. Familiar lines and layout. A close-up photograph of a toy soldier magnified to almost human scale, all the chapped plastic edges visible, the craggy, dented face, this one distorted in a cartoon rictus of pain, one arm stretched and rigid, the rifle slipping from the fingers' grasp. While with the other hand, the soldier clutched his gut over the bullet hole that had just appeared. Of all the soldiers in the set, the gunners and runners and officers, here was the one who bought it. The one at the moment of death. The one shortly to understand all that there was to understand, if indeed there was anything to understand. And under him, in the font of the political campaign poster, the letters suitable for a highway billboard: *War Is Peace.*

Eve could hear the words, and she smiled with pleasure thinking of it. *Keep up the good work, you beautiful, beautiful young artists!*

She returned to where Rabbit and Jabez were standing. A stuttering flash of sign. A shrug. Silence. Rabbit had the photograph of Ali out again. He was holding it forward, but Eve knew from the body language that Jabez was silently rebuffing Rabbit's offer to inspect the photo again.

Jabez saw her and lifted his chin, readied himself for confrontation.

Eve said: "So you know him. You're still friends and you're protecting him. I admire that. I really do."

Jabez signing. Rabbit talking. "He says yes he knows him. Yes, they're still close friends. But he doesn't know you."

Eve stood nodding. Jabez was signing further, but she interrupted. She waved her hands. Jabez turned to her. She had his full attention.

Eve said: "I watched you putting up *Freedom Is Slavery.*"

THEY CROSSED THE HILLSIDE AGAIN, jets overhead. They could hear a television playing from a high window, newscast tones. They were both hungry, so they went into a place with candlelight winking out between red curtains. She was still waiting. No actual news of Ali yet. No confirmation that Ali was actually to be seen somewhere, in the flesh.

She said: "All these secrets and double checks. You guys are like the Masons."

"It's strange, I admit," Rabbit said. "I thought Beyer would have been the one to know your brother and it turns out to be Jabez."

Some Italian place down in the East Flats. Gino's. Or Tino's. She thought how hard it was to find these sorts of restaurants on the west side where high authenticity was the order of the day. Here it was red-checkered tablecloths, candles in Chianti bottles. Shakers of parmesan and hot pepper flakes on every table. Rabbit's spaghetti smelled of garlic and basil. A real and rare curiosity was alive here, a need to know. So Eve asked the questions she thought she could ask. What about his work in Oregon?

Rabbit put his fork down. He looked around the restaurant quickly. He looked at her. Did she really want to know this? Okay, fine. He was a validation engineer. Not so interesting in retrospect. Chip layout. Circuit design. Documenting specs. Building prototypes. Running tests. Preparing logic diagrams. "Meetings I was much less good at," Rabbit told her. "I was twenty-two. I realized pretty quickly I'd made a mistake. My employer realized the same thing. It happens."

She was looking at him, a small smile coming to her face.

"You have no idea what I'm talking about," he said.

"No, I do. I've had jobs I changed my mind about. More than one. Tell me about yours, though."

"Cell phones," Rabbit said. "We were working up a new kind of cell phone architecture. Do you really find this interesting?"

Eve did find this interesting. She found Rabbit interesting and could have asked him a lot of different questions about who he was and what he'd become. What he thought about the past and the future. But Oregon had a trace of mystery in it, so she let the conversation slide to other topics on which he spoke more freely. Childhood. Here Rabbit lost his restraint. Long before working out West. Long before his parents died. Long before everything that came afterwards, there had been a town up north. There were blackberry canes in this story, mountain plateaus, a piece of land and a cabin with an out-house. There had been a vegetable garden and three-day hikes into the hills, sleeping under the stars with his mother and father. And now there was a notion, very much on his mind, that the time might be coming for a return to those same landscapes. A return to stay.

"I want to grow my own food," Rabbit said. "Don't laugh, this is all very back-to-the-earth, I realize. But I want to work with my hands."

"Don't you work with your hands already?"

"Art is between worlds, for me. Or it's a way from one world to an-other. I've started something here and I'm going to finish it. But after that, I need to be up north."

"Tell me about your parents," Eve said.

"They had me late. A last-minute change of heart about populating an overpopulated planet. They were hippies, off-gridders. We drank rainwater. Ate kale and beets and carrots from the garden. Raised our own chickens. I was homeschooled, which turned out to be something scholarship committees really liked. So off I went to a school we never could have afforded otherwise. They were good people. They were hard workers, independent, lovers of music and art, lovers of nature. Cancer got them both. My dad was stomach, my mother intestinal. In two years they were both gone. I was in university at the time. I really struggled with it, to be honest. Although a few months after it hap-pened was the worst. I almost dropped out of school. I ended up gradu-ating, but not easily."

Eve watched him while he recounted this and saw the remembered pain in the shape of his lips, a slight tension there. Those were a par-ticular kind of tears she had shed herself, six months after her father was gone, at that terrible moment when she knew he'd never return.

"Although," Rabbit said, "after a couple of years I could think of them again without the grief. The memories do eventually become a source of strength, not pain."

"They do," Eve said. Half a question, her throat tight.

He looked at her gently. "Yeah, they do."

"Tell me more," Eve said, wiping her eyes. "How do you think they most influenced you?"

He thought about that for a while. Then he told her again about being outdoors. Views of the stars. Evenings during which hardly a word was spoken and in which their peace was complete.

The table was narrow, their hands almost touching. Rabbit's leg tremored lightly in place as he spoke. She only had to drop her palm to his knee, pressing down. And Rabbit's heel leveled with the floor.

He looked at her. "We'll find your brother."

They were close. She could feel it.

"I appreciate what you're doing," she said, conscious of the music all at once. The scene. They were in a dimly lit restaurant together. Violin music in the background. The waiter looked her over when she took the bill to pay. And outside, she gave Rabbit a hug and the movement felt familiar, as if her arms and hands already had the feel of it, the sweet habit. One hand to the waist, the other finding the flat spot at the base of his spine. He held her gently, on the cusp of tomorrow. And much later, in the truck, she could still feel the places where his arms had pressed against her body. Winding down through the quiet streets, the looping concentration as she entered the West Stretch. Down Angus Crescent to Nick's house, which had been his parents' house. Their long lawn, their hedge, their oaks and azaleas. Not her house.

She parked in the driveway and turned off the truck, her watch ticking on up to midnight. She let herself in, heard Hassoman stir but not get up. Heard the house return to silence, to the serene rhythm of its programmatic sleep. Standing in the hall, still in her running clothes, she felt herself drift not just to the edge of this place, this nested series of routines, but out of its orbit entirely.

She made her way down the corridor, past the television room to the broom closet. She found it there: just what was needed for that unexpected trip across town in complicated weather. Portable food, shelter, extra clothes. And with the green canvas duffel hoisted over one shoulder, she made her way quietly back outside to the truck.

PEGG

—

DARKNESS LIKE A PRISONER'S HOOD, like a thing strapped tight around the eyes and cinched at the neck. Darkness pressing him down like a low ceiling. It bent him over, this darkness. And Pegg looked but could not find his own body.

The man had searched him, an efficient one-handed frisk. Fingers walking the creases of his sleeves and collar, a palm sliding flat down the small of his back and around his sides, thorough and well practiced. It knew the stations, this hand, and visited them without haste or hesitation. To the armpits, to the neck, around the chest for wires and into the crotch for hidden weapons, transmitters, sharpened spoons. Pegg's tape recorder was extracted from his hip pocket and inspected, then returned. The whiskey too. And down each leg now, all the way to the ankle, where a single finger reamed each sock. Brutal intimacy. Here was an organism closer than any lover. Breath and vapors, body odor and deeper scents.

"Thom Pegg," the voice had said. And here Pegg was forced to consider for the second time an accent that defied situation. This one more placeless even than Haden's. No mere pastiche of everywhere.

It was a nowhere voice. The man came from nowhere. The words came out of the blackness itself, emerging from between the folds of its material, a fabric in which light had been absent so long that it was forgotten: its weave, its current, the breath of its composite colors.

And Pegg finally had asked: "What's your name?"

"Call me Mov."

Pegg collected himself during these moments. Remembering things he was supposed to do. Rules and practices, conventions and plays. Were the children all right? And when Mov assured him they were, Pegg demanded that he be allowed to talk to them. Standard hostage-taking protocol, as per Haden's instructions. The man agreed.

Now Pegg groped and staggered. He called out in a low voice: "Anybody? Hello?"

And he heard a voice come back. A boy. Coming to Pegg through the stench of the place. Outhouse smells and popcorn, stickiness underfoot. A sniffle here and a cough over there, a slow wail rising and tapering near the back. And then a beautiful voice, not part of the darkness at all, but suspended.

"Over here."

Pegg blinked and squinted and wondered if his eyes were finally adjusting. Some granular shape was lifting from the black. A slow wash or current in the void. He realized he was seeing the slant of the theater itself, descending to the stage. He rotated his head, looked for patterns where he knew the seats would be. Any slow movement there.

Pegg felt his way along the wall, along some seats. He paid attention to a steady ticking from the gut works of the building, shafts and ducts and cables. Pegg thought of secret passages, manholes and trapdoors. He imagined soldiers crawling into their places in the ceiling overhead, getting ready to drop down on black wires and begin their killing according to the plan they had laid. The thought agitated real fear in him, his mind stumbling across unhappy images. Save us from the gas, from flash bangs and stun grenades, from the prick of lasers against the darkness.

Save us from the black hats, from those who might try to rescue us. Save us from those who think there is any way to help.

"Over here?"

"Here," the boy said.

Pegg woozy and sightless and nasally overwhelmed. But now there was a roughed-up texture in the air, the jostle of human molecules. Hello, he said. He was a journalist. Thom Pegg. Everybody all right? Nobody hurt?

They were clustered in a ragged group near the center aisle and towards the back of the theater.

"Are you here to get us out?" the boy said. "We want to get out of here."

Pegg said: "How many are you?"

"Four plus me." A teenaged voice. A certain defiance evident through the crack and strain. Heading towards their second day, the boy would have passed through fear to some other place beyond. There were five more kids near the back, the boy told him. They were separated and had been told not to move.

Ten total, Pegg thought. Getting close. At some point, as Haden himself had said, the thing resolved itself for lack of material.

"All the grown-ups are gone," the boy said. "Why are we still here?"

"How old are you?" Pegg asked.

Thirteen. The boy groped a hand out, and Pegg took it awkwardly in both of his own. The boy's name was Gerry. "Girard," he said. "But no one calls me that. Have you talked to the man? Is he letting us go now?"

"I'm sure he will," Pegg said. "Where are you from?"

Gerry was from the East Coast. He'd been in town visiting his sister and their father. She'd won three tickets and taken a friend. Their father insisted that he go along. No, she wasn't still inside. He'd gotten her out of the theater in the first rush, then come back to find the friend, who was also gone. "She got out the same time, but I didn't see her. I came back to find her because I didn't see her."

Pegg coughed. Again at the belly, the grumble of daily activity, the reawakening pain. "Can you tell me how these releases have been working, Gerry?"

"I don't know. I can't see anything."

"Does he call out names?"

"I don't know why he's doing anything. He just comes and people go with him. There's a dead man's body over there. A boy fell over it. I've told everyone not to touch it now."

It was someone from the TV show, Gerry told him. He'd come out and shouted. Then he'd been shot. Gerry saw it. Then there had been a woman who came into the theater later. They all saw the side door open and the light spilling in. Then the woman started yelling at them. "She was telling us to leave. Saying we should just go. I only came here because my dad wouldn't let my sister go by herself. These four here are good, though. They're being brave. We're not crying anymore, right? We play memory games to pass the time. Like decimals of pi. And *Star Wars*. The name of Darth Vader's super-star destroyer?"

"The Executor." A girl's voice.

"Jabba the Hut's first lieutenant?"

"Fortuna." Another boy.

"Any cell phones around?" Pegg asked.

"He took them away. I don't even live here. I don't even watch TV. I play video games but only an hour a day. Everybody just wants to go home."

"You're going home. You're doing well, though. You're all doing really well. What's your sport?"

"Chess and debate," Gerry said. "I started karate but a kid broke my nose."

"Have you all eaten?"

"He gave us some kind of cookie. We shared candy bars."

"And who else is here? Come on, all of you. Tell me who you are." Pegg was sitting now, looking back into the blackness. But he could feel the small forms here, and feel them as they came close. A hand to his arm now. Another one finding his shoulder.

Ashley, Isaac, Roshawn, Barker.

Pegg touched their shoulders, or put his hands on their heads, communicating in that way possible only by touch. We're all here. None of us are alone. There were no tears here now. Bravery indeed. Bravery and a strange silence. It didn't make Pegg proud imagining himself in the same position. He'd have run with the voice coaches, he was sadly certain. Did anything in his life allow him to think otherwise? Would he have gone back for the missing best friend of his little sister, the sister living with the father from whom it sounded like Gerry had grown entirely distant?

Gerry was telling him: "There were five or six men to start. They were actors, part of the show. Then there was a Kill. You know what that is?

"I've heard about it, yes," Pegg said.

"She's still up there in the other group, that girl. Her name is Hyacinth. I wish I hadn't given her five stars. I could have given her four and maybe this wouldn't have happened. Because after the actors, the other guy came in and started shooting. The actors ran off and left him here. He has a briefcase. It's a bomb, I think. Hyacinth is still here. Still over at the back."

"It's going to be okay," Pegg said. "Tell me where the rest of you live."

Gerry was breathing through his mouth. Smart kid, holding some five-year-old stranger in his lap. Guilty in a way he had no reason to feel. But they talked about where they lived for a while. Streets and crescents were described. High-rise developments. Favorite rooms and toys and holidays.

"Let's do pi," Gerry said.

"Three point one four . . . one five . . ."

" . . . nine two six five . . ."

"Roshawn, my man. Roshawn does what?"

"I rock the house," Roshawn said.

"He's a comic," Gerry explained. "Do some, Roshawn."

"Grandmothers are really nuts though, don't you find?" Roshawn said to Pegg, who felt himself become an audience, felt attention directed through this granular black towards him alone.

"I like this one."

"Can I go on here?"

"Go, Roshawn. Quiet, everyone."

"Like my own grandmother the other day, pushing me down the sidewalk. This other old lady stops. She's saying, like, aw he's so cute. He's so sweet. My grandmother, she's like: Oh, this is nothing. Wait'll I show you his picture."

Gerry there in the darkness, unsmiling. Unable to escape all that he'd seen. When the man was shot in the center aisle and fell to the floor, his head had rolled over towards Gerry and their eyes had met. There was no escaping the gaze. And when the woman came into the theater later, standing in the side door that opened onto the lobby, ranting that they should just get up and leave, run out, don't listen to this guy, she looked at Gerry too, he was sure of it. She was fourteen rows away, a black smudge of silhouette at the center of a blinding halo of light from the street outside. Gerry's eyes were pinched shut. And still he felt sure she was talking directly to him. Telling him to move, to do something. And he just sat there until the theater came alight with a ragged burst of flame, the stage and front seats candled into brilliance by a ragged lick of white and orange. They all saw the man onstage then, with his night-vision goggles. He was blind in that instant he fired. The tables turned. But nobody moved. The long arc of flame bridged the air between the two figures. The ghost trace. Once, twice, three times. MAC-10 or mini-Uzi. She did not fly backwards and hit the wall like in the first-person shooter games Gerry had played. She just crumpled in place in the middle of her ranting and didn't move again.

PEGG CIRCLED AWAY FROM GERRY and around the room. He talked to the others. He counted and remembered names. Laisha, Reebo, Sam, Hyacinth, Metric. That made ten total.

You'll be okay. We're going to be fine. Everybody all right? Anybody hurt? I'm going to try to help you get out of here. Tell me what you all do.

Sam did beatbox and Reebo rapped. Laisha had memorized every dish in the most recent season of *Iron Chef America* and traveled with her own copper cookware from Villedieu-les-Poêles. Metric danced pop-lock. Hyacinth, who seemed to be sitting a couple seats away to one side, said she was a singer. Her voice kept low, as if wishing not to be heard. As if she were keeping her head down.

"Come here, Hyacinth," Pegg said to her, crouching low. And he heard the little girl get up from her seat and come towards the rest of them at the end of the row. "Tell us about where you live," he asked her, reaching a hand out and finding her shoulder. He felt her hesitation. But now the others joined in, as if they too had been trying to make her speak, and failing so far. They said: *Tell us, Hyacinth. Tell us, please. We want to hear.* So she started, slowly, then went on to describe where she lived and how it had inspired her. That and Celine Dion, but mostly her home. The sound of birds in the distance. There was always a ripple of light in the trees, even at night. And if you were very still, around sunrise and dusk, the animals moved in the forests near you without fear. Elk, wolves, bears. Hyacinth was glad to have seen them, because she could think of them now. And the memories helped her.

In the darkness, Pegg's face was performing a dance of expressions, helpless to the cross-wired emotions below. KiddieFamers. Here in the darkness, they were held together by their ambitions, no matter where they learned them. The desire for fame may be long-term toxic, but was it toxic for young Hyacinth here, right at that moment? Didn't it serve her well sitting in the darkness next to a ticking bomb? If a person didn't crave living as the exception at such a moment, one might too easily accept death. And who the hell was Thom Pegg anyway to criticize?

Pegg traced the side wall forward to the front of the theater. Halfway there he decided he needed a drink to settle the acid squelching of his middle regions, relieve the pinion there, the clamp at his lower right side. He pulled out one of the half-pints and hefted it. Then he put it away without taking a sip.

"Tell me about the name," Pegg said to the man. "Mov. Is it short for something?"

They sat on the stage together, chairs just a few feet apart on either side of a low table, like actors doing improv. Pegg fumbled his tape recorder out and held it up in the darkness.

"It's fine," Mov said.

Pegg groped it down to the low table, feeling with his other hand. "The name Mov. It's not yours. It's a nom de guerre."

"Just mine for the moment," the man said. "I've taken it to honor a fallen hero. Movsar."

Pegg thought this rang a bell, but couldn't pull in the reference.

"Barayev," the man said. "Movsar Barayev."

Ah, here we go. "The incident in Moscow. I believe he was Chechen," Pegg said, starting the tape recorder. "So is this a kind of tribute, then?"

"Not exactly," Mov said. "But there are parallels."

Pegg thought about his angles here. What flattered a hostage taker? He tried the topic of those outside. How were they handling things? Did Mov think they knew what they were dealing with, really?

Mov didn't bite. He answered in monosyllables.

Pegg circled and returned. "Barayev was a drug addict," he tried. "Probably the front for some other leader, calling the shots from behind."

"Yes, well think of me as both the drug addict and the figure calling the shots."

"So what would you like me to report back? As in Moscow, so too here?"

"Not quite. I have no ethnic beef, so that's different. No subjugated homeland. No sacred codex, no articles of faith. I also have much better technology."

"How so?"

"I can see in the dark, for one. Infrared filter. These are military units."

Night-vision. Haden would probably want to hear about that as soon as possible. But he wouldn't tell him just yet, Pegg thought. Surely he'd earned the right to hear a little more of this man's story.

"Are you military?" Pegg asked.

"Not a chance. I bought two of these on eBay. And then there's the payload. The central question."

"And what is that, Mov?"

"It's a bomb. A really big one. You techie or just asking me questions on a topic designed to flatter me? Get him talking about his gear. He'll like that."

"I'm genuinely interested. Briefcase bomb?"

"Call it that. Special tweaks, though. Hand trigger."

Mov explained this detail. If his hand were to let go of the case here, the one he was holding tightly as they spoke, a pressurized capsule in the handle would expand by a millimeter, closing a circuit between electrical contacts and delivering power to an ignition chip that would then send the whole thing up, and magnificently too.

"Like someone tries to take the thing away from you and boom," Pegg said.

"Exactly that. Same thing if it gets removed from the theater."

"And how does that part work?"

"Boring stuff, technology," Mov said. "Technology is just a tool."

"I'm a journalist. I'm all about the telling detail."

"Is your tape recorder on?"

"It is, yes," Pegg said.

"In addition to the pressure trigger in the handle, the case has a GPS trip switch," Mov told him. "That switch is activated if the case is moved out of a certain zone."

Pegg coughed and then, for a moment, couldn't stop coughing. When he recovered, he asked: "How big a zone?"

Bigger than a Buick, smaller than the theater. "Beats strapping bombs to your women."

"I don't know about beats, Mov. You have children in here. This is a fairly bad scene as far as they go."

"Well yes, children. I said there were parallels. And the children are a key part of that, certainly. But an appreciation for the theater too. We want this to be remembered, don't we?"

Pegg winced in the darkness. Belly alight. Rumbles at the navel now, a blossoming within. He leaned a little backwards in his chair, which occasionally provided relief. Buzzing the internet constantly for information on his symptoms, he'd once come across the advice about leaning back. It worked for a while, temporarily convincing him that the problem was in the pancreas, the groans and complaints of which were apparently alleviated by going straight, unfurling. But then the symptoms had ripped the other way the following week, and Pegg was driven on to other ideas, other fears. Spinal tumor. Cancer of the connective tissue.

"You all right?" Mov asked him.

"Splendid," Pegg said, willing himself past the pain. "But if I remember correctly from Moscow, Barayev got the BBC World Service."

"Don't put yourself down. You were my idea."

"You read *L:MN?*"

"I do. But more importantly, I read you. I happen to like a good fall from grace. Did you lose your house? End up living in your car for a while before a rental place came through? Lose the kid? That's the one that turns people. Losing the kid."

Pegg shuffled in his chair a little. He forced his eyes to the spot in the darkness from which the voice had been emanating. From where he could hear the squeak of the wooden chair. He detected a tighter grain here and resolved to track it, staring. Pegg said: "Have we met before?"

"Never had the pleasure. Call me a fan."

Mov was making fun of him, of course. But he was doing so in a particular way. He was mocking Pegg the way Pegg himself had liked to mock people in print since his infamous fall from grace. He'd made a business of fucking with celebrities, yes. Just as Haden had said on the plane, those endless hours before. But he'd mocked the readers too. Not for their stupidity exactly. But for their self-identification as fans. Fanatics. Possessed by enthusiasm beyond reason, by a mindless enslavement not to the person being profiled—whatever actor or comedian or rising rap star—but to the precise machinery at the heart of which he and Mov presently sat, knee to knee onstage in the *KiddieFame* studio theater, bracketed around a briefcase bomb that might just vaporize them all. The machinery of yearning and dissatisfaction that delivered to people fame on the one hand and ruination on the other.

"And what was your line of work?" Pegg asked, finally.

"Languages," Mov answered. "I speak four well. Four or five others less well. I have a fantastic memory."

Pegg felt the waking alertness opposite, as if they were now both getting somewhere. He sat a little straighter himself. "Which languages, Mov?"

"Think along the lines of Arabic dialects. Although make no mistake. I'm from here. I'm one of you."

Pegg leaned back in the chair, felt the wood of it bite his back, his knees. He felt a slow wave of intestinal pressure, a steady sickness not quite rising to complete itself. He'd had many occasions to wonder what the organics of his abdomen knew that had not yet reached his brain. All that fateful knowing of hidden cysts and swelling lymph nodes. Here was such a time. The sense of knowledge there in the savvy guts.

"Why no demands, no statements, Mov? In Moscow they had demands. Troops out of Chechnya, et cetera. So tell me. Where in the world would you like them to start ordering the men back into the helicopters?"

"Ah, Thom Pegg," Mov said. "Now I know why I asked for you. Because you're really very good."

"How am I good? Help me understand."

"Where would we start with such demands?" Mov said. "These men to whom you refer. These helicopters. You ask where in the world they might be. I ask you where in the world they aren't. Afghanistan, Iraq, Israel, Jordan, Pakistan. Yes, those are the obvious places. But Libya, Morocco, Romania, Georgia, Thailand, the Philippines, Canada. These lists go on forever."

Pegg was experiencing some kind of auditory delusion while Mov was speaking. He wondered if it were being induced by sensory deprivation. Only this voice and the pressure of a small chair against the small of his back, a small chair that seemed to be slanted forward. He kept sliding down to the front of it before pushing himself back, his calves cramping with the subtle strain of it. And then these sounds, doors opening and closing in the distance, an echo, a metallic sound, footsteps on concrete.

Oh no, Pegg thought. Not this. "Languages. You were a translator."

Sounds coming from inside his own body. These clanks and clangs. His own interior alive with movement, with footsteps, with knowledge.

"Sort of. I worked for a private company that put interrogation contractors into the field."

Pancreatic winks. Gastroenterological innuendo.

"You know what that's all about, don't you, Thom Pegg? Producing information out of reluctance. Rules and techniques for making them talk."

Duodenal reckoning.

"Private company," Mov continued. "That's how it is with security these days. Public need, private profit. I didn't wear a uniform. I never saluted anyone."

Pegg took out his whiskey and slowly unscrewed the cap. "Drink?"

"Don't take the stuff. Used to, of course. I'm sure you'll quit too, eventually."

Pegg drank some and pocketed the bottle. Then he felt something pressed into his hands, tubular, with straps and mounts. He pulled the thing over his head and nestled his eyes into the goggles. For a second or two, he kept his eyes closed, as if to look all at once might blind him. But that was not the case. Teasing new information from the nether reaches of the wave spectrum, these emanations didn't sting the retina like sunlight might after an hour in a closet. They merely hummed to life. The information that all along had been flowing, seaming through the theater and out past them through the walls and on into the endless universe, those waves were now accessible to him.

Pegg opened his eyes and re-entered the world. Silver and green tones, crisp, oddly charged with depth and length. Barely a trace of shadow.

Mov sat opposite, a figure completely unexpected for how familiar he was. Overweight, shortish, balding. He wasn't dressed in combat fatigues at all, as the reports had had it. He wore a rumpled suit, shirt open, no tie. No weapon evident that Pegg could tell, no pistol bulge at the armpit either. He sat, this man, like a reflection of Pegg himself. Only holding that briefcase, hand clenched down on the handle. All that his guts had known, Pegg now felt surge to consciousness. The ordinary horror. The quiet certainty of it. The way in which Haden came to mind.

Mov looked at him across the distance. Goggles swiveling. Pegg could suddenly hear his own breathing and swallowing. His own preparation for speech.

"You worked the black sites, the secret prisons," Pegg said. It wasn't an accusation. Pegg was only repeating back to Mov the insight that he'd been offered. He was opening the way, without pressure, for the full confession. "Camp X-Ray, Abu Ghraib, Kohat, Diego Garcia," he continued, although his heart was now torquing within. "You did terrible things, Mov. I know. You hurt people behind closed doors. You broke them down with water and electricity and light."

Mov was leaning forward in the shimmery haze, his goggles reaching towards Pegg, who could appreciate with sudden intensity how they would have appeared to anyone who could see them. Like insects, like crawling things. Mandible action just now beginning under the busy apparatus of the eyes as the one opposite opened up. As he began to speak.

FRIDAY

—

OCTOBER 25

LOFTIN

—

EARLY MORNING, UNREADABLE LIGHT. There were police and militia units all through the plaza, SWAT teams and Special Forces. Members of an anti-terrorist unit were seen in the streets nearby moving from a van into a building. Police were stop-checking people, watching the entrances to the restaurants and cafés, which people might not have ultimately minded so much if the cameras hadn't also appeared. These were unsettling, mounted high on telescoping tripods. They looked like deep-space probes touched down to the pavement, with their thin aluminum members spindling, the tiny glint of a lens at the tip of each. They were aimed in all directions, at Meme and around the plaza, down the side streets. Now here came a good and sticky rumor, seemingly too detailed to be dismissed. These cameras (the rumor went) were networked via satellite to the same face-recognition system run by the big Vegas casinos to scan and catalog the millions who came through their doors every year. Sharp lenses, smart algorithms, massive banks of processors and the deep global sea of personal data.

Loftin got Pam on the line when he heard about that one. She knew the rumor was out there but couldn't say where it started.

Probably bullshit, she said. Although it was a fact that one of the sons of the Jordanian family who owned Meme Media was married to the daughter of the head of IT systems for the Bellagio Resort and Casino in Las Vegas.

Loftin had to chuckle. It was incredible how these rumors worked. Random facts beaten and hammered into patterns. "Well that's a lock then," he said.

She asked Loftin how his own story was shaping up.

It wasn't, really. He didn't tell Pam as much, but the truth was that the narrative thread was eluding him. Nobody would talk, although he could read the signs of fear, the signs that official people felt the impending weight of unknown events. No press conference since the day before, public information bleeding dry. True to form, Loftin worked his oblique angles. He shifted around. He talked to a couple of young soldiers at the barricade. They'd been schooled. They were friendly but told him nothing.

Loftin talked to paramedics and firefighters. A couple off-duty cops in baggy jeans and ball caps. These guys were in vice-narcotics but they were staying close. There was that kind of feeling in the air. People found the groups with which they identified and readied themselves to help. One of these cops followed Loftin as he strolled away around the corner of a parked ambulance.

He thought there was one other thing Loftin might want to know.

Loftin stopped and turned. He tried not to look too curious.

The woman who went inside, the cop said. The rumor going around hard at the moment was that she wasn't shot at all. Not with a bullet, that is. The guy used a ballistic knife.

Loftin raised his eyebrows. Now here was a rumor based on an arcane detail. Ballistic knife, hadn't heard about those in a while. Nasty bit of work. Banned back in the late eighties. Your thug who picked up one of these could choose between stabbing people or pulling a side-mounted trigger and launching the blade like a cross-bow bolt out of the handle.

"Pretty exotic," Loftin said.

"Russian-made," the cop said. Manufactured by the company Ostblock for the Russian Special Forces. And here, while the off-duty narcotics officer nodded slowly for emphasis, he didn't immediately close the logic loop for Loftin. He didn't assert that the hostage taker was Russian or Special Forces or anything else particularly. But something remained hanging, dangling in the unsaid.

"So what are we supposed to conclude from all that?" Loftin asked.

"Well," the man said, looking away, then looking back. His hair was greasy and long in the Hollywood style of the moment. Loftin thought how easy it must be to go undercover when all you had to do was cut your hair the way you saw in the entertainment pages. Or perhaps that made it more difficult.

"Go ahead," Loftin told the man. "I can take it."

"It's October twenty-fifth today," the man said. "Friday."

"Right," Loftin said.

"Last time October twenty-fifth fell on a Friday was 2002, eleven years ago."

Loftin nodded. "Right."

"October twenty-fifth, 2002, was what?" The man waited for him, with a satisfied half smile. Loftin might have been a serious journo but he obviously wasn't so smart.

"Moscow Theater Crisis," the man said. "The day before the end."

LOFTIN RETURNED TO HIS HOTEL and stood looking down at the narrow slice of the plaza he could see through the buildings nearby. People seething there, another fire truck creeping through. Loftin thought about the paranoid detail the cop had shared. Who would have even seen a ballistic knife in absolute darkness? Nobody, of course. The cop had seen it in his own imagination, or whoever had told him, or whoever had told the person that had told him. There had probably been many people involved in turning the fantasy of a ballistic knife into a serious point of discussion.

Forget the rumors, Loftin told himself, inventorying the facts as he knew them. A guy targeting a television show for aspiring kid celebrities. A man with the entire world to choose from who decides to tell his story to a soft-porn tabloid magazine. Thom Pegg. Pegg was a disgrace. He was a drunk who had squandered his obvious talents as a writer and a journalist. And he was a proven liar who apparently didn't even lie very well. Where these facts led Loftin in his reasoning was that they had some kind of tawdry, fame-game freak show shaping up in there, and that the real story, the story with a shot at the truth, wouldn't be inside at all.

Yes. Loftin turned to the window, looking intently down towards the plaza again. The television behind him just now returning from commercials to an interview in progress, right down there somewhere, just out of sight.

"You see these things?" one of the Black Bloc protesters was saying to a news camera. He was waving behind himself at a set of tripod-mounted cameras, rumored to be linked to spinning discs of silicon buried in armored vaults somewhere in the Mojave Desert. "You see how they do this? The corporate eye, filming us. Harassing us. But why us? Who is the enemy here, I ask you."

A black handkerchief covered his mouth and nose. He was talking about private money. Billionaires in the shadows. Just look at the people guarding the camera towers, pistols in snug nylon belt holsters but otherwise dressed in khakis and blue shirts. They looked like Microsoft employees, Google or some such.

Loftin was still standing at the glass, his idea shaping. Of course. The story wasn't inside the theater at all. To think he had briefly considered

Thom Pegg to have been in on the angle. Thom Pegg might have been someone to reckon with once, but he was on the empty story here. The common story. The sensation. The razzle-dazzle. Good for him. Let Pegg have it. What mattered was down there. Out there with the cops and the military, the Black Bloc and the Call, the pro-lifers and the law-and-order buffs. Out there among the infected and the suspicious. On the barricades. Among the spectators. Woven into the grain of that agitated and fractious mob. That's what would always distinguish Loftin from other journalists, and from Pegg too now in his degraded state: an understanding that the story was told through unexpected voices.

And while he had these thoughts, up top of the plaza—outside Loftin's field of view, beyond the adjacent buildings—the spotlights were shimmering in the angular facades of water and warping off the front of the Meme complex. The facade glared in the chaos of halogen, an angry sun, licks of hot light and harsh shadows. Everything that morning rested under a roving, searching gaze, suspicious and powerful. And in front of hundreds of people in the crowd at the south end of the square, right at that moment, Jabez and the Poets came in as if from nowhere and bombed out a statement in front of the world.

They hit the plaza in a loose crowd. They came out of the alleys in teams of three. No hoodies, no skateboards, only jeans and sports jerseys. One knapsack per team. They moved like a flight of pigeons motivated by a single distributed will to leave a roof all at once. Faster than you could understand. Some of them skipping, as if there were a hidden joy in this whole theater.

They swarmed the media circus and paint-bombed an entire row of broadcast vans before anyone watching had a clue what they were doing. It looked official. It looked like it was supposed to happen. Out of the alley and down into the street at the bottom of the plaza, just short of the trees. A beat cop just over by the hedge. A militia lieutenant on the far curb answered his cell phone ("Ride of the Valkyries" ring tone punching the air). Snipers on the roofline, the silhouettes next to chimneys, along the brickwork. A person might glance up and see them once, then glance back and they'd be gone.

The Poets strung themselves out by the white news vans parked in a row. The fountains whiting out the sound. Down to their knees and out with the gear, like time-lapse undergrowth. Hand to hand went the cans of spray paint, the banners, the stickers, the braille strips, the glow sticks tied into translucent neon ideograms. A man crouched and marked the flanks of the van while another stood to do the upper sides, and still another climbed on top to do the roof. Dense, crabbed letters from the texts chosen late the night before, sentences laying over one another: *All that was once directly lived has become mere spectacle.* And: *If someone kills the one who is sacred according to the plebiscite, it will not be considered homicide.*

These were repeated and repeated until the specific ideas were lost in another effect, a kind of vanishing. Bodies and words swallowed the vans. They never reappeared. The jungle encased them, joining seamlessly with the trees at the top of the plaza stairs and the grass boulevard. The whole thing seemed to unroll in an instant and all that hardware was suddenly part of the foliage.

The light came up in the east, still distant. The halogens cracked back from white heat to a cooler blue. The south end of the plaza now came fully alive to what had happened and crosscurrents ripped through the crowd. There were those who thought the Poets' work was part of the overall threat. Those who thought it was the perfect response. And so part of the crowd pulled back in distaste and fear; and another part raised their fists and tied black bandanas tighter across their faces, their numbers swelling. Invisible faces behind a climbing, shadowed sea. The banners multiplied. In another interview a Black Bloc spokesperson endorsed the paint-bombing as if it had been his own idea. He then declared that celebrity was a social disease and that hostage-taking was its deformed offspring. The comment might not have parsed, but it quoted. It hit the airways and exploded into a million sound bites.

The anchors rounded on the mood change, touching fingers to their ears to hear correspondents in the plaza where the noise had risen. One of the network vans had been overturned. There was no sense of official reaction to any of this, the police and militia keeping their distance away in the plaza, on their street corners and rooftops. And a quick suspicion took hold and spread among many people present: someone was letting it happen.

The Call began to sing.

We don't want your idols, the Black Bloc spokesperson said to the interviewer, his mouth moving behind the cloth. The selling of them is a corporate activity, a contemporary indulgence. We don't want your new church. And we don't want your killing machine to uphold it. People are dying in the Middle East to protect billionaires in Las Vegas and Hollywood, in Jordan and Haifa. The War on Terror is a franchise sequel.

The Call sang behind him. *O Lamb of God, who takes away the sins of the world, have mercy upon us.*

A network showed a close-up of a man in front of a shop holding a sign that read simply: *Order.* Another sign read: *Not one more child.*

Another group started up a competing chorus: *Mine eyes have seen the glory of the coming of the Lord . . .*

The Call sang louder: *O Lamb of God, who takes away the sins of the world, have mercy upon us.*

The whole bank of elevators in Loftin's hotel was jammed up with crews and executives, producers and gofers. Loftin paced for a minute waiting, then ran down thirty-nine flights of stairs and across two blocks into the plaza, panting, head spinning. There were ferns hanging here.

Open planters and waterfalls. People everywhere: chanters and singers, placards angry and distraught. The seething tension of for and against.

He saw people dancing in front of a boom box over to his left. *We don't need this fascist groove thang . . .*

And the idea came. Loftin was amazed that he hadn't seen it before: fault lines running through the crowd. The story was in the fault lines.

O Lamb of God, who takes away the sins of the world, grant us thy peace.

Everyone was adrift. The encircling authorities, the cameras, the grip of the hostage drama itself. Everyone living in fear about the end. The ending was the thing. And Loftin felt it in a flash, his own story arriving. There was a great war going on here about control over the ending. Each breath of this common air fully vested.

EVE

—

EVE CAME UP INTO THE HEIGHTS THAT MORNING, her truck down in River Park with all her survival needs. Eve on the streets in her running gear, water bladder, self-sufficiency. She walked up into the plaza past the same checkpoint, only now they were turning back anybody who didn't have work in the area. Different faces, sterner engagement.

"You work early, Evey. I thought only we had to work this early."

She made the noises, said the words. Work was work.

"You want coffee? We have hot coffee."

She thanked them, but said she had to get going.

"Be careful up there. It's all agitated. You're watching the news, I hope."

As she was leaving, another cop standing separate from the group stopped her. He put a hand on her arm. "Jeffers is bad. Take Ash and use the boulevard. That's what I'd recommend."

He didn't release her arm. He stood with his lieutenant's stripe and quiver at the jawline. "Maybe don't talk to anyone until you get to work. We're doing our best. But there's tension."

She ran to the plaza and pushed through the crowd at the corner. People were standing so tightly that as she squeezed between the shoulders and elbows she found herself on the steps down before she saw them. She stumbled forward and sank briefly among the pressed bodies. Too much warmth. Too many legs and shoes. She felt a rising panic and pulled herself up, holding on to someone. She stumbled to the bottom of the steps and through the press line, where the man waved her through without asking for credentials. Inside the barricade, Eve saw a pilot she knew from her television days. He owned a helicopter charter company they used for aerial weather reports. He came over, expression focused.

"You all right?" he asked. And when Eve told him she was just trying to get through to Jeffers, he walked her across the plaza, cutting the crowd for her with his wide-shouldered bulk. As they left the enclosure she noticed the parents grouped there, near a tent providing chairs and phones, coffee and Danish pastries. It was the first time she'd seen them, they had been so protected from the press. And here the weak sunshine was cracking free over Meme and streaming into their eyes. They all looked the same direction, standing awkwardly apart, holding Styrofoam cups. They looked up to the top of the plaza, faces flat with unknowing in the orange light. A ladder truck pulled into the street just beyond the trees. Eve realized its siren had been crying and yelping for the past several minutes as it inched through the side street into the square. Onto clear pavement, the driver cut the sound high in its arc and parked with the intense red flank of the truck to take over sight lines, reddening the light all around them, laying a reflected bloodiness into the air. The firefighters climbed out of the cab and were into some sort of conference with a couple of plainclothes cops. One held two cell phones. There were ten children left, somebody said. Just ten left. Eve suddenly heard the words all around her, but they did not add up to a hopeful sound. And Eve felt dread rising there in the warning light, like this were sure to be a new kind of day.

"What's happened?" she asked the helicopter pilot. The man's name was Connor, she remembered suddenly. Ex-forces. They said he had a bullet in his leg, although Eve had never asked him to confirm.

His eyes were rounded sadly.

"Has someone been hurt?" she asked him.

"Not as far as I know," Connor told her, his voice low and controlled. There was something he wanted to tell her. He wasn't sure if he should.

"Tell me."

"Negotiations have been ruled out," the pilot said. "Off the table."

"Why would they do that?" Eve said. "There are still kids in there."

The pilot looked away, squinting into the rising light. "Maybe they know enough about the perp to know negotiations are pointless. Maybe something else."

Eve waited.

"Maybe somebody doesn't want him to surrender. Maybe knowing who he is, somebody wants him dead."

"They're going in," Eve said. "I cannot believe this."

Again the squint. "I'm not saying this morning. But they're running out of time. And then, there is the issue of this crowd."

Over the pilot's shoulder Eve could see the parents, still standing in those first red rays of the morning.

"What about the crowd?" she asked.

"You can probably assume they're going to want people out of the plaza before they do anything," the pilot said.

"Like force them to leave."

"I don't know," the man said. "It's tricky. But I wouldn't stay down here. Take care of whatever business you have here, then clear the area."

"Thank you."

"You take care now, Eve." And his words rode with her up the side steps and out of the plaza, clear to the top of Jeffers, then down two doors to Double Vision, where she used the card, conscious of producing it out of her wallet, this totem of privilege and position that she pressed to the black box on the glass. The card triggered a distant beep and shifted some tiny catch within. A light on the door handle went from red to green and the glass sighed inwards under her palm. She was in the quiet, where she let the coolness of the marble come up through her feet, her insides settling with the chill.

THE BOARDROOM HAD ITS PICTURE-BOOK VIEW. She stood at the window and stared down Jeffers into the plaza, saw the shape and shift of the crowd. But she was thinking about Rabbit, Joey's Panda Grove. These new people moving in her life. Nick was in her thoughts, a reproachful shadow. But she turned away from thinking of him directly. Eyes to the rooftops opposite where she'd seen Rabbit the day before. She was picturing the handstand again, looking at the spot where he'd been and imagining his hands spread on the metal flashing there. Sure hands.

Marcus came into the room behind her. She smelled his clean leather smell. A fatherly safety he worked to project around him. "I was so pleased to hear you came down, Eve." Although, as she turned with a smile, as warm as she could manage, she saw the slope-away of his eyebrows. The disturbed calm, the wavering certainty. She'd been invited. Given a key. But then she'd chosen this particular day. Marcus continued, as if to explain her choice: "We've had the news on since it began. I guess we're all riveted. We can't pull our eyes away."

Eve said: "I feel like it's happening to my own friends, my own family."

"I find myself wondering what the man wants."

"Maybe he's getting what he wants already."

She turned back to the glass. Far below in the plaza, there was a flat-screen monitor mounted outside the media tent, an endless channel-surf through the febrile here and now. At this distance it flickered, oversaturated, the screen hot with color.

Marcus said he'd come back, told her to take all the time she needed. Feel free to come any time, any hour. But when the door was closed, she could picture him moving away into a place she would never know, deep into the cubicles and schemes, the data, the angles. Eve waited until she was sure he wouldn't return, then quickly moved across the room to the telescope in the corner. It had a black-and-white authority, the promise of resolution, of telling details. It offered an answer, Eve hoped, to a critical question.

She swung the lens over towards the Peavey Block, unscrewed the lens cover and let it fall to the end of its thin brass chain. She aimed the scope by hand, standing above it, wondering if she could find the object without leaning into the eyepiece. That bulge in the shadows there. That oblong attached to the metalwork. Then she bent to the viewfinder and found it immediately, fixed to the top of the highest point on the roof, a round ventilator shaft that emerged from the elevator housing.

What have you done? She addressed this question to Rabbit, out there on his roofscape somewhere. Rabbit, Rabbit. Why are you here and what have you done?

Eve sited the telescope, moving it gently, centering the object in her quivering field of view. She cracked the zoom up, one notch, then two. Full zoom. The object was black and roughly pyramidal in shape. The sloping flanks of the thing were oddly iridescent.

Outside the restaurant, the night before, Eve had mentioned Oregon again. Why was she so curious? She wasn't sure except that there seemed to be some important missing piece to the story. Rabbit conceded a little more. He'd been on the development team for a next-generation personal telecom device.

"You mean like the WaferFone?" she had asked, which made him laugh.

"The WaferFone is a toy," Rabbit had told her. "Kids' stuff."

She looked at him, quizzical. "And your phone wasn't?"

"Quite different. A more sophisticated bit of business, if I can put it that way."

And as Rabbit said that, his gaze drifted in from the high darkness over her shoulder where it had been restlessly hovering, and settled in her own eyes.

More questions about that "sophisticated bit of business" were pressing to be asked. But Rabbit was now looking at her intently, nodding fractionally, acknowledging an impulse but for once unsure. And seeing his hesitation, Eve let go her questions and acted for both of them. She wanted this next part, the unsure part, the part with no answers. So she put a hand up to his cheek to bring him closer. And as she did, Rabbit's hand came up to cover her own.

He leaned in. She thought: We're kissing. And she felt the undertow: shame, thrill.

Now Eve stood in the Double Vision boardroom, remembering the moment and staring through the viewfinder, the black object poised, the movement of her blood translated into minute tremors. She held herself away from the eyepiece, and the field of view stabilized.

The object was clad in some kind of metallic flexible material, seemingly both matte and gloss in its grain. She guessed Teflon or Gore-Tex. It had an aperture in the top with a reflective disk. Glass or hard plastic. And around one side, almost concealed from the angle she had, Eve could make out a small grid. Tiny filaments in a woven pattern, the surface giving off the silvered and blued hues of oil, of gasoline.

She pulled back from the viewfinder. A panel of some kind, facing south. Positioned deliberately, she judged, wondering now what the position might have been intended to maximize. A view, a broadcast, a projection. Or was the object a receiver? Did the signals come from the south? From some ground source, from satellites orbiting?

Eve leaned into the eyepiece and looked again. Rabbit, Rabbit. Please tell me.

The panel glinted once as the sun rose, a wink involving reflected waves, refracting in through the layers of atmosphere overhead.

Eve stood and breathed in sharply, her heartbeat suddenly elevated and prepared, her body tuning to the truth, knowing it before her mind. The grid was facing south to catch the sunshine, to maximize its receipt of light: rays, energy, power. And she felt a flood of relief, but of excitement too, a fresh and destabilizing kind.

The thing was rigged to renew itself with solar power. Whatever he had built and installed over there, Eve realized, Rabbit had fixed it up with a solar panel. Not a battery, with its finite life. He intended, instead, for this thing to recharge.

This thing he had built, Rabbit wanted it to last.

PEGG

—

PEGG ENTERED ANOTHER LAND. It built itself around him in an accretion of moments. Those first seconds of blackness, the hooded weight of it. The invasion of the one-handed search. The time spent talking with Gerry and the others, the shame he felt. The moment the night-vision went on and the silver-green images were surrendered to his eyes. These moments accumulated and he was pressed down to the floor with them. He was stripped away from this world and ushered down a long, cold corridor into another.

The land of exception, where everything mattered just as it did in the regular world, but none of the same rules and restrictions applied.

He didn't sleep in this land. He was released into it as a drifting, sleepless ghost. He visited the children. He helped one of them pee, holding him by the shoulders and aiming him at the side of the chair at the end of row 12. He got them all to sit together, and Mov, watching always from the stage, did not object.

Pegg said their names, each time he addressed them, reminding them all that they were each still there in a small group, together. Still hunched in darkness. But not absorbed by it. Laisha, Reebo,

Sam, Hyacinth, Metric. Ashley, Isaac, Roshawn, Barker and Gerry.

With his night-vision goggles, Pegg could see that Gerry was a skinny kid with an honest face and, in a single bid to fashion, square-cut glasses with metal frames. Pegg didn't tell Gerry that he could now see him. And he noticed that Gerry did not look for him when he spoke. His own eyes flatlined in the absolute zero of this darkness.

"This is Hyacinth," Pegg said to Gerry, who took her hand and helped her sit in the seat next to him.

"*Star Wars?*" Gerry said to the group. And when there were assenting murmurs he suggested brightly: "Obi-Wan's last words?"

And all of them knew the line. Pegg watched, incredulous. It had been over thirty years since he'd seen the film. But here came the famous passage: ten voices singsonging in the fetid air.

"You can't win, Darth. If you strike me down, I shall become more powerful than you can possibly imagine."

Gerry and Hyacinth holding hands. The tough comedian kid Roshawn sitting with his arms around the two youngest, Sam and Barker. Pegg wiping his nose under the lenses of the goggles and looking away. Most of all, he thought, in the land of exception he was unable to speak. He could only listen and be amazed. By this crew here, certainly. But also by Mov.

Mov stood onstage in the grainy sub-light, a silver figure, ghosted green. He beckoned and Pegg went to him. They sat in chairs opposite one another as the story was hemming in, as Mov began to speak.

You had to imagine a medium-sized city and a medium-sized life, Mov told Pegg. You had to imagine varsity ball and driving up and down through the warehouse district looking for parties. You had to imagine sex for the first time in the basement of a friend's house after the friend had dropped two tabs of blotter and disappeared into his bedroom. Chemical haze. Beer bottles clinking together. Van Halen on the stereo. Parents in Florida. And you had to imagine the friend's sister. College was coming, languages. It was like discovering that he could breathe underwater, that's what languages had been like. His parents spoke several of their own, on either side. He'd never paid much attention to the fact that he could do this thing. And then the world unfolded before him and he plunged into it hungrily.

"I'm from here," Mov said. "Went to Brookdale Elementary. Moffat College. I'm a kind of feel-good local story, Thom. East Flats Boy Made Good."

He liked the work, Mov told him. Make no mistake. It was hard to understand in the light of day, but there had been a certain internal logic to it. The other contractors were married guys, single guys. People with kids and people without. The job seemed not to tell you much about a person, that was his conclusion. Much less than learning that a person was a bus driver or a doctor.

"Everyone has their own way to keep a secret. But all those techniques are the same in the end. The secret slips in behind some larger truth. It nests in a protective layer of stories about work, family and tribe. About God frequently. But always a reference point outside the person, outside the system. If you found that reference and broke the link, people let the secret go. It lost the quality that it had, whatever made it worth protecting. That was the job right there. Listening to people for the sound of links breaking within."

There were places where this work was done. But they were all part of the same place in the end. An island in the Mediterranean belonged to the same place as a room in a hospital in Germany, which was itself connected as if by a single hallway to a shed out back of a listening post in the subarctic. These were places with separate coordinates. But in the trade, they were as contiguous as the anonymous chain hotels after which they were nicknamed. Hilton, HoJo, Best Western, Travelodge. All places where the rules didn't apply. Mov thought you could feel it walking through the door.

He had a home by then. "East Coast. Wife. I had a child. This will get more familiar as we go along."

He flew out to work, civilian. He had a credit card with a $25,000 limit. Flew night flights often, taking window seats, laid his head against the cool glass and slept until arrival. Rented a car. Went to work. He did interrogation prep, which was one of the jobs they contracted out. He didn't envy the men who extracted the actual information. They had even higher security clearances. Cover stories, lives of deceit. They left each room they entered with new secrets they were obliged to keep. It was a life that accumulated misery, and he'd met more than a few of them who would gladly admit it.

Interrogation prep meant softening up the prisoners. Getting them used to the idea of endless suffering, with talking as the single mechanism for release. Not talking now, just talking later sometime. For this purpose Mov's company hired language grads, psychology majors, guys who'd had collegiate sports careers interrupted by injury. They hired church people and heathens. It was understood by those on the inside that a trace of patriotism didn't hurt, but that they had been selected for self-interest too.

Third interview, they asked Mov why he wanted the job. "You speak what, seven languages," the guy said. "Why aren't you on a campus somewhere? Campus life. Autumn days. Nice office. Pretty co-eds."

He answered: "I'd like to help out. I believe in Western civilization. And sure, I see it facing certain threats."

The man asked him: "But what? I hear a but in that."

Then the man waited, a long pause. They were interviewing him in a bare room in an industrial park outside of a prairie city. He'd seen a grain elevator while driving in earlier, big letters across the side: *John 3:16*. Mov wasn't a believer. Although having not yet been hired, having not yet seen inside the machine, he thought that if he did believe he'd surely turn around and head back to the airport having seen that sign.

Mov gave the man an answer. Something to do with occasionally stepping up to do a duty. But there were other things he wasn't saying. He could see them hanging in the air, the other considerations. The man himself inspired something, the phantom machinery of which he was a part. There was a kind of person who wanted to be asked to do those things other people wouldn't do. Mov knew it now, if he hadn't fully then. There was a type who responded to the inner distinction of the clandestine. The hidden mark on the heart. Take this package to the man in the café. Drape a scarf out your window if you're being followed. Those who were called didn't know their full role in things, only that their role was full. In the ambiguity lay the reassurance. You were one step further inside, nearer the way things really worked. Nearer the reasons, the truths of the matter.

"It was like wanting fame, but not fame. The other related thing," Mov told Pegg. "The one you couldn't speak about. Anti-fame. I wanted that."

Pegg forced himself to breathe. "Anti-fame?"

"Some people want to be widely known and celebrated. Others want concealment and secrecy. It's gaming the system, either way. It's a bid to separate yourself from all those wandering around outside the machinery, subject to it but blind to their enslavement. *The fan is always the mark. Celebrity is a con.* Who wrote that, having seen it for himself up close and personal? What smart man, Thom Pegg?"

Pegg leaned back in his chair. He felt exhausted already but sensed that he'd barely been tested. "Go on," he said.

"I didn't like any of the weird stuff, any of the sexual play, the dogs," Mov said. "I didn't put panties on the guys' heads or have them simulate blow jobs on each other. I didn't like the whole approach of humiliation. There could be honor in it, even under the circumstances."

He worked contrasts, mainly. These were time proven, he explained. Cold cells, hot cells. He kept them in darkness and then shone a bank of quartz incandescent lights in their faces. He stood behind these lights, barely visible. Voice coming out of the blinding white. Rarely threats. Fear was a lever that worked in about one in ten cases. Middle-class secular guys caught up in the game without religious motive. But there weren't many of those, no point denying it. And once you had a kid coming out of a God School in the Pakistani highlands, your fear, the one you brought to the table, well that was ranked and ordered against other fears that eclipsed the sun.

"But I would hood them with empty sandbags and stand them spread-eagled against the wall, hands high over their heads. You pulled their feet right back, made them support their weight against the wall with their fingertips."

Sometimes he did this to a group of people. A few hours standing with six or eight of their friends arrested at the same time. At first they took a lot of strength from the collective, which was exactly how you wanted it. Four or five hours in, they might have been questioning the return on their investment. They still had sandbags over their heads. They had no idea if the brothers were still there or if they were alone because they weren't allowed to speak. The hood cut off a great deal of who they were as autonomous people.

"So hour four you ask for a show of hands. Who's ready to have a conversation? You say something like: whoa, whoa, one at a time. They have no idea who all has raised their hands. But you can see the pennies individually drop. The hands start going up."

He had compliments from the people in intelligence, spooks and wonks. Good prep, the guys would say, they're talking. He was flying around more. The inquest was spreading and taking Mov with it across that land with no borders, defined simply by wherever he appeared. He didn't mind admitting that he loved the feeling of being every-where at once and virtually invisible. Anti-fame. Well, exactly. He once saw a famous movie producer waiting for a flight, hovered over by protective flight attendants who kept autograph hounds away and then whisked the man into a corner seat in business class.

"Oscar winner," Mov told Pegg. "You know the name although it doesn't matter. The guy's Gulfstream was probably in the shop."

Mov said he remembered the sense of satisfaction he felt as he took his own seat in the opposite corner of the cabin. Between him and the movie mogul—hunched over the *Wall Street Journal* in his sunglasses—a grid of businessmen making last calls before liftoff on their cell phone earpieces, pecking out last memos on their BlackBerrys. Tense with aspiration and thwarted desire. Every one of them packing an extra twenty or thirty pounds in their light blue shirts and tassel loafers. Every one of them sipping the complimentary champagne that only Mov and the producer had declined. Me and you, pal, Mov thought. We're free. And he felt pity for the rest of them. Slaving away on the outside without a clue about how anything actually worked.

"Gaming the system, he and I," Mov said. "We were inside the machinery looking out."

"A feeling you enjoyed," Pegg said.

"You don't enjoy it?" Mov said. "You don't like it on the inside of your machine, Thom? You don't secretly thrill to the work you're doing now over the work you did before? A lot of serious journalists would have considered an interview with me to be a big opportunity. Tell me honestly: were you dying to come in here and meet me?"

"Honestly, no," Pegg said. His tongue dry and raspy. "Although I still don't see where you and I . . ."

"Oh, there's a lot of me that's a lot like you, Thom. Just listen," Mov said. "We prepped a young guy in a back room at a civilian airport once. Nineteen years old."

And Pegg could hear that one crack in the air. He sat forward, then forced himself to relax. "Civilian airport?" he said. "Where was it?"

Mov considered the question. "Eastern Europe. The United Kingdom. Canada."

Romania. Manitoba. The point was that no matter where the prisoner was physically, he was in all the places where he might conceivably have been. The other point was that the prisoner was more than a God School grad, more than an indoctrination case. What they had there was a prisoner who was genuinely religious.

Pegg made to speak again. He inhaled to ask the question, *Which God?*

But Mov's hand went up. Don't. It doesn't matter. "The point is he had one," Mov said. "Once you have a God, the only point worth making about it is that you have one."

Pegg nodded grimly. Point taken.

And a closely held God, too. This was God in the very grain of the person. In the weave of all self-reflection. Nineteen, twenty years old. A bad age to encounter this kind of thing. There hadn't been enough years lived for contrary evidence to accumulate: life's ordinary disappointments and irregularities, all the superficial nicks and edges on which faith begins to snag and fray. He didn't pray aloud or rock in place. Mov looked him over when he arrived and saw a depth there that worried him.

"They needed him ready to talk inside three days. Ticking bomb scenario. He knows something event-specific. It involves a truck full of explosives or a bomb wired to a cell phone in a locker somewhere. Everyone involved in this case has a degree of urgency and the guy's just sitting in the regular cell on a bench. We haven't started to strip things away yet. I haven't. First thing I do is tell him I'm Israeli. Of course I'm not, but I'd claim to be whatever worked. And for a lot of prisoners, at this point in history, Israeli is the one they don't want to hear. It sets the stage. It says: between you and me it's personal. And nobody cares that you're here because of exactly that, because between you and me it's personal."

Mov talks to him in his own language. He talks to him in a dialect from his region. He uses slang you'd know only if you were raised there, if you were thick with the locals. The guy listens, humming noteless rhythms under his breath.

"Not too much early physical pressure. You can drive these types into an inner chamber. They have a consciousness with trapdoors. Something happens and the catch springs, they slide down a chute into the panic room of their soul. Then they're well and truly gone. You might as well let them go."

Mov worked at subtracting things in layers. He corrects the guy's pronunciation of a word in his own language. He tells him his father and brother have been arrested and are down the hall. He moves him to a cell with no furniture, no windows. On with the hood. On with the death-metal soundtrack. The cell is soundproof so Mov doesn't have to listen to it, a scything avalanche of machine noises and guttural German screaming. The volume is randomly varied. They bring him military rations in the middle of the night. After twenty-four hours they make him stand on a box. The music hasn't stopped. The guy moans. He falls and wakes himself up. He falls and wakes himself up again. Mov hasn't even raised his voice. The guy is going through all this like he's had practice. He asks to use a toilet and Mov leaves him to soil himself. He hasn't seen the light or felt a trace of life's regular heartbeat in twenty-four hours, thirty-six hours. He has been unmoored from sanity's anchors, pattern and repeat, stable rhythm.

"Then I turn the music off. Give the cell some heat. It was about five degrees centigrade in there. I take off his hood and sit him down. He's swollen around the eyes from where he's been banging his head against the wall, lacerations. But he's still with me. I haven't lost him yet."

Mov tells him some men want to talk to him. Just questions. The guy spits on the floor. "So it's going to get a bit more physical now. You ready to hear this?"

Pegg listened in the urgent gloom. His mind racing. He was thinking of Gerry, Hyacinth and the others just then, having heard a movement in the theater, in the cluster of shapes up there. A sniffle, a whimper. Pegg felt a surge inside him, not his guts, which were strangely silent. Something from the heart. He said: "I really, really need to suggest something."

HEROISM. TICKER-TAPE PARADE STUFF. Pegg had no business doing this kind of thing and he blamed the fact that both pocket bottles were now tragically empty. All that courage was inside him now and bleeding out. Better use it while it lasted.

"I'd like to suggest we let them go. Finish up this conversation on our own. It's brilliant, I mean. The story will be told."

"You think?"

"Yes, I do. Just let them go."

"Why not choose a couple?" Mov suggested. "That's what I've been doing. Keeps things moving along. Gives the whole event directionality without bringing us to our conclusion all at once, too suddenly."

"I can't choose."

"Sure you can. Pick two."

"No, no. I refuse."

"Make it three."

Pegg in a dream. Pegg in a terrible nightmare. He stumbled up to the end of the row where Gerry and the others were sitting.

"Are we going?" Gerry asked. "I have a sick one here."

"Who's sick?"

"Isaac needs his inhaler. He dropped it somewhere."

"Take Isaac and another one," Pegg said. "You're going."

Gerry stood and then sat. Then stood again and said quite loudly, "By age. We do it by age. That's Barker and Sam."

Pegg took the boy Barker and the little girl Sam, holding both their hands in one of his. Then Isaac. Then the next youngest one, Ashley.

"I have four, Mov. There's a sick one here."

Then he moved across the sloping floor towards the side doors opening onto the lobby, pausing there. Wondering at the logistics of it for the first time.

"Take off the vision," Mov called.

Right, right. Pegg stripped away the mask and blinked into darkness again. Then he pushed open the door, slowly, slowly. "Eyes shut," he said to them. "It's bright." And then into the glass-walled lobby, which was lit from all the lights in the square outside. Into the whitest light he could remember having endured. It was painful. He took a step and waited, hoping he was seen. Another step, another long wait. They were on the marble now, broken glass underfoot. Pegg was humming to himself. He heard it suddenly, an intensely alien sound. A tune he didn't know. An impulse he didn't remember.

"It's me!" he called out. "It's Thom Pegg!"

Outside it was Friday afternoon. Indian summer with hovering storm. And in the air a thousand shivering notes at once, slips and cricks and jostles. The attention of the waiting square swiveling and locking in place. He heard the oiled movement of rifle parts and felt the crosshairs tickle his scalp. His sight was returning. People were screaming in the distance. Yells and catcalls, yelps and hollers. It sounded like sports crowd noises.

"It's me!" he called out again. "Thom Pegg."

On the steps there was now a flurry of movement, a terse economy of shapes low to the ground. Several people coming forward, scuttling up the stairs. Silent. When they were close Pegg could see that they were soldiers of the midnight black variety, everything about them oiled over and invisibilized, face paint, gloves. He released the children, who were now wailing, crying. They were scooped up and carried away. Gone instantly and over the barricades.

"I need to speak to Bruce Haden," he said to the one soldier remaining.

"Don't know him," the man said. "Tell me how many."

"He's federal, I think."

"Psychos and hostages, sir," the soldier said, taking Pegg's arm and persuading him with a single tug down to one knee. They knelt that way face to face, the man's rifle sited past Pegg, through the broken glass and into the lobby. "Please tell me now, sir. I need the how manys."

Pegg told him. One hostage taker. Pegg himself plus six kids: Gerry, Roshawn, Laisha, Reebo, Hyacinth, Metric. And the man repeated what he said into a throat mike, his words clipping in behind Pegg's. Seven total, roger that. The six kids were all together, rear placement.

"The guy is calling himself Movsar Barayev," Pegg said.

"We know that. And what does he have, sir? Bomb, guns, what else?"

Bomb, Pegg told him. Briefcase. Handle. Can't be moved. The soldier nodded and held up a gloved hand. Stop there. He was listening intently now to someone talking at the other end. "Yes sir. GPS trigger."

He listened some more. "Roger that," he said, then to Pegg: "Don't ask for any more to be released. We're going to let it flow from here."

"All right," Pegg said. "But Haden. Get to Haden and tell him the man is wearing night-vision."

"Just keep him talking. Near the stage if possible. Try to keep some distance between you two and the hostages, yes?"

Pegg nodded, bewildered. And the soldier leaned to his shoulder again, listening. He said: "Out." Then clapped Pegg on the arm, spun on his knee and scuttled off down the steps and over the barricade. Entirely non-human in his movement and speed. Like a turbo-charged crab.

ON HIS WAY BACK INSIDE, after strapping back on the vision, Pegg was crushed with guilt. It just dropped on him, this emotion of which he was keenly aware, but only in the air around him. Not so well personally acquainted. Black guilt. He'd never even thought about the producer and the paramedic woman actually lying there. He'd sort of had them in a wing of the special effects trailer. Flash, bang, they're dead and then they disappear. All very tidy.

He looked for them and found them. She lay collapsed near the front wall, just inside the door. Pegg got to his knees next to the body and touched her throat. He had never touched a corpse before and was surprised that it seemed so familiar a feeling, as if the fingers come preloaded with the knowledge of what death is, its tactile emptiness, the flatness of it, the grain of the skin as the oils lose their temperature. His fingers touched where the pulse would have been and bounced away. She was rolled to one side, not much blood or mess. Dark stains only across the chest. Body twisted and rigid. The producer wasn't far away, just up the aisle. But Pegg didn't touch him.

"And how'd that go?" Mov asked him when he approached the stage. "Out there."

Mov was sitting on the edge of the stage, legs swinging.

"What do you want to have happen here?" Pegg asked.

Mov patted the stage next to him but Pegg remained where he stood. He saw Mov's shoulders round in resignation. "In the end, they come inside. Of course."

"In a big fireball, is that it? You want that."

"Let's not get ahead of ourselves."

"What do you want from me?" Pegg asked, voice cracking.

Mov regarded him steadily. The slight tilt of the goggles might have reflected amusement. "There's one person on earth who understands your life, a single person to whom you can really tell your story, to whom you can really confess. It's never a priest. It's a mirror individual, somewhere, sometime. You're the one for me, Thom Pegg. It couldn't be clearer. You've already written my story, lived my life."

"Then let the kids go," Pegg said. "Let them go and you confess or do whatever it is you need to do."

"Just you and me?" Mov said. "Is the child all right? The sick one."

"I don't know. I don't . . ." And here Pegg was effusively sick himself into the front row of seats. It volcanoed out of him. A mercury flow of vomit. Booze puke, acid on the windpipe, scoring the throat and the back of the nose. He gagged extensively, breathed some of it back into his windpipe, exploded outwards again. Retching. Wretched. He wiped his mouth on his jacket sleeve, then tore the jacket off and threw it into the seats.

"Don't hurt them!" Pegg yelled. "Just don't hurt them!"

Mov waited. Then continued as if Pegg hadn't spoken. The prisoner. What to do next. Nudity and stress positions. Pegg collapsed to the carpet, sat in a heap.

Well, the prisoner had spit on the floor. What you might call active resistance. So physical pain was introduced. Subtle, naturally. Guised under the suggestion that it was self-inflicted. To this end: cuff the detainee and put him in a stress position. Short shackling, for example, meaning you chain him by his neck to the floor with a chain too short to let him stand. The chain from his neck up to the eyelet in the wall didn't allow him to lie down either.

"Twelve hours in that position and you don't hate the chain or the guy who fastened it there. You hate your own body. You go hostile with the envelope of your own flesh. You want it to die, and for you to continue living. A separation and a double bind. Interesting. Things that seemed like options start to go unconscious, they start to wink out."

Pegg was reviewing the possibility of being sick again, greatly facilitated in the process by the wafting aroma of his previous sick. He muttered, phlegmy: "Jesus Christ."

"Who, since you mention him, is a weak-ass wingman under these circumstances," Mov said, rising from his seat on the edge of the stage and walking back towards the two chairs where they had been sitting. "Muhammad far better, in my experience. This guy did twelve hours and said nothing. Didn't even open his eyes. And here, for the first time, I did really wonder if I'd done him. Driven him inside, down the chute to the panic room."

Pegg followed Mov and sat opposite him, his voice recorder on the table between them.

There were a range of come-back-to-me type maneuvers, Mov explained. It's not like this had never happened before. In the old days, this was the point when electricity was introduced. Now, more sensitive times meant more thoughtful escalations.

Mov slapped the guy hard in the chest, grabbed his shirt and shook him. He let him rest a minute and repeated the move, slap and shake. About the fourth time he saw the man's eyes shock open. He didn't want another one. So there they were, face to face, the world shaping itself as it had to be. Mov and the young man, no room for his God. And Mov, unlike any God he'd yet encountered, had plans and contingencies. He pulled the man's shirt up and smacked him across the belly, palm flat. It made a sound like: *pock, pock.*

"Like knocking on a coconut. Blows the breath out of him, keeps him wide awake, leaves no marks."

Pock, pock.

The guy is staring at Mov. He can't close his eyes now. Something critical has changed. And that was the sign Mov was waiting for. Out of the cell, away from the chains, the low ceiling, the chill, the buckets of water, the duct tape and cling wrap. And across the hall into a bigger room, straight chair, low lights, no pictures on the wall, no windows, no music. Time for a little Alice in Wonderland.

"Three questions at the same time. Things he couldn't possibly know. Then a single question over and over. Then silence. Changing my voice the entire time, talking falsetto, talking like Groucho Marx, talking like Elvis. There's a degree to which you push this kind of thing and the walls of a sanity start to bend. People talk just to make you stop."

"Did it work?"

"Just listen!" Mov yelled at him, lunging forward.

Pegg jolted backwards in his chair, shocked to silence.

"Of course it worked," Mov said, smiling at the effect he had achieved. "People don't like to be disoriented. You'd talk, and he did too. I held up one hand. I said: 'Save it. I just need one more thing.'"

Pegg waited. He was bruised with the story. He was beaten by it. He was in a stress position himself, chained to a wall and banging his head.

"I told him: Tell me that your God isn't here. Not that he doesn't exist somewhere. Just that he's not in this room. Not with you now. Tell me that we're alone. Tell me that your God has taken a powder and left you here with me."

And he did. A confession that had nothing to do with secrets and locations and plans, codes and targets. Only belief. Mov cracked his faith and offered his denouncement back to him, that critical-system failure, as a viable way out.

"He took it. And I left him sitting there with a cup of tea and went to make a phone call. Your man is prepped. They showed up in less than an hour. He lasted twenty-four, as best I can make out. Died during interrogation the next morning, hands shackled to a window frame behind him, doused with cold water. Some of them die when you do this, and he turned out to be one of them. I was at home, asleep."

"What happened?"

"Well we didn't get the ticking time bomb, did we? So presumably something exploded somewhere and people were killed. I never heard. There were too many of those events to keep track. I was left thinking about how the kid had renounced his God and then died."

Mov stood saying that, losing some of his calm and remove. And Pegg too felt a familiar failing within. Like losing everything. Sources exploding. Lies chasing each other around the room and out the door. It was the way the editorial director of one of the big papers told him on the phone: *Well, I guess that's the end of it then.* But Pegg knew when hanging up that it wasn't the end of anything. There was a surge, a splintering, a terrible suction as if water were rushing, oceanic distress. But that wasn't the end. That was barely the beginning of the fall, barely the start of losing it all, alone over the abyss and the abyss rising fast.

"Then you changed your mind about things," Pegg said. "And things got worse."

Regret, remorse. *Homo paenitentia.* But Mov didn't remember just becoming regretful. He remembered beginning to lose his mind. He remembered not holding it together for a week then dropping an assignment midway, after driving some old man into the panic room, never to be recovered. An important asset, that one. Mov fucked it up.

"Tell me the rest," Pegg said.

Mov told all. He confessed his guilt to his own bosses. Oddly, it wasn't the young man's death that plagued him, Mov told them. It was the idea that he'd made things complicated between the young man and his God, right at the critical moment.

"Imagine, confessing guilt to your boss about something like that," Mov said. "Nothing comes of it. The confession does nothing to help you."

He was given time off. Then he was fired.

"Ask your friend Haden about that if you like," Mov said.

"You worked for Bruce Haden."

"Haden or someone like Haden. The shadows are long and they're full of Hadens."

Pegg had only met one Haden. But that was enough to convince him that Mov was right. The shadows teemed with Hadens. "Keep going."

After being fired, things began to unspool at home too. Suppressing violence became difficult, Mov told Pegg. Some monster, strong enough to handle the tensions of the moment, stole into him and filled out his every contour. One day while taking the dog around the block for a piss, he yanked on her leash so hard the old bitch ended up at the veterinary hospital. Eye hemorrhage. And there were other things: episodes, outbreaks, meltdowns, moments of genuine fear and madness. Some spore was loose in the house, he remembered distinctly thinking. But Mov was the only one breathing it in.

She kicked him out. She kept the child.

"Your boy," Pegg said.

And here came the settling of darker times just when it seemed impossible that things could get any darker. Strange currents. An inward turning.

Mov went quiet. He said nothing for a full minute before Pegg reached down and touched the tape recorder sitting on the low table between them. Touched the key and turned the machine off.

"Just you talking," Pegg said. "Nobody listening but me."

Mov waited, then spoke. "Ever felt like you were being watched? Like you were no longer anonymous in crowds, no longer alone in your own home? Ever felt lifted out, selected and acquired, like you were a targeted individual?"

Pegg's guts rolled and flopped. His spleen bleated. His bladder did a spit-take. He felt the wet below.

Men on foot in black ball caps. Men in cars, one fender dented, one hubcap missing, aerial bent at right angles. They had a routine revolving around Mov's entering or leaving a building. When he entered they honked their horns, when he left they flicked their brights. They made themselves known.

"Gang Stalking," Pegg whispered. "They call it Gang Stalking."

"I wondered for a long time, then went online. Common symptoms, these."

Blocked off in parking lots, passed and re-passed by the same vehicles. A particular fire station seemed to be involved. Again and again he'd see the ladder truck, the chief's SUV. They'd wink their sirens at him as they passed. Smirks and glances. They had him. He was targeted. They kept it up even after he moved, left his apartment because they'd moved into the one across the way.

"Ever notice someone new in the hallway outside your apartment and then get the feeling they'd been waiting to see you? You leave and the man is just leaving his place. He stops with the door open and you can see past him to all the equipment, the stacked receivers and transmitters, the black gadgetry, the antennae and directional microphones. I'm describing madness, right?"

Pegg didn't answer.

"Madness, of course. And yet not so terribly implausible. It's not just me thinking we live in toxic times. Whom do you trust, Thom? Your doctor. Your drug company. Is the government corrupt? What about banks and billionaires? All aboveboard? Ask someone. Ask someone on the street who used to read Thom Pegg. Ask them if the system is still one that reflects who they are on the inside. Ask them if the anthems don't ring a little flat, if the flags aren't subtly but indelibly stained. Whom do they trust? You can bet the list is short and there's not a powerful person on it. Our cattle are cloned. Our seeds are terminators. Our pipelines are full of blood."

He'd arrive home and all the lights would go on at once in the building across the street. One morning, he started his truck and noticed a man in the side mirror, crouched down on the passenger side near his rear wheel. Mov got out and went around. The man had left a kitten under his tire.

"This had a certain effect on my state of mind. I saw signs everywhere. Stickers at the bottom of rear windows, especially pickup trucks. Fuzzy dice, St. Christopher medals, motorcycle club paraphernalia, marijuana flags. I saw women with kids too close in age, like they were props. The kids would be left in the vehicles when the women got out to follow me on foot. But the vehicles, those were key."

"How so?" Pegg asked.

License plate numbers, Mov told him. You could track those. They were real data.

"You wrote down the license plate numbers of people who were following you."

He wrote them down, Mov said. He also memorized them. "4SYU671, 7B91708, 2PHX588, 1800711 (TAXI), 4YQT562, 4X94202. For example."

"You've memorized license plate numbers," Pegg repeated.

"Perpetrators, stalkers," Mov said. "Just to give you an idea. 3DKA445, 16Z1021, 3STA138, 6L03811, 4LBG661, 4TEV602, DID4MEL, 2YLM477, 4GPA456, 22107, 4XAD002, 03183, 3PTR069, 2NZP651, 4BFL607, 4MVE232, 3LMC452, 3XMA297, 4CBJ974, 4EDT696, 4JLT436, 7F1850, 4JFK922, 2PLT526, LA DAD, 5CLC219, 4VLH756, 3XNC574, RRT 868 (OR), JK65587, 4VRE879, 3VAV141, 2VON186, 3VCT167, 3WNV662, P60KDK, 4WVG799."

"Okay," said Pegg. "I get the picture."

But that didn't stop the flow. Mov scrolled on through his list. Dozens of license plates. Dozens of dozens. An incomprehensible screed of letters and numbers until Pegg thought the sound of it had become a kind of torture in itself. 4MHW247, 5625511, 3NNY540, 4URH695, 5DIJ795, 2UTL078, 535TNF, 4S44767, 4ULW516, 4DUG492, 4PEB958, 5DTV565, ZEPOLL, 88A01, 4YJ4721, 3P42709, 4RGW962, 5BBE906—

"Stop!" Pegg yelled over the rising din of it. "I get it!"

"I believe you do," Mov said. "I believe you're beginning to see how it's done. This whole business. Fame and anti-fame. They both grind down to some point. Some solving value when appeasement is required, a sacrifice. And then we feed someone into the machine. We tear someone down and discard them and things return to normal. We run the video of the politician caught with the transvestite prostitute or the tape of the actor delivering a drunken, racist rant. And we feel much better about ourselves, thank you very much. Those pictures of Abu Ghraib, same thing. We didn't need to *approve* of torture to walk away from those images feeling more righteous than we had the moment before. Aren't these things that you and I know better than most, Thom?"

Pegg thought he might be having a heart attack. His chest was alive with syncopation and stutter steps. His heart doing a frantic two-step, his guts aflame. But they were getting somewhere here. Maybe the machineries of fame and anti-fame were nasty fraternal twins. The one crass, known and symbolic; the other serious, concealed and terribly real. And maybe there were kills involved either way to make us feel secure, to keep the public peace. Kills symbolic and kills real. Maybe Mov the lunatic was right in his way.

But that wasn't the story. Or not the heart of it. Because in the madness of Gang Stalking, in the madness of that long list of license plate numbers loomed a darker dimension.

"There's more to this," Pegg said, coughing, gagging, recovering. "I'm just getting it."

"And me about you too," Mov said. "Our moment has arrived. Epiphanies all around."

Two goggled creatures, surrounded by the sounds of fear, the smell of death.

"You really are sick, aren't you?" Mov said.

"Not feeling so great at the moment, I admit," Pegg answered.

"But you've actually got something. A real medical condition."

"I can't confirm or deny that," Pegg said. "But about you . . ."

"Pancreatic cancer," Mov pressed. "Sclerosis."

"This is more than revenge for you, isn't it, Mov? More than just payback. Make no demands. Remain silent. It's not revenge, or not revenge only."

"How long do you have?" Mov asked, leaning forward. "A humid summer, a lousy fall. A couple more winters and it starts getting speculative. You running on fumes, Thom?"

"It's about turning people against themselves," Pegg said. "I just realized this part. That's what you're trying to do here: turn us all in on one another. Turn the machinery onto itself."

They sat in silence for several seconds. Then Mov sat back, sharply. "Or no," he said. "No, no, no. Oh God, how could I have missed this?"

Pegg waited. He'd been right in his reading of Mov, he was certain. Now, it occurred to him, Mov was about to be right about him.

"You're a hypochondriac!" Mov said, a smile spreading across his face. "Acute, fucked-up, self-diagnostic. I love it!"

The great uncovering. From the Greek word *apokalupsis*. The two men staring at each other. And it was a little like the old days, Pegg had to agree. The story cracked open. The head-rush of truth. Only no pleasure in it for Pegg this time.

He wanted his night-vision gone. He reached up and unbuckled himself. Freed himself of sight, if not of knowing. But in the darkness there was only deeper clarity, as if he could finally see the man and all the invisible agony to which he had contributed even as it had shaped him. Pegg saw it all laid out in the blackness. Mov's final bid for restoration was a great monkey wrench thrown into the guts of the machinery that had destroyed him. And when he was finished, nobody would know who to blame, who to fight, who to hate, who to punish or sacrifice including themselves. Chaotic malfunctioning.

Generalized madness and paranoia. All against all. And not just any event could be used to precipitate such a state of affairs. Mov knew his stuff on the topic of beating out of people the response required. Keep them in darkness. Strip away the layers. Listen for the sound of links breaking within. Alice in Wonderland.

"It was critical the hostages be children, wasn't it, Mov?"

"It's not exactly a new idea," Mov said. "History is strewn with tiny, perfect skeletons and infant mummies of ideal stature. Look under the Pyramid of Tenochtitlan or on top of Mount Ampato, under the grass at Woodhenge or in the ashes of the fires at Carthage."

"But it's going to be just the one, in this case," Pegg said, his throat constricting. "You're going to drag this all out until only Hyacinth is left, aren't you, Mov?"

"They picked her, Thom. They made my job even easier than I could have predicted. I'm only following the course that was pre-selected."

"You can't do it," Pegg said. "You're saying the words. That means you understand what you're doing. That means you won't really be able to do it."

"But there's the beauty of it," Mov said. "I don't have to do anything. As soon as you leave, Thom, as soon as you're out there in front of those cameras—and you can bet there will be a lot of them—they'll come and do it for me. The men will come. The men whose names are secret, whose existence is denied. They'll come and do what they do. But there's no getting around the briefcase in my hand, either. It is what it is."

Pegg was sobbing. It was around midnight, Friday. About the point in the Moscow crisis when one of Barayev's men fired a shot out of the theater and over the barricades because he wanted to make things happen. Those ghosts in the Russian Special Forces heard him loud and clear. They consulted amongst themselves, then granted him his wish: the convulsive act by which they no doubt hoped that peace would finally be restored.

And here all of them were quite similarly poised, and hoping just as much in vain. They were waiting for nothing here, less than nothing. No amount of death would bring about the cathartic reversal, the turning aside, no matter how apocalyptic an event Mov managed to invoke. Because something had soured, all right, prepping that young man for interrogation. Something curdled, went rancid. But not just in the soul of Mov—in all of them. Killing the young man had obviously earned them nothing. No information, no temporary calm, no saved lives, no return of peace, not even a minute's worth, for their bottomless investment in death. It had only spawned more war and more death and the newspapers were full of it. And that failure wasn't just driving Mov crazy, it was driving them all crazy. It was making everybody suspicious, seeing things in the shadows behind everyday objects, people, events and currents. Gang Stalkers. Well, exactly. Pegg used to think: nine parts psychiatric to one part real. But that wasn't the explanation. Gang Stalking was one hundred percent social infection, a cultural contamination of the deadliest and most contemporary kind. It was what you got when the machinery stopped working. Distrust gone 360 degrees. Pegg knew it well, having been infected once himself. And now Mov wanted to contaminate them all. Set them shaking and shimmying downwards into patterns like this one. Huddled together in a feverish dream, counting missing hubcaps and memorizing license plate numbers. Wearing indigo ribbons in support of the Targeted Individuals who were *everywhere*. Everybody quivering in the hood of darkness, waiting for the return of normal.

And all entirely without point, since nobody would survive to tell the true story and so nothing could possibly be learned. Not from Mov clearly, who dead or alive would be someone's dark secret. Not from Pegg either, who knew in his heart that he'd been thrown into the fire.

Something sudden, Thom. But you mustn't be frightened. Wait for that critical moment. Then hit Play.

Pegg's fingers fumbling blind for the button, for the sequence of beeps that would bring the machine to life. Pegg didn't know what Haden would do on hearing this. He wasn't supposed to know. Pegg was a walking microphone, Haden's ear on the inside and nothing more. Dispensable. A sacrifice. He might push this button and cause the blade to fall. But he didn't care. Pegg needed to hear the recording himself, right that second. Nothing else mattered.

Midnight. And from the air now, a tiny voice. It warbled up from the past and into the pressed moment.

Micah Swenson Pegg. He lived with his mother in the house where they had all once lived. Pegg felt the egg crack, the yolk spill. He heard the boy say what he had said to his father, clear-eyed and unprompted: "What did the skeleton say when he walked into a bar?"

They waited a beat. One very long beat.

EVE

—

THE NIGHT BEFORE, RABBIT HAD TOLD HER that he'd meet her downstairs at the Panda Grove with whatever information Jabez was able to produce. So that afternoon, at the time they'd chosen, Eve made her way down those Stofton sidewalks, past the crowds milling in front of the corner stores, dark shapes in brown light.

In the Panda Grove front bar, Eve watched the crowds watching the news, grumbling amongst themselves. Flames and smoke were now rising from the darkening plaza, some kind of vigil bonfire. Or more than one, as there seemed to be rival camps. Tents had gone up under the raking cameras. The Call lined the far sidewalks, standing or sitting in folding deck chairs, singing *I know my savior lives . . .* while across the way the Black Bloc gave interviews and denounced the media. A camera had been broken, a crew from a cable news program chased away, pieces of brick thrown. Everywhere, sudden movements. A truck lurched to a stop, black smoke coughing from a vertical pipe. A group of young men ran from an alley. A shout went up from somewhere. A banner failed in the steady wind, ripping free of its wooden frame, the paper winging across the plaza, crumpled and tumbling.

There were jolts and starts in the air. Eve felt it as a tension in the body. A reflected jitters, as if everybody around her were poised to run, poised to do something. Act now. Act first. On the Beaufort scale, somewhere below a storm there was a rating for the kind of wind that picked up only garbage.

The release of the four children late on Friday afternoon didn't ease the mood. For the first time there was a press conference involving the released, two girls, two boys. They sat with their parents, straight and quivering. They moved hair back off their faces with open palms and tried to smile. When the questions came pouring towards them, they did not flinch, blanch, cringe. One of them, named Ashley, turned away at the end and cried in her seat. She was five. She said, *I'm sorry, I'm sorry.*

Mixed reactions on the streets. There was evidence of a deepening dread in interviews. Some horror was shaping itself. People were sure of it and nobody could avert their eyes.

"What does it mean that the hostages have been winnowed down in this fashion? From over one hundred to just six now?" a host asked an expert. "Is the breakthrough coming?"

"No," the expert said, dark circles under his eyes. Everybody working around the clock. "There's no reason this has to end soon, except that law enforcement authorities typically do not let things go very far past the third day."

Eve watched the television over the heads of the crowd. She felt the expert's discomfort, his eyes continually sliding and shifting to objects off-camera. Then they went to commercials: lawn-care products, a pet insurance program, a Mexican resort destination for single seniors. The crowd at the Grove grumbled and speculated.

In a minute, the host was back. "To clarify, we have no information at this point about any planned assault on the building. Meanwhile in financial news, markets have reacted to . . ."

A jeer went up and Eve looked away. The Grove smelled of must, mildew, hidden fungal growth. Eve could hear the Beach Boys coming from a back room: *Wouldn't it be nice . . .* She walked through a room of dancing girls, all in jeans, sockless in vintage sneakers, T-shirts and coral necklaces. She found the stairs at the back of this room and went down. In the basement she could not see Rabbit immediately and was swamped with the thought of a seven-thousand-dollar check written to a man she didn't know to help another man she didn't know. She felt her heart rate tick upwards at the idea that this all could have been such a simple and dismal thing. A con.

Then Eve saw him, and was flooded with a mix of feelings. Relief, automatic thoughts of the night before. Their faces closing, his touch. But something else, stronger, woven through the moment: anticipation. Eve felt momentum, the pull of a current, the sense of unknown events in store. It had become an unfamiliar feeling, she thought, the future brimming with surprise. It excited her.

Rabbit was sitting under a mural of a dragon breathing a rolling geyser of fire, all colors mingled and sorted at the moment of destruction, from the white core out through the spectrum of reds and oranges and violets and iridescent greens to the final black singe of smoke that licked along the trailing edges, the final syllable of what the flame had to say.

She slid in next to him and brushed his shoulder with hers. Then she put a hand over his, squeezing lightly. "Hello," she said.

He took her hand carefully in his. Then he removed a piece of paper from his pocket and folded it into her palm, gently closing her fingers around it. He held her hand closed now, looking her squarely in the eyes.

"Secret stuff," Rabbit told her. "Address, phone number. Invitation to dinner. It's all there, passed along by Jabez."

"Wow," Eve said. And she breathed in deeply.

Rabbit let go her hand and she opened the paper, smoothing it flat on the table. He watched her hands, fine fingers, clean nails. The address was written in Rabbit's neat block letters. Eve said: "East Shore."

So that was it. Ali out there, not down here. Ali in a house, with a yard, with a driveway. What could it possibly mean for her to feel disappointment learning that? She didn't know. But there it was.

Eve looked up at Rabbit. Again the sense of pull, a future with renewed possibility. "Come with me," she said.

He looked at her. "Moral support?"

"Just come," she said.

Out to the street, then. Over three blocks to the truck. The air was smoky, distant fumes. Car alarms in the distance. In the truck she paused with her hand on the key. Rabbit was tracing a crack in the vinyl dashboard with his finger.

He said: "Ever bought an art installation before?"

Eve shook her head. "Ever sold one?"

"Never."

She waited for him to say whatever else was on his mind. But he was looking past her now, distracted. A man was standing on the far sidewalk swinging a mangled baseball bat against the iron grating on the front of a convenience store. People on the sidewalk nearby were standing back, watching. He hit the grate and the metal bars rang. He might have been doing it just to hear the sound. There were posters on the wall here, advertisements. A *masterpiece. The most. The last. The first. No joke. Unbeaten.*

There was a practiced quality to the second swing. But then a man came out of the store with a gun and people scattered. He waved the weapon in the air, then lowered it and stood in a quivering stance. There were shouts from farther down the way. Blunted voices.

Rabbit turned to Eve, returning to his thought. "I don't know why I need to tell you this."

"Because you've never told anyone else," Eve said.

"Maybe that's it," Rabbit said.

She waited.

Rabbit said: "About Oregon."

SO NOW EVE ALONE KNEW WHAT HAPPENED to Rabbit in Oregon. It didn't worry her to be in that position. It galvanized her interest in him. Eve now had different mental pictures to work with. Rabbit in a clean laboratory. Rabbit in conference rooms with team members. Rabbit waking up uncomfortably to how his ideas were actually going to be used.

"Nobody was dying as a result of my work, I realize that," Rabbit told Eve. "There were jobs at Raytheon and Intel where I could have worked on control systems for cluster bombs and joint stand-off weapons. I was working on a phone. I was helping design the newest, latest, hottest version of a device most people use to order pizza, text their friends."

But what a phone. What an idea. From a technical standpoint, it had been fun to work on. Naturally it was also an internet device and a video camera and a GPS and a music player. And yes, the prototype was also designed with an integrated biometric fingerprint and retina scanner, so the device was useless if it was stolen, and it could also log user medical information like blood pressure, blood type, pulse rates, et cetera. But the fact that it could do all those things was secondary to the phone's chief innovation, which was a function that would ultimately be invisible to its users.

"And what was that?"

"It listened to you," Rabbit said.

Eve thought about that one for a second or two. "Don't all phones listen to you?"

"Not actively," Rabbit said. "They just transmit. And even so, they generally don't transmit unless you're on a call."

Eve was trying to work this through. "The phone was designed to eavesdrop?"

User intelligence, they called it. Or sometimes: behavioral finger-printing. The phone was designed to sample the life of its user: ambient noises, television shows on in the background, music choices. The system then synched that data up with all the other information collected—downloads, GPS logs, voice traffic, medical data—and built a user profile that allowed the device to assemble phone books or web links, push ads and suggestions at you through the browser, even dial 911 and transmit medical data in the case of certain medical emergencies.

"Which was maybe a little more phone than some people would want," Rabbit said. But what was a lot stranger, what really got into Rabbit's head and wouldn't come out, was the client-side request late in the project timetable for silent dial-out functions.

"Silent what?" Eve asked.

Dial-out. These capabilities enabled the phone to upload user pro-file data to pre-set third-party locations.

"As in, without people knowing," Eve said.

Rabbit shrugged. Conceivably without them knowing, yes. The phone could have been designed to do that. He, personally, never got that far with it.

"Because you realized all this would be completely illegal?" Eve asked.

"It wasn't illegal to test it," Rabbit told her. "We were designing a prototype. A feasibility study."

MADDAM, the client called it. Massively Distributable Data Acquisitions Module. Rabbit didn't remember thinking once about what the device might represent if half the country or half the world owned one until that late client request that upload features be de-veloped. And if there was any chance Rabbit was going to get his head

around that part, there was much less of a chance the following morning when a whole raft of new nondisclosure agreements were shipped
over by the client's lawyer to be signed immediately and returned.
Rabbit signed. But why the paranoia? What exactly had they been
working on?

"Maybe we really were just tossing around ideas for a super-smart
phone," Rabbit said. "But that morning I realized I just didn't know.
Maybe I was developing the most sophisticated low-maintenance
wiretap the world had ever seen. Selling people stuff and surveillance
have a big overlap, if you're seeing my point here."

"I am. And I'm scared to ask the next part," Eve said.

Rabbit nodded. He knew where this all led if you thought about it.

"Who was the client?" Eve asked.

"Short answer?" Rabbit said. "Nobody I worked with had any idea.
We used a code name in house. Blue 52."

"Blue 52," Eve said. "And who did you think that might be?"

Rabbit looked at Eve steadily. "I didn't know. I would have been
guessing, and looking at those agreements that morning it suddenly
occurred to me I didn't want to start guessing. I thought: Maybe there
is no client. The phone was our only project. Maybe Blue 52 was my
employer. You understand?"

Eve thought she did. She had different mental pictures for Rabbit
now. Rabbit alone in the evening. Something troubling him, making
him afraid. The idea that he may have been in place on a game board,
playing a role quite different than the one he'd imagined. The idea
that all along he had been playing as a mole.

"And here came the big epiphany," Rabbit said. "It was a real if-then
situation."

"What's that mean?"

"If A, then B. Meaning I understood the moment to be one of
choosing."

He went to a rep house called the Starlight Theater that same evening. He didn't even know what was playing. But he'd been thinking about his parents, who'd been gone almost two years at that point. And he suddenly needed the anonymity of darkness. Turned out it was the Errol Morris film *Gates of Heaven* with a short first: *Werner Herzog Eats His Shoe*. Rabbit was preoccupied, hardly paying attention, his mind running back and forth between childhood memories and the things he'd just learned at work. He had a sense of being involved in something sophisticated, but also crude and primitive. Something that took the world backwards. Then Werner Herzog spoke off the screen, across thirty years, to Rabbit alone.

"I'll never forget the words," Rabbit told Eve. "Herzog said: 'If you switch on television it's just ridiculous and it's destructive. It kills us. And talk shows will kill us. They kill our language. So we have to declare holy war against what we see every single day on television.'"

Holy war. Blue 52. Fewer than a dozen other people in the theater. Rabbit frozen with a handful of popcorn halfway to his mouth. There was something going on here. Some other business, vast and spreading and, Rabbit felt certain, highly toxic.

"Herzog said: 'Give us adequate images. We lack adequate images. Our civilization doesn't have adequate images. And I think a civilization is doomed or is going to die out like dinosaurs if it does not develop an adequate language or adequate images. I see it as a very dramatic situation.'"

"So what did you do?" Eve asked.

"I thought of my parents," he said. "I just focused on that. Then I stopped showing up for work. It was the craziest conviction. Like I was at the very brink of doing something terrible and just had to bow out."

"Weren't people upset?"

"They were," Rabbit said. "But I never returned any of the calls.

A couple weeks later I got a big severance check. I think they were worried."

"So nobody came after you."

"No," Rabbit said. "Although I went and lived on the beach for about four months. Anybody coming after me would have concluded I'd wigged out. Probably because I had wigged out."

Rabbit told Eve he drove out to the dunes for the first time that night he saw the film about Herzog. It was June. He lay down under a bank of sand crested over with long, soft grass that he could pull down over himself like a blanket. He lay there, hidden from the world. He slept and dreamed of high mountain fields, open views, places that reminded him of home but were not quite what he remembered from home. He woke when the moon came up, a radiant disk. Rabbit lying there in the sand, under the grass, washed in silver light. Stars exploding in their infinite patterns above. He was thinking of his parents.

If, then. Well, Rabbit thought. If I've been doing something I didn't realize all along, if I've been contributing to some project the authors and objectives of which I don't even know, then either I'm helpless and might as well go back to work, or it's time to prove that I can choose, that I can act, that I create something of my own.

THE SKY RELEASED A THIN SHEET OF WATER and there were many memories in the sound of it, striking the metal hood of the truck and making the big tires sing. The sheen of the pavement and the slap of the wipers. The shape of them carving back and forth, endlessly countering one another. Eve had slept with these in her dreams, so many times. Her father at the wheel. Ali next to her at the side window, looking out.

Rabbit held Jabez's instructions on his knee, but Eve knew the way. East Shore, the words sounding strange in her own mouth, in her thoughts. All that time and he was in East Shore.

Eve's hands were opening and closing on the wheel.

"You all right?" Rabbit asked.

"This feels so abrupt. Everything so sudden. Finding him and going out to see him. But everything else too. My whole life in motion. I don't know. Sorry, I'm nervous."

"I'm nervous half the time," Rabbit said. "It just means you're up high somewhere. You might fall. But things are happening. Things you care about." He looked over at her while she drove. "And you found your brother, so this is huge."

"It's huge," Eve said. "Sure it is."

"I'm excited for you." He was still watching her drive, and Eve felt the gaze although it didn't make her uncomfortable.

"I'm excited too," she said. "Excited. Nervous. A little angry too, honestly, finding out he's been living in East Shore all this time. He could have called."

He smiled at her profile, then turned to look back out at the street. They were crossing a bridge, the water invisible far beneath. There was a police barricade blocking traffic returning to the city. Over the hump of the bridge Eve felt herself falling into it, the old routes and throughways. Old sight lines, a familiar unfamiliar. The long slope of the hill. The rock escarpments and twisted trees. The rain came and stopped, then started again. She slowed when passing the house where they'd lived as kids, picking out the window that had been hers, the tree that her father had planted now towering over the lawn.

On the radio they were airing a live interview with a spokesperson for the police department. Do not go to the Heights. Do not drive or walk. You will be turned back. Police would be asking people already in the plaza to leave. Safety, the man was saying. It was a safety precaution. He wouldn't say any more. Safety from what, from whom? Rabbit reached over and turned the radio off.

Ali's house was down a crescent with a hidden cul-de-sac. Other houses peered from within the trees here, familiar sixties bungalows, modest faces. A simple lawn and roofline, a carport. She watched the addresses, numbers on mailboxes and front doors. And when they came to the right house, Eve pulled the truck to the shoulder, the flank of it pressing up into the shrubbery. A house like the others, its light sifting through the evening trees. A dog barked. She could hear children's voices and the sound of a television coming from one of the houses along the street. Lining the front walk of Ali's house there were small lamps in holders, a steady warmth among the fronds and leaves. Then a young woman opened the door, and she stood bathed in that light, a smile on her face.

"I'm so glad you came," the young woman said. And when she turned to call back into the house—*Ali, Ali. Your sister is here*—Eve could see that a large cross hung from the wall next to the front hall closet. A crucifix. A Christ.

Ali's wife's name was Kumi, late twenties, with a wide, unguarded face and long straight black hair. Sandals, skirt, pregnant and holding a toddler against her narrow hip. The boy's name was Francis. He had a twin sister named Yuko. Kumi was due in eight weeks, she told Eve. All this while Eve stood in the wood-floored front hall, bent over Francis. A nephew and a niece and another one on the way. She was an aunt and hadn't known that about herself.

Ali was in the room before Eve saw him. Rabbit touched her shoulder. She turned and there he was: Ali with Yuko on his lap, the little girl's black hair a straight version of Ali's dark curls, her dark skin against his pale forearm. Only Ali sat now in a low-slung wheelchair, canted solid wheels, aluminum dented from use. He rolled into the room and smiled up at Eve, swung open one arm. She leaned down into his shoulder and he squeezed her hard.

"I know, I know," Ali said. "I break my spine and I don't call."

Eve had promised herself not to, but she cried. The tears came on their own and moistened the cotton of his shirt near his neck. "Why didn't you?" she asked.

"Been away, you know."

"What happened?"

On the wall behind Ali, prints of the Buddha, a string of Tibetan prayer flags.

He said: "Four years ago. I fell off the roof of a warehouse. Don't do this if you can avoid it." Then he just held on to her and said how nice, how nice, how nice it was to see her, and it was wonderful to hear him say this even if there was still anger sifting through the mix of things she was feeling. All this sudden information released as if it had never been withheld. As if he hadn't abandoned her. But when Eve rolled her face away from him, tucking her chin down to hide her tears, Yuko was right there, very close. Up on her knees in Ali's lap. She reached up and took Eve's neck. She kissed Eve's mouth and said: "Daddy's auntie."

"*Your* auntie, baby. I'm your daddy's sister."

Rabbit stood back watching this with a half smile. He looked like he were trying to make himself small. But then Ali noticed him and extended a hand, and Kumi took his arm and pulled him towards the living room, down a hall lined with books. Eve walked past the colorful spines of hardcover volumes, names she hadn't seen since she was a child. Voltaire, Rousseau, Hume and Diderot. Books on art and archaeology. She stopped with her finger on the spine of a boxed set of Gibbon's history of Rome.

"Yeah, I know," Ali said. "Like a copy of Dad's library. Living around the block from our old house. The twists have been strange. The outcomes unexpected. Nobody is more surprised in all of this than me."

Eve didn't press the point. They'd been in each other's company for less than three minutes.

She walked into the living room where Kumi had led them, and where she tried to preside over polite pre-dinner small talk. A useless exercise. Ali had become like their father in this respect too. He did not do the human pleasantries well. And so he sat with his hands folded while Rabbit talked to Kumi. Until it was finally time to eat.

They went in to dinner. Kumi carried out a hotpot, rice and small plates. Eve saw back into the kitchen: the spice rack, the cupboards with the stainless pulls shaped like different vegetables, the food processor and the pots hanging on the far wall. Eve in turbulent, conflicted flow. She'd hoped to find him doing well, but all this domesticity threw her. She had no point of reference, no memory of him being like this before. And she knew she'd struggled herself with household routines at Nick's place. But these observations were then quickly lost in another one as Ali bent his head to pray over the food. Eve found herself staring at that remarkable sight. Ali in a wheelchair, brought down from his high places. And this: the finger to the lips, to the heart. The medieval regimen. Ali with a God.

They joined hands, awkwardly. Ali held Eve's fingers tightly just as she held Rabbit's. She couldn't close her eyes. They were locked now on the table, on her bamboo placemat. On the blue ceramic salad bowl, the near edge of which just hemmed into the top of her view. A household moon. Her neck hurt, bent down like that while her brother—roof climber, graffiti writer, shit disturber, substance abuser—her brother interceded on behalf of the troubled world. Ali prayed: " . . . that all those in the theater might be saved, the children and the hostage taker alike . . ."

They said "Amen." Kumi, Yuko, Francis, Ali last. The paternal punctuation. Rabbit sat still wearing his bemused half smile, fiddling his chopsticks in his hands. Eve put a hand on his leg under the table. He covered it with his own.

Food was served. Eve thought she could hear all of their thoughts zipping and singing through the complexities of the moment. Who should go first and what they should say. What ground to cover. All while the little dishes went around. Spinach, salmon, rice.

Then Ali began and Eve thought he had a new and unfamiliar voice. There was a certain gravity and calmness, a seeming dispassion. He had reached deep conclusions, Eve thought. Like someone to whom the world had been exposed by science. Although it wasn't science in this case but the other thing, the other source of bottomless certainty. The one they'd been taught as children to treat with aesthetic appreciation and respect—a verse, a statue, a ring that had belonged to a great-uncle who was a priest—but never to absorb into the personal system.

Ali was talking about the plaza, about Meme Media. They'd been mesmerized by the news for the past forty-eight hours, just like everybody else.

"It plays like a kind of movie," he said. "Which is probably because we all feel like we've seen something like it before."

He paused for Kumi to serve rice, his expression suspended.

Rabbit said, "I heard someone say the police have known who the hostage taker was from the beginning."

"Like we should be reassured," Ali said. "Some psychopath known to police. But I doubt it anyway."

He was taking spinach while he spoke, delicate chopsticks, quick sharp movements, the click of contact between wood and plate.

"Why doubt it?" Eve asked him.

He looked faintly uncomfortable, as if he'd now been trapped into saying something that he hadn't been planning to say. "It's just that show, *KiddieFame*," he said, glancing up at her, then back to his plate. "Maybe we should have seen it coming that someone would target that particular show."

Eve ate some rice and frowned.

"You disagree," Ali said. "I know that expression, Evey."

"I just wouldn't blame them for what happened," Eve said.

"I'm not blaming them. I'm blaming me," Ali said. "I mean me in the sense of those of us who watch the show. Don't you watch it?"

He had addressed this question to Rabbit, who shook his head, but then stopped himself. "Not regularly. I have a couple of times down at the Grove bar."

"I hate the whole idea of it," Ali said, wincing. "But if I'm clicking channels and I come across it, I can't turn the thing off."

"So it's a bad show," Eve said. "That doesn't mean kids deserve to be terrorized for being on it."

Eve got the feeling she'd awoken Ali somehow, saying so. His eyes were bright now as he formed ideas. He pointed his chopsticks at his sister. "What's looming, though? What is the threat in this situation?"

"That a child might get hurt, of course," Eve said.

"Exactly. But were we so angry when those same kids were getting lined up for one of these so-called Kills?

"I don't even watch the show," Eve said. "But this Kill thing they do is fake. In bad taste, maybe. But it's not real."

"I don't know about that," Ali said. "How alive are those kids outside of their competitive desire to be famous? How alive are we letting them be? Telling them fame is everything."

"You were a graffiti writer," Eve said, putting down her chopsticks. "What's not attention-seeking about that? I'm not criticizing. I enjoyed watching you be that person."

"Fair comment," Ali said. "I have no right to lecture. But my point remains that the show is destructive and we seem to enjoy that about it."

"Guns don't kill people," Eve said. "Celebrity does."

"Eve Latour, gold medalist, being sarcastic with me," Ali said. "Can't walk down a street without someone wanting to touch her."

Rabbit shifted in his chair beside her. Kumi too seemed poised, as if trying to think of something to say that might smoothly change the subject.

"Are we actually arguing?" Eve asked. "I haven't seen you in years."

"We shouldn't be," Ali said. "That's just my point, E. You've lived through all this yourself. You must have thought along these lines before."

She stared at her brother. Several seconds. Then she said: "Ali, where did you go? I needed you after Dad died and you were gone. That's more the lines which I've been thinking along lately."

Ali stared at her intently, leaning forward. "E, you mad at me?"

"Don't do that," she said. "I'm not laughing. I'm not seeing this as a big joke."

"It's boring, though, Evey," Ali said. "Addiction. Recovery. A bit of travel."

"Tell me about it, though. It's been a long time. And I've come here to find out what happened to you. I heard you went to Asia. Tell me about that."

"Tokyo," Ali said. "Which is where I heard about your gold medal, actually. You marrying the . . . what was he?"

"We never got married. We were engaged. He was a film director. His name was Reza."

"Eve and Reza. You know the last time I saw you?" Ali said.

Eve picked up her chopsticks again. "You better not tell me you saw me here in town and didn't even say hello."

"Shibuya," Ali said. "When I was in Tokyo, this is true, I saw your face on a huge news billboard in Shibuya."

"Well . . ." Eve said, and lost her words. She imagined her face up there above the traffic. Enormous and exposed. "Well, you should have called or e-mailed. Or texted. Meanwhile I return home and find you're gone. All the police can tell me is you didn't die here."

Ali raised his eyebrows. "You talked to the police?"

"Of course I did. You were a missing person," Eve said. "Why were you in Tokyo? Were you working there?"

Ali was teaching English and doing his art. Still hanging in there. Still trying to make it work. "But I was a failure," he said. "Bottom line."

"You weren't," Kumi said.

"I was," Ali repeated. "But fuck, I tried."

"Ali." Kumi glared at him.

He was making collages out of *hentai*. You could cut these pieces down small enough, he said, and any part of the human body could be used to make a flower, a forest. He was turning animated porn into formal Japanese flower arrangements. He never convinced a single gallery to touch the stuff.

Eve looked at her brother and saw how he had aged. Strange not to have thought of this before. In their years apart, they'd passed through some moment after which his face no longer looked just as she remembered. A bit of her father, true. But he would age into his own face, as they all did.

"Then you came back here," Eve said.

He looked across the corner of the table at her. Nodded.

"You sneaked back into town."

"I didn't sneak," he said. "Things weren't going so good for me, E. Ask Kumi. She was the one who kicked me out."

"I knew you were here," Eve said. "When Dad died. I knew you were here. Mom was on the coast. After the funeral I was so sure of it I went to the police a second time. Still nothing. Why the hell didn't you call? Why didn't you come to the funeral?"

"I was using," Ali said. "Do you have any idea what that means?"

"Using," Eve said. "I guess part of my problem was I never knew that. When I saw you the last time I knew things weren't going well. But if I'd known about the using, Ali . . . I would have tried to help."

Eve threw her napkin down onto the table and pushed back her chair. "Sorry," she said to Kumi, and she left the table, her throat tightening, her eyes threatening to release tears. But she pinched off all these symptoms, these ways to release, to vent. And when she was safely in the bathroom, the door closed quietly and locked behind her, she leaned on the counter, head down between her shoulders. Eyes closed. Shoulders silently heaving. She'd decided already that she wouldn't cry for Nick. Now it was time to decide that she wouldn't cry again for Ali either. When pushed close to tears, Eve thought, pressing her palms to her eyes, you simply had to learn something.

She washed her face. She saw that a set of stones were set up in a ring around a miniature torii gate on the counter. Some tapered candles. A long lacquered box with matches next to it. A plaque of praying hands above the toilet. She looked at herself in the mirror, looked into her own eyes. Why was she here? Because of a memory. Wind in his hair, up some structure somewhere. Ali elevated and unafraid. That memory had been so crucial to her.

You had to learn something.

Eve went back into the dining room. Ali was eating, talking to Rabbit, who looked up at her with concern. Kumi was just about to get the kids ready for bath and bed. Yuko said to Eve: "I love you."

Eve leaned down and kissed her. "I love you too, honey. I really do."

"I used to live on Sixth Street," Ali was telling Rabbit. "Bought my dope in that little park there." He was eating. Chopsticks in motion, muscles rippling along his arm. He had tattoos Eve had never seen before. Sacred heart, Celtic cross, Star of David. He was taking bean sprouts from a small dish, dipping them one by one in a dark sauce and delivering these to his mouth. He did so with a loose-wristed ease, elbow to the wooden table. A worn motion.

She sat down. "You know what I think about? I think about us climbing that radio tower. I think about how absolutely terrified I was."

Ali nodded. He said: "E, I really am sorry." He chewed and worked through his next thought. "Let me ask you something. Did you get along with Dad?"

Eve told him: "We kind of had a mutual agreement not to talk so much that we argued."

"He and I didn't have that agreement."

"Do you miss him?" Eve asked.

"I do," Ali said. "Although I also wonder why he was such a bastard."

"He always knew what he was doing," Eve said. "Why and to what end. It made him impatient."

Ali tapped his chopsticks on his plate. An unconscious, nervous movement.

Eve said: "I always thought you were the same. But with a different spirit somehow. Happier than Dad. So much freer."

Ali frowned, his fingers twisting a teacup in place on the tablecloth. The tea itself long cold. And the next thing he said seemed at first disconnected from what had come before. He looked at her, tilting his head in resignation. He told her about buying this house. About how much moving back to the neighborhood meant to him. He'd surprised himself, wanting it so much. He told her about his work too. He was part-owner of a language school downtown. Kids came from all over the world. A lot of Koreans and Chileans at the moment, but the thing went in cycles. He had partners and they'd done well financially. They'd recently expanded the facility, even bought other properties. He still went to Narcotics Anonymous meetings but had found a way to enjoy them. And Eve understood him to be telling her that whatever she thought, he was not like their father in always knowing what he was doing. Not why. Not reliably to what end.

"I didn't call," Ali said, "because I was ashamed. I was waiting for the time to be right. I'm glad you were more impatient. I'm glad you came looking. I'm lucky."

He put his hand over hers on the table. Then, after a moment, he took his hand back slowly and looked at Rabbit. "So what about you?" Ali said. "Why'd you quit the flowering alleys of Stofton? I liked those."

"I'm doing something new," Rabbit said. Then, after a pause: "You and Jabez are friends?"

Ali nodded.

"And Beyer?"

Ali smiled and nodded again. "At the beginning it was the three of us. You know that, right? Tight as thieves, Beyer and Jabez. Thinking the same thoughts and planning the same plans. That's always how it starts with mortal enemies."

After Kumi returned from the kids' room and they'd cleared the dishes, they all went into the living room to get the latest. The television sound on low. Lights shone on the front of Meme Media. The police were asking people to leave the plaza, but nobody seemed to be listening. There were thought to be as many as fifty thousand people in the area, cramming the side streets. You couldn't see the fountains. You could hardly see the trees. When the crowd moved, it rippled through itself. It had leveled up, become the larger organism. The thing with twitchy movements, limbs, reach, quantum unpredictability.

"I have to ask," Eve said, staring at the television.

Ali waited for her.

"God," she said. "Religion."

Kumi said: "We converted when I came over and we got married."

"Converted from what to what?"

Ali said: "From epicureans living in the moment to God freaks living in the moment."

"We're not God freaks, we're believers," Kumi said to Eve. Then to Ali: "And you weren't epicurean either. The term for what you were is hedonist-nihilist."

On the television a picture of people in an alley. They were tearing up the pavement and breaking it into pieces. They were loading these pieces into wheeled plastic garbage bins.

"So I'm back here. Tokyo is done. I'm strung out, putting up these line drawings on the roofs of warehouses in the approach path to the airport. These big dioramas, hands and feet and faces and fuck knows what."

Kumi said: "Language, please."

Rabbit said: "You might be interested to know that Beyer claims those now."

Ali shrugged. "Beyer was always like that. You know how Faith Wall happened? We were sitting around drinking beer and decided to put up a piece with a random word from each of us. I said faith. Beyer said wall. Jabez said revolution. Beyer dropped Jabez's word and there we were."

Rabbit laughed and shook his head. Eve watched him and knew that the revelation of beginnings did not always satisfy.

Ali went on. Before he'd left for Tokyo, the group of them had done a few of the rooftop Nazca lines together. But when he came back it had stopped. "I decided to start doing them again. Do we still have those pictures?"

Eve could hear rain on the roof, the trees sighing. A musical mobile playing in the room Yuko and Francis shared. These came in over the voices on the television, tuned low. A new condo development. A household cleaner. A line of cosmetics. Someone said: *The simple life full of grace and luxury.*

Kumi brought back a handful of photographs, nicked and bent around the edges. Eve took in a breath seeing the first one. Ali, Ali. She felt as if she were meeting him again, this time the one she remembered. Wire thin, white T-shirt. Up on a rooftop. Eve could hear Rabbit breathing next to her, looking at the same image.

Ali was looking over at the television, distracted. Armored cars. Plastic shields. Smoke billowing. "I was working on this big one, a man standing like he'd just been busted. Hands over his head. And I'd almost finished the thing. I remember I was working on the fingers of his hand. Walking backwards pouring down the powder we used, which is the same from football fields only mixed with this sparkling stuff we got from a kids' art supply store. I guess I was a little wrapped up in the moment. I was also high. In any case, I walked right off the roof."

He fell thirty feet into a parking lot. Bent the top of a light pole going down, crushed in the roof of a limousine waiting for an airport fare. He woke up in a hospital bed. "This is the cliché, right? You find God lying in a hospital bed." They contacted Kumi in Tokyo for him, and she flew over. She showed up with her duffel bag and a change of clothes. She was sitting in the chair next to Ali's bed. And they were arguing about something.

"About whether you were going to keep making art," Kumi said. "You decided you weren't."

"It was a T5 break. Very bad. I was frozen from the chest down. I'm doing better than I should be. They were telling me people just don't recover. So we're arguing. And then we finish arguing and I fall asleep. And then, sometime later, fifteen, twenty minutes, that thing happens when you half wake up."

Ali came up into the room, up under his own eyelids. He felt the room, heard the low hum of hospital machines and hallway traffic, the dry heat of the place, the cover smells, cleaning products, all just barely keeping the stench of sickness and fear at bay. And Kumi was sitting there just where she'd been when he fell asleep, but now her eyes were closed and he realized she was praying. He knew, watching her, that she was addressing her thoughts to some entity beyond. Some being they couldn't know to exist. She was saying words that required belief.

"And here comes the big epiphany," Ali said.

Rabbit moved in his chair, sharply. Eve wondered for a moment if he might leave the room. But the movement was followed by stillness.

"It just burned right through me, this thought," Ali said. "We'd been arguing about whether to keep going or to stop. A dispute over free choice, free will. We assumed freedom enough to even argue the choices. And yet where did it come from, that confidence that we could really choose? Everything that had happened to me could be explained by rational science. Inability to move legs because of nerve damage. Nerve damage because of T5 break. T5 break because of falling off a roof. This all happens because of this, which happens because of this, which stretches back through time, past me, past generations and history back to whenever it began, with whatever big explosion. Thermodynamics, quantum physics, whatever it is, it's a rational unfolding. But if that were true, if my lying there really was fully explained in those terms, molecules jostling outwards in some inviolable quantum legal framework that started at the big bang, the irreducible particles in us just doing what they do in accordance with the fantastic numbers encoded within them, then what decisions were left for me to make? Do billiard balls make decisions after the break? Do they suspend geometric laws on occasion to find the pocket of their choosing? How would a billiard ball understand choice or desire, or the notion that by choice or desire something good or bad, or beautiful or ugly, might come about? What sense could a billiard ball make of hope and regret? And yet I suddenly understood how intensely I needed just those things. Choice, desire, hope, regret. I needed these not just to feel good, but to live. Kumi praying over there. I could see her lips move. I was thinking: I need choice, I need desire, I need hope and regret not to be proteins etched on the inner lining of my cells. I need to want art or not want it. I need to want Kumi or not want her. I need to want recovery or death, or happy spirits or sad ones, or to clean up or return to junk. Why junk without choice? Why smile? Why was I smiling, lying there in my hospital bed with a broken T5 vertebra? Well sure, because my cheek muscles contracted in response to endorphin flows. But in my experience of the moment, in my memory of its texture, it was because I was falling in love with Kumi. My love for her entered the universe coming from the same place that the art came from, a big eye on the top of a warehouse, my endless, useless work. It didn't come from the network, from the phenomenal soup. It came from somewhere outside, some source beyond or before. And watching her lips move, I knew she was addressing that same source. Wherever and whatever it was. Whomever. I didn't care about religion as an institution or a set of coded practices. I still don't care about that. I care about choice. I need it. And without belief, without faith in something beyond sense, there can be no meaningful choice."

The wind was up. The trees were whipping back and forth in the yard. Rabbit, who had risen from his chair during Ali's long speech, now slipped out of the room and into the hall. Conversation flagged, it softened and lost its shape. Eve's eyes kept drifting to the window, to the trees moving there. Ali lived in a forest. The man of the rooftops having come down just far enough to nest among the branches. And even when Ali keyed up the television volume, Eve's attention remained outside the news. She thought of what Ali had said. Without belief there was no choice.

They were showing a steady shot of the plaza now, seething crowds. The camera seemed bewildered in its long, unwavering shot. No fast cuts, no slick production values. The camera stared open mouthed just as they all did. It took Eve several minutes to realize what she was watching, coasting between the images and her thoughts of Ali's new conviction. The people in the shot had started a fire in a planter, the flames and sparks now rising up. A beautiful and terrifying sight. Eve and Ali and Kumi sat as if they were in front of a fire in a hearth.

Rabbit came back into the room. He was holding a copy of 1984.

Ali caught his glance. "It's killing you, so ask."

Rabbit said: "The Poets."

Ali sighed. "All Jabez. All his. I have nothing to do with them anymore."

"The Grove."

"What about it?"

"You own the building."

"Me and a group of people. Strictly business."

"Wow," Rabbit said. "I'm finding this very bizarre. You seem to be at the root of a lot of things in my life."

Ali shrugged. "Don't start thinking anything. I'm out. Millions of people have copies of 1984."

But Rabbit was on to a new idea, and this was now coursing uncomfortably through him. "You ran the Easter Valley Railway Tunnel."

Ali looked at him in surprise. "We all ran the tunnel. Jabez wanted to *live* in the freaking tunnel. He found those rooms down there."

"Who's Alto?"

Ali's expression changed. He was amused.

"The name of an artist who failed," Ali said. "Ali Latour. Alla never quite sat right. God complex and all that."

Rabbit took a step backwards and bumped the frame of the door. On the TV, the fire grew, front and center. The on-scene reporter was saying " . . . several slightly injured . . ."

Alto.

And Rabbit was gone. Disappeared up and into the front hall. Eve could hear the front door clicking shut.

SHE WAS GOING TO FOLLOW HIM. She didn't need Ali to tell her to, although he did. He wheeled with her into the front hall and pulled her down to him again. No more tears from Eve even though he said he was sorry again, and she knew he was and that moved her. But she just held him. She inhaled his different smell, different soaps and routines, different pains and defenses. She wondered if they would now see each other occasionally or if they'd return to their separate lives. But either way, she was at peace with it. He was safe. He was still himself, still walking the path he chose. And by connecting, they had restored at least a part of what had existed between them.

Then it was open, the door in front of her. Open by her hand. Her feet taking one step after another down the flagstone walk and onto the pavement of the drive, her eyes casting around, looking for Rabbit. Choice in every instant for her too. Maybe that was something Ali had returned to her. Something like a belief in her own ability to choose. Irrational, but vital.

Rabbit was sitting in the truck, waiting. Eve climbed in herself. They sat in silence for a moment, Rabbit staring straight ahead, seemingly lost in thought. She started the truck. And when they were five or six blocks down the hill towards the river, she cracked a glance over at him. His strong profile against a blur of streetscape. Rabbit flying across the brick and glass, the mailboxes and utility poles.

He shook his head, a sharp movement, as if to startle himself awake. "Ahh," he said. "That was strange."

"Are you all right?"

"Fine. Honest, I am."

"I'm not sure I understand what happened back there. You want to tell me?"

He did, actually. He wanted to tell her a lot of things. But for now he told her about the Easter Valley Railway Tunnel and his running routine, about a mysterious hidden painting and the inspiration it had provided.

"I always knew there was a person out there somewhere who had done that piece," Rabbit said. "I just didn't necessarily want to meet them."

"Why not?" Eve asked.

It was a harder question to answer, to even think about. Because he

didn't want to meet his inspiration. He didn't want to risk having someone in his life he might then look to for approval. "Or worse," Rabbit
said. "Someone I'd end up resenting. Beyer and Jabez, they're ruined.
They used to have ideas. Now they have nothing but their rivalry."

They'd made the bridge and were stopped in a long line of cars
leading up to a checkpoint. An officer with a flashlight was coming
down the row of cars, shining the light into each. No traffic moving.

"You think you might feel rivalry towards Ali?" Eve asked.

He turned to look at her when she said that. Mineral-green eyes,
dark lashes. And having asked the question, she suddenly knew what
she wanted him to feel. She wanted Rabbit to feel that he could be
better than Ali, truer than Ali. She wanted Rabbit to feel that he could
replace Ali.

Rabbit was still looking at her steadily. "I think we're past rivalry,"
he said.

And Eve again felt the surge, like a river current, like the tug of ac-
celeration. Forward rushing. Anticipation and excitement. These delicious feelings, so recently renewed.

The officer had arrived at the truck. And when Eve buzzed down
the window, he recognized her and said: "Evey, what's up? Can't let
you across in the vehicle."

"Can we go on foot?" she asked him.

"Bit of a mess up there, to tell you the truth. We have power out on
the Slopes, down near the river too. Where you going tonight?"

"West Stretch. I have to get home."

The cop told them where to park the truck in a service station.
Then he let Eve pull out of the line of cars, turn around and head back
down the bridge. When she'd parked and locked up, Rabbit and Eve
returned to the barricade and the same police officer walked them
through. There were others there—private security, police, militia.
Some of them greeted Eve, but their minds were on other things.

Nobody spoke more than necessary, all the radios alive with incoming news. Updates from the troubled fronts of the city, while the river water surged in the darkness, far below.

When they were through, Rabbit could see where the bridge sloped off into River Park, and how beyond that the Slopes were patched with light. Uneven black squares along the hillside. At the top, somewhere over the crest, the plaza. And there were many flashing lights on the ground and in the sky. The low cloud flickered with them, pulsing in dark red tones.

"Want to run?" Rabbit said.

They were both in light clothes, so they ran together, gliding into an easy pace. Rabbit admiring her natural flow, efficient movements. She didn't over-swing the arms or over-stride. She picked up the cadence and he ran right with her. Through the light rain, the night wind picking up. Down through River Park. Something rising in the air. Crowds at the big intersection at the bottom of the Slopes made Rabbit imagine the places of gathering all over the city. People finding their way to these spots, to these local corners. Sensing some common threat.

They reached Rabbit's apartment in about twenty minutes. He showed her the place to climb the brick, fingers to the ironwork, then a long step across the rung of the ladder. She swung across like she'd done it dozens of times before, no hesitation, no second thoughts, following Rabbit up six flights as the distance to the pavement opened below. Up to the final platform. Smoke in the air. Sirens. The whole tangle of it spreading as they climbed. No television required to sense things just at the moment of combustion. Past tension, past waiting. Whatever had been about to happen was now happening, violence unfolding in the rotored air.

He climbed through the window and she followed. They entered the narrow room where he lived, empty but for a battered futon and a cable spool worktable, the far wall stacked with Rabbit's boxed macaroni and kimchi ramen. The train yards glowed mercury orange and the light came in. Ali may still have been present in both of their minds, but he was now there differently than before. Rabbit didn't want or need to know more about the man who'd been the third corner of a triangle that closed to bring him and Eve together. That man, so pivotal, was a fiction to Rabbit now. A character they'd both fleshed into the invisible scheme.

And much better that way. Rabbit had this thought as Eve lay back in the chair, breathing deeply, something resolving in her too. Better to know at the moment a thing is finished, that the inspiration you thought you had did not truly exist. That no part of the thing you were making was caused by someone else. That what had come to mind was, indeed, entirely new. Entirely your own.

Eve lay back in bands of orange light, cut by angular shadows. What sounded like gunshots at the ridgeline, cold spikes of sound. But far, far away. And when he sat next to her, she took his hand and pressed his palm against her cheek. He did the same with hers. She reached up and he laced his fingers through hers and put her hand to the side of his face, her index finger resting near the corner of his eye, her thumb just to the final crease of his lips. He said her name. And she said his. And they both felt their names enter at the fingertips, then move down their arms and into the rest of them.

What did it add up to in those moments before midnight? Rabbit could inventory and catalog and wonder later without coming to a definite answer. Only that everything had changed. Jabez and Beyer, even Alto, were fading from view. And Rabbit knew that when he put his arm around her to bring her close, his lips on hers, that he was, right in that very instant, both disappearing into her and disappearing from view. Holding her, he was already gone, already heading north to his house in the woods, to his small field, to the things that would grow there. And afterwards, when Eve was asleep, he pulled himself out from under the sheets and sat naked on the edge of the futon next to her, his hand gentle on the curve of her hip, and looked out over the yards, already calculating time. When he'd leave, when he'd be in the tunnel, wet cloth pressed to his face. When he'd pass Alto that final time. He owed no further tribute. But if there was to be a final observance of an old ritual, Rabbit wanted it to be in the earliest hours of the morning, when a new day was rising in the east. A new day that Eve had made possible.

Rabbit put clothes in his pack and cinched it tight to his chest, listening to the sounds of the city. Something happening up top of the hill now, the distant sound of a crowd raising its voice. Flickers of light up against the lowered cloud. He imagined the clash of great forces. He would leave the room the way he'd come, sliding out to the platform, pulling the window closed.

But not before leaving two gifts for her. For Eve alone.

The first, a map. Rabbit extracted this from his knapsack. He pulled it free of the various plastic bags with their wires and components. It was grimed with use, creased to the point of fraying. But he lay it gently on her clothes, crumpled on the floor next to the bed where they'd fallen.

Second: a fresh drawing for her to see on waking. A long composition on the blank wall of the apartment. Wide black strokes of felt pen. It cost him his damage deposit to leave her with a final crucial thought in lines and loops, arrows pointing north, directions and words. A diorama, a marked route, and an invitation.

You'll find it where you last saw it.

Rabbit knew she'd recognize the words.

SATURDAY TO FIRST LIGHT
—
OCTOBER 26

LOFTIN

—

EVENTS PATTERNED AROUND ONE ANOTHER in spirals, in coils. Beginnings reached out for endings. On this point, everyone in the plaza would have agreed.

Loftin was swimming in his story. He had mapped the crowd, its factions, splinters and blocs. What looked like chaos, he now knew, retained in fact an inner order. He wrote that in his notebook (his third one; there were two full of notes and a blank remaining in the side pockets of his cargo pants). *There is a fine but hidden order in this chaos. And that order is an ordering of all chaos.*

Loftin stood on a park bench on the street that flanked the east end of the plaza. It was midnight and he'd been talking to people up and down the square for the past couple of hours. Doing so, Loftin had concluded that there were actually four distinct types of people in the crowd. They arranged themselves, in his mind, on a chart with two dimensions. The first was the personal tendency to either confront or conciliate in resolving the crisis. The second was the impulse, in advocating any given position, to invoke the authority of either the rational self or a source of wisdom beyond. Hawks and doves. Materialists and

mystics. The combination resulted in four distinct orientations, and
Loftin had already named them: Hippies and the Black Bloc on the
material side, the Call and the Crusaders on the side of mystery.

And there they all were, plain enough to see once you'd cracked the
code. The Hippie kids over on the south stairs singing "Give Peace a
Chance" and strumming guitars, appealing to the peace that was believed to lie organically within. The photogenic Black Bloc who'd
taken over the planters and the fountains to the east, raising their fists,
their *Celebranoia* and *Remember Genoa* banners, agitating for a revolution in the here and now while collecting stones and fragments of
pavement in garbage cans. The stoic members of the Call held the
central area around the band riser where they were gathered in circles
with their heads bowed, holding candles, or standing by themselves
with their hands raised to heaven, entreating a benevolent father somewhere overhead. And behind Loftin, milling in the street, the sullen
and volatile Crusaders, for whom the force of the supernatural was
justice, and justice now.

Everybody talked. Loftin's interview guide was the simplest he'd
ever used. Two questions. Who is the hostage taker, do you think? And:
Why are you here? The answers were pressing hard against the inside
of the ribs, they burst out of people. Loftin's notes reflected that:

*#5 Thin girl, college. (22 yrs.) Tree planting, northern Alberta. Heard
perp = psychiatrically deranged, needs our help. Here for the cause of
peace.*

*#12 Man 60+. Cousin died Madrid 04. Bible says stand up for yourself.
Perp = Islamic terrorist. Here for justice. "This country has had enough."*

*#16 Younger man, tie/cord jacket. Paralegal local firm. "So much
suffering." Saw the Call online. Perp = obsessed celeb stalker. Here to
show God's love.*

*#24 Woman mid-30s. Arrested G20 Toronto. Non-profit work. "Military-
entertainment complex" runs country. Perp = inside job.*

Nobody said they were there to confront or disagree with any other group. But every person had a hard reason why they couldn't leave. And everybody was disturbed by the same rumors, about one new one per hour. Special military units were going in, or they had already gone in. Shots had been fired inside the theater. Or the worst rumor: executions had begun. Children were already dying. These kinds of thoughts agitated people, and Loftin observed much arguing and jostling. All the more surprising, he thought, given this factional venting, that the authorities would have been so careless about uniting people under a single complaint aimed not at the hostage taker but at the authorities themselves.

But that, in the end, is exactly what they did when they decided to bring in riot police to clear the plaza.

Loftin watched from his perch on the park bench, and was astonished. He could sense the unrest and hear the shouted arguments. He'd seen the odd rival banner torn down, even a few fights, scraps, pulled shirts. But there was no riot going on. Loftin felt the injustice. Yes, the police had tried persuading people to leave. He'd shown his own press card often enough to have accumulated a crust of resentment.

"You can't do this," he said to a young police officer who, having looked at Loftin's card, had ordered him back to a newly established media green zone. "Are you declaring martial law? I'm entitled to be here."

The cop shook his head and walked away. And when Loftin turned back to face the plaza, he could see the riot police forming a long single rank, just past the main body of Black Bloc protesters.

So this was how it was going to be. And instantly, things were alive in Loftin's peripheral vision. People pulling out garbage cans loaded up with bits of pavement and stones. Objects going hand to hand. Loftin thought: *This is crazy.*

He climbed off the bench and pushed his way forward to crouch behind a planter. What was the term the experts used? Instigating incident. The thing that pushed people over the edge. Here it came as a second rank of riot police jogged out of the side alley and squared up behind the first. People actually cheered. Loftin did too, he let out an ironic laugh to join the generalizing sound. Many, many voices now.

Loftin called out: "Oh for heaven's sake. Leave us alone."

The police were advancing, beating their plastic shields with their black batons while a voice spoke through a bullhorn from the rear. *Please leave. There will be no second chances.* And here it came. The first stones, bits of brick, pavement. A piece flashed directly over Loftin's head in the darkness. He turned and another one came, very close. He saw it approaching, tumbling end over end. He ducked. Whoosh. It was a thrill. Loftin's heart was racing.

People sang nearby. Loftin heard old church hymns and John Lennon blended. A choral weave behind the action, advancing riot police, special squads now deploying to the rear. Loftin recognized the snub-nosed rifles used to fire rubber bullets. While in the crowd all around him, he felt the shift. The factions fusing, a larger organism being born. And that organism now seethed and rocked, it washed from one side of the plaza to the other, it let its head fall into its hands. It wept for all it didn't know.

The police lines met the crowd right at the seam where the Black Bloc and the Call intersected. The Black Bloc launched their missiles. The police swung their clubs. The Call went to their knees. Hands to heaven. But that, in the end, did not save them.

Crack. Loftin heard it. A brutal sound. A cop stepped forward and did what he'd been taught to do. Slam the shield into the man's face. Knock him down. Apply baton to side of head. It sounded like a big stick of celery being snapped in two.

Crack. Blood pooling. The crowd surging. Loftin was again calling out words. He was feeling real anger now. There was simply no call for that kind of violence. And he noted a momentary lapse in police resolve too, as people rushed in to surround the fallen man. As the hail of stones began again.

The tear gas arrived. Loftin watched the arcs of smoke overhead, the cans hitting the pavement, spitting and spinning. Then his nose and eyes locked and streamed mucus. He doubled over and held his breath. Shapes danced in, faces swathed in towels or gas masks. Ski goggles. Foam padding wrapped to the shoulders and the arms, cinched in place with duct tape. The gas canisters were picked up and sent sailing back over the heads of the cops. Angels, Loftin thought. Guardian Black Bloc angels. Then someone threw a bottle corked with a burning rag and the pavement burned, Plexiglas shields winking orange and black.

Loftin's legs were cramping. He went onto his knees. He watched a man standing in the front ranks of the Black Bloc, gesturing at the police. Black leather jacket, black mask. And then a cop stepped forward, shouldering a snub-nosed rifle, and dropped the man with a rubber bullet to the side of his head from only twenty feet away. Whomp. The man spasmed grotesquely, then crashed straight down to the pavement. Leg quiver. Then nothing.

Loftin was gasping, his brain unspooling. *What the devil. That was. He didn't. He is dead. That man is dead. Heaven help us.*

And then the strangest thing. Loftin couldn't believe what he was seeing. A second man stepped out of the Black Bloc lines and approached the police directly. He was also dressed in black, with a black mask over a dark beard. But he was now waving his arms and gesturing that the police should stop. It was either incredible bravado or incredible stupidity. And Loftin winced involuntarily, waiting for what would happen to the man. But nothing did. The police actually stopped. The batons dropped. The rank of men took several shuffling steps back.

It was a miracle, Loftin thought. The bearded man was Mahatma Gandhi. He was Nelson Mandela. The crowd cheered as he crouched beside the man who'd been hit by the rubber bullet, taking his pulse and talking into a cell phone. Loftin squinted, processing these details. Then it came to him in a rush as the man clicked shut the phone and his hand went into the side pocket of his jacket, shaping around something there. Loftin guessed 9 mm. Personalized grip. Oh dear, he thought. The man was some kind of professional.

And that thought came to Loftin the instant before a helicopter thundered up over the building opposite and came rotoring in on the plaza. Pasting back the trees. Cycloning garbage. Sending people running all over. The man who'd been shot was lifted aboard. The bearded man followed and the chopper vaulted skywards and wheeled away.

Loftin was still on his knees behind the planter, but the miracle was now sour.

The riot police withdrew to a side street. And all the old rumors were now replaced by a single new one. The men evacuated in the chopper were police, or Special Forces, or intelligence. Something bad had been loose in the plaza, seeded through the crowd. And the crowd's mood now dangerously darkened. Loftin's own mood darkened. And in the hours following midnight, he listened to the sound of breaking glass and watched fires being started in the planters and the dead fountains. At three in the morning, he called his wife, very unusual for him. Mid-morning London time. "Just to say I love you," he told her. "Everything is fine, sure." He said it again, "I love you." And she said the words back to him: "I love you too."

He was off the phone less than a minute when he witnessed the beating. Firelight flickering on all of their faces. Three men with black masks grabbed another and ripped off his woolen hat. He fought back, make no mistake. But when they slammed him down to the concrete stairs he curled into a ball and tried only to survive the kicking. Dismal business, the street fight. It lasted thirty seconds, but Loftin didn't make a move. Special Forces tattoo, the men who had done the beating said afterwards. Dude's a spy. A fucking rat. There were fucking rats everywhere.

"This is terrible," Loftin said, to nobody in particular. "Did anyone even see the tattoo?"

The beaten man staggered away, disappearing into a side street, leaving a treacly spatter of blood on the pavement behind him.

The man next to Loftin turned to look him over. He didn't say a word.

"I'm a journalist," Loftin told him. "I have a press card."

There were more men around him now. There were hands feeling in his pockets, hands holding him. Notebooks out. They were leafing through the pages. #35 *Man, 26 yrs. of age. Left of center politics . . . #43 Female, 53 yrs. . . . .*

Helicopters in the lower air. Someone was yelling at the top of the plaza. Loftin could hear the words very distinctly: *It's happening. It's happening.*

So fast. So quickly. Loftin might have missed it even if the beating hadn't begun at that same moment. Fists and elbows, knees and boots. Something crushed and cracked in his central regions. His bowels released. He was falling down through plate-glass windows of pain. While up top of the plaza, the business had begun. One helicopter. One armored personnel carrier. The simplest of maneuvers. The helicopter landed on top of the complex. The armored personnel carrier backed up at high speed and smashed into the lobby of the theater.

There was nothing to see after that. No movement. No shapes visible. No formation. No plan unfurling. There was only an instant of pause, and then something like a pulse. It was barely visible. People experienced it as a sense on the skin, or at the inner ear. The building pulsed and then the plaza did too.

Loftin felt it. He couldn't be sure exactly what it was. His eyes were pinched shut and they were beating him methodically, paying much more attention to him than they had to the first man. Face and knees. Groin. Face again, this time with kicks. But something came in through his eyelids and rippled through him.

Voices all around them: *It's happening. It's happening. It's happening.*

The last one to kick Loftin had no idea that as his boot went home, there was in fact no Loftin left to kick. That was because the one who had kicked him just prior had done so artfully to the side of his head and killed him. That man was nineteen years old and was never charged. And he might have continued kicking Loftin, in his turn, were it not for that strange pulse. It seemed to come from within the theater and spread outwards invisibly. Everybody turned to look. Some people would say later that they saw the walls of the building physically move, puff outwards a fraction. That's not how Loftin would have de-scribed it, however. Had he survived to describe the last experience of his senses, he would have said that a seam of white seemed to blink out of every crack and crevice in the Meme complex at once, a glow of spotless white, the structure humming suddenly with a new and total energy. And that energy, which all those present in the plaza had col-lectively brought to life, then burst outwards, back through the crowd, penetrating and transforming them all, dissolving whatever order he'd observed there previously, making chaos into larger chaos. Had he lived, those are the things that Loftin would have said.

Twenty seconds, no more. And then everybody was poised, every-body waiting, everybody holding their collective breath.

PEGG

—

It was light.

They did it with light. In the end, that was the trick they saved for timely use. They would have had other options. There were ways they could make your bones vibrate or blenderize your inner ear, fiddle with the knobs on your stability and balance systems, make you fall over, wet your pants, liquefy your entire intestinal tract. They could project a voice into your head and make you insane. They could do that kind of thing.

Only, key point, they weren't going to use any of those techniques on someone with his fist clamped around the trigger of what might be a radiological dispersion device, a so-called dirty bomb. True, these weapons were not considered potent enough to kill a lot of people. But a nuke was a nuke, in the public eye. And the authorities would be evacuating a city if that word got out, which would surely be the black outcome, the major domo downside.

Pegg was in an ambulance, fading slowly from consciousness by the time he got around to thinking this through. They were heading somewhere, although not quickly. In fact, they were stopping and starting now through crowds that plugged every street around the plaza. Honking and wailing and welping their way through. Even strapped to a gurney, though, Pegg was able to appreciate the genius of what had been unleashed. The genius of that otherworldly light. And he, Thom Pegg, had called it forth.

"Bring me a beer," said his boy. His own lost boy. "And a mop."

And there was Pegg laughing somewhere in the deep and forgotten recesses of history.

They didn't come immediately. Pegg waited after the tape played with his eyes pinched shut, unable to imagine what Haden had in store. He listened for sounds in the ceiling, in the sewers below. He listened for explosions, soldiers breaching the walls, storming through. None of it came. And as Pegg counted off seconds, then what he assumed to be minutes, it occurred to him that he could leave the theater. Everybody was through with Thom Pegg now. He'd listened to Mov's madness from beginning to end. He'd pressed the button on his tape recorder at the moment that seemed right, just as Haden had requested. Haden hadn't sent men in to kill him immediately, so he was free to go. Free to be free. Free to live unless they were planning to sniper him down on the lobby steps in front of five hundred television cameras.

But he didn't leave. He went back to sit with the kids instead. Gerry and Hyacinth still next to one another. Roshawn. Laisha, Reebo, Metric. Pegg flashed on an image of what lay outside the theater doors, the agitated crowds there, the press and lights. And it seemed quite clear that he and these kids had more important things to discuss. The first thing on that list, naturally, was what they were going to eat when they got out. Pegg had them all hold hands sitting there in row 14. Hyacinth suggested fries. Everyone agreed. So it was unanimous. They were all going to eat french fries when they were freed. Not a long time afterwards. Immediately afterwards. And tears were streaming down Pegg's cheeks.

Gerry said: "You okay?"

I'm good. I'm good.

And then the kid said this. He actually did. "Would you like a hug?"

Pegg embraced the boy and wept onto the top of his head. Gerry gave him a squeeze. He said, "I know we're not going to die."

Pegg wasn't an adult. That's the thought he had. He couldn't possibly be an adult, because he was unable to suppress the following question: "How do you know?"

"Because I choose to believe in life," Gerry said. "I believe in all of our lives."

The boy said that too. He actually said that.

Mov had disappeared, although Pegg could still feel him in the darkness, somewhere close. Sitting on the edge of the stage, head lowered. Leaning against a nearby wall, exhausted from the effort of bringing everything to these last moments. Pegg found that even fear was hard to shape in the darkness.

As it was, they all sat tightly together in the sweating blackness. Everything suspended. Everything in that darkness having now taken on a temporary tone. They heard Mov move towards the front. Pegg thought it had been fifteen minutes since his tape played, since he'd held his breath and depressed that key. He wondered if there were any traces yet of morning light outside. Predawn. Then he heard Mov in sudden motion.

Pegg said: "On the floor, now. Everybody."

And they all wriggled their way to the sticky, stinking carpet. They all tucked their heads in under the seats. Except Pegg, who stood uselessly, stupidly.

"Is it over?" Gerry asked him from the floor.

"Right now," Pegg said.

That was the moment. *Is it over? Right now.* But Pegg could not have known the way in which it would arrive. Nobody could have seen that coming, because there was, literally, nothing to see.

Light. Unexpected and enormous. They came with light. How do the tough guys say it? *Bring it.* These were tough guys. They *brought* the light. Soundless and endless light, a celestial explosion of luminance. It gauzed the room. If Pegg were still seeing—if that's technically what he was doing through his clenched-shut eyes—then it was white and blue filaments that could be seen. White, blue, and the veins in his own eyelids. Pegg thought he could see his own platelets moving, shivering there in the incandescence. Not illumination, note. This sort of light didn't throw itself *onto* anything. It didn't reveal. It only obliterated the darkness in favor of itself. Suddenly and violently. Pegg felt it like a physical assault on his skin. The crush of a new atmosphere, a deeper pressure. The thing fisted his optic nerves and tossed him. Pegg was on his feet one second, then blown over the next. Something seemed to hammer both his temples at once, and down he went. Blinded twice in two very different ways. Maybe something the size of the universe really was fucking with him.

I've been hit, he thought. *Just like in the movies.* His face contorted, twisting into itself. He felt penetrated and afraid. His body coursing with electrical currents. He thought a spill of thoughts, like fever dreams at an accelerated pace. He thought: *They're using electricity.* He thought: *I'm going to die.* He thought: *This is the light I've heard about, the one at the moment of death.* He thought: *My body is disappearing.*

He curled shut, his fists and toes painfully cramping.

Then, the voices. And here Pegg registered something with chilling certainty: the men were not shouting. He wanted them to shout. He wanted to hear them yell. *Down! Clear! Secure!* He wanted martial action of the extreme and definitive kind. *Lock down! Stack up! Close!* Whatever the words were. He wanted the safety of the good guys' violent program. But he heard none of it. They spoke with bureaucratic, death-industry calm. Most unsettling. They moved into the room, ghosted into this inhospitable light. Pegg could feel them all around, not shadows or shapes, barely outlines. They were force fields, linked together, and they spidered through the room in programmed sequence. They seized space and held it. Hands on them all. The children were screaming. Gerry was screaming. Pegg himself might have been screaming, he couldn't have been sure. He was listening for Mov, though. Listening for the sound. And then he heard it, or he thought he heard it. The last sounds of Mov were a cadenza like this: *pop, pop, pop.*

Pegg was being handcuffed but something like vision was creeping back to life behind his eyes. There was a voice above him, distant at the command end of two hands that vised him into immobility. That voice said: "I have the second man."

This crackled through the airwaves. *Man two. Man two.* And then he saw them. The children. Six of them, Gerry in the lead. Hyacinth behind him. Then Roshawn, Laisha, Reebo, Metric. No more screaming. They were up in the dazzling, spotted brilliance, they seemed to be floating. Drifting towards the door.

"Micah," Pegg said. And then he was up himself and being carried. Dragged, really. There was a hand on either side, his legs banging painfully across a sill, a step. He smelled street air, alley air, sweet garbage, sweet urban rot. His vision returning in layers. He could see black and chrome now. The sheen of running water. He saw a sewer drain and an ambulance. He was in an ambulance. This was news. It rooted him. He was in a vehicle, in a bed. He was strapped to the gurney. Somebody was working his arm, rubbing his skin with a cold swab. He felt the needle go home and the wave of something moving inside him, not unpleasant.

"Micah," Pegg said again.

And then a familiar voice from very close. "Man two. We're mobile. Please move now, driver. Thank you." The lurch and the rattle of things in cases. Sutures and swabs, scalpels and injector pens. They were going somewhere in an ambulance.

"What happened?" Pegg asked. More vision. Haden here, creased brow, black turtleneck under a jacket with a familiar frog lapel pin. The frog winked at Pegg, as if it recognized him.

"All good," Haden said. He was leaned in very close to Pegg, their faces almost touching. Pegg realized that Haden was going through his pockets. His tape recorder. Haden was taking his tape recorder. Under normal circumstances, Pegg would have objected loudly. But it didn't really bother or surprise him at the moment.

"Tell me," Pegg said. "The light."

"Super-halogen tissue convulsant," Haden said. "Get some rest, you got dosed good. It puts you out for a minute or two, but nothing long term. You're going home."

"The kids?"

"Safe and sound. All six. Nice work, by the way. Night-vision, check. Once we knew that, the guy was fucked. A burst of super-halogen into infrared filters means your brain is never the same again." And Pegg was swept with emotion hearing all this. He had most certainly been expendable to Haden, or at least his brain had been. But he'd pulled off his night-vision and the children were alive. They were all breathing, with a future ahead and plans to eat french fries. And with this thought the ambulance seemed to swerve hard right. Gravity went sideways and stayed sideways for so long that Pegg began to wonder if it was perhaps only his own gravity. Haden looked like he was comfortably centered. He looked like he was going straight.

"What about the bomb?" Pegg asked.

Haden was staring forward now, past Pegg to the road ahead, a seam of concern working itself into place across his forehead. The ambulance was slowing, horns sounding. Haden said: "Fuck." Then glanced down at Pegg and did something unexpected. He put his hand on

Pegg's arm. He said: "The briefcase. The bomb. Once you were all down and convulsing, our guys went over and cut off his hand."

Pegg was full of wonder. He thought: *The hand. My God. What genius. How simple and efficient.* They couldn't have him letting go of the handle, so they cut off his hand. "With an axe," Haden was now saying. And he offered a thin smile.

Pegg was slammed up against one side of the gurney, on this crazy journey going somewhere around a never-ending hard right turn. Somewhere else in the city, Mov's case with his hand attached was going somewhere too. The GPS trigger had been a bit more of a challenge, Haden continued, but there was always a way with technology. "Thanks also on that score," he said to Pegg.

"For what?"

Haden's hand was still resting on Pegg's forearm. Thanks, he explained, because Pegg's tape recorder had a GPS jammer in it. It activated when Pegg played the clip of his son and blocked the transmitter in Mov's case.

Haden hummed between the bits of information he was choosing to share.

After that, they just turned the whole system off briefly. Winked out the satellites for a few minutes and deactivated the trigger. A bit hairy. They had to let the airlines know. They had a couple wobbles up there, but things came out all right.

"Now relax," he said. That was why Pegg had been given a muscle relaxant in the first place. Because there was going to be some pain and possible side effects later.

"Side effects like what?"

Haden said: "Cranial. Don't worry, it's all short-term stuff."

"Memory," Pegg said. "You're saying I'm going to lose my memory."

"Parts of it, temporarily. It's normally bits and details, recent and older stuff. But don't worry, it comes back."

"I won't forget Mov," Pegg said. "I won't forget who he was. Mov was from your world. One of your kind."

Haden looked at Pegg with a sad smile. "I know. And now you know. But nobody else will ever know, and that's for the best."

"I could write the story," Pegg said. "I took off my night-vision, Haden. I'm alive and my brain is fine. I can still tell the story."

But Haden just shook his head, without saying a word. He didn't even have to make the point that so obviously came next. Pegg could write the story, sure. He could tell the world about Mov and who he was. The source of our guilty conscience. The poison in our cultural water table. Pegg could write about how Mov cracked and went primitive, tried to induce the sacrifice by which his sins might be cleansed and peace restored. *Homo paenitentia.* Maybe even a tabloid hack could have written that story and maybe he could even have done it without his tape-recorded copy of the interview. Maybe people would have even believed him.

But not if he'd written the story once before and made it up that time. Who would believe him on the second try?

Precisely, absolutely, squarely: no one.

Pegg had to marvel at the design of his trap. Haden was very good. But now, Haden was also more seriously distracted. The ambulance had come to a standstill. And Pegg could now feel the bodies and hands pressed to the sides of the vehicle. He could hear the banging and feel the ripple of their thousandweight as they pressed against the sheet steel. Haden sat frozen, making calculations.

Pegg was slipping away, down into sleep and peace, and making his own calculations too. There was only one mistake Haden had made, and Pegg was alive to it in those fading seconds. Haden did not appreciate how central Mov remained to events unfolding. Mov would have known it. Pegg knew it without question, without even thinking. It was bone knowledge. Mov was going to become more important than anybody could possibly imagine, because Mov—an escaped prisoner from Haden's own world—well, because nobody was ever going to see Mov again. Nobody, ever. And the curiosity would gnaw at people. It would make them sick for answers.

IT WAS SIX IN THE MORNING. It was seven in the morning. It was eight in the morning. The news was spreading. And the news was mixed. The kids were safe. Nobody knew where they were being held. No press conference this time. But a deep anxiety remained. Some feeling of darkness that would not be dispelled. Suspicions grew, in crystalline complexity. You could hear the sound of them. The chatter and chew of dark ideas as they copied themselves from mind to mind.

The story about Loftin aired, but the body had been so badly beaten that he was not identified correctly at first.

"Just who was the man speaking with the riot police?" said an anchor, replaying the tape. "This is something we're trying to find out. One other man seriously hurt. And another beaten to death under strange circumstances. Three police officers injured. Chaos in the Heights."

The crowd in the plaza had been singing. The riot police were back.

"Who was the hostage taker?" yelled a Black Bloc protester into the nearest camera. "Why can no one simply say who the guy was?"

Behind him the bonfires had been fueled again with the contents of dumpsters and recycling bins, a steady wind stoking the plaza. And around the corner, in an action nobody seemed to have seen, no camera had recorded, the front glass of a coffee shop was smashed and the store was engulfed in flames.

"We have fires in the Heights. At least two. This is very tragic."

The crowd was alive again, forming and re-forming. Where were the children? Nobody knew. Where was the hostage taker? Where had he been taken?

The theater stood blankly at the top of the plaza. Fluid dynamics. Tidal rips and undertows. The riot police spread across the middle of the plaza now and began their familiar cadenced approach. The crowd formed in ranks. The rocks flew. Yet everywhere you stopped to look, at the corner of your eye, in some sparser, quieter quadrant of the plaza, someone would be standing alone watching and perplexed. As if they'd gotten off at the wrong stop and didn't recognize this part of town. In a corner of the plaza a man was playing the guitar. Another man stood nearby with a burning banner. He held it slanting out in front of him like a standard. It was dripping long nylon shreds of flame to the sidewalk. A cop raced by on a quad and didn't stop, didn't look, just as a rubber bullet was fired and knocked a man off the top of a media van where he had been trying to twist free the satellite dish. He fell into the path of an ambulance creeping down the side of the plaza. The ambulance crushed his foot, and he lay screaming.

" . . . injured in what appears to have been an accident involving an ambulance. Twenty-four years of age."

The crowd began to rock the ambulance. There were rippling waves of cheers, of calls. Some corner was turned and possibilities became certainties. The ambulance went over. The driver climbed out and scrambled up into a planter while various people set to work prying off hubcaps and kicking free the muffler. The rear doors opened and a man emerged, hands up to show he was unarmed. There seemed to be someone else in the ambulance but the crowd now surged forward again and the scene was submerged.

A press conference was canceled. The store next to the coffee shop was now burning too.

"Things are very unclear at this point. We're being told that the theater has been cleared. The hostage taker has been arrested." The man winced into the camera in the downwash of helicopter rotors. He was crouched near a bus shelter, the glass smashed out. A single shot was fired behind him.

The crowd moaned. *Urrr.* And what was poised, fell. The new organism lurched again to life, this larger beast. And stones crisscrossed the air in the plaza as militia units withdrew nervously to ring the theater, to distance themselves from this civilian chaos, as the helicopter lifted from the theater roof and sped away just feet from the rooftops. Storefronts were smashed. One after another. Rocks, fires, then this. The anger was still there. Nothing had happened yet to allow it to dissipate.

The looting began at eight-thirty Saturday morning. It seemed like the end of a long formula. Wednesday plus Thursday plus Friday. At some point there was an equals sign. And as the sum of that equation, people started taking things. Then other people joined in, many of whom would have told you that they had no thought to do so previously. The idea was so contagious that a person would have had to leave the Heights to get away from it, to find safety.

This spreading sense of owning nothing as the time ran out.

PEGG REGAINED CONSCIOUSNESS in a sideways world, a bed up against a wall. Metal cabinetry under his head. He pieced together information—medical equipment, Red Cross symbols—and decided that he was in an ambulance that was lying on its side. Then, briefly pinching his eyes shut again, he got a bit more of it. He remembered the man screaming outside the ambulance. He remembered the van going over. He remembered a head coming through the door and yelling something at him. That would have been Haden. As for his present circumstances, Pegg knew nothing much more than that and the fact that he was somehow, miraculously, uninjured.

He crawled out onto the pavement. He saw people with boxes and stacks of clothes.

He saw a young man with a video camera following two women down the row of storefronts, all the glass gone, shattered everywhere. The women were loading each other up with belts and shoes, dropping as many as they grabbed. The young man was calling to them from behind the lens: "Wow, you guys are really great. Are you really incredibly proud of yourselves?"

The women were ignoring him, as if the trailing camera and the shouted questions, while they went about ransacking a shoe store, were just part of a world they'd gotten used to.

Pegg had a card in his wallet with the name and address of his hotel, and so he returned there through the shattered streets. Across the river, where the crowds thinned and there were fewer police, you could almost imagine that nothing had happened. Still, a shocked silence hovered. Pegg read the billboards, trying to place himself in the city. *Needs Met with Passion. Plan for a Better Future. Next Stop, Great Health.*

In the lobby he was embraced by air conditioning, the sound of falling water, the smell of breakfast: waffles and strawberries. He slumped into an elevator under a video monitor with the loop of endlessly crashing waves. In his room he tormented himself with a long look in the bathroom mirror. Pain at the temples. Faint nausea. He realized that he had changed his clothes already, as if he were planning to go out. But he couldn't remember making that decision. Things from the immediate past seemed to be slipping. Memory gone sketchy. He had certain details intact. Thom Pegg. Micah Swenson Pegg. Jenny. Spratley most certainly and the girl at dinner. Mov, definitely. He wouldn't forget Mov. But the name of the kids in the theater, all of them were gone. And he regretted that. Pegg thought hard, his eyes staring into the reflection of his eyes, the reflection staring back into the original.

He left the bathroom and went to sit on the bed. He keyed on the television with the remote and thumbed through the channels.

Pictures of the city on every channel, national and local. Aerial shots, street-level shots, shots of crowds and police. Pegg said to himself: "All my life I've hated this city. I hated being raised here. What was that neighborhood called? The West Stretch. Wide lawns and narrow minds." It was the same neighborhood Jennifer had come from. Where they had lived together until the end. He should have turned Spratley down cold and never have come back. But now he was here again, cranially damaged, driven by mysteries. Sitting in front of the rolling images—smoke and broken glass, burning cars, no escaping them channel after channel—as if this city had grown so large that it had consumed the entire world.

Room-service coffee arrived. Pegg drank two cups as quickly as he could, then pulled on a jacket and walked out into the city. He didn't know where he was going. He just knew he had to move. So Pegg began a long walk that started at first light and stretched into the morning, punctuated by three notable episodes.

The first was a spectacular fish taco he bought from a street vendor somewhere towards the riverside lip of downtown, just at the edge of the escarpment on a boulevard that looked as if it were designed for much more traffic than was out today. Pegg was feeling a bit shaky. He deposited several tablespoons of hot sauce onto his shirtfront when trying to squirt it into the taco.

"You all right, man?"

"Splendid," Pegg said, then realized he had no money. Not a cent. The man looked him over with his head to one side. You gotta be kidding me.

Then—strange times, strange air—the man said: "Forget it. Be careful. Crazy what's going down over there. I'd stay on the north side if I were you."

Pegg gave the man his cufflinks and knew he didn't want to forget the exchange. Then, halfway to the river, thinking this was perhaps the best food he'd eaten in six months, it occurred to him he couldn't re-member buying it and wondered about the fact that he'd somehow left his room without putting on cufflinks.

The second thing was the receipt of news. Pegg was distracted, but he would never have seen it coming. He'd been standing near the river, near the museum — a good one, Pegg recalled, he'd been there with Jennifer and Micah any number of times — and across the way the sky was smoky and heaving. Still lots of small aircraft and helicopters wheeling around. Pegg watched these and licked hot sauce off his fingers and hoped everything would be all right. He hoped that the looting had stopped by then. He knew there was some point from which you couldn't pull back. That point was the lip of the downward-sloping and inward-turning spiral, a vortex towards eternal violence and oblivion. Maybe they were at the lip, but they were not over it. Pegg could sense that. And as his eyes were drawn up towards the Slopes, up to the Heights, he thought that something might be newly alive in the city up there. Some possibility that they could yet pull back from the brink.

He started walking with this thought, pulled by that sense of new life, new hope. It was across there somewhere, south across the river, across the falls. And he had to find it. Madness. But did he stop walk-ing, realizing it was madness? No, he did not.

Sirens and racing police cars, still. No taxis anywhere. He crossed the bridge, pausing over the falls. Then he crunched up the sidewalks through Stofton and up into the Heights. Armored cars, troops with knee pads and throat mikes, helmet-mounted cameras. And here came the unexpected news. At the brow of the hill, Pegg crossed a boulevard and a man stopped his car and rolled down the window, beckoned him over. He said: "They've cleared the plaza, it's empty now." His eyebrows angled with concern. "I was in a restaurant up there. I went home and watched on television then came back down to the plaza last night. People came because they cared. Looting is wrong but what the police did should never have happened."

The man was wearing a suit, tie loose. He'd been up for many hours, Pegg thought. They'd all been up for too many hours.

"The infiltration," the man said to him, squinting up past Pegg into the diffuse light. "That's going to cause the long-term damage. There were men dressed like protesters talking to the police. The guy shot with the rubber bullet had a Special Forces tattoo. I couldn't make that up. He was helo'd out in a medevac. Nobody else got helo'd out in a medevac. There are hundreds of people under arrest now. Could be a thousand. Detention centers on the east side, down by the tracks."

"I missed all that," Pegg said. "I wasn't in the plaza."

The man looked up at him with a kind of sorrow. There was too much that he couldn't explain to someone who hadn't been there. Then he said: "And that journalist got killed too. You hear about that?"

Pegg stared at the man. "Got killed by whom?"

"Police, maybe. I don't know. Who knows? Someone did it."

Pegg, who assumed the man was talking about him, shook his head and smiled. "No, no," he said. "The journalist didn't die. I can assure you, the journalist is quite alive."

But now the man was looking at Pegg in a sharper way, suspicions aroused. "You can't assure me of anything," the man spat. "You just said you weren't there."

"You don't understand," Pegg started, incredulous. How did these rumors come to life from nothing and then live with such ferocity?

"I do understand," the man said, voice raised. "I saw it. Kicked to death, my friend. How's that? You like that?"

Pegg watched him drive off and felt that news sink into him, news that he thought would take on darker and darker meaning as the day went by, as he learned more about the incident and who that journalist was. The one who had not been lucky. The one who had died. But then,

Pegg also wondered how much of the story he could believe. Maybe all of it. It would take no effort to believe it all. Toxic times. Cloned cattle and terminator seeds. A dead journalist. Pegg watched paper blow across the intersection. He felt the chill in the air, smelled the smoke. He felt these things inside himself. Then he walked on towards the plaza, towards the parked fire engines there, three firefighters working a hose, dousing the charred exoskeleton of a car, guts long consumed. Steam rose. Their faces were black.

And here came the third and most unexpected thing. Even in his present state, Pegg remembered enough about himself to be astonished at the feeling rising within. Rounding a corner now. Into a random street, the pavement sparkling with broken glass.

Look at her. She was something. Gold in Geneva. *Eve Latour*. And oh my, but she was lovely. As beautiful as the world knew how. Nothing of the business about her. Hair up in a rubber band. Freckles across a slightly upturned nose. Slender, long legs, all that. But unaware.

Fingernail to her cheek. Mill-town sky. That waterfall and its never-ending song in the background. She was the longing. Oh yes. The longing of our generations. The best we had. And by we, of course I mean me.

She looked up. She saw me.

THE BLUE LIGHT PROJECT

PART III. Black out, blue light

By Thom Pegg

We worked our way skyward in tiny steps. And I was terrified, make no mistake about it. I've never had much in the way of physical confidence, myself. I know and accept it. And yet there I was, the ground dropping away, spiraling beneath me as we rounded the stairwells. More a ladder than stairs really, thin steel treads with open risers, radically steep, with tiny upturned spikes for traction under your shoes. I was gasping. I was panting. My shirtfront was soaked with icy sweat. I gripped the handrails on either side with hands cramped even though I was wearing a pair of gloves. I was bent against the chill wind. Bent against myself and my every weak tendency.

When we pulled up in Eve's truck, fifteen minutes before, I'd tared up at this spindly structure and laughed out loud. You'd have to be mad. The thing was weeded over at its base, sheathed

Thom Pegg is a Los Angeles–based journalist. This is the third of three excerpts from his book, Black Out, Blue Light, *published this month. Pegg is working on his first novel.*

around in a high chain-link fence. Barbed wire, check. *No Trespassing* signs, yes indeed. It towered over us, forbidden and iconic. A bank of warning diagrams itemized a comprehensive rebuke to those who would think to enter here. One diagram showed a man shot through by a single lightning bolt. Do not climb or you will be struck dead by a vengeful God.

"What the hell is it?" I asked her, staring up. "You're not suggesting." This after a half hour's drive. Out across one of the bridges to the East Shore, then winding up through the neighborhood to the ridgeline. Already from here, the city was laid out below, comprehensible in its pieces. Downtown and the river neighborhoods. The smoky flanks of the slope rising up to the Heights where the fires were winking still.

"It's an old radio tower," Eve said. "All these warnings are overkill since the whole thing was powered down in the eighties."

"You do realize how old I am."

Eve was pacing the dry grass, expertly assessing the fence.

"I used to live out there," I told her, pointing out west across the city.

"Yes, I knew that," she said, still looking for something. "I did read about you, back in the day."

I wondered what day that might have been. A day now gone. A day now fading as ours was here. A day on which the sun was sinking in the west, making long shadows and agitating the sky with its tracer bullets of orange and red. A reflection of the city still burning below.

"Radio tower," I muttered to myself, just as she found the breech she was looking for and pulled up the wire fence. Then, in her other hand, I saw the wire cutters and realized she had made the opening herself. Evey Latour. The things you thought you knew about the famous.

We passed into the courtyard of dead thistles and beige bramble that surrounded the feet of the tower. Four enormous steel legs, splayed, and looking to be firmly enough anchored, bolted to concrete slabs. But looking up, the eye rose through ever more whimsical layers of the structure as it thinned and thinned, Eiffelesque, waisting itself into a dainty thing up there in the sky. It loomed over us, ancient. And where it touched the sky and thin traces of cloud beyond, you could see it tottering in place, groaning and creaking in its joints.

"Three hundred and fifty feet," Eve said. "Built in 1957. It's been replaced by the radio masts you see lined up on Route 45 West. But up top of this one you have your best views of the city. You think it's good from the ridge, wait until you get up there. It's like being in a helicopter."

I enunciated the words carefully for her: "You must be completely mad."

Eve smiled at me. "It's worth it. Promise."

I believed her. And she was going to show me how to do it. I'll be right there, she said. I'll be just one step ahead of you.

"Behind me might be better," I said. "That way you can catch me if I fall."

You won't fall, Eve told me. And following was indeed the far better choice. Thom Pegg the daredevil. Life, I thought, was surely upended. We crossed to the base of the tower and she showed me how the stairs down to the ground had long ago been hacksawed away. She dismissed this obstacle with a shrug, a roll of the eyes. The legs of the structure were made of wide steel lattice. She had gloves. This incredible woman had brought extra gloves for me, for just this purpose. I put them on and grabbed ahold of the steel, and up we went, one cautious step at a time to the bottom of the severed stairway. Up and on solid footing in a long walkway that squared around the inside of the tower's four legs. I could see other platforms like this overhead: rectilinear concentrics rising like some kind of gun sight for aiming moon shots.

"Good?" she said.

Thumbs-up. My breath in long, ragged pulls already. "Roger," I said.

"Then up we go." And Eve turned to the bottom of the access stairs, crisscrossing upwards in their impossible length. Up into the lowering darkness. Wind high, clearing away the cloud cover as I watched. Stars just shimmering to life up there.

I can't tell you much about what I was thinking during this climb. I was scared primarily, moving each hand with exaggerated care from one hold to the next. Gripping a railing here or the edge of the stair above me. I suppose I was thinking of her, impossible not to when you're following someone. As Eve rose above me I was comparing myself to her. I was rising up towards some vision, full of fear. Eve was bounding up the stairs ahead, step after step with unflagging commitment. She was eating up the altitude, consuming the moment at hand.

Below us the land spiraled away, dropping into the shadows of evening that were already stretching, ribbing the landscape. Shadows a hundred yards long. Houses covering the block with the black of their silhouette. I saw the spread of the small airfield near the river, then the lights of the international airport out on the eastern fringe of the city. I saw the river as it broke into view, the shining back of it, slowly twisting through the city. The silver break of the waterfall. Its sharp contour bringing back childhood views, postcards, old memories.

Up and up. High enough to see all of Stofton, River Park, the Heights. The grid of streets familiar here. I could see a church where I was taken as a child. I could see its bell tower. Our Lady of Lourdes. Hadn't thought of it in thirty years. I could see a restaurant where Jennifer and I used to go for dinner. Cheap Italian joint. When Micah came along we took him too and there was a booth table they gave us where he could kick off his shoes and lie down after eating. Jennifer and me lingering over plates of lasagna and a half carafe of sharp red.

The river arched its back below me and I could make out where the power was still out in swathes on the south side and across the East Shore below. It highlighted the scattered headlights of those few cars that were out and brought to mind the troubles, the curfew, the city still reeling.

The wind was loud enough that Eve had to raise her voice to speak to me. "It's amazing, isn't it?"

"I'm scared silly," I told her.

"Hang in there," Eve said, right up next to my ear now. "This is the last platform on the main stairs. The top deck is up a ladder."

Air currents and suspension. I felt a certain excitement I don't remember ever feeling in an airplane. Always plain dread in those circumstances. The sad dread of the helpless. Here, I was host to a different fear. I felt the age of the structure. The whole thing buzzing and wobbling in its joints and rivets. I was looking over her shoulder at the spindle of ladder to which she had gestured, my own hand gripping the railing. Maybe this kind of fear was better. Not being strapped in a seat. Not being hurtled through the air by a machine.

I looked at the ladder, my hands instinctively tightening on the rail. I was holding it as though Eve might try pulling me away. As though I might have to make a stand right there. She was smiling, rather sweetly for the horror of my dawning realization. Her head bobbing backwards to indicate that I should follow her. Eve was smiling as if she was enjoying this little thing we were sharing. And I must admit I was enjoying it too. For all my anxiety, my racing heart rate and thoughts, my self-doubt. It couldn't be denied that it was just Eve Latour and me up that tower, and I took sudden, enormous pleasure from that idea. My organs—my chatty spleen, my gossipy, insinuating inner reaches—were completely silent. Completely still.

The ladder disappeared from the middle of the platform up into a tube of lattice steel. The tube was designed to prevent you from falling outwards off the ladder, as you might if you caught even one glimpse of the ground, down there through the shredding steel below. The distance was the distance to death. That was how the normal brain worked, unwilling to suspend its faith in gravity. Its belief that gravity must ultimately win.

"I can't," I said. "I mean seriously. Isn't this high enough?"

No, it wasn't high enough. We could see the city perfectly well from this last of the inner platforms. But above us, even I could appreciate, was an experience of another order. Up there we would be past the structure and into the air that belonged to no one, that high and unsuspended place just short of the stars. The vantage point called for in the calculations she'd made just that afternoon as she cracked the code, the meaning of the map.

Hunched over the table at Kozel's. I was watching when Eve did it. She'd explained that the map had been left for her by a young man named Rabbit. That she knew it was for her to puzzle over, to solve. And then to use, somehow.

Then she said: "And I've finally gotten it. I can't believe I didn't see it earlier."

"See what?" I asked her.

"These numbers here in the margin. They're not coordinates or secret codes. Rabbit—of course. What was I thinking?"

"What are they?"

"Phone numbers."

Eve had been poring over that map. She'd run her fingers from Stofton up the Slopes, then along a series of red lines to the west. Back again. Rethinking. Retracing. Fingers to the margins to check numbers and coordinates. Then to the top of the hill, to the Heights. To one building there.

Phone numbers. She hadn't recognized them because of all the unusual exchanges. But now she put her finger on one of them, tapping in nervous excitement. New cell phones, she said. These were new cellular exchanges.

"I should have guessed Rabbit was using cell phones, but I just didn't put it together," she said to me, eyes alight.

We cored our way up that final length in fading light. And when I crawled free of the top of the ladder, gasping again for breath, I found myself on a platform less than ten feet square.

Eve already at the rail, face outwards into the wind. Standing above her city, just short of the stars.

I stayed on my knees at first, too breathless, too frightened to stand. Then I pulled myself up using the railing. The lowest rail, the middle one, the top. I stood there swaying like a toddler: ankles tentative, knees in question. And when I seemed to have steadied myself, she turned to me and I saw that she had her phone out and the map too, folded over into a tight square. She was holding these at the ready. About to make the call, throw the switch.

She asked me, "Any reason you can think of why I shouldn't do this?"

"Panic in the street?" I tried. "More rioting? Martial law?"

"Why would that happen?"

"You met this Rabbit character, not me. What do you think he had in mind?"

"Something new and without explanation," she said. "Something so beautiful nobody could be afraid."

"You could phone him and ask," I said. But I knew she couldn't, because the author of this moment, this young Rabbit, this young man whose imagination had captivated her, was now long gone.

"You don't have to tell me any of this," I said to her in Kozel's when we got to this part of the story. "We two having just met and all. Or met again."

But she wanted to. Eve wanted to tell me about waking up in a lumpy, unfamiliar bed. Naked in the sheets. She wanted to tell me about her reflection in the little mirror over the sink in the kitchen. A cracked and wavering image. It had taken her five minutes before she noticed the obvious thing that he'd left for her. A wall mural in black felt pen. A sketch of a path chosen, a rail line north, the name of a town, the name of a lane with some landmarks noted: blackberry cane, broken gate, hidden key. And across the top of this diorama Rabbit had written in block letters, in a font and phrase she remembered immediately:

You'll Find It Where You Last Saw It.

We looked down over the darkened cityscape. The guttering flames were still to be seen, the intricate dance of fire truck and police lights high on the facades of buildings as they passed, action now rising again as the evening approached. Looting. The big-box stores were surrounded by guards. Running skirmishes, chaos, flames.

I looked at her. Green eyes momentarily held, checked. Her lips were a full line, her chin sharp to its tiny dimple. I saw her eyes behind the sights of a target rifle and imagined why they would be effective there. A certain coolness and a certainty about life. She was balanced now, our Evey. And from that balance came her last moment of hesitation. She put a finger to the corner of her lips, tracing it backwards to her cheekbone.

Night was coming. It was conceivable we had climbed all this way for nothing. But Eve had an idea and I could only hope it was the right one. The idea that would throw back the cover. The idea that would reveal.

Eve keyed in the number and held the phone between us. Leaning close, I could hear the nubby tremolo of ringing.

And then, out there, far out over the expanse of the city, a prick of light. We both forgot all about where we were, let go of the railing, stood a bit straighter in the rising wind.

A pulse of blue a split second off the sound of the ring tone in both our ears. The light pulsed and held, then faded. Then pulsed and held. Halogen blue. Intense and pure. A brilliant tone on the darkened cityscape, penetrating and singular, unlike anything else to be seen on the blackened grid below. To my eye, the light seemed to come from very near the plaza. From just beyond Meme Media.

"The Peavey Block," she said.

It pulsed to life, a life waking, a brand-new idea. It came out of nowhere. Just at the crest of the hill, near the plaza. A blue beacon, fluttering. And bouncing now too, skipping somehow.

The ring tone stuttered and shifted. And there was a new blink of light below. So close as to first appear that the original light had merely shifted. That it was bouncing back and forth. Then another, then another.

Eve's hand holding the phone dropped to her side as the call-forwarding sequence unfolded below. WaferFones. Phones calling phones calling other phones, calling back. The lights launching their rhythms across the city below, a slow spread, sweeping into the western neighborhoods. There was at first no pattern to it. The lights seemed only to sparkle and cycle. Organic action. They seemed to excite one another, blinking on in shapes and lines, forming into clusters and spreading, then bouncing back, then relighting, then falling silent and still as other areas of the city ignited. It was, at first, just a beautiful thing. The maddest kind of fireworks imaginable. The city itself alight with itself. And reflecting off the low cloud. The sky alight, shimmering like the northern lights. Down the hill. On the roofs of condo towers in the Slopes. At the tip of old water towers, across the tops of billboards. Opening now to the river, where they spread and spread, spooling blue across the West and East Flats and River Park.

We stood speechless, swaying in place while the lights continued to rebound and refract. They blinked on through the blacked-out parts of the city, bridging the spaces below. The whole of the hill and the river neighborhoods pinwheeled now, an antic blue celebration at the roof level, aimed at the sky. Shooting north, east, west, south.

To the bridges. Onto the bridges.

"Look at that!"

Eve held my arm as the lights touched one bridge and then another. Then jumped out over the black of the water and headed into the city center, where even in the lights of the financial district the flickering blue could still be seen. Arcing and dancing in the hive of downtown. Beautiful yes, but more. Perhaps I only really saw it in full when it reached this height, the whole city now jumping and sparking with blue lights, dancing lines and patterns from the north, the east, the west, the south, lights racing across the East Shore directly below us, jumping from a house here to another one over there. It seemed to come from no place that could be imagined. A spectacular and inexplicable mandala. It was the universe. The before picture. Before the city, its buildings and cars, freeways and cell phone towers. Before Eve. Before me. Celestial shapes and patterns, galactic swirls, planet birth and planet death. All the deities too. I could see them patterned there, even as the lights slowly extinguished themselves below us, withdrawing, winking out, throwing last flurries across the landscape. Last flourishes. Last runs.

The final lights we saw were a single row that streaked up the hillside. A last sequencing of calls that started in Stofton and raced to the crest of the hill, to the plaza, where they seemed to launch off that originating building and disappear in a streak to the sky, which was itself now just firming up its display of stars. Winking to life as if in answer to the call.

I had my arm around Eve. I don't mind admitting that I was weeping. I had no idea why. Or I didn't for several minutes until we both noticed the standstill below. The city seemed to have fallen absolutely silent. No sirens. No rotors. No grid of diesel trucks on the hills. There were buses stopped on the bridges. I could make out cars pulled over on the riverside boulevard, people standing next to open doors.

Eve had her hand over her mouth. We both waited. One thousand, two thousand, three thousand. And then the car horns started to blow. All across the city. Some new thing unleashed. Eve put her other hand to her face, one on either side now. I was smiling uncontrollably. Spectacular, I said. Amazing. Terrific. I have never seen anything like that. Can you hear them? People are yelling down there. People are honking their horns. Which I might have done myself, had I been at ground level and seen that flowering of light above.

What had he done, Rabbit? What on earth had he done? He had lifted us. Suspended the laws of nature and made us weightless. And as we climbed down, even now, it's impossible for me to explain the sensation I was experiencing except to say that the laws remained suspended. I was hearing voices. No hallucination. Actual voices. An actual choir of them coming right out of the wind and carrying me down. Madness, I know. But better than other madnesses I have known. There it was, three-dimensional and auditory and real. No particular melody that I remember, only the sense of many voices singing the same notes. The same simple lines. Trumpets, tubas. The shimmery dance of cymbals. A beautiful madness. A saving, restoring madness.

We were laughing, reminding each other of what we'd seen. I wasn't cold. I'd lost my vertigo. We were skipping down, back to earth. Last light was an intense rose hemisphere to the west. Down and down under that floral dome, now ringing us, halo-ing us. A bid from the dying west.

I climbed down the lattice of the tower. I dropped to the ground and turned to help her but Eve jumped past me. She sprang down to the balls of her feet. And as she touched the ground, I remember how the earth shuddered through her. I can still see this, so clearly. The whole of it pushing up and touching her, rolling through her body. Eve rippled with the earth.

We stood for a moment in the wonderful chaos of the memory. My voices were still there, faintly. My feet in the grass. The honking still carrying on below. People calling. Still no sirens, not one. No helicopter sound for the first time in days. We were at a great distance from the Heights. But I felt the pressure systems slackening. And as our shoulders touched and I put my arm around her again in the falling light, here's what I imagined. I imagined that we were less helpless for the mystery of the thing we'd seen. That shimmering blue-light dance of hope.

Maybe Eve felt the same. We were not quite strangers, but we still hung on to one another there. We held each other in the long shadow of the tower. In minutes it would be dark, the rose light gone. All shadows blended to a single one. Night.

"Write about this," Eve said to me. Just a trace of wet remaining at the corner of her eyes. Of course, what came next was going to be harder for her. I only had to stay for a while. I only had to make a phone call to Spratley, do whatever had to be done there. Then stay for a while. Write about it. Sure, that's probably what I would do.

I let her go, finally. I was gripping her and she was standing there gamely, looking at me. Nicely, I have to say. I remember the look. Off she went, across the grass towards the pickup truck. "No, no," I said. "You go ahead. I'll make my own way back to the hotel."

Eve objected. "You're way up the top of East Shore here."

"Go on. I'm fine. I like to walk. I'll flag a taxi."

And I *was* fine. I knew a good East Shore intersection for the purpose of getting a cab. I remembered my hotel. Bit of a letdown getting your memory back, if you're me. Seeing in all clarity the memories I'd seen fit to assemble. My life. My project. But that's me, a lesser subject.

There Eve goes. God, look at her. Off to face what she has to face, that harder thing. Blue lights sparking in both our minds. So much beauty and mystery dancing across the face of her city just at the moment she left it. Left us.

Off north, naturally. Up that lane. To that spot in the blackberries where you turn in. To the mailbox with the hidden key. Would Rabbit be waiting there for her? Hard to say. I wasn't sure it mattered. Here's the thing I knew: that one of them would be there waiting for the other. One of them would get there first. One of them would get there and wait. I believed that. There was easily enough certainty in her stride, in her one long wave back out of the truck window as she drove away, that I could have faith in that. Eve and Rabbit had been set free. And their freedom was each other.

As for me, I'd experienced a kind of liberation too. That is,

I had no sense of wanting anything in particular. Life would continue for as long as it did. But I had all I needed for its duration, for any Mov in store.

In the meantime, just one item outstanding, and simple enough to see it through. All I had to do was cross the city sometime in the next day, or the next week. Find the playground. Some Sunday afternoon when families would be out. It wouldn't be hard for me to have a stroll down the right avenue and look over and find him up on the climbing ropes. Swinging somewhere in the middle rungs of the thing. His mother watching. Looking a little heavier through the face. Heavier and softer, fuller through the belly. I was imagining Jennifer pregnant again. I can't think why. Probably because I was imagining her happy again.

I wouldn't wave or draw attention. I wouldn't go in and try to talk. I wouldn't need that now. I could just let it be. Let them be. The looking alone would be enough. The sending of peace. And asking for it too. That would be sufficient. That would be everything I could possibly desire.

THE ARTISTS

—

This is a work of fiction. All characters and events are invented. However, some of the street art described in this book was inspired by the work of the following artists and photographers, to whom I owe very special thanks:

Andrew (Ao1) Owen

Cameraman

Emma

Jerm9 and Ninja9

Pete Jordan

Rich S

Take5

PHOTO AND ART CREDITS

—

9 o'clock transformer: Cameraman and Emma, photo by Byron Dauncey

You'll find it where you last saw it: Rabbit, photo by Byron Dauncey

Vuitton dumpster: Cameraman, photo by Byron Dauncey

Faith Wall: unknown, photo by Byron Dauncey

Dragon: Ken Foster, photo by Diyah Pera

Eye: Rich S, photo by Byron Dauncey

£?X&!: Rich S, photo by Byron Dauncey

War Is Peace: Cameraman and Rich S, photo by Byron Dauncey

Cascading Confession: Jerm9 and Ninja9, photo by Jerm9

ACKNOWLEDGMENTS

—

WONDERFUL PEOPLE:

Diane Martin, Louise Dennys, Amanda Lewis

Denise Oswald, Gillian MacKenzie

Jill Lambert, Laura Moss, Charlene Rooke, Jane Taylor

Arjun Basu, Kent Enns, Steven Galloway

PIVOTAL SCENES:

Dublin Project Arts Center

Think Café (RIP)

1111 Nicollet Mall, Minneapolis

Pigeon Park

CRITICAL INFORMATION:

Joanne Thomson, Biathlon Canada

Norman Mailer, *The Faith of Graffiti*

Shepard Fairey, *Obey: Supply & Demand*

BACKGROUND MUSIC:

Oscar Peterson, "Fly Me to the Moon"

Deerhoof, "The Perfect Me"

Carbon Dating Service, "Starbeat Academy Graduation March"

Timothy Taylor is a bestselling, award-winning novelist and journalist.
He lives in Vancouver. www.timothytaylor.ca

ALSO BY TIMOTHY TAYLOR
Stanley Park
Silent Cruise
Story House